WAYWARD SON

A Camden Ranch Novel

JILLIAN NEAL

Cover Design by
THE KILLION GROUP

Written by Jillian Neal

Cover Design by The Killion Group, Inc.

Copyright © 2018 Jillian Neal

Published by Realm Press

ISBN: 978-1-940174-43-3

Library of Congress Control Number: 2017959228

First Edition

First Printing – January 2018

To my husband, the man who taught me home is never a place, it's always a person. In his arms, I found my home.

Special thanks to:

Teresa Fordice

Ashley Stuart

Michelle Smith

Ann Suhs

Ann Riza

Chasity Patrick

CHAPTER ONE

Colton glared at the buzzing cell phone on the truck seat beside him as he flew past yet another cornfield. Sighing, he answered the fifth call from his mother in as many hours. "Still not there, Mama."

"The lawyer called again," she informed him. Her accusatory tone needled his stiff spine.

"Way I see it, both you and the lawyer can simmer down. I plan to get the lay of the land before I do anything else."

"Don't you think Gentry needs you back to work sooner rather than later?"

"Uncle Gentry understands that some things take a little time. Serve you well if you'd learn that, too."

"Don't you speak to me that way, Colton Michael Holder. You just remember your manners and honoring your mama and all."

"Mama, if that were really my name, or you were really honorable we wouldn't be in this pile of horse shit we're in, now would we? I'll call you in a few days' time. Try some more of those deep breathing things your last boyfriend went on and on about. What was his name? Asswagon or something?" Irritating the woman who'd given him birth was the only way Colton ever retaliated for the shitty parents he'd been given. If the good Lord had seen fit to let kids choose their parental units, no one would ever have picked his. Currently, his mother deserved everything he could dish out and then some.

"Anson. His name is Anson Wagden and he's going to be a world-renowned sculptor."

"Oh, I'm sure he will as soon as he blows all the money you gave him."

"Mighty high talk from a lowly cattle ranch hand."

Colt sank his teeth into his tongue to keep from cursing out his own mother.

She filled in the ensuing silence. She always did. "He was asked to study with some Pierre something or other in Oklahoma City. Anyway, I'm sure Pierre will be taken with Anson's latest sculpture." The way she giggled made Colton gag reflexively. He didn't have to ask who'd modeled for the piece. "He's known all over the world and he wanted to work with Anson."

"Sure he did. How many men named Pierre hang out in OKC and live to tell about it? I gotta go, Mama. Coming into town now."

"When are you coming home?"

Never. He bit back the retort. "Don't know. I'll be there when I get there." He ended the call and tossed the phone back onto the seat. It made for a miserable traveling companion, though moderately more welcome than his mama's voice.

He slowed the truck so he could study the Pleasant Glen city limits sign. "Population 208, huh?" he asked the stale air in the cab of his old F-250. "Bet that gets dicey from time to time." Talking to himself couldn't possibly be a good sign. He'd been in his truck too damn long.

According to the last census, which two of his aunts had helped conduct, Holder County was currently home to more than eight hundred people. He swore he knew every resident by name and family association. Occasionally, it seemed half of them were Holders.

Narrowing his eyes against the hazy sunset, he caught sight of a faint neon glow that guided him onward. A bar, it looked like. If this was the universe's way of offering him his own North Star, so be it. He could use several drinks and a week's worth of sleep.

According to the map program on his phone, he still had another hour before he could collapse into a bed in his reserved hotel room. Apparently, Pleasant Glen didn't have any kind of rooms available for rent and there was nothing but cattle ranches and cornfields for miles before the next city of any real size. That wasn't going to make his mission here any easier to accomplish. Might as well poke around town for some information before he continued on to his room.

As his boots landed on the gravel parking lot, Colt reached back to slam the door. He popped the crick out of his neck and attempted to lengthen his compacted spine, but his ass still ached from the seat. Probably too much to hope he might find a beautiful woman willing to ease the tension and stress he'd carried around for the last few weeks in exchange for him making her feel better about most anything in the world.

Shaking his head at the thought, he studied Pleasant Glen's Main Street and wondered if the tiny town had even earned its own map dot yet.

Pressing his jaw from side to side, he reviewed everything he needed to accomplish with this trip. Directly below the neon beacon he'd seen from the road—a sign declaring the honkytonk before him to be Saddleback's Bar and Grill—he noted what looked to be an old Methodist Church sign. According to the sign, happy hour was from 5:00-6:00 Tuesdays and Thursdays, they had seven beers on tap, and The Original Sinners were putting on some kind of show on Saturday night. So, the bar used a church sign for advertising. Somehow, given the nature of his visit, that seemed fitting.

Lifting his cowboy hat to a few cowgirls heading inside, he followed after them.

"Let me get that for y'all," he reached the door just behind the cowgirls. His well-developed biceps flexed as he flung open the oddly heavy door.

One of the ladies offered him a wide grin. "Where you from, cowboy? Sure isn't Nebraska, not with that accent."

Blending in wasn't going to be easy either, it seemed. Forcing a chuckle, he decided to test the waters. "Ever heard of Holder County, Oklahoma?"

They shook their heads.

"Then that's where I'm from." He gestured them inside and marched toward a stool near the bartender. A drink was no longer a want. It was a requirement.

Wishing it was customary to stand while drinking, Colt begrudgingly settled on his sore ass once again.

"Get you something to drink, sir?" the bartender asked politely. The pretty blonde standing next to him was staring up at him like he'd fixed the stars in the sky just for her. *Must be nice.* An odd sense of longing stirred in Colt's gut. In the dozens upon dozens of women he'd bedded and turned loose in the last decade, none of them had ever looked at him like that. Until that moment, it had been just fine by him. He tried to shake off the foreign sensation. Had to be the disaster he was trying to contain, or the long drive, or the town, or something.

"Uh, sure. Can I ask you something?" Might as well get on with the business at hand. He needed some information before he made his way to Camden Ranch and the bartender didn't look anything like a cattleman. Safe to say he wasn't a Camden.

Before Colt could proceed with his question, the guy's brow furrowed. His eyes narrowed a half notch. "Do I know you?"

Fuck him running. There was no way this guy already had him figured out. It was an impossibility. Ordering the panic mounting in his chest away, his fists clenched without thought. Fighting for what he wanted was how he got through this fucked-up world. This time he needed to use his brain more than his brawn. It had worked with the ladies he'd opened the door for a moment ago. No reason to switch things up unless it was required so he went on with, "Not unless you've ever spent any time in Holder County, Oklahoma."

"Never been down there. You just look familiar I guess. What can I get you?"

Colt drew a steadying breath. "I'll take a whiskey neat. This is Pleasant Glen, right?"

"The one and only. If you blink you'll miss it, so we get asked that pretty often."

All right, guy had to be local. "Can I ask you something else, man?"

"For the next three minutes, I'm the bartender here, so you can ask me anything you want."

The next three minutes? What the hell did that mean? "You get fired?" He wondered if the guy even knew how to pour whiskey. Probably should have ordered one of those on-tap beers.

"I quit. Learning to be a cattle rancher instead."

Dumbass. Colt couldn't help but laugh. Poor guy. "I wish you the best." And he did. God knew he'd need it. "Cattle ranching's a crap shoot on a good day."

"You sound like all of my brothers-in-law."

At least it sounded like the guy was going to have some help in his new profession. "Then they're probably straight shooters."

"They are, but you were gonna ask me something else."

Guy was good at reading people. That didn't bode well for getting information without a price. *To hell with it.* He proceeded anyway. "Yeah, you ever heard of the Camdens? They own some land up here or something?"

Suddenly, the woman who'd turned her back on him to put away a few glasses whirled back around. "I'm Natalie Camden. Well, actually I'm Natalie Weber but I'm still a Camden. My family owns the largest ranch in Lincoln County. Did you need something, sir?"

Shit. Shit. Shit. It was the only word his mind offered him. He hadn't been prepared to actually talk to a Camden, not yet, and he'd hoped the first one he came across would be Brock. Every confession he'd eventually have to make taunted his tongue. Bile shot to his throat burning every one of them away.

The bartender scooted his wife away, putting himself between them. "What did you say your name was?" he demanded. It was more than apparent that Natalie's husband, whatever his name was, wanted her far away from Colt. What the hell was he supposed to do now?

"Uh...my name's uh...Colton. Colton—" he bit back the truth, "—Colton Holder." He could no longer hear the jukebox or the scrape of chairs against the hardwood floors over the hum of sheer panic in his head.

"Holder, huh?" The guy moved Natalie still farther away. "Got a good friend from Oklahoma named Maddox Holder. I think he's even from Holder County. He used to be a Screaming Eagle from the 101st. He any relation to you?"

How the hell did this guy know his cousin Mad-dog? If Colton bolted, there was a better than fair chance the guy would run after him. He hadn't paid for the shot he'd been given. Why the hell had he even come in here? One comment, and he'd ruined everything. "Mad-do... No. Never heard of him."

What the fuck was wrong with him? He hadn't gone in with any kind of plan for introducing himself to the Camdens, but no one needed to tell him he was fucking this up. It was the only time in his life Colt had regretted not inheriting his father's ability to lie.

"Interesting." The bartender's nod said he hadn't believed a word out of Colt's mouth. No surprise there. "Well, my time's up. We're heading out of town. It was nice to meet you."

Lifting his hat in his customary salute, Colton prayed Natalie didn't get too curious about him yet. Her husband claimed they were going out of town. Maybe that was true. Maybe he still had time to approach the family his own way.

Taking his whiskey glass, he slunk to an empty high-top table at the back of the bar. It would be safer to stand there silently than to risk running his stupid mouth to anyone else.

The buzz of his cell phone chafed his worn nerves. Sighing as he glared at the screen, he shut the call down. Damn lawyer clearly needed more to do with his time.

Grabbing a toothpick from the jar on the table, he placed it between his teeth, wishing it were a cigarette instead. Tracing the rim of his glass, he continued his internal debate. What the hell was he supposed to do when he finally made his way to the largest ranch in Lincoln County? A sad, stupid part of him wondered if there might be a place for him somewhere on that massive ranch, not that he didn't already have a home of his own.

He loved his family. He was proud of being a Holder, even if he wasn't one by name. His great-great-great-granddaddy had been a rabble-rouser back in his day. Wanting more for his family and willing to break a few rules to get it, William Holder had hidden out in what would become Holder County so he could lay claim to the land before the rest of the Oklahoma Land Rush had begun. The rest of them had inherited that same impatience, but this was a situation that required tact, and Colt was determined to handle things right for once in his life.

The bar was less than half full. He wondered about the lives of the men and women tucked away at tables. Did they all live in this barely existent town? Cowboy hats rode high on most every patron's head. If they didn't live in Pleasant Glen, it was a safe bet they lived nearby.

The restlessness that had dogged him his whole life overrode his desire to drink, so he left his whiskey glass on the table and paced toward a bulletin board near the front door. Surely no one would think it too odd for a man to stand and read ads for a few minutes.

Standard cattle ranching notices were pinned one on top of the other, dating back as far as 1987. A fresh, crisp notice caught his eye after he had a good chuckle over the expired rodeo signs and sales from a local Feed and Seed from three Christmases before. His heart picked up pace as he jerked the flyer down.

Maybe the bar's neon sign really had been a heaven-sent beacon. None of the flyer's methodically cut tear-away tabs had been taken—and now none of them would be.

According to his Uncle Gentry, life occasionally offered a hard-working cattle rancher the very thing he needed. If Camden Ranch was looking to hire a hand for the fall cattle working, sales, and winter prep, no one else need apply. He was their man.

Maybe this whole thing wouldn't be quite as difficult as he'd imagined. Maybe this would give him the chance to get to know the Camdens a little, gather up some goodwill, before he told them the truth. Folding the notice, he shoved it in his back pocket.

The heavy door slapped his ass as it was flung open, sending his hat sailing to the floor. He turned to tell the newcomer to watch it, but the threat lodged in his throat as he stared down into a pair of the most beautiful crystal-blue eyes he'd ever seen.

"Oh my goodness, sir, I am so sorry."

Colt grabbed the door, eased the woman a little closer, and shut out the offending cold wind that seemed to have blown her right into his arms. He'd always had a thing for blue-eyed beauties, especially when those eyes accompanied a rack like hers.

"No harm done, darlin'. My ass has taken much worse."

She rolled her eyes, but a blush climbed seductively out of the V-neck of the loose tunic she wore over a pair of floral leggings, and bloomed across her features. Her long fall of wavy black hair had streaks of purple tucked throughout it. His eyes continued their inventory right to a set of full pink lips. He found himself praying they were chapped from the wind and not from some other man's bruising kisses.

"Colton." He offered her his hand. He needed to feel her touch again.

She didn't take the offer. "Nice to meet you, but I can't shake your hand because you're still holding my arm." She quirked a smile he swore sucker punched him. Sassy little thing heated his blood. His mouth filled with saliva. Just his kind of girl.

"Guess I like hanging on to you." Unable to help himself he continued to stare, trying to determine what was so different about her. His heart flew over the next few beats. Her appearance had whipped the air from his lungs like he'd been hit. He swore his cock stood up and saluted.

Skepticism and annoyance darkened those gorgeous eyes. "Yeah, well, I'm in a hurry so maybe you could find someone else to hang on to." Using the arm he'd recently freed, she pointed to the bar.

Damn, but that spite was a turn on and then some. He wasn't going down without a fight. "Can I get you a drink, honey?"

"Nope." She whisked away to the bar, leaving him standing there slack-jawed and feeling dumber than a stump.

Returning to his place at the back of the bar, he kept his eyes trained on her. Her dark hair, alabaster skin, and pink lips reminded him of one of those Disney princesses, but her ample rack and pair of hips meant for gripping reminded him of more than a few of his favorite porn stars. He'd love nothing more than to let his hands take a long, languid trip up to the top of those cute floral leggings...

"Oh, Avery, you're here. Suppose I should ask how Pearl's doing." A woman appeared behind the bar. Colton wondered if Avery picked up on her irritation and her rudeness.

"She's okay, Ms. Olson. I'll tell her you asked about her. I finally have a client this afternoon, so I thought I'd celebrate with a coffee before I get started."

"Can't imagine who on earth would let *her* set their hair. As far as I'm concerned only Satan turns hair purple," sneered a woman at a table near Colt's.

He forced his eyes from Avery's ass to glare at two old biddies more interested in Avery than their meals. The desire to let the women know precisely what he thought of their gossiping clawed at his throat. He wasn't accustomed to keeping quiet, but the fact he wished to remain relatively unnoticed—for now—kept the diatribe at bay.

"That's all you want? A coffee?" The woman behind the bar asked.

"Well, unless you happen to have—" Avery bit her lip, and she actually crossed her fingers behind her back, a gesture that made him want to make the drink for her, "—a chai tea...latte?" She cringed like she'd asked the woman to walk across hot coals on her behalf.

"A what?"

"Never mind. A great cup of coffee would be fantastic."

Ms. Olson mumbled something under her breath and Colton shook his head. *Poor kid. She doesn't fit in here any better than I do.* She was like a rare, tropical bird that had flown into the wrong cage at the zoo. He wanted to get her that chai latte, tuck her up in his arms, and forget just what the hell had brought him here.

For all he knew, they had nothing in common outside his imagination, but his heart kept up its advanced pace and his palms were oddly sweaty. His cock was hung at half-mast like he'd never seen a beautiful woman before. Something about her said she might not belong to him yet, but she was going to. Damn, he needed some sleep. He was clearly losing his mind.

Before her coffee was handed across the bar, her phone rang. He scooted closer to hear. If he was going nuts, he might as well go big or drive his ass all the way back to Holder County.

"Please, please, please don't be the school," she whispered to no one in particular. Colton understood the desperation behind those words, even if he didn't know what she meant, and he found himself silently repeating her wish.

Defeat visibly sank through her as she answered the phone. Clearly, her wish hadn't come true. "Hi, Ms. Kilroy." She squeezed her eyes shut. "I'm so sorry. I'll send him in more clothes tomorrow. It's just I only have this one client today and I really need to keep the appointment. Is there any way I can wait a little while to pick him up? This client is so important." Whatever Ms. Kilroy was saying, Avery nodded. "No, I understand. I'm on my way." Colton watched her walk right out the door without her coffee. He was quite certain he'd never seen anyone look so defeated and so determined all at once.

When Ms. Olson set the prepared to-go cup on the counter, he took it from her. "Here," he slapped enough money for both of their drinks on the bar and raced after Avery.

———

Avery Hale swore the Nebraskan winds were somehow worse than the Oklahoman winds and that was saying something. She rescued her flannel wrap from the massive Kate Spade handbag weighing down her right shoulder. A year ago, that stupid purse had been her prized possession. Now she'd give anything to be able to sell it for even half of what she'd paid for it. She threw the soft material over her shoulders, wrapping herself in a modicum of warmth along with all of her guilt and worry. How could she have even considered forcing Jaxon to endure wet underwear while she colored Holly Camden's hair? Clearly she was not cut out to be a mother.

No one had been answering any of her prayers and wishes lately, but she whispered another one as she reached her old Corolla and brought her cell phone back to her ear. "Holly, hi, I am so sorry, but the school just called again and I need to go pick up my brother. Is there any way I could reschedule your cut and color for tomorrow or Friday?" *Please. Please. Please.*

"I have to work at the clinic tomorrow and Friday. Dec's band is playing at Saddleback's Saturday night. I was kind of wanting something fun before that," Holly Camden needlessly explained. Avery already knew all of that.

"I'm so sorry. How about Saturday morning? You name the time."

"It's okay. I'll call my girl in Lincoln, but I'll catch you next time."

"Okay, sure. Anytime." Avery made a concerted effort not to rage at the leaden sky. The Camdens ran this stupid little town where no one knew what a latte was. Holly was beautiful all on her own, but Avery could've done something great with her hair. Other people would've seen it, and maybe business would have finally picked up. She flung open her car door, debating picking up dry clothes for Jaxon before she drove to the school. *What would Mom have done?* She'd been asking herself that same question for months.

"Ma'am." A husky voice she had no business wanting to hear again made its way to her ears before she shut the door. "Your coffee."

Oh God, the best-looking cowboy she'd ever seen, with the sexiest drawl she'd ever heard, and the firmest grip her arm had ever had the pleasure of feeling, was rushing toward her car with her to-go coffee in his big, capable hands.

Cinderella might've wanted a ball gown and a pair of ridiculous glass shoes, but all Avery had ever really wanted was for a man who looked, sounded, and felt like he did to care enough about her to bring her coffee.

Well, the original fantasy was that Prince Charming would bring her coffee naked the morning after a night of luscious sex where he gave her so many orgasms she temporarily forgot her own name, but she'd been without the attentions of a man for so long she'd reduced the fantasy to just the muscles and the coffee.

She stood and met him at the end of her car. She'd endured enough of her mother's incessant lectures on cowboys and their bossy, demanding ways to know better than to wish he'd whisk her away from wet underoos and perpetually empty salon chairs to his bed, where he'd make her forget every single trouble currently tightening the noose around her neck. "You didn't have to do this." She offered him what she hoped was a kind smile. "I wasn't even nice to you when you asked if you could get me a drink."

He laughed. God, that laugh. It was even better than his voice. "Do I look like the kind of man who gives up that easily?"

Did he have any idea how insanely sexy the idea of someone refusing to give up on her sounded?

"It's not in my blood, sugar. 'Sides, there ain't much in this life more important than coffee." Those caramel-brown eyes flitted to the tag on her car. "Hey, you're from Oklahoma. I live in Holder County," he announced proudly.

Realization finally snapped into place in Avery's head. "That's why you look so familiar. You're one of the Holder boys. I grew up near Oklahoma City. We just moved up here."

"Trust me, we're not that familiar. I'd never forget getting to *know* you."

The overwhelming urge to kiss that smirk off his face and run her fingertips over the perfect angle of his jaw had her clasping her hands behind her back. He was far too tempting. His familiar Oklahoman accent was a warm blanket she'd gladly trade her wrap for, and those whiskey eyes heated her with his gaze. "I used to do Olivia and Harper's hair." There, that was safe. "How's Harper's husband doing?" His face fell and her heart plummeted as well. "Oh no."

"Passed about a month ago. Harper's staying with her mama and daddy for a while."

"If you talk to her, please tell her I'm so sorry, and if there's anything I can do from up here in bumblefuck—" *oops,* "—she should give me a call." She bit back another round of longing for her old life. *You're here for a reason. It'll all work out.* Maybe she'd start believing it if she repeated it often enough. "I need to go. Kind of a rough day." Poor Jax was waiting on her and here she was chatting up some good-looking cowboy.

"Yeah, sounded like you had to get somewhere. But I can't give Harper your condolences if I don't know your name."

"Are you seriously using your cousin's loss to get my name?"

Amusement and concern fought for placement in his gaze. "I might not give up easy, but even I won't stoop that low. I really was going to call Harp."

"Oh, sorry. Rough day, I guess. My name's Avery Hale."

"You need any help with whatever you got going on, Miss Avery Hale? Couldn't help but notice you sounded kinda put out. Calling it like I see it, I have to tell you it sounded more like it's been a rough few months than a rough day."

Avery found herself sighing. Something in his weary expression told her he was no stranger to hardship. "Yeah, well, rough day, rough month, rough year, guess they all turn themselves into a rough life, right? I'll figure it out. I always do. See ya later, Colton Holder." With that, she shut the car door and headed toward the school.

CHAPTER TWO

Rushing into her aunt's trailer, Avery caught the door before it slammed shut. Aunt Pearl was sound asleep in her recliner. She was always so tired after her treatments. As quietly as she could, Avery dug deep into the laundry she'd washed and dried but hadn't yet folded. Her nail snagged on a pair of Chase's jeans. "Ouch, dammit." She whispered and then flung the jeans away and kept digging until she landed on a much smaller pair of jeans with only one knee blown out. And if there was any luck left anywhere in the whole stupid world, she'd find...

Bingo. A pair of Captain America underoos, accidentally washed with the darks, clung to the bottom of the basket. Throwing them in her bag, she tip-toed back out to her car.

The needle on her gas gauge pointed out another of her failures, aligning directly with the E. She had ten dollars in her wallet and hadn't styled a single client all week. If she didn't get a client soon, she was going to have to choose between money for Chase and Jaxon's school lunches or gasoline.

Dammit, she'd been one of the most sought after hair designers in Oklahoma City. Why the hell would no one in Pleasant Glen give her a shot? How was she supposed to take over her aunt's beloved

Cut 'n' Curl when no one wanted her hands anywhere near their hair?

Flying through the semi-circle pickup area at Pleasant Glen Elementary school, she stomped on the emergency brake as the last vestiges of her grasp on the cliff of sanity began to slip away. Randy's brand-new, jet black Mercedes was parked directly across from her Corolla, staring down at it mockingly. She'd learned in the last few weeks that remaining in motion was key to her survival, so she sprinted toward the entrance doors. Motion sure as hell wasn't progress but for now it was sink or swim and she wasn't ready to go down yet.

"What are you doing here, Randy?" she snapped as he opened the door for her.

"They called me when you didn't come. Why didn't you get here faster? If you can't take care of my son..."

"Everything is fine, much better than okay. Jax is my responsibility. I don't need your help."

"Just never forget who his father is."

"If the courts eventually say I have to let Jax spend time with you, which they will not because you had no interest in your son until he was four, then we'll talk. Until then, leave." Spinning on the heel of her ankle boots, she gulped down air laced with the scents of cafeteria food and pencil erasers. "Because he's mine and I don't need anyone's help taking care of him. I've got this."

"He isn't yours. He's mine."

"You're not the four-year-old in this situation," she snapped, "and I'm not going play tug-of-war over him like he's some toy. Jax is confused enough about everything that's happened."

"Yeah, well maybe I don't want him to grow up without a dad."

"He survived the first part of his life just fine without you." With that, she whisked down the hallway. When she was buzzed into the front office, a soaking wet Jaxon flew into her arms. "Hey, you." Avery hugged him to her, trying not to visibly cringe from what was probably getting on her favorite leggings. "Forget to ask to go potty again?"

"We were on the playground. Sometimes they don't want to stop playing long enough to come in," Melony Kilroy, the newly minted Pre-K lead teacher, offered her a concerned smile. "But this is the second time it's happened this week. He does have to be potty trained to attend Pre-K."

"He is. Well, he was. I think he's been under a lot of stress lately with the move and...everything."

"I'm sure. I'll try to get him to the restrooms more often. Look, I'm not really supposed to offer this, but if you could send him in with more clothes, I'll take care of changing him here if it happens again."

"Thank you so much. We'll work on it at home. I swear."

Melony nodded. "Uh, there was one other issue I needed to ask you about." The hesitation in the teacher's tone sent a fresh surge of panic through Avery's veins. They couldn't throw Jax out of school for wetting his pants, could they? She couldn't afford any other childcare options.

"Okay," Avery handed Jaxon the jeans and underwear she'd packed for him. "Think you can do it on your own, little man?"

"Sure, Avery. I'm a big boy like Chase."

She directed him to a back room—the same place where he'd changed the last few times this had happened.

"What did you want to ask me?"

"Well, I just thought you might like to apply for our school break-fast and lunch programs."

"He already gets lunch at the school."

"I know. This would allow him to eat here without charge." Melony handed over a manila envelope choked with stacks of paperwork.

"Really? Is that okay? I wouldn't want someone else to have to go without or anything."

This time Melony's grin was genuine. "It doesn't work like that. Everyone gets to eat as long as they've done the paperwork. It takes a few weeks to file it with the state but after that..." She shrugged. "Maybe it will take a little of the strain off."

"That would be great. Now I only need to find someone who'll let me do their hair."

"Pleasant Glen is slow to accept new things. Give us a little more time. I've been thinking about doing something a little different. Not purple but maybe a new cut." She ran her fingers through her blonde hair. The ends were frizzy and in desperate need of a trim.

"I can do anything you'd like. I won't even get out the fun colors if you don't want. You'd look great with some long layers maybe a few natural highlights. We could give you some depth of color and frame your face."

"You think?"

"Definitely." That hope, Avery couldn't seem to rid herself of no matter how many times it was dashed, began to flicker in her belly.

"I'll ask Tucker what he thinks, not that he knows anything about hair."

Fighting an inward whimper, Avery dug in deep and kept up the encouragement. "Might be fun to surprise your husband with a new look."

"Lately, I wonder if he'd even notice."

And there it was. Listening, helping, commiserating, and understanding were prerequisites for the job. Stylists were every bit as good at those things as therapists, but they didn't get paid nearly as well. "Come see me. We'll make sure he notices. I promise." Avery squeezed Melony's hand.

"You think?"

"Making them notice happens to be my specialty."

"Tucker's going with Luke and Grant Camden to a Farmers and Rancher's Alliance breakfast Saturday morning, but you're probably booked Saturday, right?"

"Nope, not at all." Quelling her own desperation, she reminded herself of one her mother's favorite pieces of advice. *If you come off as desperate, you will be. Never let on that you need help.* "I can work you in." Digging back into her purse, Avery rescued her phone from the litter lining of ancient receipts and gum wrappers. She opened the scheduling app and flipped through the empty appointment pages, putting on a good show. "Looks like I could do ten o'clock, Saturday morning?"

"That works. Maybe I'll pick up something fun to wear that night."

A spark of warmth eased up the chill that had set into her bones months ago—the day she'd taken the boys by the cemetery one last time and had driven what remained of her family to Nebraska. Maybe things were finally looking up. If Melony loved her hair, she'd probably at least tell the other teachers at the elementary school. It was a small victory, but it was a step toward being able to stand on her own two feet again.

Jaxon appeared from the room in the back, wiggling and tugging at the seat of his jeans while trying to manage the pile of wet clothes he was dragging behind him. "Here, buddy, I think your undies are on backwards again." And just like always, Avery raced to the rescue.

———

Colt stared at the rusted iron entrance sign to Camden Ranch. *Set your troubles down You are home*, it declared. The chug of his truck motor didn't drown out the low bellows of the cattle in the distance. He'd bet every head on his Uncle Gentry's portion of Holder Ranch that those who brought trouble with them wouldn't receive that warm of a welcome. But he was here...he was doing this, and there was no time like the present. Lifting his phone, he stared at the number printed on the stolen flyer. Having no idea which Camden might answer, he went on with his call.

"Hello?"

Colt cleared his throat, forcing himself to ignore the nerves fizzing in his gut. *Get it together, moron.* Never one for playing when there was work to be done he admitted to himself this situation had thrown him. The only way out was almost always through. "Uh, hi. Name's Colton Holder. I was calling about the winter ranch hand position you posted at Saddle's Bar...thing."

"You're kidding?"

What the hell did that mean? "Position already filled or something?" That'd be his luck and he didn't exactly have a plan B. Hell, he hadn't had a plan A before catching sight of the flyer now clutched in his hand.

"Nah, just can't believe anyone called. My wife, Hope, kept telling me to advertise there, but I figured it'd be word of mouth. Never hired a hand I didn't know. Oh, and it's Saddleback's. You'll get crucified around here if you call it the wrong name."

"Sorry. New in town."

"Yeah, that much was obvious. Where you from?"

"Oklahoma."

"What the hell are you doing all the way up here?"

"Uh," the quiver of his own voice betrayed the nonchalance he was going for. Dammit. "Looking for a change of scenery is all. Can I ask who I'm speaking to?"

"Sorry. This is Brock Camden. I'm the one hiring the winter hand, but my cousins might need a little help on their portions of the ranch if you're willing. You got any experience?"

The name ricocheted around in his head for far too long, freeing jagged burs of emotion through his chest. So, this was Brock. Reaching for a toothpick from the stash he kept in the ashtray, he shoved it between his teeth.

"You there?"

Yanking the toothpick back out, he cursed himself under his breath. "Yeah, sorry. You cut out for a second." Another lie to add to his guilty conscience.

"I asked if you had any experience."

"Right. Yeah, tons actually. My extended family owns nearly 450,000 acres. We run cattle on all of it."

"Damn."

"I can do anything you need. If your cousins need help, I'm game."

"Yeah, well we don't have quite that much land." He knew Brock wanted to ask why the hell he'd left Oklahoma. No cattle rancher in his right mind would leave that kind of security for a change of scenery.

"No problem. Big or small, we're all just selling grass, right?"

Brock's chuckle was distinctly familiar. "My dad used to say that all the time. Never heard anyone else outside the family say it 'fore now. When can you come by?"

"Uh, anytime. Like to get started soon."

"Good to hear. I'm spent for today. Promised my boys we'd go for a Gator ride before dark. You have any time tomorrow? Got cattle buyers coming in late next week. Love to get some help before the sale."

"I can start whenever."

"You got a horse?"

"Yeah, but not with me."

"We got plenty of spares. Meet me up at the house tomorrow after morning chores. Around nine good?"

"I'll be there. Where's your house?"

"Right. Keep forgetting you're new in town. Pleasant Glen doesn't get a lot of newcomers. You know where the ranch is?"

I'm sitting on it. "Saw some kind of big metal entrance sign off the main drag through town. That your ranch?"

"That's us. Take the dirt road to the gravel one. You'll pass a small cottage near the entrance. Keep going down the path, and you'll pass a big, white farmhouse on your right. Keep to that path and cross four cattle guards. My house is the two story on the hill. It's brown. I'll try to be out there."

"See you tomorrow."

"Daddy, you promised," Colton heard a young boy huff.

"All right, Nate, we're going. See you tomorrow, Mr. Holder." He ended the call.

"Yeah," Colton spoke to the ether yet again. "Guess you will."

Unable to keep sitting and staring at Camden Ranch, feeling both the weight of his connection to this strange land—to these strangers—and the invisible barrier separating him from it all, he backed the truck up and drove toward town. His hotel room was still an hour the opposite direction, but a cold bed all alone held no more appeal than taking hold of an electric fence. Maybe he'd go back to that bar and order a meal.

The sun was sinking low into the approaching cornfields. He flipped down the visor to save his eyes just in time to see he was gaining on a kid walking on the side of the two-lane road.

When the kid's thumb hesitantly raised, he slammed on the brakes. The scene was all too familiar. Rolling down his window, he offered the kid a smile. "Where you heading, man?"

"Anywhere but here."

"Yeah, I said those words more times than I care to remember. 'Spect you better go on home."

"I'm not riding that stupid school bus if that's what you're suggesting."

Ah. So that's what this was about. "Fine. I got nowhere to be. I'll take you home. Hop in."

"You're not gonna murder me or anything, right? You're not one of those sicko kind of guys?" Genuine fear took up residence in a pair of cool blue eyes that looked strangely familiar.

"I'm not, but that's the very reason you got no business doing what you're doing. Trust me on that. I know what I'm talking about."

The kid flung a backpack that had to weigh almost as much as he did into the bed and crawled into the seat beside Colt.

"Where's home?"

A surly huff told him the kid wasn't planning to give him a straight answer. "My home's 'bout five hundred miles that way." The kid pointed south.

"Five hundred miles, huh? That'd put you almost to OKC. I can't take you that far. I'll wager you're attending school here—" he gestured to the high school in the distance, "—so how about you let me know where you're staying in town?"

"How'd you know how far away Oklahoma City is?"

"Just drove up from there."

"Liar."

Colt chuckled. "Tell me where I'm taking you or get out, but be sure to walk further off the road, kid. Can't see you for the sun. You're gonna get yourself killed."

"It's not that far from here. Couple of trailers on a piece of property out past that big-ass ranch that takes up most of this stupid town."

"You mean Camden Ranch?"

"I guess."

"That's a long walk. You really hate the bus that bad?"

"What's it to you?"

"You're 'bout sixteen right?"

"How'd you know that?" the kid demanded.

"Took me about that long to get good and deep-down ornery. Kinda figured I wasn't the only one."

A little of the kid's icy demeanor melted. He finally looked him in the eye. "What were so you ornery about?"

Colt grinned. "What's it to you?"

"You got a name? My sister's gonna ask who brought me home."

"I have more than I care for, but you can call me Colton. How 'bout you?"

"My name's Chase."

"Nice to meet you."

"Same, I guess."

"You hate school as much as the bus, or is your orneriness reserved only for public transportation?"

"You always talk this much?"

Colton shook his head. Jesus, this kid could've been him at sixteen. "Lonely, I guess. Feeling a little lost myself."

The truth hung between them for a heartbeat. "I hate this school, too."

"Just this one?"

"Yeah. There are only like fifty kids in my whole class and they all grew up together. Half of them are related."

"You new in town?"

"Yeah." The fragmented pieces of the puzzle finally came together in Colton's mind. Oklahoma, a recent move, and those icy blue eyes.

"Hey, you any relation to Avery Hale? I met her today. She said something about being new in town, too." He sized up Chase as he slowed behind a tractor on the road. He couldn't possibly be Avery's kid.

"She's my big sister. She's also an uptight bitch, but who cares."

"Hey," Colton spat. "Don't talk that way about women, ever. I don't care how awful you think they are. If you're as ornery with her as you're being with me, I 'spect if I asked her she'd tell me you're an ungrateful brat. That the truth?"

"No." Chase seethed.

"Then give her a break. Sounds to me like she's trying to take care of you. Didn't you just say she's gonna want to know who brought you home?"

"You dating my sister or something?"

I ain't that lucky, kid. "I just met her today. I always call 'em like I see 'em. I appreciate when people shoot straight with me. Thought I'd offer you the same respect."

That brought Chase up short for a moment. Colt popped another toothpick in his mouth, giving the kid a moment to fish around for a comeback.

"Oh, so calling me a brat was you respecting me?" he finally landed on a suitable retort.

"You were being a brat, so yeah, it was."

"Stupid tractors." Chase huffed as he glared out the windshield like John Deere himself had made it his personal mission to piss him off on the regular. "So damn slow."

"Might want to cut 'em a little slack. Without tractors, you wouldn't have nothing to eat."

"You have an answer for everything?"

"Everything has an answer, kid, but I sure as hell don't have them all. Since we're gonna be behind this tractor for a while, tell me why you hate school so bad."

"No."

"Got anything to do with the fact that you're going to school with a bunch of famers' and ranchers' kids now?"

"No."

"Thought maybe that was your deal with tractors."

"I don't have a deal with tractors."

"That's right, you hate everyone and everything for no good reason. Forgot for a second."

That earned him an eye roll. It was oddly comforting that teenagers hadn't changed much since he'd been one. Driving past the ranch, he refused to so much as gaze at the expanse of land that belonged to the Camdens.

"You a Sooner or a Poke fan?" He offered the kid a lifeline. The very same lifeline his Uncle Gentry always offered him after he chewed his ass for something.

"The Pokes," Chase answered at once.

"Atta boy," Colt said with a chuckle.

"I think Rudolph's gonna pull it off this year. Beat Baylor and everything."

"You think?"

"Yeah, we have revenge on our side. That's a huge thing. Did you see the Texas Tech game? He was on fire." Clearly Colt had stumbled upon the very switch that turned the kid from surly teenager to decent human being.

"Yeah, I saw that. You're right about him being out for vengeance. You gotta want it bad to get it. Bedlam sucked though."

"Yeah, I know. But rivalry games are different. It's more emotion then skill. We're gonna do it this year. I know it."

"Hope so. Hey, you ever play football?"

"Used to. At my old school."

And there was the reason he hated *this* school. Poor kid. "You ask the coach if you could join the team here? Bet they could use a little help. Young Rodeo always gets more attention in ranching towns."

"Nah. It's too late. They probably already have their uniforms and practice schedules and everything."

"Couldn't hurt to ask. All he can say is no."

Chase chewed on that piece of advice as they made their way past Camden Ranch.

"This it?" Colton asked as they came up on an inlet of more dirt than grass and two singlewides a hundred yards apart.

"Yes, sir."

Sir? Damn. Maybe something he'd said had gotten through Chase's armor of rudeness.

"Could you not tell Avery I was thumbing?"

"I could probably do that. How did you come to end up in my truck though?"

Before they could work out a story, Avery was outside looking madder than a half-drowned cat. "Hate to tell you, man, but she already knows."

"Shit."

Colton outright laughed at that. "Say it one more time 'fore she gets to the truck, then you keep that kinda speaking to yourself. She looks like she might skin you alive as it is."

"Chase, where have you been? The bus went by ages ago. I was about to call the police. I thought you'd been kidnapped."

Her cheeks were ablaze and her eyes fierce with her fury. But there in the deep blue depths was utter relief that her brother was safe. Colt was quite certain he'd never seen anyone look more beautiful angry. Her frantic gaze landed on his and she did a double-take. "Uh, thank you for dropping him off."

"No trouble. He missed the bus. I happened to be coming by the school 'bout that time. Asked if he needed a ride."

"Is that what he told you? That he'd missed the bus? He didn't. He refuses to ride it for some ridiculous reason. I told you it's not like back home. All the kids here ride the bus." She turned her accusations on Chase.

"And I told you I'm not riding that lame-ass cheese wiener. Mom said I could get a job and buy a car when I turned sixteen."

"I know that but I can't afford the insurance, Chase. I'm sorry but that's just the way things are right now."

"Bye, Colton. Thanks for the ride." Chase's shoes hit the dirt and he ducked out of his sister's reach, beating a path to the built-on porch of one of the trailers. Avery stood in the open doorway of his truck. That was just fine by him. Would've been even better if she'd climbed on up.

"Maybe don't be too hard on him." Colt hoped he wasn't stepping on her toes, but he felt for the kid. Felt even worse for her.

Turned out Chase and Avery rolled their eyes the very same way. He shoved another toothpick in his mouth to keep from chuckling at her.

"Thank you again for bringing him home. He's been impossible ever since we moved."

"Like I said, it was no trouble. Can I offer you one more piece of advice?"

"Kind of get the impression you're going to anyway." There it was again, that strength and sass that couldn't be bogged down by whatever life had thrown at her.

"He misses playing football."

The tense frown lines around her mouth and forehead eased. "He told you that?"

"Not in so many words. I kind of put two and two together."

"Why didn't he tell me?" She sounded heartbroken suddenly.

"Sometimes you need something real to be mad about."

Two quick blinks of her long eyelashes and the furrow of her brow said she was digesting that. "Thanks for telling me, Colton. You've saved my ass twice today. I guess I owe you."

She didn't sound too thrilled about owing him much of anything and her choice of words had his imagination running wild. There were plenty of other things he'd like to do with her ass. Namely, take hold of it, maybe paddle it on occasion if she was into it, and a few other things he had no business thinking about with her brother standing on the front porch watching them.

"Avery, doll, who is that?" A woman twice Avery's age with a floral scarf wrapped around what appeared to be her bald head made her way toward the truck.

"Aunt Pearl, you're supposed to be resting. I've almost got supper made." Avery headed toward her aunt.

"I'm sick and tired of resting. Now, who do we have here?" She offered him a sly grin that said she knew something she wasn't sharing. Colton wondered just what that might be. He wasn't ready for the people around here to know anything about him.

"This is Colton Holder, Aunt Pearl. I met him today at Saddleback's. He bought me coffee and gave Chase a ride home from school."

"Isn't that interesting. And where might you be from, Colton? I've never seen you around town."

"Uh, no, ma'am." Having had manners beaten into him by all of his aunts, he stepped out of his truck and removed his hat. He offered the woman his hand. "I'm from Holder County, Oklahoma, ma'am. Came here on some business."

"You a cattle buyer?"

"No, ma'am."

"Stock supplier?"

"No," Colton shook his head. "I'm a..."

"I know." The aunt's deep green eyes widened. "You must be here to look at that land Lincoln County is putting up on the block next week. The Rasmussen property. If anyone ever listened to me, which they don't but they should, I coulda told all of 'em that man was filthier than a tusked pig in a pile of cow shit. Why don't you come on inside with me and we'll talk all about everything I think should be done with that property." She linked her arms around his bicep and guided him toward the trailer.

"If you ask me, and as I mentioned, you always should, this town is in dire need of one of those coffee shops or maybe another restaurant. Of course, the Fitches tried with that ridiculous buffet thing several years back, but you cannot put a buffet in a cattle ranching town. Lord knows cowboys will eat themselves sick especially if you're charging them a fixed price for all they can eat. Something with a fancy twist where couples can go for a drink or quiet meal. What do you think, Mr. Holder?"

By the time she stopped talking, they were standing in the living room of the small trailer. Brown leatherette furniture took up most of the space. Some kind of plants appeared to be giving up the will to live near the windows and action figures littered a large section of linoleum in the adjoining kitchen. "Uh, ma'am, I'm a cattle rancher by trade, so I'd know a good deal more about eating like a cowboy than I do about running any kind of restaurant."

Avery giggled. The sound zinged from his ears straight to his cock. Jesus, what was it about this chick? He'd never let a woman get under his skin like this.

"A cattle rancher? Did you buy land up here or something?" Pearl demanded.

"No, ma'am. I'm hoping to get hired on at Camden Ranch actually. Going to talk to them in the morning."

Pearl's eyes narrowed slightly. She brought the glasses hanging on a chain around her neck to her nose and studied him. Colt tried not to panic. "Isn't that interesting. Ev and Jessie are sweet as pie. They'll take good care of you. Now, come eat. Avery's a great cook and I had her make extra tonight. I kept telling her Chase would show up for supper. One thing about teenage boys, they'll always show up for food."

"Just like cowboys, huh?" Colton quirked a grin.

Avery, who'd followed them in and shut the door behind them, gave him a fully formed smile. His chest vibrated as his heart beat out its approval.

"She likes to talk," Avery mouthed silently.

"Everybody needs to on occasion." Colton winked at her. "Can I help you with that?" He wasn't going to turn down a meal with her even if he did feel like an interloper. If practice made perfect, he had to be the MVP of being unwanted anyway.

Suddenly, something smacked into his right leg and hung on. A little boy latched his arms and legs onto Colton with a vice grip. "Uh..." Colt stared down at the blond head attached to his knee before shooting Avery a confused gaze.

"Want to meet my Randy?" the kid asked.

"That's me." A man dressed in a fancy suit waltzed in through the back door and Colton instantly hated the guy simply for being in the house with Avery. Who the fuck was he, anyway? And whose kid was this? "I'm Randy Buttridge. I'm Jaxon's father."

Avery made no effort to hide her eye roll. Interesting.

Leveling a cool glare on the guy, Colt begrudgingly shook his hand. So, Avery had a kid with this punk-ass loser. He searched for wedding rings on either of them and came up empty. Hope sparked inside him insistently, and he called himself an idiot. He was in town to get a job done and, if the opportunity presented itself, to get to know the Camdens. Not romance anybody. If only he could convince his cock of that.

"All right, Randy, if you insist on staying, we're eating. Find a seat." Pearl directed them to two card tables placed side by side between the small kitchen and living room. Assuming the kid would loosen his grip if he started walking, Colton headed toward the table. No such luck. The kid went along for the ride.

"Jax, take a seat." Avery tried to pry him loose.

"I want to sit by him. Miss Glenda says cowboys are like real-life heroes. I'm gonna be a cowboy when I grow up."

A grin played on Colt's lips. The kid was all right. His father didn't look any too thrilled with the assessment. *Shitlicker.* Hell bent on impressing Avery and pissing off her ex, he reached down and lifted the kid into the air. "If your mama's sure she doesn't mind me staying, you sit right here—" he sat Jaxon down into a chair, "—and I'll sit here." He took the seat beside it.

"My mama went to heaven to be an angel," Jaxon stated with a great deal of conviction. "Now, Avery takes care of me." All sound was vacuumed from the room. Avery trembled as she set a bowl of potatoes on one end of the table.

Instinctively, Colton steadied her. "I'm sorry. I assumed," he whispered quietly. Him and his big mouth. Longing to fold her into his arms and erase every stupid thing he'd assumed, he kept his hand on her for a moment, rubbing his thumb along the crook of her arm as if that might somehow soothe her.

"It's fine," she insisted. "Let's eat."

The clatter of bowls and dishes being passed around assaulted the silence. Determined to stop sticking his boot in his mouth, Colton studied the trailer instead of speaking. An odd compilation of floral scarves and handbags were juxtaposed with the furniture and ancient carpeting. Three baskets full of laundry were lined up by the kitchen counters consuming most of the available space.

Chase reappeared, drawn in by the food, and they all tucked in to their dinner.

"So, uh, Chase, do you want to ask the football coach if you could join the team?" Avery asked pointedly after a few minutes. Colt grimaced at her lack of finesse.

"No." Chase shoveled another spoonful of macaroni and cheese into his mouth.

"Why not?"

"I just don't," he grunted through a mouthful of food.

Avery cringed. "Don't talk with your mouth full."

He swallowed the bite down with a swig of milk. "Then don't ask me stupid questions when I'm trying to eat."

Colt raised his left brow and glared. Boy needed the attitude worked out of him. "It wasn't a stupid question."

With his hate-fueled gaze flitting between Colton and his sister, Chase huffed, "How would we pay for it, Avery? They don't just let you on because you can throw a ball."

Jesus Christ, Colt was batting exactly zero tonight. Should've kept his mouth shut about the football thing, too.

"Well, there might be some way," Avery tried. Bless her heart, she really was trying, and if the weary weight in those gorgeous eyes said anything at all, it was that she'd been trying for too damn long and needed some help.

His entire life, Colt had been territorial and possessive. Never having much to call his own, he never took kindly to someone trying to take something that belonged to him. But this was different. This was more. Protective instincts he never even knew he possessed took up residence in every muscle of his body. He drew a deep breath trying to create room in his chest to keep them contained. Protecting her above all others became his life's mission in that moment of sheer insanity. He would help her do most anything in the world. Sweet little spitfire who clearly looked life right in the eye and winked as it took yet another blow.

"Did you have any walk-ins today, sweetheart?" Pearl attempted to rescue her niece.

"No. Sally had several but not me."

"What business are you in?" There, surely that wasn't a dumbass thing to ask. He'd overheard those women in the bar talking about hair, but he didn't want to let on that the old gossips had been jawing about her.

"I'm a hair stylist."

"Do you like it?" Colton knew exactly nothing about hair other than that he let his own hair grow past his ears before he dragged his ass to the barber. He didn't care for being a captive audience to forced conversation. But if it made her happy, so be it.

"I love it, or I used to."

"She's the best I've ever seen," Pearl said proudly. "And I keep telling her you have to give people in the Glen a little time to get used to something new. We're not highly adaptable way out here in the prairies. And Sally's right, too, you know."

Avery rolled her eyes. "Sally is also a few bubbles off the beam, Aunt Pearl."

"You'll mind your tongue about my best friend, thank you very much, Miss Priss. She knows what she's talking about. If you had a boyfriend, all the rancher's wives would feel better about you doing their husbands' hair."

Wasn't that an interesting little tidbit? Colton wondered if there was any truth in it. He'd never kept a woman around long enough to call her his girlfriend. It was the worst possible time in the world for him to offer himself up, but damn, being able to call her his own was more than appealing. If it would help her get customers, why not go on and leap out of the frying pan and into the fire?

CHAPTER THREE

"You know, my aunt was right." Avery kept babbling even though Colton had insisted he needed to go. She shouldn't be talking his ear off as she walked him out to his truck. Not when Chase almost certainly wasn't doing his homework and Jax needed a bath. Intoxicated by the heat rolling off of him and the raw masculinity of his voice, she wasn't ready for him to leave.

His left eyebrow lifted in intrigue. "About what exactly?"

"This town needing a coffee shop. That coffee from the bar isn't very good."

"Oh yeah? I'm not all that picky about coffee. As long as it's hot and in my hand I'm happy."

"Did you ever go to Grips and Grinds in OKC? They had the best chai tea lattes." Desperate for someone to reassure her that her life before hadn't all been some kind of dream, she kept talking.

"Little place out on Cedar Grove?"

"Yes!"

"Pretty sure I did go in there once. Name's a little confusing. I didn't really know it was a coffee shop 'til I got through the door. Did have a good cup of coffee though." Even his smirks were gorgeous.

Avery couldn't remember the last time she'd laughed twice in one day. The muscles in her cheeks were practically rusty from lack of use. "I take it you were looking for some gripping and grinding, not mugs and coffee."

"I might be an even bigger fan of gripping and grinding than I am of coffee and that's saying something." He waggled his eyebrows, and the heat of his gaze intensified. It settled low in her belly, almost at the apex of her thighs, and radiated up her spine. He didn't touch her. He didn't have to.

His eyes slowly crept down the length of her body. Appreciation and lust seemed to ride on the sweep of his tongue over his bottom lip, like she was a feast and he'd been starving for most of his life. "You know if you need someone to pretend to be your boyfriend, I volunteer."

God, he was gorgeous. That unruly golden-brown hair parted wherever it liked and almost touched his cheeks. He had a few days' worth of old beard unable to completely conceal his dimples. All bad boy... with dimples. Holder through and through. He looked every bit the part. Only this particular bad boy was actually a good man—the way he'd helped her earlier, his kindness to Chase, and his patience with Jaxon. He was exactly the kind of man she could fall for if that were in the cards for her, which it most certainly wasn't.

She shook her head, more at herself than at him. A lifetime ago, she would've taken him up on his offer and then challenged him to a few gripping and grinding sessions and would've loved every minute of it. But she'd buried that life she'd loved so much, right along with her mother. "You don't have to do that. Surely this town isn't that crazy. I meant to thank you for getting Randy to leave after dinner, though. He keeps threatening to take custody of Jax away from me."

"Yeah, I picked up on that. I took a bet. He seemed like the kind of guy who'd sell his soul for better cell service. Did you see how fast he flew when I mentioned how many calls I'd been missing since I got out here?" Colton chuckled and several of the butterflies that had resided in her stomach so long ago were birthed anew. That laugh was going to be the end of her. "It was a good bet. All he really cares about is money as far as I can tell."

"Yeah, well, I figure if you hate him, I'll hate him, too." Gently cupping her chin in the palm of his capable hands, he traced her cheek back and forth with his thumb. Every nerve ending in her body applauded the caress.

"I don't believe in hating people. It's not worth the effort." She barely recognized her own voice weighted with need.

"Oh yeah?"

"Yeah. It takes so much energy. He doesn't deserve that."

When Colt's thumb made one last pass, she forgot to breathe. Her lips parted in a silent plea for him to kiss her so hard he shattered every horrible moment of her day into an oblivion.

"You're too damn beautiful to hate so I get that. How 'bout I'll hate him for you?"

"You don't have to do that for me. You've already done enough on my behalf."

"Oh, honey, I'm just getting started. Can I be nosy before I go though?"

"You can be anything you want." The words sailed off of her tongue with far too much ease. It took her a moment to realize she was flirting. How long had it been since she'd flirted? The butterflies birthed a split second before in her stomach that were now swarming with reckless abandon said it had been far too long since she'd felt the fizzy, addictive sensation of a new crush.

He edged closer, crowding her near his truck. His sleeves were rolled up despite the brutal wind. She wondered if there was some kind of prize for forearms that looked like his. Maybe there should be one of those cowboy calendars for charity. If his muscular thighs and pecs matched those chiseled arms, he could be Mr. January through to Mr. December. "Good to know."

"I'm sorry. What?" She tried to remember what he'd said before she'd gotten lost in thought over his thighs and that...whoa baby...bulge behind his zipper line. Blinking rapidly, she ordered her traitorous eyes to return to his face. They refused.

The rough glide of his fingertips on her chin lifted her head. He guided her gaze to meet his own. His half grin had morphed into an all-knowing smirk. "You're needing something more than someone to tell Jaxon's dad to get lost aren't you, darlin'?"

Oh God, yes! "Uh, just to say thank you and..."

"I can think of more than a few things I intend to have you thanking me for, but getting that asswipe to leave ain't even on the short list."

Her brain short-circuited and she found herself blabbing out her life story. "My mom was only nineteen when she had me. Jaxon and Chase are both my half-brothers, but Chase isn't Randy's. I don't actually know Chase's dad, and neither does he. Randy and my mom were never married. She...she was never married at all." The confessions took flight from her heart.

"I'm sorry she passed on, darlin'. My mama knew my sperm-donor less than twenty-four hours before they up and decided to make me. Both of 'em have been a thorn in my side since birth, so I get it. Believe me." She'd half expected judgment or at the very least shock. The genuine sorrow in his tone settled the tension knotting in her stomach.

"Thanks for saying that."

"You have an awful lot on your plate, taking care of your aunt, too. Seems to me somebody oughta be taking good care of you."

"I can handle it. My mom and my aunt are the ones who taught me to be a stylist when I was a teenager. I'm supposed to take over her salon here. But yeah, I'm helping Aunt Pearl with her medical bills and making a home here for Jax and Chase. It's not going quite as well as I'd hoped, but I'll figure it out." As the unending list of responsibilities once again settled on her shoulders, she felt herself sink farther into the cold Nebraskan dirt.

"Not sure exactly how long I'll be in town, but I intend to help you do all of that. I know more than I care to about family obligations."

"You're too kind, Colton. I guess if you see Chase out thumbing again, it would be great if you could pick him up. Other than that, I'll handle this on my own."

"You ever think maybe we're not meant to do everything on our own?"

"I'll be fine."

"I intend to see to it." He lifted his hat before climbing back in his truck.

Figuring she deserved a few free indulgences, she unabashedly admired his ass as he made his ascent. Her fingertips itched to sink themselves into that ass while he drove inside her. Longing to feel his weight on top of her own flooded her mouth with saliva. It had been so long. *Maybe he could have been yours a lifetime ago, Avery, and you could have stayed in bed with him all weekend, but you can't be that girl anymore.*

"Okay, but I still have no freaking clue what X is, Av, and what the hell do I do with the Y?" Chase asked the very questions swarming in Avery's head. They were seated side by side at one of the card tables, puzzling over a set of problems that might as well have been Egyptian hieroglyphics for all the sense it made.

"You will literally never use this in real life," she ground out. The numbers swam on the notebook paper she was trying to decipher.

"But I do have to graduate so I can get a job in real life and we can actually afford to raise Jax," he rebutted.

Defeat continued to mortar itself brick by brick in her soul. "I don't want you to worry about Jax. I'll figure it out. I want you to go to college and meet a nice girl and be happy."

"You always say you'll figure it out," he said, swiping a hand through his hair, "but we can't even figure out what X is in this stupid problem."

"That's because Algebra is ridiculous."

"I'm going to bed. I'll go in early and ask my teacher or something."

"I'll take you."

"Did you get gas?" The accusation in his eyes said he already knew the answer.

"No."

"Then I'll walk."

"No you won't. I'll..."

"Figure it out. Yeah, I know. Night, sis."

"Hey, no more hitchhiking."

"Maybe that's part of how I'm figuring it out." The door to the boys' bedroom closed behind him. Blowing her bangs out of her eyes, Avery got up and heaved one of the laundry baskets into the chair she'd vacated. She folded clothes until her eyes began to water. When her eyelids protested staying open any longer, she carried her stack of clothes to her room, leaving the rest on the table.

Stowing the stack of clothes on top of the dresser, she plucked her favorite nightgown off the top and slipped it on. The constant chill in the air of the trailer tightened her nipples. What she wouldn't give for a nice set of muscles to keep her warm and safe. She glared at the back door to the trailer, which just happened to be in her bedroom. She'd stacked boxes in front of it, certain some kind of monster was going to come through it at any moment to murder her in her sleep.

A quick shiver shot through her. Using her very last reserves of energy to exercise control over her own thoughts, she shoved terrifying images of '80s horror flick monsters from her mind and replaced them with what Colton Holder might look like sprawled naked in her bed, beckoning to her.

The Holder boys were notorious players. Wild as they came, each generation more unrestrained than the one before. But he'd seemed different. She'd be willing to bet whoever finally got him to settle down would never have nightmares. He'd always keep her safe.

It was weird he was up there looking for work. As far as she knew, the Holders had more money than Jesus. Maybe he really had come to town to buy up land. The Holders were as notorious for being real-estate tycoons as much as they were cattle ranchers. They owned more land than any other family in the entire state of Oklahoma. But it had been sweet of him to offer to help her. At this point, she'd take a mercy fuck from a man like that just so she wouldn't feel so damn alone in this world, to ease the icy chill that had set up in the very marrow of her bones.

The buzz of her phone in her handbag shook her free from the erotic thoughts she'd allowed to go on for far too long. "Samantha? It's so late. Are you okay?"

"No, I'm not. You're not here and this is the best party I've been to in a while." Her friend's laughter assured her she was perfectly safe. She was just being Sam.

"Are you drunk?"

"No, Mom," she sneered. "Just checking on you. You haven't called since you moved yourself up to the frozen tundra or wherever the hell you are." Avery wondered if she'd ever sounded that vapid. Certainty she had at some point made her cringe.

"I have called. Like a dozen times. You haven't answered."

"Been busy with the new job I took for shits and giggles, oh...and cash. Lots and lots of cash."

Avery stood and started pacing in the three feet of space between her bed and bathroom door. Samantha had dropped out of Cosmetology school, Real Estate Licensing school, and Dental Hygienist school in that order in two months' time. She had no real marketable skills as far as Avery knew. "What kind of job?"

"You'll die when I tell you."

"I'm half-dead as it is so just tell me. You're not selling drugs, are you?"

"Ave, come on. Even I wouldn't do that. Mom and Dad gave me the big you have to pay your own way speech."

"Well, you are thirty." Avery couldn't help but roll her eyes, more at the girl she'd been than at Sam.

"Yeah, yeah. I knew it was coming, but I'm not a nine-to-five kind of girl, ya know?"

"Oh, I know." Avery shook her head. Currently, she'd donate her own toes to have clients from nine to five any day of the week.

"So, I wanted a job where I could party."

"Which is what?"

"And I get to put all of our years of ballet to good use, which, I mean, is kind of awesome because Lord knows we spent more time in those studios than we did our own freaking homes."

"That wasn't always a bad thing." Avery's opinion of her own home usually depended on which man was keeping her mother's bed warm from moment to moment.

"I know. Anyway, I got a job dancing at Scarlet A's."

"What's Scarlet A's?"

"Ave, come on, *Scarlet* A's."

Avery could almost hear Samantha's eye roll from five hundred miles away. She tried to remember something named Scarlet's in Oklahoma City. Suddenly a neon image surfaced in her brain. "The strip club?"

"Yep. Get this, I made eighteen hundred dollars in tips just last week. And I've made almost that much this week and it's not even the weekend yet."

"Holy crap."

"Yeah, I plan to shake it for a few months for some lonely dudes with more money than sense and then figure out what I want to do with my life. I'll have enough to live on for a while. I paid off an entire credit card in one week. Hey, do you think I'd make a good nurse? I'm thinking about nursing school."

Trying to imagine what she would do if someone handed her eighteen hundred dollars, Avery took a minute to process Sam's question. "Let's go back to the way you reacted to the skeletal jaw in hygienist school. I'm betting nursing school has even more skeletons."

"Ugh, that was gross. Okay, what about a party planner?"

"I could actually see that working for you."

"Yeah?"

"Definitely."

"I do throw a great party. But what about you? How's Nebraska? How's your new salon? I bet you're making everyone up there beautiful."

"Not my salon until my aunt and her best friend finally decide to retire, and Nebraska pretty much sucks so far."

"Then come home, Ave. Please. We miss you so much."

"I can't. I'm not even allowed to take Jax across state lines without Randy's permission. Besides, my aunt needs me to take her for her treatments, and I've always wanted to run my own shop. It's the only one in like a hundred-mile radius. If I made a few changes, we'd be so busy we could hire a few more stylists, but Pearl and Sally are happy with the way things are now. Which means Sally has clients all day and I have none."

"Hey, you listen to me, you are the best stylist, the best sister, and the best friend anyone could ever ask for. No one fights for shit they want harder than you do. Everyone will figure out how amazing you are. Give them some time. You're gonna figure this out. You always do."

Everyone kept saying that to her—give it some time—and she

finally spoke the rebuttal to Sam that she'd wanted to give the rest of them. "I don't have time to give anymore. I am officially out of time. Things keep getting worse and worse."

"Want me to send you some money?"

"No, Sam, but thanks. You keep all of your tips. I love you but I do not want money that's touched your ass or your vaj."

Samantha giggled hysterically. "Hey, it all spends the same. Maybe I could run it through the laundry."

Avery scowled. "I have to take Chase to school early tomorrow. Fill me in on everything and then I have to go to bed."

"Everything here is pretty much boring. Oh, I drove by Mirror, Mirror yesterday. Maybe it's good you aren't here to see it."

The ragged fragments of Avery's heart sank to her feet. "What are they doing with it?"

"Well, it's not so much an *it* anymore."

"What?" She wished Sam would just spit it out. Whatever had happened to her mother's legacy, the one the probate courts and county had seized to cover the debts, she wanted to know.

"They leveled it." Sam's voice was barely a whisper.

"What? Why? It was a fantastic salon. What about the yoga studio and that smoothie shop that went in beside it last year?"

"They're all gone. Some real estate investment firm came in and they're putting in another shopping mall out there. They've been buying up those stores along Carson Avenue. But let's talk about something else. Something fun. I don't like sad things." The forced change of tenor rubbed Avery raw. "You're up in cattle country, right? There have to be cute cowboys around. You have a cowboy's hat hanging on your bedpost yet?"

"Very funny." But a remnant of the girl she was before sparkled in the depths of her mind. She grasped it knowing the fool's gold was ultimately worthless, just like the party girl life she wasn't truly sorry she'd left behind. "Actually, you'll never guess who I met up here today."

"Is he cute?"

"Extremely."

"Who?"

"Colton Holder."

"Wait, like a Holder from here?" Samantha sounded far more excited than she should.

"Yep."

"Is it the one who does the rodeo stuff?"

"No, that's Jase Holder."

"Did I sleep with him once?"

"Quite possibly." Avery sighed.

"Oh, is he the one who's in the army?"

"I think that's Maddox, but don't quote me on that." Avery tried to recall all of the conversations she'd had with a few of the Holder women while they were in her chair.

"Is he the one that's a firefighter?"

"That's Jamie."

"Did you take some kind of Holder family class or something?"

"No, but I used to style some of their hair. They talked. I listened," Avery explained.

"Well, which one is Colton then?"

The best one. "All I know is he's one of the cowboy ones." Avery told herself she had no business smiling as much as she was currently.

"That's most of them."

"Which makes sense because they do own the largest cattle ranch in Oklahoma."

"Yeah, so what's he doing in Nebraska?"

"I'm not sure but I intend to find out."

When Avery ended the call, she slunk to the bathroom, remembered to lock the door from the hallway while leaving the one to her bedroom open, and tipped the lavender cleansing oil her mother had taught her to make onto a cotton ball. She methodically rubbed it over her eyes and cheeks, removing her makeup just the way she'd been instructed.

The stillness of the end of the day cemented her bare feet to the cold linoleum. A freezing blast of Nebraskan wind made its way around the shut window. The creaks and pops of the trailer jarred her. Why did it always have to sound like someone was coming in?

The ever-expanding knot in her throat grew larger. She trembled and dropped the cotton ball. Taking another from the Mason jar on her counter, she could almost hear her mother's voice. "Take care of your skin, my beautiful Avery, and it will take care of you. Never put anything on your body you wouldn't put in your body." A single tear trailed down her cheek, dissolving the oil. This was why she clung to the constant motion of her current life. As soon as she stopped moving, the bitter sadness and the anger caught her.

————

"Spread your legs for me, baby. Show me that wet pussy. Show me how ready you are for me." Jerking upright from the stale hotel room sheets, Colt scrubbed his hands over his face. He stared at the empty spot beside him and then at his own fingers. Dry as a bone. He would've sworn they were soaked with Avery's juices, ripe with need. Dammit, it had only been a dream, but what a dream... His heart rode hard in his chest, unappreciative of the interruption.

He staggered out of the bed, his feet protesting the prick of the cold carpeting. That blasted heater was loud enough to wake the dead, but he turned it up anyway. He had a job to do. Might as well get on with it.

After grabbing some breakfast and making the drive back to Pleasant Glen, Colt drove beneath that damned sign assuring the Camdens they could set their troubles down.

The fist of tension and dread in his gut tightened with every inch he progressed. The envelopes, one addressed to Ev and Jessie, and then one for Brock and each of the five kids, were shoved in the old briefcase his Uncle Wyn had let him borrow.

He knew their names but not their faces. His very soul was severed. Half of him was desperate to know them, whatever the cost. The other half wanted to turn his truck around and drive all the way back to Oklahoma, not stop until he crossed the Holder County Line. Damned lawyer could go on to hell. No one had the right to drop something like this on a family who believed they could lay down their troubles at the gates of their home. Every family deserved something like that, some defining belief about who they were, where they belonged, and what it all meant. He was about to decimate it all.

Yet, he drove on. The rough grind and slide of his truck tires over the first cattle guard registered in his mind. And there was the farmhouse on the right. The wrap-around porch and chimneys stood tall and proud and the front door was open. A screened door was the only barricade to intruders, as if no one was concerned about much of anything.

Another cattle guard vibrated under his tires. He kept count to keep sane. *Nothing more than a yellow-bellied coward.* Those were the last words his father had spoken to him, and at that moment, he felt certain there was a great deal of truth in them. There was one thing that gave him the strength to get out of the truck when he saw Brock Camden standing with a little boy in his arms in front of his brown house—the idea that he was only there for a job interview. The rest would keep. Of course, he'd never actually interviewed for a job before. It had been understood from the time of his birth that he would work Holder land until he died. For the most part, that had been fine by him.

"Mr. Holder?" Brock offered him a kind smile.

"Yeah. You Brock Camden?"

He laughed. The memory of a similar laugh—no, the very same one —frayed Colton's remaining nerves. "The one and only." He offered his hand. Colt accepted. He searched Brock's face for any recognition when their hands met but saw none. Brock's son had his father's and his grandfather's eyes. The Camden lineage stared back at him curiously.

"Well, this is it. Camden Ranch. My wife'll be out in a second to get him and we'll head over to the barns." The little boy in his arms lolled his head onto his father's shoulder, shoulders that matched Colton's in breadth and width from their shared life's work. "I'm this many." The little guy held up an entire hand's worth of fingers.

Brock chuckled again. Colt smiled at the little boy, wishing he had something to give him, something to let him know if he ever needed anything he would help him out.

"Uh, let's try this many." Brock helped his son lower his thumb and pinky. "There we go. You're that many. And this is Evan, my youngest for the moment."

"Hey, little man." Colton forced a smile. It took longer than it should have for Brock's words to register. "For the moment, huh? I take it you got another in the oven?"

"Nathan, my six-year-old, is at school, and yeah, my wife's pregnant again. That's another reason I need some help. She's awful sick with this one. Makes me wonder if it's a girl this time." Brock's storybook family stabbed through Colt. That same twinge that had rubbed him raw the day before in the bar when he saw Natalie with her husband chaffed over him again. What would it be like to have a wife and kids of his own with land to provide for them? He'd most likely never know.

"Congrats, man. Hope she feels better soon."

Brock grinned. "Hope's her name, actually. Here she comes." A cute brunette headed down the front steps. She couldn't have been very pregnant. She wasn't showing as far as he could see. She did have a slight green tinge to her though. Poor thing.

"Hey, baby, this is... I'm sorry, did I ever get your first name? I'm terrible with names."

"Colton. Just call me Colton."

"Okay, this is Colton. He's here about the ranch hand position."

"It's so nice to meet you, Colton. Gosh, you look familiar. Are you from around here?"

Shit. Colt ordered his mind to come up with some other phrase. It refused to follow orders. "Uh, no, ma'am. Must have one of those faces."

"Yeah, I was thinking that, too," Brock said as he handed Evan off to his wife. "Maybe we met in another life or something."

That was just a little too good of a guess. Colt slunk back away from the family. "Maybe so."

"Want to get the lay of the land?"

"Lead the way."

They spent the next two hours touring the ranch in Brock's truck. He talked off and on about the family business. Colt focused on breathing normally and mentally calling himself a pussy. One thing was glaringly obvious—Brock was nothing like Mick.

"You said your family had land down in Oklahoma. What brings you up here?" Brock tried again.

"Like I said, just a change of scenery."

"Guess I get that. Spent quite a few years living down on a beach in North Carolina. Met Hope down there. She was the best thing about being down there though. Couldn't wait to get back up here."

Gypsy Beach. The address on the will. Colt shook off that information. "Oh yeah? Kinda funny. Got my sights set on a girl from up here. She's the prettiest part of the scenery as far as I can tell."

Brock grinned as if a woman were a perfectly legitimate reason to leave Holder Ranch. "That makes more sense. What's her name?"

"Avery Hale."

"Avery?" Brock's brow furrowed. A half-second later realization echoed between their identical eyes. "Miss Pearl's niece, right?"

"Yeah, that's her."

"Haven't met her officially yet. I don't get into town too often. She's got all the holy-rollers up in arms about her purple hair or something, right? Hope was telling me about what some of them were saying. She's too sweet to tell 'em all what she really thinks of all of 'em. She'll probably come home with some new do out of solidarity."

"I like the way Avery wears her hair. It suits her."

"Whatever floats your boat, man. Miss Pearl's one of my favorite people. I used to go hide out at the Cut 'n' Curl when my dad was on one of his binges and out looking for me."

Holy fuck. What had Mick done to him? "She seemed real nice." Colt could barely breathe over the words. Brock seemed to sense his distress. He changed the subject.

"Basically, if you can ride, drive cattle from one field to another, drive a semi, and don't mind helping me bust up frozen ponds, you're hired."

"Spent my whole life doing all of that. Just need a horse." Every word he refused to speak burned like battery acid on his tongue.

"Well, like I said, we got plenty of 'em." Brock stopped at a large paddock. Three copper quarter horses were chewing hay like they didn't have a care in the world. Colton envied them.

"When can I start?" The chasm in his soul continued to expand. *Never want to leave. Should never have come.* He had no idea which he wanted more.

"You think you could start now? I got some calves to work this afternoon. If you want to take tomorrow off to get settled in that's fine."

"Sure thing. I promised a friend of mine I'd give him a ride this afternoon when school gets out. Think we'll be done with the working by four?" As much as Colt wanted to work he wasn't going to let Chase thumb a ride home with anyone else.

"Shouldn't take that long. We need to get the late calves worked from two pastures before the first snow."

"Count me in. You should be proud. You've got a beautiful ranch."

"It's home and it's mine. There's nothing better than that."

"Yeah." Having never had any land to call his own he couldn't relate. He'd tried to see the other half of Brock's ranch on their drive but Brock had stuck to the feed truck runs and his cousins' land.

"Oh, hey, here's a few of my cousins. Come meet them." They exited the truck and Colton swallowed down another round of dread. "This is Luke, Grant, and Austin. Their sister Holly is working at the free psych clinic in town today and their sister Natalie is off on her honeymoon. I'm running her portion of the ranch for her while she's gone. Guys, this is Colton Holder. He's my new winter hand."

More guilt piled in Colton's gut. He certainly couldn't stay in Nebraska through the winter. He'd used this job as an excuse to get to know the Camdens before he broke the news, but he'd told his uncles he'd be back in Holder County in a week or two.

"Good. We need some help." Luke offered his hand. "And you actually look like you know your way around a ranch. Had an idiot show up yesterday in a suit and alligator skin loafers, looking for a job. Believed he was gonna get richer learning to run a ranch."

"Greenhorns," all of the men present retorted at the same moment. That elicited a hearty round of laughter.

Austin extended his hand. "You kinda look familiar. You ever on the circuit? Or you got relations up here or something?"

"Came up ranching down in Oklahoma. Got a cousin on the circuit. Jase Holder. Kinda lost his edge lately. And no, no relations here." Bile singed his throat. He needed a toothpick. "But it's an honor to meet you. They show your ride in Vegas on the PBR network all the time. Helluva ride."

Austin gave him a single nod but didn't seem to appreciate the admiration.

"Oklahoma?" Luke chimed in. "We have a wheatgrass backlot property 'bout sixty miles due south of Oklahoma City. Out near Moore."

No. You used to have a wheatgrass property in Moore. "Really? Never been out there. Mostly stick to Holder County."

"That's north of the city, right? Think I've driven through there carrying calves," Grant commented.

"Yeah. Northwest of the city. From here you can't get to Moore without going through Holder lands." The Camden men shared glances that required no interpretation. *Then why the hell are you here?*

"We gonna work calves, boys, or are we working on our winter tans?" A voice that sounded so much like Mick Camden's Colt spun around prepared to see a ghost called out to them. Colt stared down what had to be Everett Camden. Mick's brother joined the gathered bunch, pulling on a pair of deerskin gloves.

"We're getting to it, Dad. Don't get your panties in a wad. Just meeting our new winter hand. This here is Colton Holder," Austin made introductions.

"Sir." Colt choked on the single word as he offered his hand.

"Ev Camden. Hey, did you happen into Saddleback's yesterday? My son-in-law came by here all up in arms over somebody asking about the Camdens."

Dammit. "Yes, sir. That was probably me. I'd heard you had need of a hand and I'm new in town, so I wanted to apply." *You are nothing but a filthy liar, just like your daddy.* Revulsion had him swaying in the incessant breeze.

"I figured it was something like that. He gets worked up about things. On the one hand, it's unnecessary. On the other, I like him being protective of my baby girl, not that either one of them bothered to call me and tell me they got up that mountain safely, mind you."

"Dad." Grant shook his head and laughed at his father. "Trust me, you don't want Nat calling from her honeymoon. And if Aaron is half as good as I am, he won't give her time to make a call."

Luke and Brock both groaned.

"He ain't a Camden. Let's not give him accolades, now," Austin goaded.

Ev glared at his sons. "I don't even want to think about it. All I'm saying is they coulda let me know she was all right. Driving to Colorado when we got a storm coming in..."

Colt studied the clear blue skies dotted with a few sparse clouds. If there was a storm coming, it was news to him.

"Notice he really don't give a shit if Aaron's okay. It's Nat he's worried about," Luke chimed in.

"Hush up, son, and go get the calf table ready. I intend to get this done and get back up to the house in case she does call."

"We using a table?" Colt asked, trying to drown out his thoughts by focusing on the job at hand.

"Yeah, it's not that many calves and most are big 'uns," Brock explained. "Be easier to table 'em and it won't take us as long. You'll be able to leave in time to pick up your friend."

"I appreciate that." Desperate to share any truth of himself he could to make up for the lies he'd been spewing, he went on. "It's Avery's little brother. She's got a lot on her plate and he's being every bit of sixteen he could possibly be."

All of the Camdens gave him approving smiles.

"Avery, huh?" Luke picked the single word out of his explanation. "That Miss Pearl's niece?"

"That's her," Brock answered for him.

"'Spect you'd like to impress Miss Pearl's niece right out of being a friend and right into being something more than that. That sound about right?" Ev had called him on the carpet, or rather the prairie grass.

Looking the older man in the eye, he nodded. "Might go something like that, sir."

Ev laughed and slapped Colton on the shoulder. "I ever tell you how I met my wife, son?"

Son? Holy shit. Where had that come from?

"Ah geez, here he goes," Austin sighed.

"How would you have told him, Uncle Ev? He just got here." Brock chuckled.

"Well, that's how I usually start the story. Don't mess up my flow, boy."

Colt helped Brock and Luke hoist the calf table out and set it up. The thing was a classic.

"How many calves you figure we've sent through here, Dad?" Grant asked.

"Been using it since me and your uncle Mick was boys. Gotta be more than a hundred thousand, but you ain't distracting me outta my story, so pick your post and shut your mouth."

Colton's head swam as he tried to envision Mick as a child. "I can guide 'em or stand in the hole." He preferred to volunteer for the worst jobs, which kept him from being ordered to do them. A choice was always easier to swallow than a command. It helped him keep up the illusion that his uncles considered him as much a part of the Holder family as his cousins.

"Nah, we got it." Brock shook his head. "I'll guide 'em if you can catch?"

"You sure?" The guide was going to be wearing enough cow shit to fertilize four football fields by the time they were done. The guy catching the calves and closing the table would remain relatively clean.

"Yeah, it's fine. Just don't get knocked down. Like I said, some of 'em are big."

"Been doing this since the calves were taller than me. I'm good." The trick of it was to catch the calf with your hands and your might before he rammed headlong into your groin, which would bring you to your knees in a heartbeat.

Austin made quick work of driving the gathered calves toward the table. Clearly the guy's skills weren't limited to hanging on to a bull.

When they started working, Ev naturally guided his family and Colton, exactly like a father should. "Pull." His guttural command flowed from him on instinct.

Quickly finding his rhythm, Colt caught the calf's neck, shut the table, and pulled the mechanism to lay the animal on its side. Luke jumped in with the vaccination shots. Brock stamped a BC brand on the calf's hind quarters, and Grant took care of the castration. Took less than thirty seconds. The Camdens worked together like a well-oiled machine.

Ev leapt back into his story once they'd established a rhythm. "I have a good buddy, Nash Tillerson. Right after he got back from Vietnam, he inherited enough cash from his grandpa's passing to open a ranching equipment supply store out in Ogallala. Said he needed me and another buddy of ours, Tandy Monroe, to come out and help him drive tractors into the store for the display and what not."

"In exchange for what?" Grant asked as he carried on with his job. The bucket of nuts continued to fill.

"What'd I tell you 'bout interrupting me?"

"We've heard this story near 'bout as many times as this table has seen calves, Dad. I'm trying to make it more interesting."

"It oughta interest you since it's how we got you here. Now, hush up or I'll start telling honeymoon stories."

All of the Camden shuddered and gagged their disapproval. Colt only chuckled.

"Anyway, we got the tractors loaded into the shop without too much destruction. Nash asked me if I'd mind letting him ride back to the Glen with us since his truck was loaded down with cattle feed to be sold. Since we was all the way in Ogallala, naturally we stopped in for Runzas."

"What's a Runza?" Colt got caught up in the story.

The Camdens all grinned.

"It's the only kind of sandwich that matters, city boy," Grant teased.

"Have to see if I can find one, I guess."

"Closest Runza restaurant is out where we were in Ogallala, which is about an hour due west from here," Ev supplied. "Jessie'll be wanting one here soon, gets a craving for 'em now and again. Maybe we can all go out there."

Colt didn't mention that he was staying at a hotel in Ogallala. Good to know he could occasionally keep his mouth shut. The easy way Ev had added him to a future family outing had shaken him. It felt good, probably too good, but it also reminded him of why he was really there.

"After our Runzas, we headed back to the Glen. I was driving and we were cutting up. I near about sideswiped a car pulled off the road out on Rural Route 276. I'd been ornery all afternoon, uneasy like. Felt like something was coming—a storm—and I couldn't stop it. Wasn't entirely sure I *wanted* to stop it. Ended up being the most beautiful storm I'd ever laid eyes on."

Colt grinned at Ev's determination to tell his story through to the end without cutting corners. Truthfully, he wanted to hear it as badly as Ev wanted to tell it.

None of these men were anything like Mick. They were the kind of men who'd give you the shirt off their back if you needed it. The kind of men he wanted to be.

"Now hear this, son, the Camden name means a whole lot of things," Ev vowed. Shock gripped Colt by the short hairs. Did he know?

Brock let another calf through and he missed this one. He turned just in time to be butted in his hip instead of his 'nads.

"And I tell you this 'cause I expect anyone working for Camden Ranch to understand that as long as you're working here, you're family. You're to go out and do good for this town, for this county, for this state. Hell, even for this country that's so damned and determined to tear itself apart at the seams."

Colt's heart jolted back to life and then attempted to sprint out of his chest. Desperate to focus on the task at hand, he repositioned the calf and tried to pretend nothing had happened. Dammit, he was going to be black and blue come morning.

This was nothing more than a *don't ruin the Camden name while you're associated* speech. He could handle that. He'd grown up hearing the same thing about the Holder name.

"One of the things Camden stands for is cattle rancher, another is respectful men who take care of anyone who might need a little help. When I pulled up next to that car that day out on 276, I saw her slumped over the steering wheel. I jumped outta my truck and headed toward her. She lifted her head, tears pouring outta them pretty green eyes. It was the weirdest thing. My heart near about beat out of my chest and I couldn't have held glue in my hands they were so sweaty. I'll tell you right now, I woulda rather been hit by one of them bulls my son used to throw himself off of than to see her like that. I opened that car door and she stood up and tried to explain to me that she'd run out of gas, but she ended up falling into my chest. That was it. I was sold. No going back.

"She was scared and exhausted and needed someone to look after her. That's why the good Lord put me here on this earth. I figured it out then and there. She told me she was bad lost and I found myself wanting to tell her she was home. You shoulda seen her trying to climb in the cab of my old truck between three cowboy hats. Brought her back here, convinced her to marry me, and then made her raise these yahoos. Bless her. Woman deserves three crowns in heaven."

"And here comes the *this is the way of the Camden men* portion of the tale," Luke goaded his father. "Hang tight, Colton. He's almost done."

"When did you meet Indie Jane, Luke Camden?" Ev demanded of his oldest son.

Luke rolled his eyes. "First day of high school."

"And when did you fall in love with her?"

"First day of high school," Luke conceded.

"Grant?" Ev continued down the line. Colt had no idea what they were getting at.

Grant's eye roll was a duplicate of his brother's. "Yeah, yeah, the Camden thing. We know, Dad. My baby drove her Honda into the hitch of my truck. We got married a few months later."

"Brock?" Ev ordered next.

"Uncle Ev, mine was a little different." Brock jerked an old handkerchief out of his back pocket and mopped his brow. He wouldn't look his uncle in the eye.

"No, it wasn't, boy. You don't have to be mine to be a Camden. Go on with it."

"All right, fine, first time I saw Hope I wanted her. Took me several years to get us there, but he's right that some part of me knew right off."

"Worked the same way for my girls and Austin, too. See, we

Camdens know as soon as we meet the person we're meant to spend our whole lives with," Ev explained. "Might be like that for you, too. Never know. Can't just be a Camden thing. Maybe this girl you're trying to impress is your one and only, son."

Certain his tongue had turned to sand, Colt tried to come up with some kind of appropriate response. "Doubt I'm that lucky, sir," summed it up.

Not lucky enough to really be a Camden. Not lucky enough to really be a Holder, either. And certainly not lucky enough to ever claim strong, sexy, sassy Avery Hale with hips thick as honey and lips that had to be twice as sweet, as his own no matter how many times she'd shown up in his dirty dreams the night before.

"Well, it's good to see we've already inundated Brock's new hand with your stories, Everett." A short, auburn-headed woman sporting a smirk exited a Suburban carrying a basket with thermoses from varying ranching supply stores. "I brought you all some coffee."

"Thanks, Aunt Jess." Brock motioned to Austin to keep the rest of the calves back in the corral. "This is Colton Holder."

Colt started to offer his hand but cringed. "Sorry, ma'am. Hands are filthy."

Jessie Camden stared at him like she'd seen a ghost. She said nothing about his hands. She said nothing at all. She just stared at him with her mouth hanging open.

Panic twisted his gut and shot outward through his veins in painful jolts.

She shook her head. "What did you say your name was, son?"

"Uh... I'm Colton... Holder."

CHAPTER FOUR

Wondering if it burned more fuel to idle than it would to turn her car off and then try to re-crank it, Avery touched her father's name on her contact list. She cringed as soon as her father answered her call but attempted to summon bravery she was quickly running out of. "Hey, Daddy."

"There's my girl. How are you? Sharon and I are worried sick about you."

"I'm okay. I kind of need...a little help. I can pay you back." Somehow she sank lower in the freezing seat of her car. She didn't have enough gas to run the heater.

This wasn't how her life was supposed to go. She was a grown woman asking her father for money. Jesus, how had she gotten it all so screwed up?

"Baby girl, I put a few hundred bucks in your account last night. I wish you'd let me help you more than this and you will absolutely not pay me back. I may not have gotten along with your mother, but I know what she meant to you. I still can't believe you've decided to take on the boys all by yourself."

"Thank you for the money. I swear I can do this. It's what Mama wanted and I do want to take over the salon here. Besides, Aunt Pearl needs my help. She's offered me money several times, but you wouldn't believe how much we have to pay for her medicines on top of the chemo."

"Don't get me started on healthcare in this country. I can send Pearl a little to help out as well. I don't have an endless supply but it kills me how sad you sound, Avie."

"I'll try to sound happier when I call."

"Sweetheart, I don't want you to sound happier. I want you to *be* happier."

"I want that, too, but Aunt Pearl would never accept your help."

"Well, that must be where you get your stubbornness from. Her and your mother."

"Thanks for the money. I *will* pay you back. I need to get gas and get to work. Can't fix hair if I'm not there."

"Don't work too hard. You get that trait from me."

"Yeah, I know. Love you, Daddy."

"Love you, too, my Avie."

As soon as Avery arrived at the Cut 'n' Curl, she dug through her bag until she located one of the special K-cups from the stash her step-mother had packed up for her. She saved them for when she really needed a boost. Popping the organic fair-trade French roast pod in the Keurig, she watched her favorite mug fill with the dark, delectable liquid and then added a hearty shot of cream from the mini fridge. If only coffee were as capable of curing empty bank accounts as it was bad moods.

The first sip helped her see beyond the hanging dryers, which had been on life support since the Ford administration, and the chiffon pink styling chairs old enough to have given birth to her. A little spit and polish and a whole lot of love would turn it into a real salon someday.

Someday. She allowed herself a long moment to imagine it as she added a packet of sugar to her coffee. Someday, she'd start making money the way she used to. She'd replace the ancient chairs and the oxidizing mirrors. Install some slick tile flooring. Upgrade everything. Have a computer created in this century instead of that appointment book Sally used to write notes on changes she felt the producers of

Days of Our Lives should make instead of keeping track of actual appointments. She'd build a display case for the organic, homemade beauty products she'd always made with her mother.

Someday she'd have herself a real salon.

Her heart leapt when the bell on the front door jingled. Sally wasn't there yet. Maybe this would be her chance at a walk-in client. Her hope was dashed immediately. Sally's poodle, Theodora, dragged Sally, who was trying to hang on to the leash, through the front door.

Avery attempted to sink her teeth into her tongue, but the words came spilling out. "Sally, the State Board is going to be in to check this place out. We're going to get shut down for cleanliness issues if you keep bringing Theodora to work."

"You sound like my son. You kids and your wanting everyone to follow the rules. I'll have you know the inspector is a big fan of mine."

"That doesn't matter. I just got my license in Nebraska, and when they come check on me, they're going to see *her* and shut us down." As she said this, Theodora leaped up into Sally's chair and Sally put a pink floral cape on the damned dog.

"No one's going to shut us down, Avery. Like I said, the state inspector and I are *friends*."

Avery narrowed her eyes. "What kind of friends?"

"The kind who keep each other from getting lonely on cold winter nights." She waggled her eyebrows.

Avery fought not to gag. "I see."

When Sally got out the special perm rollers she saved only for Theodora, Avery wondered how hard she'd have to hit her head on her station to put herself out of her misery.

"Cold winter nights brings me to what we were talking about yesterday. If I've heard it once, I've heard it two dozen times. The ladies aren't real keen on you cutting their husbands' hair with you being unattached and all."

"That is ridiculous and it makes no sense. Even if the ladies don't want me cutting their husbands' hair, my relationship status shouldn't stop *them* from sitting in my chair."

"They're just wanting to see a little of your work. Have to give them time." There it was again, that sentiment about time, but Sally wasn't nearly finished. "But besides all that, you need a warm set of muscles to keep you nice and hot this winter. You think the weather in Oklahoma was cold. You ain't seen nothing yet, girly. Might put you in a better mood, too." She grumbled under her breath as if Avery couldn't hear her.

"And where would this hypothetical set of muscles keep me warm?" she spat out. "I live with my aunt and my two younger brothers." The logistical argument would get her nowhere but she dug her heels in anyway. Her stubbornness was her only friend as of late.

Sally pursed her lips. "No man in his right mind's gonna take you on with that attitude, young lady."

I'm thirty. She longed to rage in Sally's face. To insist she would not be treated like a child. Her mother had thought she was capable of taking all of this on, so she had to be. End of story.

Before she could come up with a retort, the bell on the door jingled again. Whirling around with the expectation of seeing the state inspector, she prepared to apologize and plead for mercy only to find a sweet little old lady easing inside with the use of her walker.

"Oh, goodness, let me help you, ma'am." Rushing to the door, she guided the woman in out of the cold.

"How are ya, Gretchen?" Sally bellowed from the other side of the shop.

"I'm all right, Sally. How's Pearl?"

"Fighting hard, which is all any of us can ask of her. Poor thing doesn't have anyone to help her. Now she's taken in her sister's kids. It's a mess."

Avery gasped her disdain. In the last two months, she'd driven her aunt all the way to Lincoln for chemo treatments, gotten her medications, made certain she took them on time, cleaned the house, cooked the food, checked on her aunt constantly, and helped out in any other way she possibly could.

Sally ignored her irritated sound.

"Well, I'll see if I can't get one of my cakes to her next week. That's good for what ails ya. Now, when you're finished with Theodora's perm, I'm here for my regular wash and set."

"I could do your hair, ma'am. That way you wouldn't have to wait."

Avery gestured to her chair, refusing the hope that stupidly kept sparking in her chest like one of those ridiculous re-lighting candles her mother used to put on her birthday cakes.

Gretchen eyed her cautiously, her lips pursed. Avery debated offering her the almond lip cream she created that would help with wrinkles.

"Uh, I graduated top of my class in Cosmetology school. I've been doing this for years. I'll take good care of you."

"Yes, well, I wouldn't care for my hair to be purple. Can't fathom what gets into some people."

"Oh." Avery shook her head. "No problem. We can keep it simple. Whatever you prefer."

"She's Pearl's niece. She's real good," Sally vowed, much to Avery's shock.

"I do need to get over to Reverend Higgins's house to discuss last week's sermon with him. I have a few notes he should heed for this Sunday."

Glancing skyward in a silent prayer for the reverend, which she was certain he was going to need, Avery forced a smile. "You know, I could do a rinse and deep conditioning treatment that would really bring out your gray and make it shine. We could cut it a little differently in the back to give you some fullness and a little height, which would high-light your cheekbones. Give me a shot."

"I've been trying to downplay my gray for the last thirty years. What do you mean you're going to bring it out? Don't we want it to go back in?"

"Women are beautiful no matter what age they are or what hair color they have. My aunt is still stunningly beautiful and she has no hair at all right now. We all have beauty inside of us. It's my job to help you take care of you. I'm just going to make your outside as pretty as your inside."

That did it. Gretchen let Avery help her up into the chair. "I happen to think it would be better if women wouldn't show off so much of what they've decided is pretty. I for one have always believed it was an egregious error that 'blessed are the chaste' was left out of the sermon on the mount." She pointed to Avery's cleavage. "I will admit

I'm interested in seeing what you can do with my hair. But vanity has always been my struggle and I do not intend to indulge in it, so I'll just have my regular wash and set."

Avery and her mother used to joke that someone should write a book on things stylists wished they could say out loud to their clients. She mentally added, *You may not like my tits, sweetheart, but I'm rather fond of them and I won't be told how I should exist in this world,* prude to the book. She refused to believe even a woman as uptight and sanctimonious as Gretchen couldn't be softened a little and taught how to find the ample strength in her femininity. Instead of making her as beautiful outside as she was inside, Avery would have to make her prettier on the outside and she'd pray the inside caught up.

There was the small matter that she didn't actually know how to do a wash and set. They hadn't been taught in cosmetology school in the past two decades. Stylists tended to age with their clients. Wash and sets were standard fare for women of a certain age. That age just happened to be forty years older than Avery. But hair was her medium and she could make this work. She refused to have any doubt. Algebra, arguing with Sally, and being a stellar stand-in mom might not be her specialty but hair certainly was.

———

When they finished up the last of the calves, Grant and Luke volunteered to turn them back out in Brock's pastures. Weighted with guilt and unease from the way Jessie Camden had studied him, Colt went on with one of the things he needed to accomplish.

For all the time he'd spent with the Camdens today, he'd done nothing to further the Holders' mission. Determined to prove he was more than a coward bastard, he climbed up into Brock's truck. "You mind showing me the rest of the land I'll be working? I'd like to get the lay of things."

"Sure. I need to check Nat's calves first, but then we can take the long way back to my house."

On ragged edge, Colton reached for the pack of toothpicks he kept in his pocket. As he shoved one in his mouth, he noted the old CB radio hook up in the truck. "Haven't seen one of them in a day or two." He wondered how old the truck was.

Brock chuckled. "Yeah, we used 'em up here longer than I 'spect you all used them down in Oklahoma. Took us years to get cell towers all the way out here. You know, my old man used to do that toothpick thing once he quit smoking."

Colton yanked the toothpick out of his mouth. "Oh yeah?" He couldn't recall seeing Mick with a toothpick ever. Of course, for most of his life when Mick came around he stayed as far away as he could.

"Yeah, he was an ornery asshole of the highest caliber."

I know. "Yeah. My...uh...dad was like that, too. Guess we have that in common."

Brock offered him a genuine, sympathetic glance. "My old man used to go out on drinking binges and then drive. We used the CB in the trucks to let the whole town know to keep off the roads when he was on 'em. That's how I knew when to stay at Uncle Ev and Aunt Jessie's, too, or to head to Miss Pearl's like I was telling you."

Colton cracked the window. He needed some air. His lungs had momentarily forgotten how to take it in. Jesus, he'd always known Mick was an ass. He just hadn't had to exist in the same world with him on a daily basis. Mick would show up in Holder County for a week or two every few months.

Brock kept talking, seeming to understand that Colt couldn't at the moment. "When Hope and I first moved back up here, the closest cell tower was between here and Ogallala. We got okay reception until the snow came in. Whole town switched right back to the CBs every winter. We were bundled up in the truck one night when we heard Betty Morris come over the air demanding to know where Old Bud was and when he'd be home for supper."

A grin automatically formed on Colt's features. A foreign sensation, like some other entity had taken over his face. Was this how it could've been if everything hadn't gotten so fucked-up? Hearing the old stories. Making fun of other ranching families in the area. He managed a chuckle. "Bet that pissed Bud off."

"Bud didn't answer and that got Betty fired up. She made three or four other calls demanding to know when he'd be home to eat his meatloaf. When he still didn't answer, she proceeded to tell him off over the radio, knowing full well that at least fifty other ranchers could hear her. Went as far as announcing that he'd gone from being a stallion to a jackass before he made it off his horse and back to his truck to answer her."

"Poor guy. Rough having the whole fucking town know you can't get your cowboy saddled up for a rodeo anymore."

"Jesus, you sound like Austin. You're gonna fit in around here just fine. Anyway, Hope and I were cracking up. We weren't the only ones of course. By Monday morning, the entire town had picked sides. Either you were on Betty's side and thought Bud shoulda told her when he'd be in for supper or you were on Bud's side and knew that sometimes chores don't quite go as quickly as you'd like. People drew up petitions. Preacher kept preaching on love being patient and kind. Ed Olsen, who owns Saddleback's, refused to serve anyone who wasn't on Bud's side. The Ladies Aid Society refused to make their Sunday school breakfast the first Sunday of the month unless the preacher declared Betty was right. 'Bout four months later, the city council made sure we had two cell towers out here. They even had one of those ribbon cutting ceremonies for them."

"My great-granddaddy Holder used to say there's no bigger bully than a small town, but there ain't anywhere that's better either."

"Ain't that God's honest truth."

"Hey, you got a calf out there." Colton pointed to the small animal burrowed down in the grass. The herds were nowhere nearby.

"Shit. You got a good eye."

"Been doing this my whole life."

Brock studied him for a second and then said, "Can you help me get her?"

"Of course."

They got the calf loaded in the truck and up to the barn. Colt and Brock stood by while Luke checked her out. "Needs a heater and a little love. You check any of the mamas to see if they're baying for her?"

"Wanted to get her up here to you first," Brock explained.

"I can go do that if you don't mind me taking your truck," Colton volunteered. Taking the calves from their mamas was the worst part of being a rancher. He always volunteered to help pair them back up if given the chance.

"Thought you needed to pick somebody up at the school?" Grant asked.

"Shit. Is it that late?" He checked his watch. It was nearing lunch time.

"Nah, but it might take you a few to find the mama. Nat runs a thousand head."

"It's fine. I don't need to head to the school 'til four. I'm hoping to catch the football coach before he leaves for the day."

"Oh yeah?" Grant smiled. "Well, you could talk to the assistant coach right now."

"Seriously?"

"Yeah, but my Katy's getting on into her second trimester. I told Coach Wilhelm I'd help him out until my newest one makes his appearance."

"His?" Luke laughed. "You know something we all don't? Thought Katy didn't want to know with this one."

"I figure unlike my big brother—" Grant smacked Luke's shoulder, "—I only make boys."

Brock rolled his eyes. "You figured that out after having only one."

If Colt closed his eyes and listened, the Camdens would be almost indistinguishable from a few of his Holder cousins harassing each other about their kids. "Hate to interrupt a good pissing contest, but what were you saying about being one of the football coaches?"

The Camdens all laughed.

"I like him." Luke nodded to Colt.

"Sorry. Got distracted by my own manliness," Grant goaded. Everyone else groaned. "Anyway, what'd you need with Coach Wilhelm?"

"The kid I was telling you about, Avery's brother. He's hating life six ways from Sunday. Used to play football at his old school but figures he can't play here until next season."

"I thought we were the only cowboys who said shit was six ways from Sunday." Austin looked impressed.

Colton rushed through his request in an effort to cover his panic. "I thought I'd ask the coach if he could walk on. I played through school. It's pretty much the only reason I graduated."

"Oh yeah?" Brock lit up at that information. "What position did you play?"

"Receiver."

"No way." Luke and Brock shared a reminiscent grin. "Brock was the best receiver we had 'til he up and moved, leaving me high and dry."

"Nah," Brock shook off the praise. "You did fine without me, but I sure as hell get football being the only reason you got through school."

Grant leapt back into the conversation. "You're really going all out for this girl. She's the one with the purple hair, right?" Grant asked.

"Yeah, that's her."

"She must be something for all you're doing for her."

She is. Colton's mouth watered as he recalled the few quick instances he'd had the pleasure to be in the company of Avery. "I'm trying to be a friend to her. She's had a rough go for a while from what I can tell."

"I figure Dad was right. You're thinking helping her out will ultimately get her to your bed." Grant smirked.

"Sure as hell wouldn't mind if that was the outcome, but I'd like to help her even if it don't end up that way."

"Dad didn't mention this in his lecture, but helping a brother get laid is something else the Camden name means." Austin stuck the tip of his tongue between his teeth and chuckled.

"Guess I'd be much obliged then." Lowering his guard for just a second, he allowed himself to feel like he was genuinely one of them. Like maybe he belonged here.

"We don't have any rules about walk-ons. We don't have enough players to be picky about shit like that," Grant explained. "What's the kid's name?"

"Chase." Colt paused. Avery's last name was Hale and Chase didn't know his sperm donor. "Not sure about his last name truthfully."

"You know what position he played?"

"No idea, but there's fire in him."

"There's a Young Rodeo competition tonight, so we're not having practice, but tell him to come see the coach tomorrow at school. We'll get him suited up."

"I appreciate it, and hey, any fees or uniform costs or anything I'll cover."

CHAPTER FIVE

"There we go." Avery beamed. "What do you think, Gretchen?" Ignoring the awful screech the chair made as she forced it to spin back toward the mirror, she whipped the cape off and showed off her hard work. It was a masterpiece if she did say so herself.

"I think you should call me Mrs. Parsons since you have neither the wisdom nor position to call me Gretchen."

Avery's heart sank through the storm roiling in her stomach and landed somewhere in the vicinity of her feet.

"However," Mrs. Parsons turned from side to side. Her green eyes lit and sparkled. Though clearly trying to maintain her severe demeanor, she couldn't keep from smiling.

Avery's heart made a quick return trip to her chest. Damn thing was making her woozy. "You like it? I think it looks fantastic."

"Don't gush, child. How did you manage this exactly?"

"I make my own aloe deep conditioning treatment for gray hair. It softens it and brings out the shine. Then I did a vinegar wash. The harsh water up here can dull hair. After that I did a blue shampoo and rinse. With this cut, it brings out all of your best features." Accomplishment rushed through Avery's veins. God, she'd missed this.

"And can I purchase this conditioning thing you did? Mind you, I do not spend money on worldly things like hair."

Avery bit the side of her mouth to keep from giggling. "Not yet. I'm hoping to have enough made to sell in the shop by spring. My aloe plants haven't handled the move all that well."

When Mrs. Parsons started to stand, Avery handed her the cane and guided her upwards. Maybe she could start her repayment program to her father with her tip. She totaled up the treatments and cut and announced the price.

"Thirty-five dollars!" Mrs. Parson's gasped. "You cannot be serious. A wash and set is eight dollars. Has been for years. I'll have you know I started driving all the way into Ogallala when Pearl and Sally raised the price from five fifty, didn't I, Sally?"

Sally was combing out Theodora's perm. "She did. But you came back real quick like when you saw what they were charging out there. Hush up and pay her, Gretch. You look great. She earned it."

"I did do several additional treatments, plus your cut, which isn't part of a wash and set." Avery hoped that was actually true.

"Well." Mrs. Parsons spent the next five minutes meticulously filling out a check, of all things. She mumbled something about vanity, rich men, and eyes of needles. When she finally handed it over, Avery stared at the number. Thirty-five dollars. No tip. Gall rode on the bile that shot to her throat as the awful woman made her way out of the shop.

"She didn't tip me," Avery spat out as soon as Mrs. Parsons was in her car.

"Gretch doesn't tip for anything. Says she won't pay one penny more for services. Thinks waitresses, hair dressers, and anyone working in a hotel shoulda considered that before they took on that job," Sally explained.

Avery slammed the cash register drawer shut with her hip and ground her teeth. Before she could continue bitching, the phone rang. Hope once again flickered to life under her skin. She wondered how many times she'd have to be disappointed before it would quit that foolishness. "The Cut 'n' Curl, Avery speaking," she answered. "Oh—" she cringed, "—hold on one second." She covered the ancient receiver. "It's a funeral home for you, Sally. I hope every-thing's okay."

Sally didn't look terribly concerned as she took the call. "Hey, Burt, you need us today? Uh-huh. Oh, dear, well they lived a good long life I s'pose. Nah, Pearl ain't able to come out there and I got appointments all afternoon. Wish they'd died a little earlier."

Avery told herself she could not possibly have heard that correctly.

"Hey, you know we got Pearl's niece working out here now. She's needing the work and I bet she'd do a real fine job. Knock you dead so to speak," Sally and the man on the phone both howled with laughter.

Avery rubbed her temples. Dear God, where had she moved?

"I'll send her out your way. She'll make 'em look real nice for their showing tonight."

Their showing?

"All right, have a good one, Burt. We'll see you later." Sally hung up the phone. "Seems Mr. and Mrs. Lancaster have passed on to their heavenly home. He was ninety-seven. She was ninety-five. Died yesterday morning in each other's arms. Married seventy-three years."

"Oh, I'm so sorry. Were they friends of yours?"

"I didn't know them that well. They lived out in Kempton."

"That's so sweet though. I didn't know there were any couples like that around anymore."

"Oh, that's nonsense. You just gotta find yourself the right man and then drive him all the right kinds of crazy so he don't want to up and die on you 'til you're ready to go yourself. And that's that."

Avery suspected there was a great deal more to it than that, but the part of her that still believed in fairy-tale endings wished it were that easy. What she wouldn't give to find a man who'd willingly walk through this life and into the next with her.

For some ridiculous reason, Colton Holder's face appeared in her mind. Just like that hope she couldn't rid herself of, the idea of him being hers was just as insane. No man in their right mind would will-ingly agree to take her on with both of her brothers.

"They need you to go out and do their hair and makeup for the visi-tation tonight." The harsh scrape of Sally's voice jerked Avery back to the present.

"Wait. What?"

"Normally Pearl handles the mortuary visits, but seeing as she can't I figured you could use the money. Plus, you did Gretchen up real nice. You can handle Harvey and Nora. Just watch the blush. The dead ought not look like they're about to fill in as back up dancers in the main tent for a circus freak show."

"I know." Quelling her sense of panic, she took a two deep breaths. "I did my mother's makeup and hair."

"Good. Now get going. Visitation starts at five."

"You have my cell phone number if you need me," Avery reminded her.

"I've got it. Go on now. I've got to get Marion Denton's neck waxed before *Days* comes on."

Hair is hair. Avery repeated the mantra to herself as she attempted to find Kempton, the next ranching town over, on the map on her phone. Kempton had the funeral home and a few little shops but Pleasant Glen had the honkytonk and the feed store.

Poor Siri struggled out in the sticks. When the directions finally registered, she cranked the car heater up as high as it would go and pulled out onto the main drag. "It's not that I don't like dead people," she spoke to the ether. "It's just I'm better with live ones." That was true. Her mother had taught her to cultivate life in everything she touched. But her mother wasn't here anymore. "I can do this."

———

Satisfied as he watched the calf reunite with her mama, Colt took Brock up on his offer to wash up at his house. "You sure you don't need me tomorrow?"

He wished Brock would tell him to come back in the morning. They hadn't driven over the other half of the ranch, and truth be told, he'd like to spend more time with him.

"Nah, take the day. I'm sure you know a day off is worth more than gold to a rancher."

Colt nodded to Hope, who was lying on the couch with a weary look in her eyes. "Hope you feel better, ma'am."

She sat up. "Don't call me ma'am. I'm not that old." She laughed. "And I will feel better in about seven months."

"Congratulations. You have a nice family." Once again, he clipped his own words short.

"Thanks. I swear I've been tired ever since I birthed that one." She pointed to their oldest, who was holding a cookie over his head and out of the reach of his little brother. "Nate, give him the cookie," Hope ordered.

Colt chuckled. "I'll see you later."

His cell phone was ringing before he climbed back in his truck. At least it wasn't that damned lawyer. "Hey, Uncle Gentry."

"You sound like hell, son. I take it this ain't going quite as smoothly as my little sister thinks it ought to."

"When is anything ever as easy as my mother thinks it oughta be?"

"That's a better than fair point. You met the Camdens yet?"

"Yes, sir."

"You told 'em who you are?"

"No, sir."

His uncle's smooth, even laughter eased his soul. "Hey, you got every right in the world to take your time with this. Just remember the world keeps right on spinning even when we wish it'd slow down."

"Yeah, I know, but it's not something you just drop on someone." Colt was well aware he was doing everything he could to buy more time.

"Damn straight. 'Specially considering everything else tied up in all this."

"That's what I keep trying to tell that damned lawyer."

"Yeah, well lawyers want everyone doing their work for 'em to get it done yesterday, but when they're charging by the hour it takes seven weeks of Sundays."

"You forgettin' you have a niece that's a lawyer, Uncle Gent?"

"Well, she's the exception to the rule. Give that lawyer my number. I ain't having you harassed about all this."

Colton knew any of his uncles would've made the same offer. Holders through and through. You crossed one, you got 'em all. He reminded himself of how much he loved his family. "I'll be all right. How's the ranch?"

"Missing you. Bailey rode Rio for you, she said he was missing your ass on his back."

Chuckling at that, Colton felt a pang of regret for even agreeing to all of this. "Tell 'em I'll be back in a few weeks."

"You think it'll take that long?"

"Like I said, I don't want to drop all of this on them and I kinda sorta might have something else I need to do while I'm up here."

"What's her name?"

"That obvious?"

"You're a Holder. Every single one of you kids has more wild oats than the Quaker family harvests each year. There's a reason there's dozens of grandkids in this family. We're a virile lot. And you ain't ever let your bed stay cold for too long," Gentry stated pointedly.

Unable to argue that, Colt let the familiar ease of talking with his uncle wash through him. "Her name's Avery."

"Careful now. Wasn't it you that your Uncle Wyn caught with not one but two buckle bunnies the last time the PBR came through town?"

"I'm never gonna live that down, am I?"

"I'll tell you the truth. I didn't know whether to shake your hand or whip your ass that night."

"I wouldn't say it was one of my finest moments."

"The fact that you'll admit to that tells me maybe you're on the downward slope of Fool's Hill. I'll be the first to tell ya good judgment comes from experience and experience comes from a whole lot of bad judgment. And speaking of you getting experience, Wyn and I talked the Jenkins boy out of pressing assault charges. I still wouldn't rush back to Holder County, but at least he's not out for Holder blood anymore."

"Charges woulda been a bunch of bullshit anyway. He got mouthy and slapped his wife. I won't have that and neither would you. I stepped in but he threw the first punch."

"Which might give you something to stand on if you didn't have three priors. Does this Avery know about your penchant for fucking and fighting?"

Colt laughed. "Nah. I figured I wouldn't have much of a shot if she saw my fucked-up resume right off."

"You know I met your Aunt Leigh because she was the nurse who bandaged me up in the Emergency Room after a bar fight. Almost got in another fight in the room with your Uncle Barrett 'cause he flirted with her. Took her more than a day or two to cool my temper."

"You saying maybe there's hope for me yet?" Colton goaded.

"All I'm saying is all the other women you've bedded and turned out never seemed to have names when I asked. There's something different about this one."

Colt had been telling himself that very thing all morning. "Not sure it matters either way. I'd just like to help her out if I can." *I'd like a chance to be a man instead of an asshole.*

"Mmm-hmm, said that to myself when I met your Aunt Leigh, too."

"You know, Ev Camden kinda reminds me of you." Colt's truck bounced as he drove from the gravel road to the dirt to leave Camden Ranch.

"He the senior Camden?"

"Yeah, but he's Mick's younger brother."

"He a good man?"

"Yeah. He is."

"Then I'm much obliged, Colt. You stay up there long enough to get to know all them Camdens, then you work out your deal. And you just take care of Avery while you're there. You know, for all I was able to help your Aunt Leigh manage when we first started seeing each other, it was really her that saved me from my sorry self."

"You and I both know I ain't worth saving. But thanks for letting me take my time with this."

"I don't know that at all, son."

Colton had no response to that. His uncle rescued him from the silence. "'Course there's the body to consider."

"Yeah, I know. I'm heading out to the funeral home mentioned in the will. Figured I can at least get that started. Camdens don't have to know about it right yet."

"Good plan. Maybe get all of the details worked out and then ease 'em into it real gentle like. You get a look at the land?"

"Not yet."

"You know a few of 'em are gonna have to come down here to get all of this insanity from the will straightened out. A few of us Holders might have to make a trip to Nebraska as well. If you need my help, just say the word. I'll be on the next flight." Colt could hear a few head of Holder cattle bellowing in the background. Regret cinched tight in his chest. Homesickness on top of everything else sucked.

But he didn't need their help. He could handle himself, but he did want a little more information. "Can I ask you something kinda crazy, Uncle Gent?"

"Better than any of my kids."

Colt laughed. "When you met Aunt Leigh, did you think she was the one that you were gonna marry and settle down for?" *The one who was going to save you from yourself.*

His uncle was quiet for several seconds. "I've missed shooting the bull with you."

"That ain't an answer."

"That's 'cause you ain't gonna like my answer."

"So, you didn't know she was the one then?" That nonsense Ev had spewed earlier must be something he told his kids to keep them in line or his wife because she thought it was romantic. He'd only let himself get turned around by all of that talk because this situation was messing with his head. *And because of Avery.*

"There you go."

Colt could almost hear his uncle smiling five hundred miles away. "What?"

"You wanted me to say that I knew Leigh was gonna save me from my sorry-ass self. What that tells me is you want this Avery to be the one that makes you act like the man we all knew you were gonna be someday. You want to pretend you don't have a choice in the matter. Son, listen to me, if you want something in this life, you go out and make your own fate. And if you aren't real sure what it is you want, I've always found I make the best decisions while the quarter's still in the air."

"Thanks, Uncle Gent. I'll be home soon. Take care of Rio for me."

"You know we will. Do me a favor too if you don't mind."

"Anything."

"Don't forget you're a Holder no matter who your daddy is, and no matter what name you bear."

"I know, Uncle Gent. Believe me, I know."

CHAPTER SIX

"The family has gone home to work on a few more arrangements. They left the makeup and a few photographs. Just let me know if you need anything." Burt, the funeral home director, shut the door leaving Avery alone in the tiny space with two bodies. There was barely room for the three of them.

A shiver shot through her, making her grip one of the tables. Why must every room in Nebraska feel like a freezer? She supposed this time there was a good reason.

Reaching into her boots, she pulled her old leg warmers up to her knees. Her coat and knit cap would have to stay on.

She closed her eyes, trying to focus her intentions. It was her job to bring out the beauty of this couple, for their family and friends and for the life they'd shared here on earth.

Pulling off her gloves, she stared down at Mrs. Lancaster first. "I hope you had a beautiful life, ma'am," she whispered. For some reason her voice didn't echo the way it always seemed to when she talked to herself. Maybe they heard her. Trembling, she brushed a loose curl out of the woman's face and tried to picture how she might've preferred to wear her hair.

She studied the photographs left by the family. They were at least twenty years old and a few were black and white. That didn't tell her much. She stared for several heartbeats at a color photograph of the couple seated before a cake with a 50 prominently displayed. They were surrounded by their children and grandchildren. Three sons and two daughters from the looks of it. Even in the old photograph the love between the couple was apparent in their smiles.

Avery's eyes flitted back to Mrs. Lancaster. "Too bad you can't tell me how you managed this."

The bag of makeup sitting on the table beside Mrs. Lancaster was crammed full of blushes, mascaras, and eye liner pencils. She smiled at what had to have been the four-hundredth jar of Pond's Cold Cream in the woman's life. "I bet you didn't need all of this to be beautiful," Avery whispered as she began planning the best ways to make people who were no longer living look alive once more.

Leaning over Mrs. Lancaster, she began methodically brushing on a little foundation.

The blare of her cell phone shot through her. She jerked upright. Her head collided with the low-hung light fixture. Pain seared from her crown through her jaw and brought a rush of hot tears to her eyes. Racing to grab the phone to end the incessant ringing, she clipped the corner of Mr. Lancaster's table with her hip. "Ouch, dammit." The body shifted slightly. Great, now on top of being a broke, single mother of children who were not her own, she was also a tremendous klutz.

She finally located the phone at the very bottom of her cavernous bag and answered the call. "Hello?"

She ground her teeth as she heard a recording from Pleasant Glen High School informing her that Chase had inexplicably missed second period. "I'm going to ki..." She glanced at the dead bodies in the room with her. "Okay, I'm just going to shake him. Chase, can't you cut me a break?" The Lancasters had no opinion on the matter, so she ended the call and got back to work.

Her head still ached and her hip protested her every movement, but she fought through the pain. Pain was all a part of her job. Her feet and back had ached every single night since she'd become a stylist.

Digging through the woman's makeup bag, Avery couldn't find

anything to add shadow to her face. Lying down with her eyes closed meant she had no depth of features. Debating, she finally located her own favorite bronzer in her purse. "I'll get another one someday," she explained to Mrs. Lancaster as she set to work. The fact that it was only sold in posh boutiques in Oklahoma City didn't really matter. Maybe someday she'd get to go back and visit and she could pick up a few things. *With what money, Avery?*

Shaking off that irritating point, she applied a hefty dose of mascara to Mrs. Lancaster and then carefully moved on to blush. "I bet you were a great mom and wife. You probably knew just what to do when one of your kids misbehaved...and I'll bet you always knew what was wrong even if they wouldn't tell you. You made them feel loved. I can see that in the pictures.

"I bet you had a nice home where you always cooked their favorite meals for their birthdays. And you had special presents for everyone all wrapped under the Christmas tree each year. I bet you knew what to say to them when everything went wrong. You did good while you were here. No one can ask for more than that, right?"

When she finished Mrs. Lancaster, she moved on to her husband, careful not to make him look made up. "I bet you took good care of her, didn't you, sir?" She couldn't stand the silence of the funeral home, or the knowledge that the putrid scent of flowers was outside the door, so she kept speaking to the Lancasters. It helped her ignore the fact that she was, once again, in a place where life and death walked far too closely together.

She wanted no part of it all again. She couldn't stand the powdery veil funeral homes draped over death. If she never smelled another carnation, it would be too soon. She tried not to think about her mother.

Besides, she knew she would have appreciated the effort if it were her loved ones someone else was preparing. Putting make up on someone was a personal thing, and it only seemed right that she should try to get to know them. "I bet you took care of her and of your kids. That you worked hard and that you were her hero. I can tell you were a good man. The kind of man who played ball with his kids in the yard after work and helped them with their homework. I bet you even knew what to do with X and Y. Or maybe she was good at math and you were better at reading them stories. The kind where the good guys always win and life works out the way it's supposed to in the end. I bet she burned suppers for the entire first year you were married and you told her they were the best things you'd ever tasted. I bet you were her everything, sir. I know she loved you. I know she still does."

Turning back, she brushed a final coat of lipstick on Mrs. Lancaster's thin lips. "You look beautiful and peaceful. Go on home, both of you." She touched her fingertips to her own lips and then touched each of the Lancasters' foreheads. Leaning to scoop up her bag, she collided with Mr. Lancaster's table. The body moved again and suddenly the dead man's hand slid against her ass and her grip on reality faltered.

Gasping, she raced from the room, her heart beating in her ears. Burt was nowhere to be found and the cloying scent of carnations immediately assaulted her senses.

This was the twin of the funeral home where she'd paid to have a service for her mother. The same painting of Jesus with his hands extended had pride of placement across from some ridiculous picture of heaven done by a hack artist. Beneath the vividly colored print sat the very same podium from the other funeral home, holding a similar guest book. Odd statues of disembodied clasped hands were situated everywhere. And did every freaking funeral parlor in the Midwest get a bulk rate on that striped wallpaper?

She couldn't do this again. She had to get out of there. Now.

She gained ground down the long hallway with each step. The whisper of her boots on the thick carpeting was deafening. Bile lodged in her throat. She ran faster and faster. Where was Burt? She kept her eyes on the door, eager for a way out.

The creak of the hinge on the pushing mechanism was like nails on a chalkboard. Her boots hit the walkway and she gulped in fresh air right before she ran straight into Colton Holder's arms.

"Whoa, there, baby." His arms wrapped her up in a sanctuary of protective muscle and the mingled scent of hay and cologne. "You okay?"

She tried to catch her breath. He planted a kiss on top of her head like he'd known her for years and not only one day.

"Shh, it's all right. I've got you, baby. Can you tell me what happened?" His strength never faltered. His boots were rooted to the ground, keeping her upright. She'd needed a steady foundation her entire life, and for some unfathomable reason her heart told her she'd just been handed one.

"I don't know. I was talking to this dead guy and then he grabbed my ass," erupted from her nonsensically.

———

Keeping her head pressed to his chest allowed Colt a moment to compose himself. *Poor baby. Do not laugh at her.* "I've got you, sugar. You tell me where this dead guy is, and I'll whip his ass for touching yours."

She lifted her head, revealing bright pink cheeks. A minuscule smile played at her lips, but tears still threatened her eyes. *"She was scared and exhausted and needed someone to look after her. That's why the good Lord put me here on this earth. I figured it out right then and there. She told me she was bad lost. I wanted to tell her she was home."*

Could she feel his heart hammering its way out of his chest? Did she understand his desperation to protect her no matter what? When she burrowed her head against his soft flannel shirt and clung to him for dear life, he understood that she did.

This strange connection he felt for her was something she felt, too. It was right there pressed between them. It made no damn sense. He didn't need it to. He'd been searching for a place to belong his entire life. He'd finally found it.

"Come on. Let's get out of here, okay?"

She nodded against him.

"Ms. Hale?" A short, bald man with his cheap tie tucked into his suit pants burst through the door. The name tag on his coat declaring him the head funeral director was entirely unnecessary.

"Oh, Burt. I'm sorry. Uh, I finished up. I just...uh...guess you need to pay me." If she kept gnawing that lip, she was gonna draw blood.

"I peeked in on them. Beautiful job. The family will be thrilled. You left your gloves." He handed over a nice pair of black knit gloves.

"Thanks."

"Nope." Keeping her tucked in his arms, Colt accepted the gloves on her behalf. "You want to get her payment, sir? We need to be gettin' on." He hadn't wanted any part of this portion of his mission anyway. Getting her the hell out of this place and taking her most anywhere else suited him just fine.

"We usually pay Pearl at the end of the month. We don't deal with any cash here."

Colton felt Avery slump in defeat against him. "There any way you could write her a check?"

"Accountant only comes in once a month to make payments. I'm sorry, ma'am."

Despite his efforts to keep her tucked close to him, she jerked out of his grip. "It's fine, sir. Don't worry about it."

From the looks of her weary eyes and the tense set of her delicate jaw, it appeared Avery was willing to do all the worrying for the entire world.

No more.

"Let's get out of here. I've got you." He took her hand and guided her out to his truck.

"Wait, why were you here? Do you know the Lancasters?" She still couldn't quite seem to understand what was happening. Something in there had scared her stiff, not that he could blame her. Place gave him the willies.

"I was here on family business. Don't worry about it. I'd just as soon put it off another day or two anyway. I'd much rather take you to get something to eat or to find a good cup of coffee."

Hope lit in her eyes. "Really?"

"Oh yeah. Have you had lunch? It's getting late."

"No, but I am hungry." Defeat quickly drove away the excitement in her gaze. "I can't go get lunch with you, Colton. I don't have any..." she spoke to the cement pavement instead of to him.

Tired of cowardly backing away from what needed to be done, let alone from what he *wanted*, he gripped her chin, letting the feeling of her soft skin feed his need for her, and tipped her head back up. "Let's get a few things straight. I am taking you to lunch and I plan to buy you as much coffee as you think you can drink. From here on out, I aim to help you with anything else I can. You have anything to say about that, you can tell me all about it while I drive you to the restaurant. But fair warning, I'm 'bout as stubborn as they come and when I want something I go out and get it. Now, get your sexy ass in the truck."

"So, you think you can just pick me up from some funeral home and start ordering me around like a rude knight in a Ford truck? Is that it?" she seethed.

"And the spitfire finds her voice." He chuckled. "I knew it was in there. Just gotten a little lost lately, hasn't it, darlin'?" Damn but that fire in her lit him up like nothing ever had. She needed someone to help her kindle those flames, and he was the man for the job. Together they could create enough heat to keep the prairies ablaze for years.

She stared at him like he was one of those desert mirages. If he was a betting man, which he wasn't, he'd say she wasn't yet sure she liked what she saw.

"Sorry I'm coming on a little strong. Got a lot of shit going on and I like you. There, I said it. Isn't that what women are always saying they want us to do, tell you how we feel?"

"What do you mean you like me? You barely know me."

"I plan to remedy that situation as soon as possible and I still want to know more about this dead guy who made a pass." He couldn't help but grin at that. "I'm territorial as fuck, even if they are no longer with us."

"Jerk."

"Him or me?" He made no effort to hide his laughter.

"You. Mr. Lancaster was a nice man, who wouldn't have done that if I hadn't kept bumping into his table."

"Tempted to say you can bump into my table any time you'd like, but I suspect that might get me smacked, so how about this? We're both new in this ass-backwards little town. Why can't we be friends?"

"Friends, huh? That all you want?"

"Hell no, but I ain't opposed to turning this friendship into something more if you're willing."

"And if I'm not?" The flare of heat in her cool blue eyes and the way she fidgeted with those legwarmers pulled up over her tights said she was.

"You are. And even if you insist on telling yourself you're not for a while I still want to help you out with Chase and the little one and your aunt and all you got going on."

"I don't need anyone's help."

"Do you have enough money on you to buy yourself a cup of coffee to recover from whatever sent you running out of a mortuary and into my arms?"

She crossed her arms over her chest. "No."

"Then you do need a little help."

"You cannot help me, Colton."

Stubborn through and through. "I don't take too kindly to people telling me what I *can't* do."

"Me either." So he'd noticed and damn it if it didn't make her more alluring.

"Then let's see if we can't make this friendship work out for both of us."

"I live with both of my brothers and my aunt. I do not have time to date. I don't even have time to think about dating. And I don't have a private place in which to be with a guy I might like to think about dating. I barely have time to breathe. I get that you Holders don't understand this, but I have to figure out some way to make enough money to take over my aunt's shop, and pay for her medicine, and drive her to Lincoln twice a week for her treatments. I have...too much to figure out to even consider dating or friendship or anything else."

"Then let me help you with all of your figuring, sugar. Maybe if we figure enough, we'll come up with a spare moment or two where you can give dating some consideration. And don't make assumptions about the Holders and me and money. You have no idea what you're talking about. Now, come on." He hopped out of the truck, finally pleased with something he'd done.

Accomplishment spiked his blood. Until this morning with Brock, he'd never backed down from any task he'd taken on. If it needed to be done, he did it. This insanity with the Camdens could simmer for a day or two. Figuring out Miss Avery Hale held far more appeal.

CHAPTER SEVEN

A whirlwind of confusion whipped through Avery as Colton wrapped his arm possessively over her shoulders and guided her to a table in the back corner of an admittedly adorable coffee shop across the street from the funeral parlor. When he pulled out her chair, she rolled her eyes. "I'm perfectly capable of doing that myself. I'm not helpless."

"Sit your ass down, honey, 'fore I turn it over my knee."

Every single cell in her body was on high alert. Her heart pounded out its approval. Stupid, ridiculous thing. His threat to spank her should have had her dumping frigid water in his lap to freeze a little of his ridiculous ego. Instead, she was intrigued to the point of imaging his hand smacking her ass, of being naked against him, growing wetter with each strike. She hated that the most intriguing part of all was the idea that he might really want to be her friend.

He hung his coat on the back of his chair and sank into the seat like he didn't have a care in the world. He was still sporting that pompous smirk. Half of her wanted to slap it off his face. The other half wanted to kiss it off and then kiss her way into that button-down shirt and all the way down to those Wranglers that were rubbed in all the right places. She'd clearly lost her mind.

Furious with herself, she ground her teeth and refused to even look at him. *This is what happens when the most action you've gotten in the last six months is from a dead guy.*

When the waitress came over, she softened her expression. This woman was working hard and didn't deserve to bear the brunt of Avery's awful day. She'd save that for the man across the table from her, the one who thought she needed to be rescued.

"She'll have something called a chai tea latte. I'll have a large coffee with extra cream and would you mind bringing over one of the menus? Been working cattle all morning and I'm hungry enough to eat my horse." He gave the waitress that infuriatingly flirty, sexy grin and she blushed.

Avery rolled her eyes.

"I can bring you both coffee but we don't make lattes. Sorry. Anything else I can get for you or *do* for you?"

He chuckled at her barely concealed innuendo. Avery stuck her finger in her mouth, pretending to gag when the waitress wasn't looking. That brought on more laughter from Colton. "You just take real good care of my baby. If she wants it, you get it for her." He gestured to Avery.

"Lucky girl," the waitress breathed out as she went on her way.

"Oh my dear God," Avery fumed. "Your baby?"

His eyes narrowed a half-notch. Somehow it only made him look more determined. "What's your deal with not wanting anyone to help you do anything, *baby*?" he taunted.

"That has nothing to do with me not actually agreeing to date you, Mr. Holder."

"I told you not to make any assumptions about me and the Holders. And you didn't say you *didn't* want to date me. You said you had too much on your plate. But you didn't seem to mind sizing me up at all, so to speak, in your front yard last night. So, no, I don't believe for one minute that you ain't interested in seeing just where this might go.

"And look at us sitting across from each other in a darn near citified coffee shop, having a spat that could end in one helluva make up session. I could get you all hot and bothered, work out all of that stubborn orneriness in my bed, and then simmer you down slow and steady-like, wear your little body out 'til you become more sex kitten than angry tiger mama. Looks to me like you *do* have time to date, sugar."

"You always so full of yourself?"

Another smirk. "Trust me, darlin', I don't exaggerate and you're intrigued."

"So, what, I'm supposed to blow off my little brothers and my aunt, who, by the way, looks precisely the same way my mom did six months before she died, so I can become another notch in a Holder bedpost? I know all about the wild Holder boys, remember, Colton?"

All of the egotism and arrogance bled from his features. Was that...? No way. She watched his Adam's apple contract harshly. Even his neck was sexy but all of that bravado and might couldn't conceal the hurt in his eyes.

"Is that what you really think? You think I'd offer to help you just to get you in bed? I'll readily admit I have a few cousins who might do shit like that, but I'm not that kind of man, Avery. You ever think I might want to help you because of Chase? I *was* the kid with no daddy, hitching my way home because either no one cared enough or had time to get me from school? You ever think that maybe I could use a friend, too?"

His words tore the breath from her lungs. A rocklike enclosure cemented in her throat.

He put a hundred dollar bill down on the table and grabbed his coat. "Get whatever you want and a coffee to go. Your car's right across the street. I'll see you around."

"Wait! Colton, I'm sorry. Please don't leave."

"Why? You're damned and determined to do it all on your own."

"I am, but you have to understand..." She didn't owe him an explanation, but the idea of him leaving made her chest ache and the acid in her empty stomach swirl ominously.

"Understand what?" He pulled on his gloves.

"Please don't leave."

"Why?"

"Because I could really use a friend, a real friend, not all the irresponsible party girls I used to hang out with. I guess I do need some help, too. I'm just too damn stubborn to admit it, like you said."

When he shrugged back out of his coat, her heart located a steady beat. When his ass settled back in the seat, breath returned to her lungs. "I would never push myself on you. I would never do anything you didn't want me to do. I come on strong, but that's because I know what I want." His head sank so he was speaking more to the fake woodgrain table top than to her. She had to lean in to hear him. "The way my life works I tend to take everything I can get 'cause I don't ever know when somebody else might try to take it from me. I take care of what's mine. I don't take nothing for granted. You would never ever be a notch in a bedpost to me. You got that?"

"I'm sorry I said that."

The waitress set down their coffee and the menus. "To friendship." He lifted the cardboard-sleeved cup.

"To maybe more than friendship," she allowed as she met the toast.

"That's my girl." A hint of a smile returned to those rugged features she had precious little hope of being able to resist for much longer.

"Not your girl yet, Colton."

"Told you I come on strong." He gave her another one of those winks that she swore tied her in knots she'd never be able to undo.

"I didn't ask you to stop."

"Tell me about all this with your mama."

———

"She died about three months ago."

Unable to sit there and watch her reel from life itself without offering any comfort, he reached across the table, eased her glove from her hand, and placed her warm fingers inside his own.

He was lost, too, dammit, but if he couldn't solve his own problems, at least he could be her lifeline. His Uncle Gent was right—he had a choice and this was it. If she needed someone to guide her home, he'd be her lighthouse. If she needed a buoy, he'd be her anchor.

"Mama didn't believe in doctors."

Ah, geez. So this story started out bad and only had the possibility of getting worse. "I'm sorry, sugar."

She shrugged. "I don't know if they could've helped. I don't know what she had. I couldn't afford an official autopsy or anything. I had to sneak Jaxon to the free clinic back home to get his immunizations so she wouldn't know and he could go to school. I loved my mom but I had to work around her most of my life. A lot of the time I felt like I was raising her."

Damn. Girl was fierce. He'd known from the first moment he laid eyes on her. "Believe me, sugar. I get that. Pretty sure I'm still trying to raise mine and she just keeps getting worse. When'd you become a hair cutter person thing? Jay-sus that's probably the dumbest thing I've ever said to you and that's saying something."

She giggled. Music to his ears, his heart, and his cock. "Stylist," she corrected.

"Yeah. That."

"Mama ran Mirror, Mirror Salon in Slatern Hills. Some part of me wanted to be just like her. I went through the cosmetology program at my high school, so I was licensed by the time I graduated. I love making people as pretty on the outside as they are on the inside. She taught me to make the all-natural beauty and health products we sold in the shop. They're amazing. I mean they really do work even though she should've let a real doctor help her when she got sick."

"The past can be a bitch, baby. Believe me, I know. There's always could'ves and should'ves and none of them change a damn thing." He squeezed her hand. His own past reared its ugly head far more often than he would like.

"Were you two going to order?" the waitress interrupted.

He hadn't even noticed her approach. For a cattle rancher trained to notice everything, that was disconcerting. Figuring he'd already made an ass of himself by indulging his caveman tendencies, he grinned at Avery. "I'll have whatever she's having."

That pleased her, which pleased him. She glanced over the menu. "Let's see. I'll have the chicken spinach wrap and a bowl of your vegetarian vegetable soup, please."

A frustrated grunt he couldn't halt escaped his throat. "Scratch that. I'll take a burger with two patties, medium rare, with extra cheese. And a double order of fries with extra salt and barbecue sauce."

"No problem. I'll be right back with your orders." The waitress gathered the menus and headed back to the kitchen.

Avery was shaking her head and outright laughing at him.

"What? I'm a man. I eat like a man, not a fucking rabbit on a diet. What the hell is vegetarian vegetable soup, anyway? Ain't the vegetables in it vegetarian enough? One of 'em is unnecessary."

With a decidedly mischievous smirk, she giggled. "I don't eat red meat."

"I'm putting that right at the top of the list of things I plan on saving you from."

"I don't need saving."

"Says the girl that don't eat real meat." Another one of those addictive giggles escaped her lush lips and he changed course. "Maybe I need to tell myself I'm saving somebody. Does mighty things for my ego. I'd be much obliged if you'd let me go on with my superhero complex."

She rolled her eyes and he took the bait. "Surely there's a few things I could do for you that you can't do for yourself." He waggled his eyebrows. "Or even if you can do them by yourself, I'll bet they're not as much fun."

The cutest little mischievous grin he'd ever seen formed on her features. "I'm tempted to take you up on that offer. How about I'll let you save me from the long cold nights if you manage to find one single place back in Pleasant Glen where we can be alone for any length of time."

"Now that right there is a dare I'll take. Be ready for me, sugar."

"Bring it on, cowboy."

"Oh honey, trust me, I'll be bringing it."

Consideration darkened her eyes. "It cannot be a hay loft, anywhere in a truck, or anywhere that has a parking lot."

"You got any more conditions, city girl?"

"Probably, and I reserve the right to change the rules as we play."

"Then I reserve the right to paddle your ass when you get out of hand and to call you my baby whenever I feel like. Now, you were telling me about your mama."

"Why don't you tell me what the heck you were doing at the funeral home?" she came right back.

"I told you it was family business."

"Yeah, but your family has an entire county in Oklahoma named after them, so how are you handling family business all the way up here?"

"That's a long-ass story I ain't getting into right now. If you don't want to talk about your mama, tell me about taking over the salon thing."

Her eyes lit with excitement and the muscles that had tensed in his chest relaxed.

"Well, see, I used to help mom run the shop portion of Mirror, Mirror but I didn't really know much about the books." With that statement her excitement quickly darkened. Colt rubbed the tender patch of skin between her thumb and index finger, hoping to ease whatever had upset her.

"I didn't know until after Mom died that we were in so much debt. The day I found out the probate court was going to sell off the salon to pay her debts back was the same day I found out Randy was going to try to take custody of Jax from me. I moved up here hoping to get him to agree to sharing custody and my Aunt Pearl offered to let me run the Cut 'n' Curl. She said she and Sally were ready to retire."

"Damn, baby. It kills me I wasn't there for you that day, or any of the days leading up to it. Sounds like you were walking straight through hell all alone." Something he'd never allow again.

"Yeah, kind of felt that way. Still kind of feels that way. But you know what they say about hell—the only way out is through. Other than all of the bad stuff, I'm excited about the salon. I have so many ideas. See, my mom and my Aunt Pearl were both stylists. My grand-mother was a stylist too, back in the day. I love thinking about her doing all those big bouffants and pin curls like Ava Gardner back in the forties. It's a family tradition, I guess. But Aunt Pearl met my Uncle Les, God rest his soul, and she moved up here with him. She opened the Cut 'n' Curl years ago. When Mom knew...you know...she wasn't going to make it she asked me to raise the boys near her family.

Between that and all of the stuff with Randy, Oklahoma just wasn't an option anymore.

"The only problem with Pleasant Glen is no one will give me a chance. That's why I don't have any money. I've had one client all month and she didn't tip me."

"Why didn't she tip you?" Gall ticked in Colton's blood. He didn't like to think about his baby's hard work going unappreciated. Damn, but he was already in this with both feet.

"According to Sally, this witch doesn't believe in tipping."

"Town's half crazy."

"I guess it has its good points," she said with a shrug. "Aunt Pearl says you just have to settle in to Pleasant Glen."

The delivery of their food quelled conversation. She was practically drooling as she watched him throw barbecue-sauce-laden fries in his mouth one after another. "Sure as hell hope you look at my cock the way you're looking at these fries someday, sugar. Hope you lick your lips like that for me, too."

"You are just so polite and gentlemanly. You must woo all the ladies with your elocution and manners," she teased.

"I don't know what half of the words you just said mean, but I do know how to woo you." He lined up four thick fries, dipped them in the sauce, and laid them on her spinach covered plate. His left eyebrow ticked upwards as he waited on her to cave.

"Why does temptation always have to look so good?" She whimpered and then succumbed, shoveling the fries into her mouth all at once.

"I could ask you the same thing." He scrubbed his face with the paper napkin he had placed in his lap, despite her insinuation that he didn't have manners. Settling back in his chair, he pushed the plate with his remaining fries toward her and crossed his arms over his chest.

"You can't possibly mean me?" She abandoned the spinach-covered shit altogether and went for the fries. He was certain the smirk she elicited from him was going to become a permanent fixture.

"You are twice as tempting as sin on a Sunday and more appealing than any one woman has a right to be."

"And how many women have you said that to back in Holder County?"

Fuck. She wasn't cutting him any slack. In true Holder fashion, and hell, probably Camden fashion as well, he doubled down. "You really sitting there trying to tell me you ain't ever had another guy's...fries?"

"Touché, Mr. Holder."

"Stop calling me that and finish up. We got shit to do."

"What do we have to do?"

"We have to get back to the Glen so you can cut my hair and I can pick up Chase from school."

All traces of flirty banter melted from her features. "You're really going to pick up Chase?"

"Someday maybe you'll believe me, Avery. I intend to help you as much as I plan on helping myself *to* you. And I ain't having him out walking that road while the sun sets. It's dangerous. 'Sides he needs to know somebody on this planet besides you is looking out for him." *He needs to know somebody is going to hold his ass to the line.*

CHAPTER EIGHT

Avery tried to remember the precise course of events that had led her to Colton Holder being in the truck behind her car driving toward the Cut 'n' Curl. She'd given that witch a haircut, then she'd headed over to the funeral home and picked up the call about Chase cutting class—she still needed to throttle him for that—Mr. Lancaster had grabbed her ass. She'd breathed in the smell of death and carnations, and Colton had whisked her away to get a better than decent cup of coffee, and now she'd agreed to...

What the hell?

He'd never in a million years find a place in Pleasant Glen where they could be alone. She hadn't truly felt alone more than once or twice since the move to Nebraska. Well, if he was really willing to be her friend, and Chase's friend, too, then she could at least return the favor. And who was she kidding? He was a dirty, sexy, sinfully seductive temptation and she wanted him more than she'd ever wanted anything in her entire life.

Besides, for now he was just getting a haircut. There was no denying she needed the money and he'd certainly tip her well. That was far more palatable than letting him buy her things.

"You're sure you want to do this?" she asked him again as they climbed out of their vehicles and onto the gravel parking lot. School would be out soon. If he was determined to get Chase, she was going to have to hurry.

He whipped off his cowboy hat. "You tell me, sugar."

"You could use a trim, but I kind of like the length."

He shoved the hat back on his head and had an arm back around her in a split second. A low chuckle sounded in her ears. His eyes were full of that dark fire that warned her she was in way over her head. "Do ya now? Bet you'll like the width, too. As long as you're with me, you won't have to worry about that ridiculous shit boys shovel about it not being the size of the ship that matters. Trust me."

Cocking her jaw to the side, she rolled her eyes at him and started walking toward the salon. "You are so full of shit," she said as she opened the door and led him inside. There was no sign of Sally, though it would be too optimistic of her to hope she'd gone home or gone off somewhere.

"Careful now. Remember what I said about you getting out of hand. Now, do I sit here?" He pointed to her styling chair.

"Have you never been to a salon?" It was unfair that his hair was naturally that gorgeous without any help.

"Been to more than a few barber shops, but this is a little different."

Theodora moved in, the prick of her paws on the linoleum announcing her arrival. Before Avery could apologize and tell the dog to go find Sally in the back room, Colton was letting her lick his hands and petting her. "Hey there, girl." He scratched behind her newly permed ears. "Who's this?"

"That's a very good question." Sally appeared from the back room. "That's my sweet little Theodora, but who are *you*?"

"Name's Colton. I'm a friend of Avery's."

"Really?" Delight danced in Sally's eyes. Avery's stomach did a few unnecessary flips. "How good of a friend?"

"Sally," Avery scolded.

"Not as good as I'd like to be, I'll say that. She's running hot and cold on me though. I plan to put a stop to that in a day or two."

"You're perfect!" Sally declared.

"Sally." Avery ground out her name in warning this time. Why did he have to be so infuriating and so freaking sexy all at the same time?

"Simmer down, darlin', I've never minded women telling me I'm perfect."

"Oh, good grief." Avery slapped one of the pink and green floral capes over him and then laughed hysterically at the sight of the big, tall hunk of cowboy covered in pink and green flowers. "Now, where did I put those purple sponge rollers?"

"You come at me with anything but a comb and a pair of scissors, it will definitely be considered getting out of hand. And I don't much care who's watching. Keep that in mind."

Avery plucked the hat from his head giggling at his reflexive scowl. "I'll take good care of it." She set it aside and ran her fingers through his hair. She noted the shift of his body as she pressed gently against his scalp. He tensed. His eyes went from pensive to lustful.

On the next pass, he grunted out a curse word. She grinned at that.

"Why are you doing that?" he asked.

"I'm learning the shape of your scalp and the direction your hair naturally falls. Working with the natural shape is much easier than trying to force your hair to do something it was never meant to do."

"It feels good." If she wasn't mistaken, he'd lost a little of his natural bravado.

"Good. Hope you say that about my..." Before she could mimic his outrageously dirty banter about french fries, she remembered Sally was watching their every move.

His eyes flashed out a carnal warning. "About your what, doll baby?"

"Nothing. Just let me work."

———

Every movement of her hands on his head strung him harder than a railroad spike. He knew he had no business challenging her to be more than friends but by God he wanted her more than he wanted to draw his next breath.

He jerked away from her when she began spraying cold water through his hair. Her gorgeous lips pursed. "Would you relax?"

Settling back in the chair, he clenched his jaw. Relaxation was not something he was capable of feeling at the moment. Not when she was close enough to him that her breasts, soft and ample, occasionally brushed his shoulders. Not when his every breath brought in a lungful of her scent. The mixture of sweet vanilla cream and spicy nectar that was all her. He wanted to bury himself inside her until they both forgot, if only for a moment, every single thing in their lives that wasn't going right. He longed to sink himself so deep inside her he obliterated every worry that made her so certain everyone in the world was out to get her.

He watched her every motion in the mirror as she moved the scissors over his cheeks.

She'd piled on layers of clothing like armor. Another pair of those damned inviting floral yoga pants, a pair of leg warmers he'd seen a few of his female cousins wear when they were taking dance, a long black sweatshirt he swore they could fit in together was cut low enough to show off that rack that made him ache, and a sexy pair of black leather boots no self-respecting cowgirl would ever be seen in.

She wanted him to relax. He wanted to know just what kind of panties she had on. She seemed like one of those girls who wore matching bra and panty sets. Fuck him running if he wasn't dying to find out. His mind instantly conjured up an image of her in nothing but black—no, she was too soft and sweet for black lace. Maybe an innocent white lace bra that couldn't quite contain her tits and a matching G-string that was meant to hold nothing at all.

Saliva flooded his mouth. His palms itched to pull her into his arms and take both of them to heaven. He wanted to thread his fingers in all of that thick black and purple hair and bring her mouth to his cock, let her suck away all the need so heavy in his sac he burned with it. His blood heated and his breaths came in quick, disintegrating huffs.

"What's wrong?" Her hot breath over his ear made him grunt.

"Not a damn thing."

"You sure? You look like I'm hurting you."

More than you'll ever know, sugar. "You are." He went on with the truth. The rest of his life was currently ensnared in lies. He didn't want to lie to her, too.

She dropped her hands and studied him. "I'm sorry. Did I pull your hair?"

Throwing his elbows out like wings until he escaped one side of that ridiculous cape she'd put him in, he reached back and grabbed her hand. She grinned. He guided her to his side. "You didn't pull my hair. I want you so bad I can't see straight. In fact, if you really want to pull my hair just wait 'til I get my face between them gorgeous thighs."

Blood flooded her features. Utter delight filled him. But a moment later, hesitation clouded her gaze. That wasn't a good sign at all. "Colton, it's like I said...I can't really do a relationship right now. As much as I might like to. Surely you know that."

"I don't know that at all, and I might as well warn you—until you stop telling me you *can't* and start telling me you don't want to, I'm going to find a way to make this work." He kept his voice to a whisper since she didn't seem to care for the other woman to hear them.

He watched her delicate shoulders lift as she filled her chest with air. "I can't tell you that I don't want to because...that would be an outright lie."

"That's all I needed to hear."

"You are a really bad idea, Colton."

"Maybe, but I promise to be a really *good* bad idea."

A man's deep chuckle ripped the haze of lust out from around them.

Shit. Grant Camden was standing at the counter of the beauty salon laughing at him. "Dude, they'll get you a black cape thing if you ask. You ain't gotta wear the flower one."

"Hey, Grant, how's the family?" Sally grinned at him and waved him over to her chair.

"Katy's good. Little Keith's fine. Finally got him sleeping through the night just in time for the next one. Can you trim a little around my ears and clean up my neck, Sally? It's getting on my nerves."

"How are your folks?"

"Mama says to ask how Miss Pearl's doing."

"She's all right. Avery's taking good care of her."

Colt smiled at that, but Avery's mouth hung open for a solid second before it snapped shut. She'd stopped clipping his hair again. "Sally, you told that awful Gretchen woman that I wasn't helping Aunt Pearl at all," finally leapt out of her mouth.

"Oh, I was only making conversation," Sally said, grabbing a black cape from the back room and settling it around Grant's shoulders. "I knew Pearl would like one of her cakes and there's no way Gretchen would get off of her self-righteous ass and bake her one if she thought all was well. You have to learn how to make this town work for you, girly. Now, get back to Mr. Holder's cut."

Shaking her head at that, Avery did as she was told. Colton wondered what she'd be like in bed with him. Sweet and docile or the spitfire he'd seen at lunch, cutting him no slack and giving him no ground. Both, he hoped.

"Hey, Avery, Colton was telling me your brother wants to play football," Grant called.

"You asked him about Chase?"

Colt couldn't quite describe the look in her eyes. She was clearly touched, but there was more to it. She looked...shocked. Like no one had ever stepped in on her behalf and gotten something done for her. Well, that was all about to end right then.

"Yeah, baby. He's the assistant football coach."

Her eyes closed like she was trying to dam back tears. *Oh fuck. Please don't cry.* He had no idea what to do with a crying woman, especially when he was trapped in what looked like his Great Aunt Edna's draperies. "Thank you," she finally whispered.

"How's it going on your current mission, my man? I see you're pulling out all the stops." Grant asked Colt.

"I'm getting there."

"You're getting where?" Avery asked.

"Real near to you, sugar bee."

"And you asked Grant about that too, I take it."

Grant offered Colton an apologetic glance. "You know, my granddaddy's fond of reminding me that it's a whole lot easier to let the cat out of the bag than it is to get it back in, so I think I'm gonna sit here quiet-like and let you ladies keep right on working."

"What's he talking about?" Avery turned her accusations on Colton.

"I mighta told him I want to help out with Chase and that I'm interested in being more than a friend to you."

His honesty seemed to shock her. "So, you've been blabbing your mouth all over town about me?" Her coy grin said she didn't really mind.

"If it's on my mind, it's usually coming out of my mouth." He glanced back over at Grant. "'Cept maybe for a few personal things."

Her left eyebrow lifted. "There better be several things you keep to yourself."

"Don't you worry. I can keep my mouth shut when I need to. When I was talking to him about Chase, I didn't need to."

"Good." When she finished snipping, she grabbed another spray bottle and went to town.

"What the hell is that for?" he batted away the wet particles floating across his vision with his free hand.

She giggled again. Damn but that sound was addictive as hell. "It's hair volumizer."

"That gonna make my hair louder or something?"

That did it. She doubled over laughing hysterically. If he could just keep her doing that, maybe he'd figure the rest of his shit out and hers, too.

"No," she finally managed. "It gives it a little texture and body."

"You got all the body I'll ever need, baby. And you are aware that I'm slapping that hat back on the moment I pay you, right?"

"Cowboys." She rolled her eyes.

"Are God's gift to the land, the cattle, and all of women-kind," Grant bellowed from the other chair.

"Hear, hear," Colton called back.

"Oh dear, God, there are two of you. Please tell me you're somehow related and this isn't a deep-seeded belief shared by all egotistical cattle ranchers everywhere."

"Aww come on, now, Miss Avery, I bet my boy Colton can get you saddled right on up and show you how to ride," Grant teased.

Refusing to comment on her quip that they might be related, Colt gestured both hands to his crotch. "Come on, city girl, save a horse."

"So full of yourself. It's really unbelievable."

"I keep trying to tell you it's you who's gonna be full of me, sugar."

Before she could come up with another retort, Sally leapt into the conversation. "You know, Colton, Grant's brother-in-law's band is putting on a big fancy show at Saddleback's Saturday night. I happen to know Avery doesn't have a date and everyone will be there."

"Sally," Avery whimpered.

"That so?"

"I cannot go to the concert. I have no one to watch the boys. Besides, it's a terrible idea for someone who's taking care of a cancer patient to drink. What if Aunt Pearl needed me to take her to the hospital or something? No way. I'm not even chancing something like that."

There, in her crystal-blue eyes, he could see the shadows of every person she put before herself.

"We ain't gotta drink," he pointed out. "We don't even have to stay long. God himself knows you need a night off. I bet Sally'd be more than happy to stay with Pearl and Chase is plenty old enough to keep up with the little guy. In fact, he needs a little responsibility." Colt laid out the evening plan he intended to enact.

"I'd love to sit with Pearl. She's my best friend, you know," Sally confirmed the very thing Colton had suspected. You could read people same way you could cattle and horses. She had that twitchy, put-out look about her that Rio always got when Colt rode another horse. She was feeling more than a little replaced and useless. It wasn't only Avery and Pearl's lives that'd been turned upside down. Every human being on the planet wanted to feel like they were needed.

"You're welcome over there anytime, Sally," Avery vowed. Her tone told him she'd picked up on Sally's feelings as well.

"I know, but I don't want to be in the way."

"She'd love to see you. You're never in the way," Avery assured her.

"Well then, I'll sit with Pearl and help Chase with Jaxon. You two go out and have fun. Make sure everyone sees you together."

"Dec puts on a helluva good show," Grant added helpfully. Clearly he hadn't been exaggerating earlier—the Camdens were willing to help a brother get laid. "And you wouldn't be the only one not drinking. We're all going and I ain't quite sure about Indie yet, but I 'spect every single one of the Camden wives are expecting. They'll all be there sipping soda water and whatnot."

"What time does this thing start?" Colt inquired.

"Dec's taking the stage at eight, but we'll all be there early." He nodded to Sally, who'd taken off his black cape thing and declared him done. He pulled out his wallet to pay her.

"See y'all later," he said, sparing a grin for Colton on his way out.

"Come on, baby, let me spin you around the dance floor."

"You actually dance?" She sounded shocked.

"Hell yeah. You ever met a cowboy that don't?"

"I don't think I've ever really dated a cowboy before, so I'm not sure."

"I dance. Plan on dancing you right on into—"

"Your bed. Yeah, I know. All right, fine, as long as we don't stay out too late."

Before he could agree, her phone rang. "Oh no." She raced for the bag she'd stowed behind the counter. Colt wondered what that was all about. He also wondered when he could take off the curtains and put his hat back on.

"I'm so sorry. I forgot. They're sitting on our kitchen table. I meant to put them in his bag and it slipped my mind this morning. I promise I'll be right there. Please do not call Randy," she ordered whomever was on the other end of that call. The sharp edges of defeat pricked and punctured his baby. He had to put a stop to this. When she ended the call, she was gnawing that lip again.

"Here, I'll finish Colton up and you go pick up Jaxon," Sally volunteered.

"I'm so sorry," Avery offered.

"Is he sick, darlin'? You want me to go with you?"

"He's not sick. He just keeps doing this and I can't figure out why. I need to go to the school before they call Randy again. Are you sure you don't mind picking up Chase?"

"Not at all. I'll meet you back at your house in a little while." He wanted to kiss her goodbye. He wanted to know what had happened to his little buddy. He wanted to decimate anything in the world that had made her feel like she wasn't good enough. And most of all, he wanted to erase that failure from her eyes.

She was gone before he could do anything at all.

"Poor thing," Sally tsked as she ran a towel through Colton's hair and then made a few last snips around his ears. "If you really are willing to help her, Mr. Holder, she sure could use it."

"Mr. Holder is my uncle, but what's going on with Jaxon?"

"I don't know how much she wants you to know. Poor thing has been through more than any child should ever have to go through. There. You're all done. She did a real nice job."

"If it's all right with you, I'll pay her directly."

"You do that."

"You think you could encourage her to let me help her some?" he asked.

"Avery's just as stubborn as Pearl. They don't like to rely on other people and that's because a lot of people in their life, including Avery's mama, let them down time and time again. But I'll do everything I can. I have a few tricks up my sleeve. I've always said times change, but people—and most certainly falling in love—don't change and it never will."

CHAPTER NINE

Colt grimaced as he sat in his truck with the motor chugging outside the high school football practice field. Chase was looking down at a pretty young girl in a cheerleading uniform like she'd hung the moon. In reality, she was probably the first girl he'd ever noticed.

When she handed over a binder and what looked like a textbook, Colton cringed. Kid was reliving his life and he wanted so much more for Chase than that. Taking the long way over fool's hill was a bitch.

"Chase," he called, rolling down the truck window as Chase headed toward the road. "Thought I told you if you were gonna walk not to do it on the side of the road."

"You taking me home?" Hope made a hesitant showing in those eyes that were duplicates of his big sister's.

"I ain't sitting here for my own health. Get in. It's cold."

Repeating the movements he'd made the day before, Chase crawled in the passenger seat. Colt had never been all that good at small talk, so he went straight to the heart of it. "What's her name?"

"Who?"

"Don't give me that crap," he said as he pulled back onto the road. "The chick you're doing homework for."

Chase's spine went stiff as a board and a scowl formed on his face. "How'd you know that?"

Colt sighed. "I did my fair share of homework for pretty girls in my day."

"Kami."

"You sure Kami ain't using you for your brains?"

"It's a group project."

"And are you the part of the group that does all the work while she bats her eyes at you and rubs her hand real close to where you'd like it to be?"

Hate replaced the momentary hope in Chase's eyes. His lip curled and that was all the answer Colt needed. "That's what I thought."

Chase searched Colton's appearance. "You let Avery cut your hair. You're just picking me up and interfering in my life so you can get between my sister's legs." He scowled.

"What goes on between me and your sister is between me and your sister. I'm helping her out because I care about all of you, no matter what happens between us. And if things do work out with Kami, don't be talking shit with your friends about what she lets you do with her. Be a man."

"I don't have any friends." The barely audible confession socked Colt in the gut.

"Hey, uh, I talked to the assistant football coach today. He said they'd love to see you at practice tomorrow."

"There's a hundred-dollar uniform and booster club fee, dumbass," Chase snarled.

"I covered it and watch your mouth. By the way, you're babysitting Jaxon Saturday night and it looks to me like the grass between the trailers needs to be mowed. You can do that, too. You want to keep up the name calling, I'll take you out to Camden Ranch and let you shovel manure, see if we can't work some manners into you."

"Hey, you think maybe you could get me a job there, too?" Suddenly all of the irritation was erased from Chase's features. Damn if the kid didn't keep him guessing. Beneath all the surliness and anger he carried around, he could be a decent human being. Teenagers.

"I might could do that, but it's gonna be hard to play ball and work."

"I need to help Avery make money."

"How 'bout you show up to practice tomorrow and see how it goes and I'll talk to the Camdens about you doing some work when you're not practicing as long as you keep your grades up."

"I don't need a dad," Chase huffed.

"Good thing, 'cause I don't have a clue in the world how to be one. Never had one myself."

"Really?"

"Really. Hey, you know why Avery keeps getting calls from Jaxon's school in the afternoons?"

"Yeah, he keeps wetting his pants. Oh, and I am not changing his wet butt when I babysit him, just so you know."

"Isn't he too old for that?" Seemed to him his cousins' kids had outgrown that before they went to school. Then again, Jaxon had been through a lot in his short time on this earth.

"Yeah. Little twerp's gonna get thrown out of school if he keeps it up. That's part of why I need you to talk to the Camdens for me. Avery can't afford a babysitter for him if he can't go to the state preschool program. I'm gonna end up dropping out and going to work. One of us has to actually earn money."

Damn. "You're not dropping out of school. We'll figure something out."

"You sound like Avery," Chase said, shooting a quick glance at him. "Seems to me somebody needs to stop trying to figure shit out and actually fix something."

"I intend to do just that."

———

When Colton's impressive mass filled most of the entryway to the trailer behind Chase, Avery reminded herself this was not her life. She could not get used to having him around. Eventually he'd be done with whatever he was doing at Camden Ranch and she would be on her own again. He would be way back in Oklahoma, where life just wasn't this difficult.

"Hey, stop," he grasped her wrists as she heaved a large pot of water onto the stove to boil spaghetti noodles.

"I can't stop. Everyone needs to eat."

"Then let's go out. My treat. I hear Runzas are good. Pearl must be sick of looking at these four walls all the time."

"I'd love a Runza," her aunt called over the blare of *Wheel of Fortune* reruns.

"See."

Going out to eat should not be an aphrodisiac, she reminded herself. "I think you just don't want to eat my turkey spaghetti."

"I'll eat most anything you fix, but we have to get you over this fear of red meat. Now, get your coat on and let's get."

"I can't. Chase has homework and...oh, speaking of that..." She grabbed the collar of Chase's T-shirt before he could escape to his room. "What were you thinking skipping second period? Isn't that math?"

"How'd you...? I had something else I needed to do." Guilt was written all over his face. And all-knowing certainty was written on Colton's.

"Bet it had something to do with Kami and that cheerleading skirt." Colt shook his head at him.

"I don't need you two telling me how to live my life," he snarled. "You're not Mom."

If he'd actually backhanded her, it wouldn't have hurt as much as those three words. Her eyes closed. "I know," escaped her lips without her permission. Suddenly, Colton's arms were drawing her to his chest. That feeling she had no business entertaining returned, the one that said this was the foundation she'd needed her whole life.

"He didn't mean that, baby," he whispered against her hair before he planted another one of those kisses on top of her head.

"Pretty sure he did."

"Come on, let me take you all out. Let's get some fresh air."

She had no will left to argue, or to cook, or to wash more of Jaxon's soaking wet jeans and underoos. She wanted to collapse in Colton's arms and sleep for the next week. After that, maybe she could fight again.

"Pearl, get your hat on. We're going out," he called to her aunt.

"I knew I liked you." Aunt Pearl was up and out of that chair quicker than Avery had seen her move in the last week.

At that moment, Jaxon raced into the kitchen. "I want french fries."

Colton chuckled. The motion rocked Avery to the core. "You got it, little buddy. But first let's you and me go have a chat man–to–man."

Avery lifted her head. "I thought we were going out. And what's a Runza anyway? And where are whatever they are?"

"According to the Camdens, they're the only sandwiches that matter. We are going out, just let me chat with the little man for a minute."

"Yeah, man–to–man." Jaxon arched his back, puffing himself up like Colton had declared he was the head of the Avengers. Avery had never seen him react that way with Randy or anyone else.

"He, uh, he does have on dry clothes, doesn't he?" Colton cringed.

Avery gave him a weary nod.

"Come on, little man." He hoisted Jaxon up into his arms and headed to the front door of the trailer.

"Where are you taking him?" Avery called after them.

"Men do all their best thinking out of doors and we got some thinking to do, don't we, Jax?"

"Yep, we do."

The front door shut behind them and Avery cracked the kitchen window despite the cold. She wanted to hear this.

"All right, now, you were just telling me last night all about how you're gonna be a cowboy superhero, right?" Colt set Jaxon's wiggling form down on the grass.

Somehow, Avery smiled. She hadn't even felt capable of forcing a smile three minutes before.

"Yep, like Captain America and like *you*!" Jax raced past the window blasting imaginary foes with his hands and then throwing his nonexistent shield.

"All right, then. What's this I hear about you wetting them drawers every day at school? Can't fight Red Skull or drive cattle with wet britches."

"You can't?"

"Nah, I 'spect that'd make your horse real ornery-like. Plus, it'd be awfully uncomfortable."

Avery clasped her chest and whispered a silent prayer that this might work. She wasn't even sure how he'd found out about Jaxon's bathroom issues. She also didn't care.

"But if you have an accident at my school, then Avery comes and gets you and you don't gotta stay no more. You can come home, and she'll clean you up and watch TV with you."

"I see." Colt nodded.

Emotion clogged Avery's throat. So that was it.

"Don't you like school, little man?"

"Yeah, and I gots to be the line leader today."

"Hey, that's an important job."

"I know, but one time I went to my old school and I gots to be the line leader and when I gots home Mama wasn't there no more."

"You kinda worried maybe if you stay at school too long Avery won't be here when you get back?"

"Yes, sir." He shot a few more mortal enemies and then performed a few karate chops in the air. Tears tracked down Avery's face. The tender prick in Colton's voice said he did care about all of them just like he'd promised.

He lifted Jax back up in the air and settled him on his shoulders. "How about we make a deal?"

"A cowboy deal?"

"Yep, and that's the best kinda deal you can make 'cause cowboys always try to tell you the truth and take care of the people who are important to them."

"Am I important?"

"You are very important, little man, trust me on that."

"I take care of people, too. I take care of Avery and of Chase and of Aunt Pearl, even when she won't let me play with my shield."

"I know you do, but listen to me for a minute. How about if I promise you Avery's gonna be here when you get home every single day, and if she isn't here, then I will be. And if you try real, real hard not to have any more accidents, I'll take you out and let you see a bunch of cowboys working sometimes while I'm here."

"Can I ride on a tractor?"

"Sure thing."

"Will you watch TV with me?"

"You got it."

"Wow! I won't have no more accidents. I promise."

"Put her there." Avery watched him offer Jaxon his hand to shake. He shouldn't have promised something like that, and yet she didn't have it in her heart to scold him. Stupid her, she'd already fallen for him.

Her fragile heart still hadn't recovered from her mother's death and now she was placing it in the callused, willful hands of a much too slick cattle rancher who was inevitably going to break it again. She wasn't certain she'd survive with him or without him.

Avery scrubbed her hands over her face as he carried Jax back inside.

"Hey, Colton, can I have one more thing for not having no more accidents?" she heard her baby brother ask.

"What's that, Captain America?"

"Can you make it so Avery's not so sad all the time?"

"I'm gonna do everything I possibly can to see to that, Cap."

CHAPTER TEN

Willing away the exhaustion setting up residence in his bones, Colt scooped Jaxon out of his car seat and carried him inside the trailer. He'd fallen asleep somewhere between the Runza in Ogallala and Pleasant Glen. Little guy was tuckered out.

Colt would've given anything to put the boy to bed and then slip into Avery's room and sleep with her tucked in next to him until morning. As it stood, he had another hour-long drive back to Ogallala ahead of him.

He laid him in his bed and Avery pulled the covers over him and whispered a kiss on his cheek.

"I need to head on, baby," Colt whispered.

She followed him out to his truck. "Thank you for all you did tonight." Her sweet whisper slipped through his ears and warmed his weary body.

"I didn't do anything much. Runzas are a little weird, but they're not bad. 'Course you wouldn't know 'cause you only ate a salad."

"It was a decent salad for a sandwich place."

Soon as he found himself a stove, he was going to make her a fucking filet and watch her eat the whole damn thing. He grunted out his disdain.

"Thanks for what you said to Jax about wetting his pants. I heard you."

"You spying on me, baby?"

"My brothers will always be my first priority. Kind of goes with the whole guardianship deal."

He'd never ask for it to be any other way. "You're the strongest person I've ever met. You know that?"

"I don't feel very strong."

He had to get on the road if he was going to make it back to his hotel without falling asleep at the wheel. "That's the thing about strength. When you feel like you just don't got nothing left to give, but you keep on going, that's the strongest you've ever been."

"Maybe. Hey, what was all that with Chase and the cheerleader?" They'd come to a stop beside his truck. The heat of her breaths were visible in the frigid night. He slipped out of his coat and draped it over her shoulders. He had every intention of making a claim, however small, that evening and he didn't want her to freeze.

"Time will tell, but I believe he's crushing on a girl that ain't worth his time. I'll talk to him more after football practice tomorrow. He'll leave some of that excess testosterone on the field. After that, I 'spect he'll make better decisions for about twenty minutes 'til it builds right back up again."

Even her laughter sounded exhausted. "So, I need to time my lectures in twenty-minute blocks after football?"

She was mere millimeters away from him and yet it just wasn't close enough. Lust hummed constantly under his skin. She tucked a wayward strand of hair behind her ear and he was fascinated with her every minute movement. The tender seduction of her scent filled his lungs along with the thin night air. He focused on those lush pink lips desperately trying and failing to really hear her words. "If you can, that'd work best, but I'll see if I can't get through to him. Too bad I can't offer to take him on a tractor ride and get him to quit being sixteen."

The low-hung moon glimmered in her darkened eyes. Her lips glistened enticingly. "You shouldn't have told Jax you'll be here when he gets home."

"Why not?"

"Because eventually whatever it is you're doing up here is going to be done and you'll go back to Holder County."

Damn, why didn't she just drive his Stockman knife through his chest? "I said one of us would be here. You already trying to get rid of me?"

"No. I'm trying to save myself from a whole lot of heartbreak."

"Why are you so convinced I'm gonna break your heart?"

"Because you are."

"No, I'm not."

"Would you shut up and kiss me before I'm able to remember why we're such a terrible idea?"

"Dammit, Avery, we are not a terrible idea."

"As you cowboys like to say, bullshit."

"Why are you so convinced I brought you out here to kiss you, anyway?" Her smirk said she had no doubt of his intentions. With her fingertip, she traced a slow, torturous outline over the denim around his cock, making him pulse and grunt. Unable to help himself, he covered her hand with his own, reveling in the warmth of her palm spilling against him. Jesus, he needed her touch.

Victory rang in her moonlit gaze. "That's how I know."

Turning, so he had her trapped between him and the bed of his truck, he threaded his fingers through her hair with one hand and wrapped the other around that full, luscious ass, the very one he intended to take hold of while he plowed into her from every available angle. She needed to get a few things straight and he was all out of words that night. He was going to let his actions talk on his behalf.

Her tongue darted over her lips. Her chest rose and fell as her breaths dissolved into rapid pants. Sick to death of all of her back and forth about the two of them, he jerked her forward until her pussy collided with his erection, so hard and hungry for her he wasn't certain he'd be able to drive.

"Feel what you do to me, Avery," he commanded as he rubbed her up and down the ridge created by his overly anxious cock. "You make me so fucking hard for you. And someday soon, honey, I'm gonna let you feel it deep inside of you. I'm gonna fuck you so hard you won't be able to walk. I'll show you just how good we're gonna be together."

"Oh God, yes," she gasped in his face.

"Mmm-hmm that's what I thought. You need it every bit as badly as I do. And I'm gonna take it, baby. Wear your little body out. Make you so slick with wanting, the only thing that will make it better is more of me."

Her pleading moan was so loud he was worried she was going to wake her little brother. He trapped it with his own lips, crushing them down on hers and quelling those needy noises that made him crazy.

Her lips were soft and hungry. Willing and supple. Even better than his dirty dreams. Like a man possessed, he licked the seam until she opened for him. A low, ragged growl spilled from his lungs as he finally tasted her. Warm vanilla, sugary confections, and there it was at last—that sinful spice he knew she tried so hard to keep at bay.

Her hands wrapped around his shoulders and pulled him closer. He thrust against her again, driving home his point. She was his. All his. He would show her that if it was last fucking thing he ever did.

Another thrust. She whimpered out her need. Heat spilled through those yoga pants as he ground against her. He knew she was swollen and wet for him. Caressing her cheek as he turned his head and dove back in for an even deeper kiss, devouring her flavors, he let his fingertips traverse a heat-seeking path directly to the left cup of her bra. Her nipple puckered obediently against what felt like delicate lace under that thick top.

She arched her back into his caress and pressed her pussy against him, empty but so hungry to be filled.

"Feels good doesn't it, sugar? Feels good rubbing up against my cock." Catching her nipple between his thumb and forefinger, he gave a hesitant squeeze.

"Yes," shattered from her.

"That's my girl. We're gonna get nice and naughty, baby. I promise you that. I'll fuck you 'til you understand that I'm not gonna walk away and leave you."

"Now." She sucked in a haggard breath.

"Damn, I like you begging for me. I'm gonna need to hear that real,

real often, but tonight this is all you get." He gave another dedicated thrust. She trembled in his arms.

Her lips were going to be bruised. Good. Every time she looked in that mirror, she needed to remember who she belonged to now. That she wasn't on this earth fighting all alone.

When the front door slammed open, they broke apart like two teenagers caught red-handed. Chase glared at both of them.

"When you're finished choking on his tongue and letting him feel you up, Aunt Pearl needs help with her nightgown, Avery."

A tremor shot through her as she tried to stand on her own. Colt kept her upright. Damn, but she needed to be thoroughly undone, and soon.

"I'll be right there."

"Whatever."

"I need to go." Her voice was laced with desperation.

"Baby, we're going to figure everything out together, okay? I swear to you."

"That's an amazing thought, Colton. It really is. Thank you for all you've already done."

"I'll see you tomorrow. I'm picking him up from practice."

She managed a ragged nod. "Bye." She raced up the front steps. Fear swept into his chest with his next lungful of freezing cold air. He hated that she always seemed to be running away from him.

———

Finally alone in her room after she'd gotten Pearl in bed and had ordered Chase to do the biology review his teacher had assigned them, Avery stared down at her pillow. There was another one of those hundred dollar bills Colton seemed to have in endless supply attached to a note, *Best hair cut I ever got. I'll see you tomorrow.*

She didn't even have his phone number. How was that possible? He didn't have hers either. This whole entire thing was insane. She couldn't let herself rely on him. No matter what he said, she knew he wouldn't always be around. Yet that ridiculous, fizzy, flustered feeling continued to do the backstroke through her veins and to cloud her vision. It felt so good. No, it felt fantastic. The invisible tether between them continued to strengthen its hold. His touches were solid and familiar like she'd known them her entire life.

A faint trace of his flavors remained on her tongue. All man, cologne, and sweat. All cowboy, leather, and hay. All Colton. She desperately wanted more. Her lips were still swollen. Like his kiss was so full of sin, it actually contained venom.

Take it one moment at a time, Avery. You can't manage more than that.

Turning the shower water on to let it get hot, she grabbed her cell phone and texted Samantha. *I kissed a cowboy and I really, really liked it.*

Her phone rang two point four seconds later. Smiling at that, she answered the call.

"O-M-G are you seriously going to bed one of the Holder boys? I'm so freaking proud of you," Samantha shrieked.

"Could we stop speaking in adolescent verbiage maybe?"

"Would you get off your granny rocker and tell me more about this stud? Oh, and by the way, I went to grab a latte with Juliet Simps today. You remember her. She went to school in Holder County but she took dance with us that one summer. Anyway, she said she doesn't remember a Colton Holder at all."

Annoyed with Samantha's fascination with Colton because of his last name, Avery regretted her text. "Maybe he graduated before her. I pretty sure he's older than we are."

"Oh. An older man. Very saucy."

"Not an older man...just...never mind. I need to go."

"Not until you tell me about this kiss and when you plan on getting him in bed. You deserve fun in your life, Ave. Heck, you deserve Holder-level fun and that's saying something."

The next morning, Avery got the boys to school and came back to the trailer to clean up and check on her aunt before she headed to the Cut 'n' Curl.

"This just can't be right." Aunt Pearl stared down at some paperwork Avery hadn't gotten to yet.

"What can't be right?" Avery took the paper from her. She didn't want her aunt to worry about anything. Stress only made her feel worse. After reading half of the words and running her eyes down the right hand column of numbers, she gasped. "They can't do this."

"I don't understand what they're saying they won't pay for," Pearl explained.

"They're denying you the new medication your doctor put you on because they say there's another drug that's cheaper. But they already tried the other one and it didn't work. And they don't want to pay for your patch. I have to call the doctor and the insurance company. They can't just say they won't pay for medicine you need."

"Well, how much is the medicine if they won't pay?"

Avery's eyes fell to the final line on the invoice. "It's...uh..." She tried to take a deep breath, but the air singed her lungs. "It's several hundred dollars per pill. I'll figure it out, Aunt Pearl. I won't let them do this to you."

"I don't know what I'd do without you, Avery."

"It's fine. I'll handle it. I'll figure it out."

By ten o'clock, Avery had yelled at the insurance company twice and had gotten nowhere. The oncologist's office hadn't called her back and her chair had been empty all morning. So far, Melony Kilroy hadn't cancelled her appointment the next morning. Avery clung to that.

She could make this work. She had to. There was no other option.

Another burst of infuriating hope bubbled up when the bell on the front door opened. "Yes, sir, can I help you?" She leapt to her feet.

"Possibly. I'm here to serve a Miss Avery Hale."

"Serve me what?"

"Custody papers, ma'am."

CHAPTER ELEVEN

Restless, Colton couldn't stand to look at the walls in his hotel room any longer. Even if it was freezing, outside was always better than in. As he flung open the door, he huffed. The sky wasn't any better, a bleak gray that blended in with the air around him. His head was as foggy as the morning sky and he felt like he was drowning in some kind of abyss.

It hadn't occurred to him until he'd gotten back to his room the night before that he didn't even have Avery's number yet. *Dumbass.*

He forced his truck to drive without heating it up. It was less than a mile to the local Denny's though, so he went with it. Pitching himself in a booth, he debated his next moves. In hindsight, he'd fucked up more than a few times already, both with Avery and the Camdens.

A plump waitress with wind-pricked cheeks appeared to take his order. She sized him up. "Honey, you look like you could use something much stronger than anything we serve here."

"You're not kidding, but it's barely nine in the morning."

"What's her name?"

"Avery."

"She break your heart, darlin'?"

"Nah, but she seems more than convinced I'm gonna break hers.

Didn't exactly do much to assure her I wouldn't. Pardon my language, but it's all kinds of fucked-up. Plus, I got no clue why I'm telling you all this."

Her laughter was pleasant enough he supposed, but he missed Avery's mischievous little giggles. "Ain't it always that way. I'm a wait-ress and I asked how you were in a roundabout way so you're supposed to tell me. Now, how 'bout a coffee and a Lumberjack Slam?"

"I ain't a lumberjack."

"Oh sweetie, I know. You cowboys always seem to dig your boots in at the wrong times. My Sal gets his britches caught up on his own pitchfork most of the time."

"What's that mean?" He was sure it was standard diner waitress advice that might or might not cover myriad situations.

"Means sometimes when you finally figure out that you're in a hole the best thing to do is stop digging. I'll be right back with your coffee."

That sounded a lot like giving up to Colton and that was the one option in this shitstorm he'd created that he would absolutely never accept. He'd figure out some way to make something work out for himself. He was going to stop being the bastard kid who screwed everything up.

He slowly ate eggs, ham, and bacon with a hearty side of regret. She'd been scared. He'd told her how hard he was going to fuck her like that would magically erase the lengthy list of complications in this non-relationship. She knew he would ultimately have to go back to Holder County, a fact he'd been conveniently ignoring in favor of playing pretend with the Camdens. He had no business making promises to Jaxon and he shouldn't have come down on Chase about Kami. Wasn't his place. Jesus, he needed a drink and he missed Rio.

The caffeine shifted his brain into gear, finally. He might not know her number, but he knew where she'd be. He fished out his phone, googled the Cut 'n' Curl, and then touched the number.

"Cut 'n' Curl, this is Sally. Can I help ya?"

"Hey, Sally, this is Colton. I was wondering if I could talk to Avery." As badly as he wanted to fix what he'd done, he'd gladly wait if she had a customer.

"Well, hey there, Colton. You know, Avery went home. Not sure what all she has going on but, she said she needed to make some phone calls. I kinda hoped she was sneaking out to see you."

I wish. "No, uh, I haven't seen her today. Hey, I should've already gotten this, but I don't have her phone number. You mind sharing it with me?"

"Of course. Hang on, let me see where I wrote that."

"I'm much obliged, ma'am."

When he ended the call with Sally, he immediately entered Avery's contact information and called her. No answer. He tried three more times in a matter of ten minutes, shoveling down three pieces of toast between rings. Still no answer.

Maybe she's in the shower. A low grunt lodged in his throat from the vision his mind instantly conjured. Hot water and soap slipping down those killer curves. What he wouldn't give to watch. What he wouldn't give to be the one holding her slick and slippery against him. What he wouldn't give for his hands to be...

Blinking away the filthy images, he ordered his cock to give him a break. Currently, he wasn't going to be able to stand to walk out of the diner.

The waitress left him to his irritation but kept his coffee mug full, which he appreciated. An hour later, his plates were long since empty and Avery still wasn't answering her phone. He'd left two messages. Dammit, where was she? Was she pissed? Probably. Last night, she'd acted like she didn't want him to leave, but the good Lord only knew what could've happened to change her mind since then. Women.

He needed a drink.

The next time the waitress came around, he asked her for the bill and thanked her for letting him take up the booth for so long. "Hey, you know of a bar anywhere around here that's open this early?"

"This is a dry county, honey, but I know just where you need to go. It's a little drive and weather's looking rough out there. But they have great whiskey and the wings have won awards. It's Sal's favorite."

"I got tire chains. Where is this place?"

"It's about twenty miles toward the Wyoming line out on 80."

Colton opened his map program. "What's it called?"

"The Dew Drop."

"Much obliged." He left two twenties on the table, shrugged into his coat, and headed out. The waitress was right. The weather had gone from bad to worse. It now perfectly matched his current mood. Angry, irritable, and freezing cold. The wind found its way through the weave of his Carhartt and chafed at his skin. His hot breath curled in the air as he hot-footed it to the truck. Cranking it to let it warm up, he tried Avery again. Still no answer. Dammit.

Minuscule fragments of ice pelted his windshield. Great. When his phone rang, he answered it on the first ring. "Avery?"

His uncle's chuckle didn't calm him this time. "That can't be a good sign. What happened?"

"Nothing, Uncle Gent. You okay?"

"Lawyer's taken to calling me instead of you, which I'm okay with, but he ain't happy with the time delay. You made any headway with the Camdens?"

"No, sir."

"Let's change course. You made any headway with your Avery?"

"Not really. As usual I was a dumbass."

"I doubt that, but I can't tell you for sure 'til you tell me what you did."

"I have no business messing around with her." True, though it hadn't stopped him from calling her phone again and again. "She's got enough on her plate to cover every single one of the plates at our Holder family reunions."

A low whistle slid between his uncle's teeth. Colt had seen him do that dozens of times in his life. He knew exactly which expression his uncle was wearing and just then he missed his family something fierce. He missed knowing somebody was going to be there to bail him out or at least tell him how to fix his latest mistake.

"Did you think about maybe seeing if you could take a little off of her plate?"

"Yeah, that's what I was trying to do, but I think I might have scared her more. She keeps going back and forth on me."

"What do you do with a skittish horse, son?"

"You pull up hard on the reins." He answered without much thought. He'd been riding his entire life.

"There you go."

"I'm not so sure that's what she needs just yet. It's kinda like much as she stumbles she really is galloping."

"You sitting down?"

"Yes, sir. Warming up my truck."

"Good because it sounds to me like you're in love with this girl."

"That ain't even possible. I've known her a grand total of two days."

"That's plenty long enough. I'll tell you this, the man I'm speaking to on the phone right this moment ain't the angry, indignant guy who drove off my ranch cursing his life, his daddy, and his mama."

"I'm still furious at both of 'em."

"Rightfully so."

"What am I supposed to do about that and about Avery? She's trying real hard to make a life here and things keep going wrong for her."

"Last time I checked, you were a part of a big-ass family that happens to own most of the land in western Oklahoma. You ever think about seeing if that life she's trying to build up there might be real easy to erect down here?"

"No, she's got family up here."

"You got family down here. Listen to me for a minute, and for once in your life maybe try doing it the way I tell ya the first time."

Colt slowed the truck as the snow and ice mix started to gather on the roads. "I'm listening."

"I'm about to sound like a pussy. You ever tell any of my brothers I said any of this, I'll string you up."

Colton laughed at that. "I'll keep it between you and me."

"Good. Now, here it is, if you're gonna give a woman something, give her a place to lay her head on your chest. Give her some peace. Something real to hold on to. Hold her while she sleeps without fucking her senseless beforehand. Make damn well sure she knows you're gonna be standing there holding her when the whole world falls apart, because trust me, it will. Make sure she knows that you're gonna be standing there holding on to her making sure she don't get caught up in the rubble. And then you take that rubble and you rebuild her world brick by brick. Never make her doubt. Let her hear your heartbeat when you lay her down on your chest at night. Let her know it beats for her."

"Damn."

"I can be darn near poetic when I put my mind to it."

"Yeah. Still got no clue how to do any of that when I leave here."

"Why don't you try doing it now while you're there and see which way the world spins next."

"Currently, she won't even talk to me."

"Well, now, best way to eat crow is while it's warm. Gets mighty hard to swallow once it's cold."

Colt slowed the truck as he saw a sign directing him down a two-lane to the Dew Drop bar. "I'll find her and talk to her."

"Sounds like a plan."

"Thanks, Uncle Gentry."

"My pleasure. I'm happy you've found someone special. But Colton, do remember why you're there. This ain't just gonna go away as much as you keep wishing it would. It's got to be dealt with."

"I know." He turned into the empty parking lot. Bar certainly didn't look open. He made a wide u-turn, intent on heading straight to Pleasant Glen. That was when he saw several cars parked in the lot behind the bar. When his eyes landed on a tan, late-model Corolla with an Oklahoma tag, he stomped on the brake. What the hell?

———

Vomit swirled ominously in Avery's belly. Chill bumps raised every hair on her body, like some kind of armor trying to protect her. Pure terror filled her stomach until she was certain she would choke on it. She was going to be sick. She could feel it. A dizzying flash of heat burned her cheeks and then her entire body went frigid.

She swayed as she stared up at the pole in the middle of the stage in front of her. How was this even happening? Her mouth felt fuzzy. Her brain refused to offer her any kind of plan. Two human-sized cages with leaden bars glared down at her from their perches on either side of the stage.

Her seeking gaze located three men and two women waiting on her to climb up on that stage to try out for something she'd never, ever wanted to do.

"So...uh...I just go up there and...dance?"

"Yeah," huffed the big gruff one who'd threatened her when she'd tried to back out a few minutes before. "We need to make sure you look good nekkid."

"You can borrow some of my heels if you need 'em," offered one of the women, who'd been introduced as a dancer.

Heels. Right. Avery stared down at her ballet flats. She'd danced on stages most of her childhood and well into her high school years. Surely this wasn't all that different. Samantha had made it sound like an easy transition.

"Uh, okay." Setting down the bag she'd stupidly packed full of old leotards and her lucky toe shoes, she braced her hands on the stage and hoisted herself up.

"That'd get the patrons going," one of the men sneered.

The big one agreed, "She's got a nice ass, long as it's smooth." Tattoos bulged ominously out of his wife-beater T-shirt. It was less than ten degrees outside, but they had the heat cranking. The air was too thick to breathe.

Yet cold sweat gathered at the dip in her lower back. The room spun. Hesitantly, like reaching her hand into a nest of copperheads, she touched the pole. She flinched. It was oddly cold.

Focus, Avery. Aunt Pearl needs medicine. You have to get a lawyer. You could only work on Sundays when the shop's closed. They said so. You could make enough to pay your dad back and get the medicine in just a few weeks.

Music started to play from somewhere, but the air was so thick it muted the low bass tones. Or maybe she was losing the ability to hear properly. The stage started to pulse. She held on to the pole to keep from falling.

"Get on with it. I don't have all morning, sweetheart," a smaller man with a nasally drawl demanded. "We'll have customers here in an hour."

Her uncooperative brain stumbled around in her head until it landed on the last routine she'd performed with the Oklahoma City Ballet. She took fifth position, arms high over her head, abdomen locked, spine extended, shoulders back, toes pointed, and began to move.

She even managed to work spinning around the pole into her routine.

When the door slammed open so loudly it shook the stage, she gasped and lost her place.

"What the fucking hell do you think you are doing?"

In that moment, she was quite certain she'd never been happier to see anyone than she was to see Colton Holder in the doorway. "Get the hell off of that stage or so help me, I will burn this motherfucking place to the ground," he roared.

It took her far too long to understand that he was enraged.

"Hey, dude, what's your issue? She ain't even shown us anything yet," the big one spat out stupidly.

Colton shoved him aside and then suddenly he was on the stage. Fury was ablaze in his eyes, every angle of his body was drawn to a harsh point, every muscle was flexed. Even his jaw was locked tight. It took her another breath to understand that the world itself wasn't vibrating. He was so angry he was *shaking*. He circled her. She swayed as he wrapped a rock-solid arm around her waist from behind. He cradled her against his body, which was about as unyielding as a concrete wall.

Despite his obvious anger, the tight wire of tension strung from her shoulders all the way down her spine somehow eased. She was safe.

He did not lead her, did not guide her—no, he dragged her off of the stage like she was some kind of rag doll. And she let him.

But the big guy stepped in front of Colton. The only thought Avery could formulate was the man was obviously even dumber than he looked.

"Move or be moved, motherfucker," Colton snarled. He never let her go.

"She ain't leaving 'til I get a good look at those tits." And there it was. The declaration of war hung in the thick air for a single heartbeat.

Avery gulped in a quick breath as Colton released her. His right fist sailed through the air. There was a horrifying snap and crunch as it met the guy's face. He offered no reprieve after his first strike but instead pummeled the man's gut until he could barely stand.

The soft whisper of Colton's hat hitting the dirty carpet juxtaposed with the grunts and groans and filthy taunts that spewed from the men.

"Come on, Reggie. You really gonna take that?" The dancer taunted.

"Shut up," Avery finally located her voice. Was this woman completely insane?

Reggie finally landed a single strike in Colton's chest. Incensed, Colton brought him to the ground. One of the smaller men leapt in to defend Reggie.

Vomit filled Avery's mouth as fists and fury flew all around her. Surely even Colton couldn't take down three men. She covered her face, allowing herself only to peek through her own fingers. How could she have done this? How had her life gotten so far out of hand?

"Stop. Please. Please, don't hurt him," she begged as one guy managed to twist away from Colton enough to drive a fist into his throat. Colton gagged.

"Please, please stop."

The other man—the bartender, she thought—took a swing at Colton's back. He jerked out of the way as the third man dove for him, making contact with his gut.

In one blink, Colton was struggling to stand. In another, he was back up and landing his boot in the bartender's groin. He went down with a sickening groan. Spinning rapidly, Colton took on the final guy, who ran at him head first. He caught the charging beast and threw him to the ground.

Catching the collar of the third guy's T-shirt, he twisted it tight, leaving his opponent no air. "Want some more, fucker? I've got plenty left to give." The third man went down, landing on top of the bartender. Colton planted a boot on his chest, rendering him unable to do anything but gasp for breath.

He spat in the man's face before grabbing his hat, her bag, and her.

They were standing beside his truck before she realized she'd been holding her breath. A vicious combination of snow and ice beat at her skin. She deserved it. She shivered as the wind flew through the thin yoga pants she was wearing.

He still hadn't spoken to her. He flung open the passenger side door. "Get in."

"My car." The wind whipped her whispered words away.

"Now," he growled.

She complied, attempting to take up as little room in the cab as she could manage. Half of her wanted to yell at him and tell him he could've been hurt and that she couldn't stand to think about anything or anyone hurting him. The other half wanted to thank him over and over and over again.

CHAPTER TWELVE

His cheek was a garish purple and blood from his knuckles was pooling in the light hair on his hands. Avery had no idea what to say. Now that they were away from that place, the initial relief had faded. He'd had no right to do that, really. And yet, "I'm sorry" seemed the only fitting response. She *was* sorry. Sorry he'd gotten hurt. Even more sorry she was the reason why.

He said nothing. His gaze remained locked on the highway. He hadn't looked her in the eye since he'd yanked her off that stage.

Snow gathered in jagged hills along the sides of the road. The wind whipped against the truck, trying to push it to the side. He kept it steady, never wavering.

He continued to put miles between her and the only gentlemen's club she'd been able to find anywhere near Pleasant Glen. The silence was deafening. She wanted to scream. She had to do something to mark herself in this time and this place. Something that made this real. She'd somehow been vacuumed from her own reality and deposited in some alternate version. She was watching her own life through a grainy screen. How had she even gotten there? What happened now?

"Colton, please say something. Anything."

"You sure as hell don't want to hear what I'm thinking right now."

"Do you think your cheekbone might be broken?"

"Hush."

Several agonizingly long minutes later, they were coming back into Ogallala. He had to slow the truck more as the vicious wind took brutal blows against it and ice hit the windshield with harsh cracks.

They crawled down the main drag, though there wasn't much traffic, passing the restaurant where he'd taken them the evening before. The familiar landmark was an anchor. Something real. She clung to the memories of watching him pretend to sword fight with Jaxon with ketchup-tipped french fries.

Oh my God. Jaxon. How was she going to pick him up from aftercare without a car? Why was Colton turning the truck onto a two-lane? Where were they going? She had to go home.

Before she could voice any of this, he'd pulled into a motel lot and stomped his boot on the parking brake. He yanked the cowboy hat off of his head and sank it down on hers. She watched him whip off his coat. "Put this on," he ordered.

He flung open his door and shut it with enough force to rock the truck back and forth. A half second later, he opened her door. He stood there in nothing but a button-down shirt and waited on her to finish sticking her arms through the long sleeves of the warmest coat she'd ever worn.

She didn't want him to freeze, so she pulled it on quickly as her feet hit the snow-covered cement. She slipped. He caught her instinctively. The gentleness of his grip shocked her after seeing what he could do with those massive hands.

He wrapped his arm around her and pulled her into his side as he led her toward one of the doors, taking on the elements himself, shielding her from the wind and slaps of ice. Still struggling with logical thought, she took a minute to process that he had a key to this room because this was where he'd been staying.

The absence of the wind was the first thing her mind registered when he sealed the door shut behind them. The maids must not have been by yet. The bed was unmade. Two suitcases and a briefcase were shoved in one corner. The room held no more color than the sky outside.

He began to pace. "How could you...?" He shook his head and beat one more path up and down between the bed and the dresser. "What the fuck were you...?" Another trip to the bathroom door and back. "Do you have any idea what could've...? Do you know what goes on in clubs like...?" Another head shake.

He closed his eyes. She couldn't even blink. When he grabbed a hand towel off of the bed, she cowered, certain he was going to hurl it against the wall. Instead, he wrapped it around his right hand and took several deep breaths.

She had to say something. At some point she had to remind him that he'd had no business showing up and throwing punches. She didn't need a hero. She needed money. "I'm sorry you got in a fight. That wasn't necessary. At least I don't think it was necessary. Maybe." Truthfully, she wasn't sure they would've let her leave if he hadn't shown up even if she had gotten around to actually stripping.

Something told her it was nothing like the place Samantha was working. Sam said she always felt safe when she was at work. Safe was the very last thing Avery had felt until Colton had shown up at the door.

"You don't think it was necessary, huh?" he huffed. "Honest to Christ, Avery, I can't even..." He bit back the rest of the comment.

"Just say whatever it is you're wanting to say."

"Fine. I want the answer to one question. Am I such a bad idea that you'd rather do that—" he threw his bloody hand toward the door, "—than ask me for help?"

"My friend Samantha has been dancing at Scarlet A's. She said she was making a lot of money."

He shook his head and whipped the towel off of his hand. It hit the floor as he took two big steps across the room and came to a stop directly in front of her. His hand lifted to caress her cheek. He eased her head up so she had no choice but to look him in the eye. "Scarlet A's is a club owned and operated by women. It's safe. They make sure of it. They pay fair and they don't put up with the likes of the assholes I just beat the piss out of. They keep it clean. No drugs. The dancers only drink non-alcoholic drinks so they're always in control. The bouncers outnumber the dancers and there sure as hell aren't any cages. Didn't it seem off to you that there was no sign or anything advertising it as a strip club?"

Her slight head shake moved his hands against her skin. It steadied her. "I didn't think about it."

"You didn't think at all. You panicked, and instead of asking for my help, you decided to do everything on your own."

That did it. She jerked away from him. "I have no choice. Don't you get it? I can't allow anyone else to fail my brothers or my aunt. I'm it. I have to figure out how to do everything because I am the only one I know won't let them down."

———

Colt's blood continued to race hot and fast through his veins. Gall throbbed in his head. It was all he could do to see her through the haze of incensed red before his eyes. "Trust no one. Is that it? What happens when you're just not enough? What happens when you can't do it all on your own?"

"I can. I will."

"Not if it means doing that."

She sank down on his bed and his heart sank right along with her. She drew her legs up to her chest. "Then I'm out of options. I won't be able to afford my aunt's medicine, and if she doesn't get it, she won't... be here. And now I'm going to lose Jaxon, too. I'll lose all of them just like I lost my mom."

Shaking his head, desperate to swear to her that he'd rebuild her world for her brick by brick, he settled on the bed beside her. "Why can't I be your option?"

"You barely know me." She spoke into her knees.

"I know enough to know I want to help. Let me prove myself to you. I won't let you down."

She eased away. "I really appreciate that you rescued me and that you want to help. I swear I do. I was so scared." Her chin trembled. It shook his soul. "I'm always so scared."

"I know, baby." He drew her to him and kissed the top of her head. "Please let me help you."

Scrubbing her hands over her face as she sat up and stared him down. "What happens when you have to go back to Holder County and the boys and I are attached to you? What happens when I fall in love with you and you leave me, too?"

And wasn't that the crux of it? She'd said the same thing yesterday and it had kept him up all night. Half-formed words clogged his throat. He had no truth to offer, so he served up an evasion. "I'm not on any kind of real timeline. I don't have to go back anytime soon. Can't we just try this? Can't I help as much as I can?"

"According to you, I have no other options."

This time irritation filtered through his blood. "Do you want other options? Do you want me to write you a damned check and get the hell out of your life? Because if that's what you want, I'll do it."

"No. No, I don't want that at all. I'm just so tired of fighting everything and everyone. I'm so tired of doing everything wrong. I'm exhausted and there's no end in sight."

"Come here to me." Working around her, he shoved the covers back, lay on the bed, and guided her onto his chest. Reaching down, he cosseted the sheets and blankets around them. His face hurt like a bitch and he needed to scrub the blood off his hands, but just then there was nothing more important than giving her a place to lay her head, just like his uncle had said.

She curled up warm and sweet on his chest and the ache that had been there a moment before eased. He'd been hit in the face but he didn't have a concussion. He'd had enough of those between football and fighting to know the symptoms. When she tangled her legs between his, he knew there was nowhere else on earth he needed to be.

He'd wanted to take her to bed since the moment he'd laid eyes on her. The man he'd been two days ago would've balked at holding her in his arms without having his cock buried deep inside her. The man he'd been two days ago was a bastard.

He woke up sometime later when a warm, wet cloth was tenderly swiped over his face. His eyes blinked open and she offered him a timid smile. "I was worried it would get worse if we didn't get my arnica cream on it soon."

She pressed gently. Her fingertips brushed his cheek. A sigh he couldn't hold in escaped his lips. "Most beautiful nurse I've ever had," he whispered.

"Does anything else hurt?" She looked so worried it broke his heart.

"He buried his fist in my ribcage, but I've had worse."

"Can you take your shirt off for me?"

Easing upright, he slipped the shirt up over his elbows. The movement made him cringe, but he clenched his teeth and went on with it.

"That looks bad," she gasped. "I'm so sorry."

"Hey," he cupped her face in his hand, stroking her cheek with his thumb. So soft. So pretty. So sweet. He wasn't certain he wasn't dreaming. "I'm okay."

"Thank you for coming there. How did you know where to find me?" She brought the wet cloth to his side. Her tender touch restored his soul. He was able to draw a full breath and her sweet vanilla cream scent filled his lungs. Damn but he needed that.

"I didn't. Seems fate's determined to bring us together. I was looking for a drink and it's a dry county. Some chick at Denny's said that place had good whiskey. I was about to leave because it looked sketchy as fuck and I realized what I really wanted was to see you. But then I saw your car. I didn't know it was a strip joint until I got to the door."

"Do you believe in fate?" She lifted his right hand and tenderly wiped away the dried blood.

"My uncle says you make your own fate. My dad's brother thinks fate drives the whole ship. We get no say. I guess I believe something in between."

Her brow furrowed. "Wouldn't your dad's brother also be your uncle?"

"Kind of."

"Kind of?"

"That has to do with why I'm up in Pleasant Glen in the first place."

When his skin was free of blood, she rummaged in some kind of makeup bag and produced three small screw-top jars. "I made these. This is calendula cream." She pointed to them each in turn. "And this is arnica blend. It has green tea and vitamin K in it. And this one is coconut oil. They'll heal your cuts and bruises, and take the sting out. May I?"

He nodded.

She scooped some of the cream onto her fingertips and rubbed it on his chest. "I'm so sorry you got hurt because of me."

"If I get you to agree to let me help you, it'll be more than worth it. Not my first fight, baby."

"Yeah, I figured that out when you decimated all of them. If I let you help me, will you tell me why you're in Pleasant Glen? About your dad or his brother or whatever. And why you were at the funeral home yesterday? Maybe I could help you, too."

The entirety of the blasted story danced on his tongue. God, he needed to tell someone outside the Holder family the whole damn thing, needed someone else to make sense of it all. "You don't need one more thing to worry about."

"Please, it would make me feel like less of a complete loser."

"Stop it." He placed his finger over her lips. "Everyone needs help every now and then. Nothing about needing help makes you a loser."

"Mama used to say that women who relied on men were naive and weak. She never needed anyone's help. Wouldn't even let my dad do anything but pay for my ballet lessons and she refused to ever see me dance because she hadn't paid for me to learn. She taught me that strong women rely only on themselves."

"Accepting help, especially from someone who's eager to give it, doesn't make you weak. She was wrong."

"You shouldn't say things like that about the dead."

"Baby, I can see how much you miss her. I can see it whenever you talk about her, and in the way you take care of the boys. But that doesn't mean she was without fault. Might be easier to deal with her death if you remember that. There ain't nothing wrong with leaning on someone when you need to, male or female."

"Maybe she was wrong, but I never remember one single time in her whole life that she asked for help."

"Yes, you do."

"No, I don't. How would you even know that?" she huffed.

"When she knew she was dying, she asked you to take care of her sons. She didn't have to ask anyone for help but you because, my God, Avery, you just always came through, didn't you, sweetheart? Never even hesitated. She needed you and you never once questioned it. You told me yesterday you were the one raising her most of the time. That's how incredibly strong you are. Try to remember that for me."

"Some man I've never even seen before brought in papers to the salon this morning. Randy went through with it. He's suing me for full custody of Jax. I thought we were going to be able to work something out where he saw him occasionally but nothing more. Now, all of a sudden he wants him full time. He got them to set a temporary custody hearing in ten days. I have to get a lawyer now." Her voice shattered as she made the confession. "And the insurance company is refusing to pay for Aunt Pearl's medicine and for the patch that helps her recover from chemo. Without that, I'll have to take her all the way back to Lincoln the day after her treatments. That would be four days a week. I'll never be able to work if I have to do that. I...I don't know how to fix it all. Before, I could always figure something out and now... I just can't."

At least that explained why he'd found her on stage at that shithole.

"We're going to figure it out. I promise you. Do you have the papers on you?"

Standing, she located the bag she must've packed for the strip club. His stomach churned as he watched her pull a thin flannel blanket and a pair of ballet shoes complete with the ribbon things from her bag. "Did you seriously bring ballet shoes to try out at a strip club?" If his head hadn't been pounding, he would've laughed.

"I didn't really know what to bring. They said I had to come dance for them. I was a ballerina most of my life. That was the only thing that made sense to me. Plus, you know, I thought maybe my dance experience would help me get the job."

Colt swung his legs off of the bed and sat up. "That explains why you didn't think that place was sketchy. You ain't ever been to a strip club, have you, darlin'?"

She shook her head. "No, but I can tell you have by how much you know about Scarlet A's."

"Guilty as charged, but what I did before I met you has no bearing on us. As long as we're together, I'd never go looking for satisfaction anywhere but in your arms."

"So...we're together?"

"We're together. Get used to the idea."

"You could've asked," she mumbled.

"Yeah, well, I'm real done asking. Get ready. I'm pulling up on the reins. We're together. We'll figure out all of the shit that might come out of that later. Right now, show me the papers."

She handed over a relatively slim manila file folder. "I have to get a lawyer. I read a book on legal mediation and I thought I could work something out with him, but now, I have to fight him. I even signed some paper a few weeks ago agreeing not to take Jaxon out of Nebraska without Randy's permission. The book said the way mediation worked was to give something to get something. I thought if I did that he would give me something but he didn't. I will not lose my brother. Jax doesn't even know Randy. The guy just showed up at my mother's memorial service and announced that he'd like to be a part of Jaxon's life. I will not let him get away with this."

"You aren't allowed to take him out of the state?" Colt gasped.

"No. I shouldn't have signed it. I was stupid. I keep messing up, like I said."

"You were trying to do right by his father. That's not stupid. I have a cousin that's a lawyer. You mind if I call her and ask about this?"

"Do you mean Meridian? Do you think she could help me? I'll come up with some way to pay her. Maybe I could have a payment plan or something. Do lawyers do that?"

His fraying nerves continued to unravel. "Avery, if she needs money, I'll take care of it. I thought you were going to let me help. And yes, I mean Meridian. Do you know her?"

"Well, we never defined how you would be helping exactly and I cut her hair a few times."

"We're gonna start with money and go from there."

"Then you have to tell me why you're in town and let me help you, too."

"What if you helping me with that means I have to go back to Holder County sooner?"

CHAPTER THIRTEEN

"I don't want to think about that." Avery fixed her eyes on Colton. The bruises on his face were fading from the arnica. They'd only known each other three days. How was he suddenly someone she couldn't bear to think about living without? "I'm going to get you a fresh washcloth. That'll help with the swelling on your cheek." She busied herself in the bathroom, wishing she could wash her guilt and poor decisions down the sink with the water.

He followed her. Taking the washcloth from her hand, he set it on the marble counter and she found herself locked tightly in the sanctuary of his arms once again. "My face is fine. You don't want to think about me leaving and I don't really want to talk about why I'd have to, so let's leave it for the time being. We need to head back to Pleasant Glen. I want to see if Chase is still going to get to practice with the team today. I don't know how bad the weather has to be up here for them to cancel."

"What are you going to tell him about your face?"

"Don't guess you want me telling him the truth."

Another surge of guilt threatened to choke her. "I am totally aware that I should've thought of that…of what the boys would think…before I ever Googled that awful place."

Whatever he wanted to say, he appeared to be physically holding it back with the might of his molars.

"What? Just say it? I deserve to know how stupid I was."

"You're not stupid, Avery. I ain't ever met a human or an animal that made good decisions in a state of panic. But did it ever even enter your mind that Randy telling some judge that you were dancing at a strip club wouldn't have looked good for your custody deal? This ain't Oklahoma City, baby. Everybody in tiny towns knows everything there is to know about everybody else. You've got to remember that."

Crushed by her own naiveté, she leaned back into his arms "I kept thinking I'd only have to do it for a few weeks. Like I could somehow segment those weeks from my life as a whole. I told myself no one would find out."

"Believe me, I get that. Taken me thirty-something years to figure out there's no way out of your only life. The only way to carry on is to make all the parts work for the whole. There are parts of my life I'd wish away in a heartbeat but it's occurred to me lately that if it weren't for the shittiest parts of my life I wouldn't be right here holding you and I swear, baby, there is nowhere else I want to be." He gave her a squeeze before releasing her. "I'll figure out something to tell Chase. But we better get on."

As she packed up her bag, she located her phone.

"Like ten of those missed calls were from me by the way. Sally gave me your number." Colt searched for the jacket he'd put her in.

"Wish I'd answered. But look, it's only one o'clock." Between the closed blackout motel curtains, the overcast sky outside, and their nap, time seemed oddly variable. That morning at the strip club could've been a week ago. Somehow she wished it were. Putting it in her past was extremely appealing. "We have a little while before Chase's tryouts. I packed him three extra snacks and extra lunch money. I hope that helps him."

"He'll do just fine."

"The oncologist's office called me twice. Let me call Aunt Pearl and check on her and then call the doctor back. Then I want you to tell me why you were really at the funeral home yesterday. Don't think I've forgotten." She had to prepare herself for the certainty that he would eventually have to leave before this even began.

"Will you put this on your eye?" she added. "I'm so sorry you got hurt because of me."

Colton took the cold rag. An irritated grunt escaped him as he brought it to his face with a slight wince. "Not the first time I've had a busted cheek, believe me."

Avery returned to the king-sized bed to make her calls. "I take it you fight often?" She scolded herself for her reaction to the violence. The way he'd moved, the way he'd dominated his opponents, taking them on all at one time, the way he'd pressed on with seemingly no doubt...sacrificing his own safety to protect her. No one had ever done anything like that before. It had touched some primal part of her soul. Incongruent emotions went to war deep inside her. She wanted to both shut away the primal instincts and embrace and explore them with him.

"Not as much as I did in my early twenties. Maybe I've learned a thing or two since then. Used to be a weekend event. Go out, get shit-faced, wait on some idiot to get mouthy with his girl, use him to beat out all of my aggressions. I was an ignorant ass with something to prove."

"Did you ever prove it?"

"No. Turns out you can't beat your purpose out of someone else's hide. There isn't a way to prove yourself to the world 'til you know what it is you want to show everyone. It's an endless cycle that gets you nowhere. I was a dumbass, like I said."

"I don't think that's true. Maybe figuring out that you weren't entirely sure what you wanted to prove was exactly what you needed. I can't stand to think about you fighting, but I'm awfully glad you're so good at it."

A smile spread the width of his face, displaying his dimples. Every cell in her body zinged in appreciation. "Careful, baby. You keep talking like that I might just fall head over dirty boots for you and then what would we do?"

"I have no idea," she lied. She knew exactly what they would do.

He'd somehow forget all about Holder County or Oklahoma or his whole entire huge family and make a life with her right there.

She went on and called herself selfish and completely impractical as she touched her aunt's name on her phone. "Hey, Aunt Pearl, are you feeling okay?" Avery heard Jaxon's voice in the background. Her heart pounded another round of guilt into her skull. "Oh no, why is he home? Did he have another accident? Did you have to go get him? I'm so sorry!"

Her aunt began talking rapidly, something about a storm and school closing.

"Wait. What? What storm are you talking about?" Whisking to the door, she flung it open, only to be met with a shin-high wall of snow. Her mouth hung open as a blast of frigid wind knocked her backwards. Colton came up behind her and slammed the door shut.

"Shit," he spat out under his breath.

Sure, her aunt's lymphatic system was on the fritz, but there was nothing wrong with her hearing. "You with Colton, honey?"

"Uh, yes, ma'am. I'm in Ogallala with him."

His left brow arched and his grin turned decidedly wicked. This time it wasn't her cells that rejoiced. It was somewhere between her thighs.

"Oh, well that's a relief. You had me worried sick. Sally picked up little Jaxon. They've pulled the plows off the roads because of the wind. Chase willingly rode the bus home when they shut them down early. Sally's gonna stay the night with us. You and Colton have fun and stay wherever you are. They'll be able to get the plows back out early tomorrow I'm sure."

"I have an appointment with Melony Kilroy tomorrow at ten. I have to get back."

"Avery, honey, breathe for me. Miss Melony will be just fine if you have to move her appointment. You cannot get here from Ogallala safely until they get the plows back out. The wind is brutal but we're all gonna be okay."

"Do you have enough firewood?" A list of things her family might need formed instantly in her head.

"Firewood's stocked and generator has gas. You had the man come out and check it twice a week ago, remember?"

"I just want you to be safe. Don't forget your pills this evening."

"You know I did live all on my own not too long ago. I'm feeling good today. Let me enjoy it," Pearl insisted.

"Okay, I love you, Aunt Pearl. Call me if you need anything."

"I love you, too, honey. Enjoy your night. You deserve some time for yourself."

That wasn't true. She didn't deserve much of anything after the way she'd handled herself. "Bye."

From the sounds of it, Colt was trapped in a hotel room with Avery Hale. He owed the man upstairs at least a week's paycheck, maybe more. His heart pumped impatience through his veins. He stared her down as she ended the call with her aunt. "Roads closed?" His voice had taken on the consistency of gravel. He didn't care.

She gave him a timid nod before she started gnawing that lip again.

"Lay off that lip. I plan on doing that for you."

He watched blood fill her cheeks. No doubt it was filling her lower set as well, preparing her for him.

"It's just I feel bad. We told Jax one of us would be there when he got home if he didn't wet his pants."

Sweet how she was taking the blame for his mistake. "Get 'em back on the phone," he ordered. She obeyed. His cock stood up and took notice. It was a sign that he was earning her trust.

"Hey, Aunt Pearl, it's me again. Can I talk to Jax?" Her brow furrowed as Colt took the phone from her hands.

"Hey, little buddy, I need a favor." He smiled as Jaxon immediately vowed to do anything he needed him to. "Avery and I aren't gonna be able to get back to your house tonight because there were a few bad guys we had to take care of."

"Wow! Did you use your shield?"

Colt considered for a moment. He'd used his fists but doubted Avery would want him to say so. "Uh, kinda. But listen to me, you remember the other thing you asked if I could do besides taking you for a tractor ride?"

"The part about Avery not being sad so much?"

"Yep, that part. I'm gonna get that taken care of today so I can take you out on the tractor. Bet the Camdens will let us clear snow with it. But I'm sorry we won't be there tonight."

"It's okay. How are you gonna make Avery not sad no more?"

A soft chuckle escaped Colt's mouth. *You are not near old enough to hear about that, Captain America.* "I'll take good care of her. We'll see you tomorrow, okay, Cap?"

"Okay. Next time, can I fight the bad guys with you?"

"Let's hope there aren't any more bad guys, okay?"

"I guess." Jaxon sounded thoroughly disappointed. "Avengers is on. Gotta go, Colton."

"Have fun." He ended the call.

"You're completely amazing," Avery's vow was soft and fragile, laced with tension. He intended to erase all that needless worry she clung to from existence.

"I'm aware this isn't Pleasant Glen, baby, but we are most certainly alone and this isn't a hay loft or the bed of my truck."

"Very much alone." A harsh swallow contracted the long, delicate column of her neck. A quick tremor worked through her. She settled on the bed and drew her legs up to her chest again like she didn't think it was her right to stretch out, to take up space. She kept her gaze on the rumpled sheets.

Dammit. "Avery, look at me." He settled near her, careful to give her some space. "Do I scare you?"

"A little," she offered apologetically.

"Honey, all that shit that happened in the club and me talking about fighting, I need you to know that I would never, ever hurt you."

"I do know that."

"I would never force anything on you either. Tell me you know that."

"I know that, too. That's not what I'm afraid of. Not at all," she vowed.

"Then what is it?"

The storm outside held nothing on the layers of raw emotion stir-ring in those crystal-blue eyes as she stared up at him. "I love people with my whole heart. I don't even know how not to. I'm not worried about you ever hurting me physically. But I am terrified you're going to shatter my heart into a million, billion irreparable pieces."

"Why? Why do you keep saying that?"

"I know that's where this is headed, but I want you so much I'm losing my mind. So, if my choices are hurting now from trying not to fall for you or hurting later when you inevitably leave, I choose later."

"Dammit, Avery, I'm gonna prove you wrong. I'm not gonna break your heart."

She laughed. She actually laughed in his face. He quelled the desire to shove his fist through the wall. Ten years before, he would've done just that and not given a damn.

"Does that mean you're going to figure out some way to stay in Pleasant Glen forever even though your entire life is in Holder County?"

"You don't want me forever, sweetheart, trust me."

"Not even as a friend? I'm pretty sure I do."

"I don't know. Maybe I could stay." No. That wasn't an option. He knew it. She knew it. He just couldn't cop to it right yet.

"*Maybe* has probably broken more hearts than love ever did."

"I will not hurt you."

"Okay." Her eyes betrayed her lie. She didn't believe him. If it was the last thing he ever did, he'd prove her wrong. Determination set up house in the marrow of his bones.

Standing beside her, he offered her his hand.

"That an invitation to sin, Colton?"

"If ever there was one."

"Thought you were finally going to tell me why you're really in town."

"Later. Right now I'm gonna show you how it's gonna be between us. Fair warning, I'm insatiable. Never satisfied and always hungry. It's who I am. I'll want you constantly. I won't give a damn what people think, either. I'll show up at the beauty shop, take you in that back room, cover your mouth to keep you nice and quiet, pull down those leggings that I swear drive me to drinking, and ride your tight little pussy like I paid for it.

"I'll take you out to my truck and we'll steam up the windows while you ride my cock hard and fast. Hell, I'll even climb in through your bedroom window so the boys don't see me, crawl into your bed, and have you over and over again until you're so spent you got no hopes of walking straight the next morning.

"I'll fuck you slow and sweet staring into your eyes. I'll show you how much I care about you, and then I'll turn you over, leave my handprints on your ass, and show you how fucking dirty, no, scratch that, filthy it's gonna be between us. When I say. Where I say, and I don't just mean the room we're in, sugar, I mean *on* your body. How hard I say and how long I say. Sound good to you, my sweet baby?"

"Oh my God." Lightning lit the storm that had been brewing in her eyes. Her lips parted in intrigue. He watched her process his warnings. Her chest rose and fell as her breaths shattered with awareness. He could just make out the sweetened tips of her tits standing and pleading for attention under that tight leotard-type shirt she was wearing. He'd bet his very life if he eased his hand down those leggings until he reached her pussy he'd find her swollen, ripe and juicy for him. Her sweet little body knew how to ask for what she needed.

"Yeah, you'll be screaming that when you're not screaming out my name, which you'll also do when I say." Once again, he upped the ante.

"I'm about to be more honest than I've ever been with anyone in my life," she admitted.

"Good." He knew what she was going to say, knew what she so desperately needed and he was going to provide.

"I feel like you just read a script right out of my dirtiest fantasies, so yeah, it sounds really, really good to me."

"I had a feeling that might be the case."

"Like I said, bring it on, cowboy."

"So fucking tempted to turn you over my knee and paddle that sweet ass for you thinking you can show off what's mine to other men."

That mischievous smirk he always wanted to kiss right off her face appeared. "Believe me, I have no issue with it being for your eyes only but I'm not opposed to being reminded either."

A low rumbled groan wrenched from low in Colt's gut. "How wet would that make you, baby? How wet would you get if I made your sexy little rear end as pink as I intend to leave your pussy? I ain't ever been this close to heaven but believe me I have no issue paddling you, my little angel."

Her entire body jolted like she'd pressed her hands to a live wire. The wariness he'd seen in her eyes when they'd first met was long gone, replaced with pure, unadultered lust. "Trust me, the thoughts I've had about you definitely haven't been angelic."

A wicked chuckle escaped is mouth. "You been thinking about doing dirty things with me, sugar?"

"Constantly." She choked over the admittance, losing a little of her certainty. Colt hated to see her hide away her desires yet again.

"Good. That makes two of us. My fantasies about you come by the dirty dozen. One other thing I need to know 'fore we get down to business."

"I'm hoping you're about to ask me what I want to eat because I'm starving." Dammit. So much for being determined to take care of her every need. He'd nearly forgotten to feed her. Unless that wasn't actually it. "You really hungry, or are you putting me off?"

"I'm starving but maybe a little putting you off, too."

"Why?"

"Once we go there we can't come back."

"I take it you don't mean down to the Coke machines."

Her laughter was half-haunted with sadness. "No, I don't mean that."

"Then what do you mean?"

"I told you it's like you stepped right out of one of my fantasies." Rosy heat climbed seductively up her neck until it bloomed across her beautiful face. "If you're even half as good as I've imagined, I'll be so far off the ground I may never be able to dance again."

Damn woman was doing a mighty fine job of stroking his ego. It was riding almost as high as his cock at that moment. Reaching down, he adjusted to give Colton Jr. room to breathe. "Trust me, sugar, I don't do anything in half-measure. You keep coming up with those dirty fantasies. I'm about to make them all a reality. Your feet might not touch the ground again, but here's the thing, you won't want them to."

"Yeah. That's what I'm afraid of."

"Then I'd say it's high time you cowgirl up and ride. Let's get you some food. You're gonna need your strength. Fair warning, this place ain't fancy. It's got a few decent snack machines and a little cafe of sorts. We need to get down there before everything gets gone. But I want to know who lives in that other trailer on your aunt's property?"

Her brow furrowed. "No one. My uncle used to live in it before he passed."

What the hell? "You mean to tell me she lived in one trailer and he lived in the other? Tell me he wasn't some kind of hard ass or something. If you're about to say he hit her, I'll dig him up and kill him again."

Her giggle did more to him than that cute little smirk of hers. "He would never have hurt her. I promise. I come from a long line of very strong women, maybe sometimes a little too strong. About ten years ago, Aunt Pearl up and announced she was sick to death of cleaning up after him. He was kind of a slob and refused to ever get rid of anything. She ordered another trailer to be delivered to their property and moved him out there. That's why the trailers are so close together. He was allowed to come over to eat and sleep, but he had to keep all of his crap in the other trailer."

"Sweet Jesus, you'd think he would've just picked up his shit."

"You would think. They were both stubborn. Plus, I kind of think they liked having their own space. But I can tell she regrets it now that he's gone."

"I don't like space. I've had nothing but space my whole damn life." If she could be honest, so could he.

"Good." This time she gave him one of her rare, full-on smiles, the kind that lit up the whole room, and most likely flung open the gates of heaven. "Space isn't something I'm after when it comes to you, but why did you want to know about the trailer?"

"'Cause I'm moving in it."

"You're what?"

"I just told you I don't want space. Plus, the drive between here and Pleasant Glen is a bitch. If I'm there, I can help you do more stuff."

"You can't just move in. Can you?"

"Don't see why not as long as Pearl doesn't mind. I'll pay rent. You need money and seem mighty opposed to me flat-out giving it to you, so I'll do it this way."

"You've thought of everything, haven't you?"

"Oh, sugar, I've been thinking about ways to get near you since you almost knocked me on my ass at that bar three days ago."

CHAPTER FOURTEEN

"You have anything warmer than what you're wearing?"

"I have leg warmers." Avery dug around in her bag until she located her favorite lavender pair. His constant concern about her juxtaposed with his gruff, demanding warnings about the way their sex life would work, kept Avery walking an unraveling tightrope of need. The pit of heartbreak and fear beneath her had no net and she knew there were only two real options. Hurt now. Hurt later. The fraying rope continued to unwind, string by loosened string, the pops audible in her mind, as he dug in his suitcase and extracted a wool waffle-weave shirt.

"Put those on and then come here to me."

His instructions carried the weight of commands. She complied. Settling on the bed, she slipped the leg warmers over her yoga pants and pulled them up to her midthigh.

"Damn," he grunted.

Smiling at that, she stood. "What?"

"Someday soon I want you in my bed wearing nothing but those. But you've got to start dressing warmer. This isn't Oklahoma. You're gonna end up losing your toes to frost bite and then what would I suck when I want to get you going."

"I have a feeling you could come up with a few things," she teased as he pulled his shirt over the one she was wearing.

"I do like to get creative." Next, he put one of his thick flannel shirts on her.

"I feel like that kid in *A Christmas Story*," she giggled.

"Oh yeah, well next time I expect you to be dressed like that leg lamp. Now, let's get you some food." He put his Carhartt coat on her once again. Before she could protest, he held up his hand and pulled another quilted coat from his bag for himself. Clearly, he'd come to Nebraska far better prepared than she had.

He went as far as pulling the hood over her hair and tightening the strings so tight she could barely see or move her mouth. She was certain she looked ridiculous, but when a heavy handful of ice hit the windows, blown in by the wind, she decided not to argue.

A low curse reached her ears as the wind almost stole the cowboy hat from his head the moment they left the room. He rushed them to the lobby doors. Avery's cheeks burned. Her lips protested as the wind stripped them of any moisture. Water rushed to her eyes. She tried to blink it away, but the motion was far more difficult than it should've been. If she hadn't been clinging to the might of his arm, she swore she would've landed in Kansas minus the ruby-red slippers.

Finally, he swung open the lobby doors and scooted her inside. A blast of warmth welcomed them into a room decorated in varying shades of brown. Massive, over-stuffed leather couches and chairs were arranged invitingly around a roaring fire.

Moving toward it instinctively, they both let the heat lick at their freezing bodies until feeling had returned. "Holy fuck, that's some storm," he breathed.

"It's only October. How much worse does it get here?" Oklahoma got its fair share of snow every winter but she'd never experienced anything like this.

"Much. I'm betting this is an early storm. It'll melt off before they really get packed in for winter."

The single word *they* whipped ominously through her mind, leaving lashes of worry in his wake. *They* would get packed in for winter. Not him. Not them. Just the residents of Nebraska, which did not include him and never would.

"You okay, baby doll?" He wrapped her up in his arms, sending another round of intoxicating heat through her body. She nodded out her lie.

"Guess I'm an Oklahoma girl at heart. I've outrun my fair share of twisters but never snow like that."

His eyes and hair were the precise shade of a hayfield right before it was cut. Something in them glowed to life at her declaration. His jaw clenched like he was trapping a secret behind those hungry lips concealed with his scruffy beard and mustache.

She wanted to ask him what he was thinking. Did he like that she was an Oklahoma girl? Did it remind him of home or something? She untied the hood of his coat and buried her face against him instead. Right then she didn't want to be either an Oklahoma girl or a Nebraska girl. She only wanted to be his girl.

"Mr. Camden." A woman in a uniform rushed toward them. "I'm so glad you're here. I was worried about you." She gasped and pointed to his face. "Honey, what have you gotten into? That's gonna be a shiner by morning. Tell me you haven't been fighting. My word, you cowboys are all the same. Come on over here and eat. Whenever they shut the roads down—which ain't too often, mind you—I make a batch of my potato soup. It'll stick to your bones and warm you up from the inside out." Halting abruptly, the woman seemed to have just noticed Avery. "Well, since this is a nice family place, I'm gonna go ahead and assume this must be Mrs. Camden." Her kind green eyes sparkled with mischief.

Avery's mouth gaped as she stared from the woman to Colton, trying to process the one piece of information she'd pulled from that speech. "Camden?"

"Not now," he said through his clenched teeth.

Not now worked for the moment because Avery had no idea what to say. His last name was Holder. That's what he'd said. Wasn't it? Reviewing all of their previous conversations, she tried to recall exactly what he'd said. He'd told her not to make assumptions about the Holder's money and not to call him Colton *Holder*. Holy fuck. So, who the hell was he?

The cold outside was nothing compared to the frigid spike of nerves that shot down her spine. Keeping his arm around her shoulders, he followed after the woman. Avery's feet faltered. His steady hands caught her before her face became a fixture on the western rug covering the tile flooring. "I never told you my name was Holder," he choked out. Pulling out a chair at one of the many empty tables, he guided her into the seat. His eyes were panicked, as he flung himself in the seat beside her.

Camden. The name she knew so well felt foreign. He couldn't possibly be a Camden. If he was a Camden, why hadn't he grown up in Pleasant Glen like the rest of them? Why didn't he have that dark brown hair all of the Camden men had? Even Holly and Natalie favored their brothers.

Colton looked like a *Holder*. She'd been inundated with Holders her whole life. Cocky smirk, check; surly attitude lightened by dirty comments or teasing quips, check; dirty blonde hair, check; wild, determined, and dominating, hell yes.

This made no sense. What if this entire day was some kind of fevered dream? She hadn't really been stupid enough to go to that strip club. She wasn't really sitting here with Colton as some woman she'd never seen before fussed over them and placed a bowl of steaming potato soup in front of her. This couldn't be real because in real life he was Colton Holder.

And yet, there he was, his pleading eyes begging for understanding on behalf of his silent mouth. His right hand tightly grasping her left like he feared she might run if he let go. "I'm sorry," he managed.

"For what?"

"For whatever I did to make you look at me like that."

"Who are you?" Shocked at her ability to remain seated and come up with relatively sane questions, she stared him down. "Tell me."

"Not here." His eyes drifted to an elderly couple enjoying their soup at a table in the back corner before snapping back to her face.

"I don't... I don't understand," she admitted.

"Yeah, well, I'm in it deep and I don't fully understand it either. I swear, Avery, I'll tell you everything, but there's a lot riding on me keeping my mouth shut...including my ability to stay here with you for as long as we can make this work."

"Are you seriously using my confession that I don't want you to leave against me right now?"

"No," he ground out. "Maybe. I don't know. I just know I need you to keep your mouth shut until we get back to the room. Please." Keeping his right hand on hers, he used his left to shovel hot soup into his mouth. "Eat," he pled.

Her shaking fingers clattered the spoon against the edge of the thick ceramic bowl. She leaned her head closer to it and managed a tiny bite. Dozens of questions seemed to swim in the creamy mixture before her. She was effectively stuck in a hotel room with the man beside her and she didn't have a single clue in the freezing cold, cruel world who he really was and why he was in Pleasant Glen.

————

"Please, baby, breathe," Colton begged as all color bled from her features. Her face was frozen in a mask of shock and confusion. Pure terror had taken up residence in those clear blue eyes. "Nothing about the man I am, the one who wants to help you and protect you, has anything to do with my last name. Trust me on that."

"But why...?" she squeaked.

"I swear I will tell you every single gory detail as soon as we're alone. Remember what I told you about the kinds of decisions we all make when we panic."

Somehow that seemed to pacify her for the moment. She brought another spoonful of the soup he couldn't really taste to her lips. "But..." she started up again as soon as she swallowed.

"Not now."

He was all too aware of just how many people in this state knew Everett Camden. Had the man in the back corner heard Mrs. Peterson call him Mr. Camden?

Bile churned in his gut and then lodged in his throat. He'd intended to pay for the hotel with cash. He'd been informed the night of his arrival that it wasn't allowed. Too tired to argue, he'd turned over his credit card and prayed the owners of the hotel didn't know the Camdens. It had worked. Everything was just fine until that damned storm had blown them in there.

"I don't want anymore," she fussed. The bowl was more than half full. He didn't blame her. He couldn't eat either, but he also couldn't let her starve.

"Okay, come on." Keeping his hands on some portion of her body constantly was the only way he could keep sane. He tried to guide her toward the vending machines to stock up for the night. Mrs. Peterson halted their progress and Colt tried to remember some semblance of manners.

"Thanks for the soup, ma'am. I think we're gonna head back to the room." His voice sounded hollow to his own ears.

"All right, honey. We've got the generators ready to go in case the power goes out."

"Thank you for the soup, ma'am." Avery's voice was barely a breath.

"We take care of our own, Mrs. Camden," Mrs. Peterson winked at her.

"Please don't call me that." Her tone regained volume. "It isn't my name." She shot him a cold glare that threw an invisible noose around his neck.

That noose tightened with every slick step he helped her traverse back to his room. Painfully aware that any chance he had with her hung in the balance of telling her every gut wrenching detail, right down to the parts he hated most, he flung open the door.

She spun inside, stripped off all of the extra clothing he'd put her in, and seated herself at the desk. "Talk. Now."

He called himself a pussy as he lowered himself to the bed slowly, buying a few more precious seconds. "Not exactly sure where to begin."

"Well, you could start with why the hell you don't seem to mind people thinking you're a Holder when that woman in there seemed quite certain you're really a Camden, which makes absolutely no sense at all."

He held up his hands in surrender. "Okay, I'm just gonna talk, and if something doesn't make sense speak up. My mother's a Holder, so it isn't a total lie."

Her scowl said a lie was a lie without margins.

"Okay, then," he sighed. "How about I start with a couple of weeks ago? My father parked his car at my mama's house once again, just like he's done a few times a year for as long as I can remember. Only this time, he up and died sitting at her kitchen table."

"Oh." A little of her affronted incredulity faded away. "I'm sorry."

"Don't be. The world's a helluvalot better without him in it."

That earned him two confused blinks of her long black eyelashes.

"He was an ornery SOB his whole life from what I can tell. Drank too much. Gambled constantly. Loved to take out his irritations with his fists or the tip of a lit cigarette." Rolling up the sleeve of his shirt, he showed her the scars.

"Oh my God. He did that to you?"

"Yeah, but it doesn't even matter. Remember me telling you I liked to fight?"

She nodded.

"The thing that finally got me to tone it down, until recently, was when I realized that even though I'd never take my fists to a kid or a woman, I was acting just like him. I got in a fight three weeks ago because I saw this fuckstick backhand his girlfriend and it reminded me so much of my father I lost my mind."

With that, her face transformed into a look of pity. "I'm so sorry, Colton. Wait that is your real first name, right?"

"Yeah, but people that really know me call me Colt. And I don't need you to feel sorry. I need you not to hate me."

"I don't believe in..."

"Hate. Yeah, I know, but I ain't finished this story, so leave yourself some room for it just in case."

"I would never hate you. But keep on talking. I want to hear it all."

"Right, so he died. Massive heart attack 'cause he'd ruined his liver and his lungs with the smoking and the drinking. He'd gotten several of his teeth knocked out at some point prior to visiting my mother, so the beating might've had something to do with it. I don't know. Honest to God, I didn't think too much of it, or I tried not to. I hated him. I was glad I wouldn't have to see his car in her driveway anymore. My mother never cared that he was nothing more than a shitlicker. Whenever he showed up, she'd ignore whatever man had her attentions at the moment and roll out the fucking red carpet for Mick Camden."

"Wow."

"Yeah. That's one way to describe it I guess." He shook his head, still unable to believe everything that had happened. "Anyway, I went on with my life. Figured my uncles would end paying to bury his sorry ass and that would be the end of it. See, back in the day, Mama sold her portion of Holder Ranch back to my four uncles so she could have enough money to buy whatever she wanted for the rest of her life. Her land was supposed to be handed down to me when I turned twenty-one, but..." He shrugged out his disdain. "I live in a small house on my Uncle Gentry's land. I help him run it." He had nothing to call his own, not really.

Suddenly, she was on the bed beside him. Her fingers laced through his. "Keep going."

Clinging to her hands, he tried to sort through the story. "He died."

"You keep saying that. He really is gone. I know even if you hated him it's hard to wrap your head around one of your parents being gone."

"Yeah, guess you would." He brought their clasped hands to his face and nuzzled the soft, smooth skin of hers against his cheek before he kissed between her knuckles. "Thing is, I spent my whole life without him around mostly, and then he'd show up as soon as I let myself relax. I still kind of expect him to come back through like a twister that tears everything up and doesn't give a shit who has to clean up after him.

"Anyway," he said, lowering their still-clasped hands to his lap. "I was all ready to put on a suit and wish the bastard a quick flight to the devil's shindig when I got a call from a lawyer in some beach town in North Carolina of all places. Mind you, I've never even been to North Carolina, not even sure I could find it on a map."

"I hate lawyers. They always seem to bring awful news." She sighed. "What did the North Carolina lawyer say?"

"That I was the executor of a fresh will Mick had drafted one month before he died. I knew nothing about it, but according to this will, he can't be buried in Oklahoma."

"Why not?"

"Because—" Colton rolled his eyes, "—he wants to be buried on Camden Ranch. The Camdens have a family plot like most old ranching families. Holders have one, too, but Mick wants back into his family's."

"Oh...my gosh. Did you know? I mean when you were growing up...? Did you know he had another...? Oh my gosh."

Somehow she made this story bearable. Taking a chance, he kissed her forehead, wishing she'd let him curl up in her arms and hide away from his whole stupid life like a kid, something he'd never really gotten to be.

"I knew he had another family, but he never mattered to me, so neither did they, until I figured...I don't know...it's stupid."

"It's not stupid. Tell me."

Shame threatened to gag him but his beautiful angel was sitting there beside him awaiting his confessions. He had no hope of ever denying anything she ever wanted. "Until it occurred to me that I had a brother. Brock Camden is my brother, not just a cousin, someone who'd endured Mick Camden, some blood that's kind of the same as mine."

Her brow was laced with worry. She stroked his cheek with her free hand.

His eyes closed as her gentle touch steadied his breath and enlivened his body. "I figured out yesterday when I was talking to Brock that Mick must've moved his other family out to North Carolina while Brock was in high school or something. Whole thing is so fucked-up I don't know whether I'm washing or hanging on a line."

"Wait. Did you tell the Camdens who you are? What did they say?"

Guilt clawed under his skin. Ripping it away from his soul would require a blade. "I didn't tell them. I took a fucking job on their land like a coward."

"Hey." She shook her head. "You are not a coward."

"I am. But it's not even just who I am that I have to tell them.

Jesus, if only that were it. I think I'd sell my soul for that to be all there was to this."

"Don't sell it. I want to get to know it better. Pretty sure I've already fallen for it. Finish your story."

"I don't deserve that, Avery."

"That isn't true and even if it were we don't get to decide that. Now, keep going."

The confessions rose from his chest as if they'd simply been waiting for someone to usher them forth. If she wanted a part of him, he wanted to give her the very best parts. "I keep praying no one notices how much we favor each other. Different coloring and all, but we're both built just like our father. When Brock moved back up to Pleasant Glen, Ev, my uncle, gave him back the half of Camden Ranch that they'd been working...the part that actually belonged to my dad. Or our dad. Jesus that's weird."

"Okay, so Brock owns half of Camden Ranch. And Holly and Grant and all of them own the other half, right?"

"Yeah. Do you know them well?"

"Not well, but enough to know their family runs Pleasant Glen."

"Ain't that the truth. Anyway, we're getting to the part about how badly Mick fucked all of us over. Dad left me half of Brock's land. Brock doesn't even know he's dead yet."

Her mouth hung open just as wide as her eyes.

"Close your mouth, baby doll. You're giving me all kinds of ideas, and I aim to finish this story even if it kills me."

Her jaw snapped shut and then immediately unhinged again. "Is he allowed to do that?"

"According to Meridian, he is. If he owned the land before his death, he had the ability to will it to whoever he chose. The Camdens also own a small wheatgrass property where they backlot calves out in Moore, Oklahoma. Mick left half of that to my Uncle Gentry. Of course, since they haven't seen the will, they assume everything is the way it's always been, that they own all the land they ever thought they did. Legally, that's not so. But it gets worse."

"How could it possibly get worse? How could he have done this to all of you without saying a word?"

"Oh, Mick was a real piece of work. Here's the part that sucks for the Holders. There's a massive lake on a piece of land that borders my Uncle Barrett's property. It's in Holder County but has always belonged to Tex Monroe. We've been paying him quarterly for years for use of the lake to water Barrett's family's cattle. It's the closest watering source to Barrett's part of the ranch. But Tex always had a gambling problem and so did my old man. Only difference Tex almost always lost and Mick always won. I don't think any of the Camdens know this but from what the lawyer tells me it looks like Mick had a small-time gambling ring out in North Carolina and he had another one he ran remotely in Oklahoma. I'm sure he had no trouble beating people into paying but he'd take bets on anything. Lawyer said he even took bets on the high school football games for a while."

Avery scowled. "People actually bet on high school football?"

"People'll bet on anything. Point is, Mick had a steady income even though he wasn't working Camden Ranch anymore. My Uncle Barrett always tried to make sure Tex wasn't gambling away the money we were paying him but he's a grown-ass man. From what I can figure, he must have been in it bad with some bookies from somewhere. Day before Mick showed up in Holder County, I saw Tex in The Broken Bowery looking like he'd been beat up one side and down another with a two by four."

"This is awful." Avery cringed.

"Yeah, it is. Mick must've gone to see Tex before he ever showed his face on Holder Ranch. He paid off Tex's debts in exchange for the deed to the lake and land we'd been leasing. Knowing Mick, he waited on Tex to get his ass whipped before he stepped in. Then he gave the land to Brock in his will. He went as far as to pay Tex not to let us use the land until Brock comes down there and signs off saying we can. We had to haul thousands of head to other Holder pastures because they can't live without water. But all of my uncles run full capacity, which means there isn't enough grass for Barrett's cattle plus all of theirs on their land for an extended period of time."

"Wow."

"Yeah. I'm going ahead and telling ya how fucked-up I am so you can get that whole getting to know my soul thing out of your system."

"I doubt that."

"When I first saw that I'd been given land in that stupid will, I was excited." There. He'd said it. The truth felt like shattered glass against his tongue. Shame knotted in his chest and his own ridiculous inferiority might as well have been branded on him with an iron.

"Because your father had finally given you something you deserved?" Her tender voice prodded at the knot of shame in his throat.

"I don't know. Kinda. It just always seemed to me that a cattle rancher ain't worth a thing without land. Mick used to say all the time that every rancher was the same, nothing more than a grass salesman. He said a lot of shit in his time, but that's the truth of it. The land is everything. Without it, you're nothing. Guess somewhere deep in me I always wanted a ranch to call my own."

She shot up off of the bed and got in his face. "You listen to me, Colt Camden." His own name on her lips shocked him with enough voltage to make him gasp. "You are not nothing. I mean, look at all you've already done for me and for Chase and Jaxon. You don't even really know us yet, but you've helped us more than anyone else has even tried. Stop selling yourself short. You told me the name doesn't make the man. You were right. You don't need the Camdens or the Holders to be an amazing person."

"Doesn't mean my own brother's not gonna hate me when I finally grow a pair and tell him who I am and that our father wants to be buried on his land."

"You mean your land."

"Whichever."

"Why are you so certain Brock won't like you? What his father did is not your fault."

"No one ever wants to have to look their father's mistakes in the eye."

"You aren't a mistake," she vowed. "Do you hear me? You are *not* a mistake."

"I'm the bastard kid, baby. Never will be anything more than that."

"That isn't true but is that why you were at the funeral home? Because of your dad?" She settled back down.

"Yeah, the body's still at the funeral home back in Holder County. They're waiting on the funeral home up here to sign some paperwork so they can release the body. Of course 'til I convince the Camdens to let me bury him there, I have nowhere to tell them to send him. At some point, I have to man up and tell them the truth. I have to offer Brock back his half of Camden Ranch in hopes that he'll be willing to give the Holders back the property Uncle Barrett needs to run his portion of our ranch."

"But if you always wanted land and you do work out a trade with Brock why don't you get to keep the land with the lake?"

"I would never do that to my family, baby. They raised me, made me who I am today. That ain't how family works."

"Yeah, you're right. Guess I'd rather look out for you instead of the entire Holder family."

"I'm much obliged but other than last name I'm a lot more Holder than I am Camden. That land was legally leased by my uncle. Mick essentially stole it. It just isn't right for me to come in as his bastard kid and take it away from my uncles."

"So, your plan is to give him this land and the other land in Moore in exchange for him giving back the land with the lake to your Uncle Barrett?"

"I don't see any other way to do it. But that property with the lake is pretty prime real estate. I don't know what Brock will want to do with it and I have no say."

CHAPTER FIFTEEN

The only thing that made any sense to Avery was to take Colt in her arms and try to soothe all of the damage he'd sustained from his father, from the family that acknowledged him but saw no reason to give him anything to call his own, and from the family that didn't even know he belonged to them. When all was said and done, assuming everything worked out the way he seemed to want it to, things would go back to the way they'd been before Mick Camden had decided to twist everyone's lives up in a vicious knot as his final act. And when everything went back to the way it had been, it would leave Colt, once again, with nothing.

"Do you ever think about buying your own piece of land in Holder County or here or anywhere?"

"My uncles have no interest in selling any property to any of their own kids at this point, much less to me. Thing is..." He shrugged and refused to look her in the eye.

"The thing is what?"

That final paintbrush stroke created an image she understood. He wanted land but he also wanted a family, not only someone to belong to but a place where he knew he was supposed to be. Didn't everyone want that? Didn't everyone deserve that?

Wanting him to know she understood, she dug deep into the well of her own life experiences, squeezed his hand, and said, "When I was a little girl, if school was out for some reason, my mom would leave me at home when she went to work at the salon. I wasn't really old enough to be on my own, but she couldn't afford a babysitter. It took her years to make Mirror, Mirror a success.

"Anyway, I'd be all right for a little while, but then I would get so lonely I thought I'd go crazy. So I used to imagine that I had a sister the same age as me. Someone to play with...to talk to. I know I should probably see a shrink, but ever since Mama died, I've kind of pretended I have a sister again. Just a subconscious someone to go through all of this with me, someone that grew up the way I did and knows what all I have to accomplish. I know it's just an extension of myself. I'm only telling you this because I understand why you want to spend time with Brock before you kind of have to tear the rug out from under him. I don't think there's anything wrong with wanting to know your father's side of the family."

Staring at her like he couldn't quite believe she was real, he tenderly brushed a strand of loose hair behind her ear. A quick shiver rocked through her. *Please touch me again.* She wanted it badly enough to beg.

"I keep telling myself that, but I'm digging the hole deeper. The more I'm there, the more I'm lying to them." He sighed.

From somewhere in those wells she kept plunging, an idea rushed to the forefront of her mind. He deserved to know where he came from and who his family was. Perhaps this was the one way she could help him. "Then do it for me."

"What?" Hope made a hesitant appearance in the depths of his eyes.

"Do it for me. I don't want you to tell them right now. I want you to wait. I know it makes me the most selfish human being on the planet, but I need you to stay here for a little while. I think...no, I know what we have is special. I can feel it and we haven't even slept together yet. I felt it the first time you grabbed my arm in Saddleback's. My whole world tipped sideways when you ran my coffee out to me. I know that sounds crazy, but I swear it's true. When you stormed in that awful club today, I'd never been so relieved to see anyone in my whole life.

"When you kissed me last night, something changed in me. For the first time, I felt like I was more than a function of my mother. I was a person all on my own. A person who belongs in your arms. I can't believe I'm telling you this but the whole time we were kissing last night I kept wishing to anyone with any power in the universe that you could be my *last* first kiss.

"So, I don't want you to tell them yet. When you tell them, everything goes away, right? All of the land will have to change hands, you'll bury him, but then you'll have to go back to Oklahoma. I don't think I can possibly lose you when we haven't even figured out what we have yet. So, please, for me, don't tell them yet."

———

For the first time in weeks, Colt drew a breath that didn't bring the fire of shame to his lungs. He stared at his saving grace, finally understanding that's what she really was—call it fate, call it chance, call it whatever the hell you wanted—she was an angel sent to pull him straight up out of the depths of hell. "Okay."

Do it for her? In a heartbeat. If the constant lies bought him more time with her, it was more than worth it. If it allowed him to get to know his brother? That was what he'd wanted all along, anyway. The whole reason he kept putting off the inevitable.

Suddenly, his spoken vow simply wasn't enough. He needed to give her more. He needed her. Needed to be a part of her. Now that there was nothing unspoken between them, he wanted no physical barriers between them either.

His right hand tangled in that long, silken fall of black and purple hair. Her tongue and her teeth made a quick exploration of her bottom lip just before he caught the gasp of breath that escaped her mouth with his own.

Her eyes closed as he mated their lips, tasting her, exploring her. Her hands circled his neck and drew him closer, like she needed this as much as he did. Perfection. Bracing his hands around her nipped in waist, he drew her onto his lap.

Obediently, her legs parted, bringing her soft flesh against his rapidly hardening cock. Her pulse quivered visibly in her throat. He kissed a trail of fire from her chin to her neck, licking and sucking the delicate skin.

She rose up on her knees, brushing his chin with her breasts, and then sank downward, drawing the cloth-covered folds of her pussy over the denim ridge created by his cock. Any patience he'd ever possessed went up in flames, never to be regained. He'd seen the way those shitlickers at that club were looking at her. Fresh rage scorched his blood. She was his and he aimed to prove it.

Speed was far more important than finesse. He jerked the shirt she was wearing up over her head, fuming at the light pink satin and lace camisole that kept his hands from what he required to survive. A dark purple bra, the precise shade of the dye in her hair, created an erotic silhouette of her breasts beneath the satin top. Beautiful, but there were far too fucking many layers. He needed to feel her warmth in his hands. Needed the heft of her breasts to spill through his fingers. Needed to know she wanted this just as much as he did.

Sensing his frustration, she smirked. "I love lingerie and I thought you wanted me to dress warm?"

"I want you nekkid," he demanded. "I'll keep you nice and hot after that."

"Yes, sir." She dispensed with the fancy underthing, leaving his hands free to cup the ample globes of her ass, pressing her to his erection desperate for relief.

"Like hearing that, too, honey. When I saw you up on that stage I damn near lost my mind."

He groped her ass savagely abrading her skin with the lace of the panties that did indeed match her bra. He worked his hands up the smooth planes of her back. All of her muscles were pulled taut. He popped the clasp of the delicate bra, letting her breasts spilled forth, freed from their trappings. Like a man possessed, he tore it away from her. "So fucking gorgeous."

She came alive in his arms. Her head fell back and her body rolled.

Her tits swayed before his eyes, their rosy tips beckoning to his mouth and his hands. He couldn't decide which he wanted more, to taste or feel. Both.

"So damned beautiful. All mine." His tone held more notes of warning than of admiration, just as he'd intended. "I swear, if any of those fuckers had gotten to see you like this, I would've clawed their eyes out of their skulls. This is all for me, baby. I don't fucking share. Say you understand that."

Her entire body trembled in his arms. The soft feminine scent of her filled his flaring nostrils. He wanted to drown himself in her, fit her so tightly to him, they became two parts of a whole.

"Please, Colt, please," she whimpered.

"Oh, baby, you getting greedy for me already? I know what you're needing and I'm gonna give it to you but not until you tell me who you belong to, who opens you, who fucks you, who makes you come so hard you beg for it. Me and no one else."

CHAPTER SIXTEEN

A darkness she hadn't expected shadowed Colt's eyes as he made his demands. Her heart, already dangerously teetering on the precipice of a cliff, swelled further and beat faster. Its frantic dance allowed only quick pants of air to reach her lungs. That tight rope she was walking wobbled.

"Say it. I want to hear it. Who do you belong to?" The primal urgency in his words somehow made him more than a man. The hidden boyish charms that came with his half grins and his dimples vanished. His dark, demanding gaze ate her up with possession. He became all cowboy.

"You," she supplied readily. More than willing to stroke his alpha side, to discover the parts of himself he was trying to dam back, she readily complied. She wanted them all. She wanted to see the things he kept locked away, the parts of himself he was ashamed of, the parts he was certain no one would accept. She wanted to show him that *she* would. For a man who had nothing to call his own, he wanted her and she wanted nothing more than to lose herself in him. "Show me. Show me what you want to do to me. I need it," she begged.

She was drowning in custody papers, insurance claims, unused hair solutions, and self-doubt. She couldn't see her way out of it all, couldn't decipher the path back to herself.

God, she needed to feel alive, like something more than a not-good-enough duplicate of her mother. He stood, keeping her cradled in his arms like she weighed nothing at all, and then laid her out on the bed.

She wondered if he bench-pressed cattle instead of just caring for them.

He stood over her, his molten gaze burning past all of her barriers, and licked his lips like she was a platter of prime rib he intended to devour. "You really want that, sugar? You really want all of the fucking filthy things I want to do to you? Think carefully about your answer because once I start I have no intention of stopping."

The cool hotel sheets pricked at her back, rough to the touch. She didn't care. Her body burned warm enough to set them both on fire. The friction against her skin was nothing compared to what she craved from him. "Please. I want them. I *need* them."

"I'll fuck every other man who's ever even thought about you right out of your system. Fuck you so hard and so thoroughly, it'll be like there's never been anyone else whose hands have touched what's mine."

The words shot shivers over her body. She decided not to inform him that it wouldn't require the level of intention she could see in the dark fire of his eyes. They hadn't been terribly memorable in the first place.

She wanted every ounce of the hot-leaded determination that flowed through his veins, through his... Her eyes zeroed in on his denim-trapped cock, so hard and thick it stood like a steel-pipe attempting to escape his zipper line. Oh yeah, she wanted it all. "Take me. Now."

Although she'd been completely unable to summon an ounce of sexuality on that stupid stage, her own femininity surged up inside her as she sat up and stared at him. Swinging her legs up onto the bed, with all of the grace she'd once possessed as a ballerina, she rose up on her knees and let her hands trail down over her breasts.

His eyes rounded and a husky grunt escaped his lips. Her nipples stood in peaks so tight and stiff they ached. She let her fingertips fall to her waist, intent on stripping off the yoga pants.

"Touch them," he demanded.

"What?" The rough demand threw her off. She hadn't expected an instruction while she stripped.

Gathering her hands in his own, he brought them back to her breasts. His rope-callused fingers abraded her tender flesh. "Jesus, so soft. Do they hurt, baby?"

"Yes."

"Touch them. Show me, honey. Show me how much you can handle. I'm not feeling too fucking gentle right now."

At one point in her life, she'd hated her breasts. They'd shown up in ample supply right around her fifteenth birthday. Two years later, her hips had made an appearance, effectively ending her career as a ballerina.

But one night, alone in the dark of her room, she'd noticed how good the soft lace abrasion of her night gown felt against her nipples. Intrigued, her hands had gone on an exploratory mission. By the end, she no longer held any disdain for her breasts. He wanted to know how much she could take? She'd gladly show him.

She cupped her breasts in her palms and splayed her fingers, imagining it was his hands instead of her own. She caught her nipples between her index and middle fingers and rubbed them back and forth.

A low, hungry growl rumbled from him.

Working with more vigor, she rolled them between her thumbs and forefingers now. His eager gaze fastened her to the bed. A slight moan accompanied the shiver that quaked through her. She'd never had an audience before, not for a dance quite like this.

Suddenly, he was on her, his hands lifting her and laying her out on the bed. Her stomach rose and fluttered, rendering her breathless. She was already flying and he hadn't even gotten started.

As he stripped her of the yoga pants and socks, she mentally tossed her fears away as well. Later. She'd deal with the pain and heart break and terror of it all. Later, after he'd told the Camdens, after he'd gone back to Holder County, when she was alone in a tight ball in her bed.

Right now, she craved the pervasive pleasure that would skirt a delicious pain. Something he could surely give her.

"My God, baby, you are beautiful." His eyes slowly, methodically tracing down the curves of her body. "So many things I want to do to you. So many things I want you to feel."

"Do them." Yearning filled her. She wanted to drown in his masculine scent, wanted to taste him, wanted the burning heat of his hands all over her body, craved his fullness inside her.

The heated path his eyes were traversing down her body halted abruptly at her thighs. A low, ragged growl ripped from his mouth. His fingertips gently traced over her bare mound. "I know this wasn't for me," he huffed.

"It's for me," she informed him before her eyes closed involuntarily as he continued to taunt her exposed skin. She was raw with need. "One of the many perks of fucking a stylist. We can wax ourselves."

"Damn." He fell to his knees and jerked her toward him. The rough scrape of her back on the sheets made her gasp. Her legs fell to the sides in invitation.

"So fucking thirsty for you." He continued to torture her, drifting his rough fingers down her inner thighs in long strokes that were making her crazy. She bucked toward his mouth. "Do you taste as sweet as you are, sugar, or are you hot and spicy for me? I bet you're both. I want to know."

"Yes," she whimpered. Why was he waiting? A dark chuckle was his only response. She rocked her hips against the mattress, desperate to lure his mouth to her pussy.

"Look how wet you are for me. Look how wet I can get you without even touching you." Two fingertips traced either side of her slit. She arched up off of the bed, feeling herself weep for him.

"Colt, please," she whimpered.

"My name sounds so fucking good on your lips, sugar. Someday soon I'll take my time with you, but right now I'm so damned hungry for you I can't fucking wait." The soft rasp of his tongue at the apex of her mound made her tremble. He feathered his tongue down her slit, never entering her, driving her out of her mind.

"More. Please. I need more."

"Do you, baby? You need to be opened, don't you?" His thumbs parted her drenched tissues and a ravenous growl ignited the warmth gathering low in her belly. "So swollen and pink. So wet. You are perfect." The wet glide of his tongue melted her thoroughly. "Mmm, so sweet, baby. Like candy made just for me. Let's see just how wet I can make you. I want you so wet I can hear it when I fuck this sweet little snatch. What do you need to get there?" He traced her inner folds with his index finger. Every pulse point on her body throbbed with need. Her thighs tensed from the overwhelming sensation. It was too much. Too good. "I bet I know what my sweet girl needs." She swore every nerve ending in her body rejoiced as he drew his tongue to the hood of her clitoris and unleashed unrelenting devastation.

———

"Oh my...yes..." she cried as he bathed that tender, slippery little bundle of nerves with his tongue. Colt grinned against her silky folds.

"Figured this would do it. But, darlin', I'm just getting started." He gauged her constantly, watching and listening to her reactions as he moved slowly and gently and then with more force. He wanted to drown in her juices. He needed to lose whoever the hell he was deep inside her.

Her body pitched back and forth, so anxious for his tongue. Using only a little of his strength, he pinned her thighs open against the bed, halting her movements. She got wetter still.

His eyes coasted up her abdomen and ascended to the steep, voluptuous mounds of her breasts. They swayed with every slight movement he allowed her. The rough stubble of his beard rubbed against her creamy folds. Another one of those needy moans whimpered from her. He swore it reached through his chest and wrapped tightly around his cock. "Your needy little moans are gonna be the end of me," he warned.

He intended to give her tender pussy his single-minded focus, but her tits were swollen, full and round, almost as needy. Heat settled high in her cheeks and streaked down her body—ripe pink perfection. She was so beautiful he almost forgot to breathe, and when he forced a gasp of air down his lungs, it was filled with her musk, complete with a chaser of reckless abandon. "So fucking good," he groaned as he returned to his work.

He hadn't exactly gone about this in normal order. He was rounding the bases in the wrong direction. He told himself keeping her off balance was more important. Having every intention of spending hours with his mouth and his hands and his cock on her breasts and against her lips, just then he was proving a point.

Her sweet, spicy nectar flowed readily now. He scraped his teeth along her folds. Her fingers threaded through his hair and she attempted to hold his face in place, so needy it drove him wild. Primal carnality whipped through his veins.

He spread her legs farther, spun his tongue in the tender spot where her right leg and her pussy joined, and then sucked hard, branding her, marking her as his.

Her head raised up off the mattress and she stared him down with heavy-lidded, hungry eyes. Her lips were drawn into a sex-soaked pout. "Make me come," she panted.

"Say please, baby doll. Say please and I'll let your juices drip down my throat."

"Please, Colt."

"That's a good girl."

He circled her opening with his index finger and zeroed his tongue in on her clit. Her moans turned to pleas. Too far gone to draw this out longer, he dipped two fingers deep within her. Her body drew him in. Raw need throbbed through him with every breath he managed. Her satisfaction took center stage in his mind. It was the only thing that mattered.

Keeping his tongue soft, he increased the friction with his fingers constantly and sucked her juicy pearl until she came in a rush of wet heat and broken syllables of ecstasy. He delved deep and steeped his tongue in her juices.

The demand for breath from his lungs finally had him lifting his head. He watched her body tense and roll as the climax overtook her. Damn, damn, damn. She was gorgeous. A heady sense of accomplishment should've had him riding high in his saddle. Instead, regret rubbed him raw.

He'd barely even kissed her before going straight for what he wanted. Hell, he'd acted like she was any other woman when she was anything but. This was different. It required him to be better. Better than he'd ever been before. She'd wanted him to be her last first kiss and he'd just kissed the wrong set of lips. She deserved better.

Fuck. Lambasting himself, he crawled in the bed beside her and wrapped her up in his arms. Soft and sweet, still needy, she curled into him.

"I did that all wrong. I'm just so fucking weak when it comes to you," he managed to explain.

She lifted her head. Her hair hung in a messy cloud of jet black and shimmering purple. It streaked over her chest and curled around her nipples, threatening to erase his resolve to do this right.

"Nothing about that was wrong in any way at all," she vowed.

Though he was pleased she thought so, he still felt the need to speak his mind. "Sugar, I've spent way more time getting to know your sweet little pussy lips than I have these." He stroked his thumb gently over the lips on her face. "While I loved every minute of that, it ain't right. I put ten wagons ahead of the horse every single time I get near you."

"Just so you know, I'm taking that as a compliment."

"I sure as hell didn't say it wasn't enjoyable as fuck, just that I owe you better."

"What makes you think I don't like the way everything has gone down between us?"

"This." Angling her head up, he let their heated breaths mingle as he studied the length of her eyelashes, the little dip that drew her lips into a perfect bow, the corners of her mouth, and the tender spots where her ear lobes met her jawline. "Taste yourself in my mouth, honey. Kiss me. Let me do this right."

Forcing himself to slow, to memorize the flavors of her mouth this time, he brushed his lips over hers. Pushing an agenda all her own, she tugged his shirt from his jeans and pressed her hands to his abs. He grunted from the skin-to-skin connection. Every nerve ending in his chest wanted to applaud her caresses.

Summoning more patience than he was aware he even possessed, he kept his lips soft and tempted hers with his tongue. She opened for him readily. His groan spilled into her mouth and her hands continued their northbound trip up his chest.

They skated over the bruises, their warmth easing a little of the weary ache that resided between his ribs. When she arched her back, anxious for breath, he trailed kisses to her jawline and then to her neck. He languished open-mouthed kisses just under her ear and along her hairline. This time her moans were sweeter and softer, almost more satisfied, but she was still on a mission all her own.

Dragging his shirt up, she feebly attempted to remove it from his body. "You smell so damned sweet right here," he informed her as he spun his tongue in the hollow above her collarbone.

"It's my lotion and I don't want to be the only one who's naked," she fussed.

"It's you, baby, not any kind of lotion, and I take it you'd like some help with that."

"Yes." As much as he was trying to slow this down, he'd never deny her anything at all. He'd let his stubborn, possessive side run the show long enough. It had incensed him that other men were gawking at her up on a stage complete with cages, but that didn't mean he'd had to be an asshole about it.

His sense of entitlement had gotten the better of him. She wasn't a fucking conquest. She was so much more than that. He called himself an ass for good measure as he removed his T-shirt.

The last time he'd done that, she'd been focused on his battle wounds. This time her visual inventory moved slowly until it settled on the large Holder brand tattooed on his right shoulder. It bled into the bull skull on his chest. In an epic bout of pure stupidity three weeks after his eighteenth birthday, he'd had a topless cowgirl wearing nothing but a hat, a pair of boots, and a strategically located holster tattooed on his back.

Though he tried to pull off his shirt without giving her a view of his back, she caught a glimpse. A smirk formed on those pretty pink lips of hers as she crawled up his chest and peeked over. "She's pretty," she giggled.

"Believe I've been more than forthcoming with my own dumb-assery."

Her giggle morphed into full-belly laughter. Music to his soul and his cock. Her cheeks flushed again. A cocktail of mischief with a dash of shame danced in her eyes. She rolled over, presenting his starving eyes with the feast of her back, her satisfyingly thick womanly thighs, calves he swore had to have been professionally sculpted, and the finest ass he'd ever had the pleasure of viewing. But there was a decent-sized pair of pink lips at the crest of her right cheek, set off by her alabaster skin. The word, smack, was artfully drawn on the bottom lip.

He bit his own lips together, trying to dam back a chuckle, but her giggle set his free. "Guess there's a whole other set I get to learn as well."

"Twenty-first birthday, far too many strawberry lemonade vodkas, and friends who have terrible ideas on how a girl should celebrate."

He nodded his understanding. "On my eighteenth birthday, I announced I was getting a tat. All of my uncles told me it was a chick-enshit thing to do, which only made me want to do it all the more. The raunchier the better." Wishing he could go back and beat just a little of the stupid out of his teenage self, he sighed. "I refused to wear a shirt most of that summer while we were working so everyone could see her. 'Course I also got myself a second-degree sunburn on my shoulders and the worst case of hay rash the doc had ever seen. Ended up having to get cortisone shots, which hurt like a mother. Like I said, dumbass through and through."

"I was seriously wearing an *I'm legal, buy me a drink* tiara when I got mine, so I'd say we're even."

"Wish I'd been there to take you up on that." He winked at her. That automatic grin she gave him whenever he did that still made him weak.

"Well, I kind of wish I'd been there to model for yours."

He grunted at the very idea of her dressed as such. "Damn, baby, if you'll dress up like that for me, I'll get another one done."

She shook her head at him. "And this?" She gently traced the

Holder brand and the bull's horns. Every connection she made with his skin shot a dose of pure lust straight to his cock. *You owe her more, Colt. Conversations and kisses. Get your shit together.* His own lectures weren't doing much to quell his libido.

He shrugged as she continued to trace her fingers over the H and R.

"Who you want to be, who you were, or who you are?" she whispered the words like she was almost afraid of the question.

"All three. None of them. I have no clue."

"Maybe I can help you figure that out," she offered.

"Maybe I'd rather be right here with you right now."

"Maybe so."

Eyes locked on hers, he leaned in for a kiss and indulged in another hit of those candy-sweetened lips. Damn, if only he could keep himself from thinking about those same lips stretching around the head of his cock.

She was completely naked in his bed. Her body moved instinctively with his and Lord knew he was far from a saint. His right hand trailed up her side. She wiggled and pinned her arm to restrict his access. "Ticklish, baby? Have to remember that." But tickling her wasn't part of his plan right then. He looped his fingertips over her shoulder and then traced that perfectly imperfect pink circle surrounding her nipple.

"Yes," she sighed out a throaty plea for more. Her back arched. He loved that she was showing him exactly what she wanted, and for the moment, he was more than happy to indulge her desires. Lifting her right breast, he swirled his tongue over the turgid peek. Her entire body trembled. Interesting.

He suckled and then nipped, letting his teeth linger on her skin. She was panting by the time he drew her breast back into the heat of his mouth and sucked in earnest. Her every fragmented breath shook him as much as it did her. The lengthy rope of patience he'd tried so hard to extend turned out to be kerosene-soaked—and she'd just lit another match.

"Spread your legs. Let me feel how wet you get when I'm sucking your gorgeous tits, baby doll."

Wispy moans punctuated by those need-you noises mewled from her as she lifted her leg on top of his own. Fucking hell, she was killing him.

He pressed his entire hand to her pussy and took another hard drag of her breast before he released her to see what she made of his force. Her entire body was writhing beside him. "Does it make me an asshole that I love you bare and silky all for me?" He let his middle finger explore between the swollen lips of her pussy, only to encounter more of her sweet honey.

Those ocean blue eyes of hers lit up with pleasure. Her lips formed a knowing smile as she shook her head. "Not unless it makes me some kind of not-nice name because I love the way your fingers feel on my bare skin with nothing between us. Can't wait to feel your cock there, too, for that matter."

Damned woman was going to be the death of him. "You like that, baby?" He spread her legs farther and painted his fingers up and down over her lips. He slipped one finger back to tempt that puckered rosebud in her ass to see what she'd make of it.

Her gasp of shock was followed quickly by a guttural moan of appreciation. "Feels good, doesn't it? I'm gonna make everything feel good. I promise. I'm gonna let you feel it all." He dipped his head back to her breasts, bathing the left with his affections this time. "You get so nice and wet. You're gonna feel like heaven."

"How long are you going to make me wait?" she fussed so sweetly it speared his heart. Dammit, he'd been trying to do right by her, not frustrate her.

"You sure you're ready to do this? It's like you said—once we go there, we can't come back."

"So ready. Please. But that doesn't mean I want you to stop kissing me or feeling me up."

"Deal, baby. I'm gonna take good care of you. I'm gonna give you everything you need and everything you're so afraid to ask for. I promise you that."

CHAPTER SEVENTEEN

Pure need sizzled over every centimeter of Avery's body. The connection of his fingertips to her skin stoked the flames. He was torturing her and seemed largely unaware. Okay, so maybe she should have insisted they do a little more kissing and a little more talking before she let him strip her bare, but that tether of connection she didn't fully understand between them continued to strengthen. Her soul recognized his. She wondered if he felt the magnetism between them as much as she did.

She required this connection between them, as if her next breath and next heartbeat hinged on his hands being on her skin. She longed to dance in the space where they existed together. Her body demanded it.

"Take your clothes off." She'd beg if she had to.

"Like I could ever deny you that." He stood from the bed. She was unable to take her eyes off his dangerously muscular torso, his golden skin slightly darker than his dirty blonde hair. The jangle of his belt buckle and audible pop of the snap on his jeans sent her pulse into overdrive.

His left eyebrow lifted in intrigue as he slipped the belt from the loops. Leather on denim. The sound drew a timid moan from her. "You are looking to get naughty, aren't you, darlin'?"

"Keep going." This time her plea was breathless. Her mouth flooded with saliva as he shoved his jeans down and stepped out of them. His cock tented his boxers. Her eyes honed in on the bulge. Her mind begged him to strip bare. Like he'd somehow heard her mental imploring, he gave her another one of those dark chuckles as he shed the boxers.

Avery was quite certain she must've done something very, very good at some point in her life because this was clearly a reward. Her voracious eyes followed the thin trail of dark blonde hair that led her to his thick length rising proudly from a thatch of coarse curls. He was fully engorged, thickened veins protruding from the smooth length. His crown swollen in a technicolor display of male perfection. Drops of moisture clung to his slit. Her breath stuttered in her lungs. Her mind overloaded with all the things she wanted to experience with him.

Reaching out from her location on the bed, she trailed her fingers through the pearly drops of pre-cum and wrapped her hand around him. Her fingers barely touched. A low curse slipped between his teeth as he rocked forward into her touch.

His teeth sank into his lip and his eyes closed as he allowed her to explore. He was fevered to the touch, which only added more heat to the fire in her blood. "I want you inside of me. Now."

"Demanding little thing, aren't you?"

She wanted to sit on his face and rid him of that infuriating smirk.

"But that works real well for me because I'm dying to sink myself so deep inside of you both of us forget everything else in this whole damned world."

Instead of joining her in the bed, he wrapped his hand around hers, jacking himself. She trailed her thumb over his slit again, enjoying the sweet, filthy half-grunted words that came from him when she did that.

"I have a rule, sugar." He finally formulated a complete sentence.

"What's that?" Her voice was nothing more than a frustrated whimper.

"You have to come on my fingers before you're allowed to come on my cock."

"Then get to it, cowboy."

"Get on your hands and knees and put that pretty ass up in the air for me. Let me see them lips, doll baby."

Well, that was a little different, but the demanding edge in his tone and the dark need in his eyes said he wasn't kidding, so she complied. "That's it." His rough fingers once again slid down the crack of her ass, making her wiggle. That earned her another dark chuckle. Then he plied her lips open, sending her nerve endings into a frenzy.

"Spread your thighs more," he commanded. She immediately obeyed. "Such a good girl," he said roughly as his fingers speared inside her. No longer was he the tender man he'd been moments before. He was back to being her rough, demanding cowboy, precisely what she required.

Delighted bliss had her pressing back against his hand. Her position granted him deep access to her G-spot. "Keep your head down, sugar." He gripped her hips with his other hand and drew them to a sharper angle. Like he'd been handed a chart of all the hidden treasures of her body, the ones she could never locate on her own, he timed his strokes to the music of her soul. "Just like that. It's right there isn't it?" He pounded into her and reached around her with the other hand to coax her clit.

She shook with the satisfaction, her brain narrowing to only her own pleasure with every pass of his powerful fingers. "Do you hear yourself, baby? Do you hear how juicy I get you?"

She wanted to be embarrassed. Her own needy musk perfumed the air, but he sounded so thoroughly pleased she could locate no shame. "Oh God, mmm," she whimpered as he pushed her closer and closer to the edge of no return. Her body cinched around his touch, desperate and greedy. She gripped fistfuls of the sheets, clinging to anything that might keep her grounded. It was useless. He was going to make her fly again.

"Come on my fingers, Avery. I can feel how bad you need to. It's right there, baby." He pressed that spot deep inside her like his hand was hardwired to her brain. The knot of pressure at the base of her spine began to unfurl. "Come for me like a good girl."

His demand shot white-hot ecstasy from the tip of her scalp down to her toes. She shook and then collapsed to the mattress. She tensed in extended waves that left her breathless and almost incoherent with pleasure.

Before she could free-float back to the earth, his hands were on her hips, hoisting her back into position. "This one's for me, baby, then I'll give you yours," was the only warning she received before she heard the tear of a condom wrapper. A half-second later, he slammed inside her. The thick intrusion robbed her of breath. She could barely contain him, yet she never wanted him to vacate. Adjusting her position, she sighed at the delicious, constant pressure.

"You okay, baby?" His voice trembled with depravation. He slowed his strokes. There was his sweet side. "So fucking tight," he grunted. "Am I hurting you?" He all but whimpered like a puppy. Since every welcomed inch triggered the perfect cocktail of pain and pleasure, she pressed back to meet him.

"You're not going to break me, cowboy."

That did it. He gripped her hips hard once again and snapped her backward so fast his sac slapped at her ass. His thighs met hers in quick touch points that only added to the growing avalanche of gratification gathering in her belly.

His hands kneaded her ass as he drove her hard.

"So good. So, so good," were the only words she was capable of speaking.

"It's fucking incredible. Damn, tell me you feel that."

"So good," she tried again, but those were the only words she could manage.

His breaths were ragged enough she could feel their heat on her back. His groans were hungry on his retreats and full of satisfaction with every thrust. "My name, baby. Let me hear you scream my name when it feels good."

His name flew readily from her lips, primal and eager to give him what he wanted. His crown centered on her G-spot once again. Her entire body erupted from the dedicated assault. She couldn't think.

She couldn't breathe. She could only feel and she'd never felt so delicious.

Her thighs trembled.

Her pussy clenched so tightly around him, her abdomen spasmed. "Fuck, yeah." He roared out his dominance. "Milk me, baby. Just like that." She tried. But her legs gave out. She brought him down to the mattress on top of her as she came in a rapid succession of tensed, ragged tremors. Her teeth sank into a nearby pillow as she tried to silence her screams of his name.

———

Colt watched her beautiful body recover as breath slowly worked its way back to her lungs. Gently, he turned her over and cradled her to him. "Look at me, Avery," he whispered.

Those cool blue eyes were still seeking. He wanted her to *see* him, to look through him and find the man he needed to be for her. That was all that mattered. If she could find him, could locate the man he was meant to be amidst the insanity threatening to consume them both, they would survive. It was the only thing in the world he'd ever need.

"Nice and easy this time, sweetheart." He cradled her in his arms and then worked her underneath him, holding himself over her. "I know what you need. I'll always know, sweetheart."

He eased forward once more and his cock sank deep between her soaking wet lips. The sensation overwhelmed him, tight slip of silky heaven drawing him deep. Her eyes closed once again. He opened her and then withdrew. Gripping his cock with his own hand he dragged it over her clit and then dipped deep once again. He kept the rhythm constant, her pleasure his only goal. "I know when you need it slow and steady. Jesus Christ, you feel like heaven." He grunted. "And I know when you need to be owned thoroughly."

"Oh God, that's amazing." Her eyes flashed open and locked on his.

"I'll always take good care of you, honey. Always." Did she understand the sanctification he found when she was in his arms? Ev Camden might've known at first glance that his purpose was to love and care for the woman who would become his wife. It had taken Colton a little longer to catch on, but he was more and more certain he'd been put here to love and protect Avery.

Another prod of her clit. Another baptism deep inside to the warm fount of her, the only one that could wash him clean, his own personal promised land. Deep inside her he existed with no need for a last name, no shame, no confusion. He existed fully for her.

When her breaths dissolved into quick gasps and her sweet little moans turned to broken syllables, he let himself feel the pressure of her swollen walls, allowed himself to drown in her honey.

His muscles shook, ridding him of the pieces of his life he'd never wanted and would never understand. Her body squeezed him so tightly he lost any sense of where he stopped and she began, just the way it was supposed to be.

Her eyes opened. Understanding lit their blue depths, his own personal lighthouse on the rocky shore.

"Tell me you feel that. Tell me it's different," he begged as he rocked against her. There in her eyes he swore he saw his future, the only one he'd ever want.

"It is." She writhed. "Oh God, I'm gonna..."

He wrapped her up in his arms as his orgasm barreled through him. He lost it all, filling the condom in hot spurts that he longed to bathe her in.

This time she came with a timid whisper of his name. "Colt."

Terrified to let her go after what they'd experienced together, he prayed she'd just lay on his chest and let him keep her cradled to his body.

"That was amazing." Her voice was barely audible in the invisible cloud surrounding them, linking them together.

He longed to ask if she was referring to the physical act or if she'd felt the emotional impact he had. He still wasn't certain what she'd meant when he'd asked her in the throes of passion. "I was thinking the same thing. Sorry for being a little rough at first. Like I said, I lose all sense when I get near you."

"Don't be sorry. It's just like you said, you knew precisely what I needed and I happen to like your rough side."

So, she had been listening to his vows. Did she understand that he'd meant every word? "You figure it's only a side not the whole deal?" *Please, say you see more than that.*

"I know it's not the whole deal. I told you we were a bad idea."

"Stop saying that. Now." She'd dissolved all of his guards like they'd been made of dust. How could they be a bad idea?

"Don't you get it?" she whispered.

"No." He pulled her closer, held her tighter, begged the universe to let him stay right there with her forever.

"My whole life I kept thinking someday I'd put all of the pieces together. I'd figure out the right combination and I'd get to be all of the things I've always wanted to be. Salon owner, mom, wife. It finally hit me on my thirtieth birthday that no one's life is perfect. There are no right pieces. Then my mom died and left me with the pieces to *her* puzzle that I have to try to make fit into mine. And I'm good with that, but I gave up on the idea that I could find a man who'd fit right inside my puzzle, the biggest piece, the one who'd help me make every-thing else work. I told myself the man I wanted didn't exist. A bad boy, rough and rugged when that's what I want. A good man, protective and gentle, when that's what I need. And now I'm laying here, naked in your bed, and I am in so much trouble."

It staggered him how badly he wanted to be that piece in her puzzle. It should have scared him into bolting. Instead, he longed to transform himself so he could fit anywhere she needed him to be.

Brushing her hair behind her shoulders, he traced her cheekbone with his thumb. "Hey." He planted a kiss on her forehead. "I'm not going anywhere. We're going to figure this out."

"Long-distance relationships never work."

"Stop telling me what won't work. We're going to find something that will."

"I'm going to believe that because I want to so badly."

"Good. You do that."

"Will you do me a favor?" she whispered.

"Anything."

"Will you not tell Chase about my tattoo? He's hellbent on getting one and I don't want him to know I have one."

Of all of the things he'd thought she might ask that wasn't even on the long list. He laughed and kept her cradled in his arms. "Baby, I can assure you I would never in this lifetime or the next say something to Chase about his sister having a pair of lips on her ass, right where I can't wait to slap it."

Another one of those infectious giggles sounded against his chest. "I just have to cover all of my bases."

"I've got all of your bases covered, sugar. Trust me."

"I do. And that's a big, huge deal for me."

"I know it is. And I won't let you down."

CHAPTER EIGHTEEN

A low rumble and then a muted roar awoke Colt in the middle of the night. Momentary panic shot through the haze of confusion. Her safety and her sleep, the things he knew she needed, rankled in his mind. He cradled her closer.

Avery's soft rhythmic breaths were still cascading over his bare chest. Her sweet body was curled up on his, warm and tender and lusciously naked, which was precisely how he'd prefer she stay. He swore he was holding heaven in his hands. What the hell had she done to him?

Blinking away the haze of sleep, he listened intently. A distinctive grating scrape was followed by an annoying rhythmic beeping. Snow plows. He grunted. The winds had died down enough for the plows to be out at—he checked his phone on the bedside table—two thirty in the morning. Great.

He hated the clash of metal on concrete as much as he hated the fact that they'd be able to get back to Pleasant Glen. The momentary reprieve from their responsibilities hadn't lasted long enough.

There were plenty of things that simply couldn't be ignored tugging them back toward Pleasant Glen. She'd said something about an appointment with someone at the hair salon that morning and there was no denying it had sounded important to her.

He'd promised Jaxon a tractor ride, meaning he had to talk Brock into letting him clear snow that day. Plus, he and Avery had a date that night at some concert at Saddleback's. All of that was worth returning for, and yet he still wished the world came with a pause button.

Every single day he delayed telling the Camdens who he was and why he was there tightened the snare he was caught in. The other people involved wouldn't wait on him forever and he couldn't just let Mick rot on a table somewhere, could he? If Mick hadn't pulled all of those ridiculous stunts determined to ruin two families' lives, Colt never would've met her. He hated owing his father anything. Staring down at the streak of moonlight peeking around the shades and dancing in her hair he wondered if he didn't owe him everything.

Remembering the vow of temporary silence he'd made to Avery, his mind settled. She needed him and he was bound and determined to be there for her.

Making certain she was still tucked under all the covers, he closed his eyes and made a negotiation with the man upstairs. If He'd give him just a little more time with her, Colt would quit lying to the Camdens and come clean...eventually.

Three hours later, she shifted against him. "Shh, I got you, baby," he soothed and tried to cuddle her back to sleep.

Her sleepy giggle finally woke him fully. "I love when you say that, but I have to get up."

"Why?"

"Need to pee." She wrinkled her nose.

"Guess I'll allow that."

"It would really be best if you did."

He stared unapologetically at her ass as it jiggled with every step she made in the hesitant sunlight reflecting off the snow still gathered in the bushes outside the window. His morning wood stiffened painfully. She really was going to kill him.

Climbing out of bed, he started throwing his belongings into his suitcases. Moving into the empty trailer would make everything more tolerable. He heard the shower water kick on and his cock immediately suggested a slight delay to their return to Pleasant Glen.

He knocked on the bathroom door. She met him with a wicked grin and a look that said she had the very same thoughts.

An hour and a half later, he was shoving both of their bags into the extended cab of his truck. Ogallala was starting to awaken after the storm. The gas stations were open and there were a few cars out on the newly plowed roads, but most of the businesses were still closed.

He saw the rolling curtains lift in the shop windows of Tillerson's Tractor Supply. The name sounded familiar, but he couldn't for the life of him remember why. He returned to the room to get the rest of his things and headed back out to the truck alone, not wanting Avery to venture out into the freezing cold until it was necessary.

Every hair on his body stood up and took notice of the man standing beside his truck, the same man who'd been having soup in the hotel restaurant the day before. Shit.

"Sir." Colt nodded but refused to meet his eye.

The man lifted his cowboy hat in a customary salute. "I'm being nosy I s'pose, but Edna and I go get some of Clara's soup every time a storm comes through, so we were in there yesterday when you and your lady-friend came in."

"Okay." The reminder was unnecessary.

"Thing is, I've been friends with Ev Camden since we were knee high to the calves we weren't allowed to ride. I heard Clara call you Mr. Camden and I wondered if you was any relation to Ev and Jessie? I know you ain't one of Ev's boys, but...?"

"No, sir." His pulse thundered in his ears. Shit. Shit. Shit. "Uh, must just be a common last name. I'm from...uh...North Carolina." Fuck, where had that come from? Damn Mick.

"Oh, well what are you doing all the way up here?"

Suddenly, Avery was beside him, bundled up in one of his coats. "I have family up here, Mr.?"

"Tillerson."

"Nice to meet you. Anyway, Colt brought me up here to visit my... sister. She lives in Cheyenne. We got caught here in the storm, but we'll be on our way now."

"I see. Well, have a nice trip. Like I said, I've never met another Camden that wasn't a relation, so I figured I'd go on with my nosier side. Forgive me."

"No problem, sir." Avery waved at him.

"Thanks." Colt wrapped her up in his arms when Tillerson made his way back across the street. *Tillerson*. The memory shook loose from the recesses of his mind. Ev had helped Tillerson load tractors in a supply store in...Ogallala. Holy fuck. He squeezed Avery tighter.

If that was some kind of sign that he was holding fate in his arms, he wished God would take to using sticky notes or something. One thing was for certain, the quarter was in the air and he already knew what he wanted.

"Hey, you're keeping this charade up for me, right? That was the least I could do. I know you don't want to go back in there—" she gestured to the motel lobby, "—but I'm starving. Is there anywhere we could eat before we drive back? I don't want to be late for Melony, but I'm starved."

"Let me go get checked out and I'll find us some breakfast." He stared up and down the street and smirked at their available offerings. "Looks like your choices are the Kum 'n' Kwik or the Pump in Her Panties, baby."

She erupted in more of those hysterical giggles that righted every wrong in the universe. "Um, I believe that says the Pump 'n' Pantry, darling," she said, gesturing to the gas station he'd renamed.

"I like my way better."

"I'm sure you do."

"It's lady's choice. Hot dog, gas station sausage, or I could probably come up with something else shaped that way you could swallow." He waggled his eyebrows.

"You are terrible and I cannot believe they named their gas stations that."

"Terrible? That ain't at all what you were just saying in the shower, sweet thang."

"Maybe they have granola bars in there somewhere."

"Hippie chicks." Colton shook his head at her. "They ain't ever gonna let you on Camden Ranch unless you change those garden gobbler ways, honey."

"And why would I ever need to be on Camden Ranch?" She came right back.

Lifting her up out of the snow, he loaded her into his truck. She threw her head back laughing. *Keep her laughing, Camden. Laughing and moaning.*

He'd started the truck ten minutes before, so it was warm. After a quick trip inside to check out of his room, he drove across the street to the Kum 'n' Kwik. "I'm offended," he informed her.

"You are?" She looked horrified. Sweet baby. "Why?"

He quirked a grin, letting her know he was teasing. "I figured you might be just as addicted to my body as I am to yours and you'd sneak onto the ranch for a round of this." He parked the truck and gestured to his crotch.

————

Addicted didn't even begin to cover it. The sheer number of times he'd made her laugh that morning alone was astonishing. The reverence that burned in his eyes when he looked at her, the tender care in his touch—juxtaposed with a forceful, voracious hunger—and the way his every thought seemed to be about her wellbeing was otherworldly. She couldn't possibly deserve someone who cared about her the way he did.

Avery wondered if this beautiful thing between them might disappear as soon as they crossed the Pleasant Glen city limits. The weight of her whole world awaited her there. Ready to pile on again. Ready to trap her and choke the life out of her. She was a fly willingly entangling herself in a spider's web. Somehow knowing he was going to be living a few feet away made it seem bearable. "I am definitely addicted, Colt Camden. I might even eat a steak for you. Maybe. If you're very good."

"I'm much better at being bad and you seem to like that." His reminder shot a hot stream of blood to her cheeks.

"I do." No sense in lying.

"Then I'm holding you to that steak promise. Let's see if we can find you something to eat. Surely they have some tofu crunch nuggets or some other vegetarian shit somewhere."

"I don't eat tofu." She rolled her eyes. "I just don't eat red meat. It's better for the environment."

"Jesus, you are aware of what I do for a living, right? If you don't quit talking like that, they aren't ever gonna let me back in the Cattlemen's. Definitely gonna have to fill your mouth up with something meaty."

Her entire body felt like he'd set it on fire this time. "Seriously, you say the most gentlemanly things."

"Believe we've been all over the fact that I ain't a gentleman."

"So, a cattleman but not a gentleman?"

"Live and die by the cattleman code. Never had any interest in being some kind of pussy gent. Now, come on, my little vegan ballerina."

"I'm not vegan... Never mind." She accepted his offered hand and leapt out of his truck. Not a gentlemen, her ass. No one had ever taken care of her the way he did.

The vulgarly named convenience store was severely lacking in even semi-healthy options. She stared at salt-laden bags of mixed nuts, fruit that appeared to have been dried a decade before, protein bars that felt hard enough to crack a tooth, and chocolate-covered raisins. Sighing, she tried to discreetly watch Colton. His height and presence commanded authority even standing at a counter with hot dogs on some kind of odd roller machine.

The woman fixing the chili cheese dogs he'd ordered kept arching her back, trying to show off her cleavage in her uniform. Avery couldn't even dislike her for trying. He was so gorgeous it almost hurt to look at him.

He caught her spying on him and winked at her. She suspected that was for the benefit of the hot dog girl, but it still set the butterflies in her belly into rapid flight. And, like always, they rose into her chest and sent her heart fluttering right along with them.

Like his wink was some kind of summoning, she abandoned the mixed nuts and tucked herself under his arm. He planted another kiss on top of her head and squeezed her tight. For a moment she allowed herself to believe he was strong enough to put her whole life back together. She could hear her mother's disdain in her head. *Never let a man help you, Avery. He'll think he owns you.*

For the first time in her life, she didn't care.

"Cheese, sir?" the woman asked.

"Hell yeah. Extra cheese and put more mustard on them and some of those onions."

"Some say cheese. Some say plastic," Avery goaded.

"Don't even deny that plastic tastes good, princess."

She hated to admit that the chili dogs looked and smelled amazing. Her stomach chose that moment to whine about its empty state. It practically echoed. She was thoroughly embarrassed and he looked utterly horrified. "Baby, go find something you'll eat. My God. I can't believe I didn't feed you last night."

"You tried," she reminded him.

"Go." He pointed back to the snack food aisles.

Her gaze lingered longingly on the hot dogs before traitorously shifting to the bags of hot fries, and then to the soda dispensers. He came up behind her carrying a white sack full of his chili cheese dogs. "You want a big gulp of something, baby? I can take care of that."

Clearly, he was wanting a blow job, or maybe he just loved making her blush. Probably both. Deciding two could play his little game, she whirled around, made certain no one was nearby, and smirked. "You know I love to swallow."

His eyes rounded and an involuntary grunt rumbled from his chest. She laughed triumphantly. "That shut you up. Now, here." She grabbed a few bags of the nuts, the raisins, the one available granola bar that she was sure had more sugar in it than a Snickers, and appeased her stomach by grabbing two bags of hot fries. She shoved all of the food in his available arm.

He was still staring at her like he couldn't quite believe she was real. "Close your mouth, cowboy. I may not be stripper material, but I can definitely be naughty."

"Damn," was his only response.

"That's all I get?" she continued to taunt.

"Oh trust me, I have plenty more to say, just not in here. I already got you some hot fry things. You still want these too?"

Avery's brow furrowed. "You did?"

"Yeah, I saw you eyeing them when we walked in. I told you I'm gonna take good care of every single thing you need. Grape soda or you want an orange one?"

"How did you...?"

"I pay attention, sweetheart."

"Grape."

"Go turn the truck on and get warm." He handed her his keys. Yeah, this being taken care of thing was awfully addictive.

He climbed in the truck a few minutes later balancing their drinks and all of the food. "One request."

"What's that?" she grinned.

"Don't spill this in my truck." He handed over the drink.

"I've heard about cowboys and their trucks. I'll be extra careful."

"I mean if you spilled the drink because you leaned your head over in my lap to swallow for me, I'd probably be willing to overlook it."

"And if I spilled it without having my mouth on your dick?"

"Then I'd probably turn you over my knee and paddle those lips on your ass."

"Had a feeling you'd say something like that."

"Oh yeah? Then why'd you ask?" He unwrapped one of his hot dogs.

"Maybe because I like hearing you say stuff like that."

"You are aware I have to drive you back safely on icy roads, right? You've got me strung so tight I could hammer nails with my cock."

"Rather you hammer me with it."

"Fucking hell, you are a little minx."

She dissolved in another fit of giggles. She never wanted this to end. It felt so good to be here with him. To be loose and happy and free and herself.

"Oh, and as for your comment about not being stripper material, I'm gonna prove you wrong. You're gonna strip to the skin for me over and over again, sugar. Be ready."

"Mmm, do you tip well?"

His huff turned into a sexy chuckle. "I'm more of a taker than a giver."

"No you're not but I'll let you go on thinking that." She dug in the bag of food willing to eat most anything at that point. "You got six hot dogs?" Clearly she wasn't the only one who was starving.

"Two of them are for you."

"But I can't..."

"Damn, these are good." He sunk his teeth into a hot dog stacked high with chili, onions, and cheese. Her mouth watered. She tore the crinkly plastic wrapper to open the granola bar and had to peel it free from the sticky oats.

Her mouth rejected it instantly. It was stale, salty, and the peanuts pricked at her tongue. The dried fruit was syrupy sweet and took far too long to chew.

"Do you think the hot dogs are pork or beef?" She told herself pork would be better than beef, except she'd seen an article recently about inhumane treatment of pigs. Okay, so beef would be better. Maybe. But the environment...

"These are all beef, sug. Damned good, too."

She had seen a locally sourced sign somewhere in that shop, hadn't she? That was something. It'd be kind of like helping the local ranchers. If they weren't shipping the cattle far, that was better. Right?

"Maybe I'll have a little of one."

"Uh-huh, thought you might. Squirt a little more mustard on there for me." He handed her half of his as he pulled out of the parking lot and onto the road that ran from Ogallala to Pleasant Glen. "There's more packets down in the bag."

Avery stared at the hot dog slathered in chili and cheese. The bun was soft and warm and smelled like it had just come out of an oven, a sweetened yeasty masterpiece.

The last thing she'd eaten besides the four bites of soup she'd choked down the afternoon before was a bowl of her aunt's Grape Nuts. Her stomach was on the verge of digesting itself.

The heater in the truck carried the rich, spicy, onion-laced scent to her nose. Ever since she'd indulged in Colt the afternoon before, it seemed she'd lost all ability to deny herself the things she wanted.

Before she could quite process what she was doing, she sank her teeth into his chili dog, plastic cheese and all, and it was the best damned thing she'd tasted in a decade.

Her eyes closed as she followed the first bite with a second and moaned through the bun.

"Or skip the mustard and go on and eat mine." He laughed at her outright. "Just promise me you'll make them same noises when you have me in your mouth."

"Oh my God, this is what heaven tastes like."

"Yeah, you can say that when you're finished, too."

"Would you shut up? I'm in hot dog nirvana."

He rolled his eyes and shook his head at her. Lifting her soda out of the cup holder, he handed it to her. "Swallow it down with that, then you can call it nirvana. And when you finish up, would you make me one of the others with some of them mustard packets? 'Less you plan on eating all six of them."

"I might."

"I won't deny you. 'Course I'll never let you live it down either. Least you ain't one of them chicks that starves themselves. You had me worried with all of your granola goddess bullcrap. Looks to me like you're all carnivore, honey, just my kind of girl."

She polished off the hot dog and didn't hesitate to lick the remnants of cheese and chili from her lips. "Why did I wait so long to eat that?" She dug in the bag for two more. "Sorry I ate yours though."

"I'll live."

She added a full pack of mustard to another one of the dogs and handed it to him before she gave in to temptation and ate that one as well.

"Do I get all of this one?"

"Yes." She rolled her eyes.

"Much obliged."

"You can't seriously have wondered if I eat. I mean, you've seen me naked."

"Damned beautiful sight, too. Feminine curves that go on for country miles, baby. Hips meant for grabbing and titties so full I'm still fantasizing about what they feel like in my hands. Drives a man wild."

"I like driving you wild but not eating isn't something to joke about. I was a ballerina, remember. I had to quit because of my boobs and my hips. I couldn't ever figure out how to do the finger down my throat thing, but that's what most of the other dancers did to stay so thin."

Colt shook his head. "World's so damned fucked-up. Real men have no interest in dating a shovel handle in a dress. A real man wants something to grab on to when he buries himself in hard and fast, and something soft and thick to wrap up in his arms when he ain't. I'll say this though—if you quit 'cause of those hips and tits, ballet's loss was definitely my gain."

Yep, you keep saying things like that, Colt Camden, and I'll go on and fall completely in love with you. When she'd polished off one and a half of the other hot dogs she offered the remaining half to him.

"You eat it, baby doll. It's my fault you barely had any of that soup yesterday."

She needed precious little encouragement to do just that. Sated with protein and fat, she settled back in the truck. "How are we going to get my car back from that awful place?"

"You have any idea how good it is to hear you say *we* instead of I?"

"Do you have any idea how good it feels to know I don't have to handle it alone?"

He laced his fingers through hers, managing the recently cleared roads with more ease than she ever would've been able to. "I've been thinking about that. Obviously, I can't show back up there alone and I'm sure as hell not taking you back out there. They'll be waiting on me and it wouldn't shock me if they wanted to fight dirty this time. I'm kinda hoping they'll have it towed out of spite. That'd make it easier. Guess if they don't, I could maybe see if my brother would go back out there with me."

"Does it feel weird to call him that?"

"Yeah, that's why I was trying it out with you to see how it felt."

"He has to know how awful your dad was. Maybe he's always wanted a brother, too."

"Who said anything about me wanting a brother?"

You didn't have to say it out loud. She folded her lips between her teeth momentarily to keep from explaining that. He likely wasn't ready to hear it. "I love my brothers most of the time. I just thought maybe you'd like to have a real one, too."

"Never really thought much about it 'til now. Still have no idea how he'll handle the news. Like I said, no one wants to stare their father's mistakes in the eye."

"You aren't a mistake. I'm going to keep saying that until you believe me. And that will isn't your fault either. If he wants to hate someone, he should hate your dad."

"Got the impression he already does."

"Can I change the subject?" she asked.

"Wish you would."

"It's still a serious topic."

He turned to study her. "I'm okay with serious, baby."

"Good. When we were having sex yesterday, you asked me if it was different. It was really different for me, but I wondered what you were feeling to have asked me that."

"Damn, when you go deep you go all the way, don't you?"

"We could go back to you and Brock, but yes, I do. I told you I love hard. I don't know how not to."

"I'm sure it won't shock you to hear me say I've had more than my fair share of women in my bed. I ain't proud of it, but I get the impression you want the truth."

"I do."

"So, there it is. I've slept around, but with you it was…more, better, I don't know. I'm not so good at deep. Kinda like when everything was said and done with the others I couldn't wait to get away. With you, all I wanted was to hold you and protect you. Like I don't ever want to get away from you. Should scare me, to be honest, but it doesn't."

Avery stared at him, wondering what her life would look like in a week and then a month. Would he still be there? Would he listen to that part of him that never wanted to get away, or would he go back to Holder County where he already had a life? "I get the scared part. I really, really do."

CHAPTER NINETEEN

Colt got them back to the beauty shop at 9:50. The road through Pleasant Glen had been plowed as well. No more snow was falling, but it was still colder than a witch's tit outside. Avery threw her arms around his neck as soon as he parked, making it all worth it in his book. "Thank you so much for getting me here on time. Maybe I'll actually start getting customers if she loves her hair."

"I told you I'm gonna take good care of you. Come on. I'll walk you in, then I gotta figure out a way to get Jaxon on a tractor."

"You know I can never repay you for everything you're doing for us." Those crystal-blue eyes were earnest in what she obviously considered her own defeat. He had to figure out some way to make her stop thinking like that.

"Baby, I don't want your repayment. I just want you."

"You have me."

"Then hush up and come here to me." He stroked under her chin as she leaned in and lifted her lips to his. Those sweet pink lips turned sinful in a heartbeat. This time he opened for *her* tongue. A heartbeat later he was sucking it the same way he'd done her clit.

One of those sexy little coos she made filled his mouth. Damn but she was too good. Her comment about swallowing still had him tied up in knots. The way she'd devoured those juicy hot dogs had been one of the most erotic things he'd ever seen.

His right hand slipped to her left breast. He stroked gently this time, building the tension. He planned to keep her on edge most of the day and the night. When they got back from the concert, he'd sneak her into what was about to become his trailer and slowly, skillfully undo her. Another hungry moan sounded from her. Her legs spread and she leaned closer. "Needy, baby?"

"Yes." When she pulled away to answer, he trailed tender kisses down her neck.

"Good. Let that build for me. By the time I get you nekkid tonight I want you soaking wet and begging for it."

"Not a problem."

"Such a good girl. But we better quit because someone just pulled up."

She jerked back and opened the truck door before he could do it for her. "Wait that's not Melony. That's Holly Camden's truck."

Holly. She was still in her truck with a cowgirl hat pulled down low. Colt hadn't met her yet. This should be interesting. He helped Avery out of the truck and scooted her into the shop.

"I wonder why she's here. She told me she couldn't come in today." Avery whisked around the shop, turning on the coffee maker and lights.

"Tell me where you keep Jaxon's warmest clothes and coats. If he's gonna go to the ranch with me, he's gotta be bundled up."

"I bought the boys long johns, big coats, and snow stuff when we moved up here. It's all in their closet."

Something about the way she'd said that galled him. "You bought them snow stuff but none for yourself, right?"

"It was a lot of money." She kept her back to him as she stared out the front window.

He started to scold her but thought better of it. He didn't want anything to ruin her morning. He'd go buy her a good coat and snow pants after he got Jax back home by a fire. "Clearly gonna have to keep you hot myself then."

She turned toward him and grinned. "See, not buying all of that stuff worked out well for me."

"Just so you know, I am biting holes in my tongue."

Before she could formulate a comeback, Holly Camden stomped the snow off of her boots and scurried inside. That hat was pulled down so low Colt couldn't make out her eyes.

"Uh, Holly? You okay?" Avery shot her a confused look.

"No." Holly whimpered.

"Oh. The hat." Avery cringed. "Tell me exactly what happened and everything you did."

What the hell was she talking about? Women made no damned sense at all.

"I couldn't get in with my stylist before tonight, so I thought I'd try something fun myself." Holly drew a deep breath and then whipped off the cowgirl hat. "Look at me. Dec was literally speechless. My husband is a psychologist. He is never, ever speechless. He always knows what to say. This time his mouth just kept opening and closing and opening again. He wouldn't stop doing that even when I threatened to hit him. I rescheduled all of my appointments this morning. You have to fix this."

Colt's mouth was mimicking those very movements her husband's had.

Holly, whom he assumed was a natural brunette like the other Camdens he'd met, was currently sporting a head full of bizarrely colored hair. There were splotches of bleached blonde intermixed with reddish pinks and day-glo oranges. The front of her hair was spiked upwards and the back hung at odd lengths. He didn't know much about hair, but he assumed deranged rhino wasn't the look she'd been going for.

"I watched this..." Holly attempted to explain.

"YouTube video," Avery answered for her.

"Yes. So stupid. Can you fix it? Please, please say you can fix it."

"I can fix it, but I have an appointment at ten, so I'll have to do it after Melony's."

"But you can fix it before tonight, right? I cannot let Dec's entire band see me this way. My brothers are still howling with laughter, assholes that they are."

"I'll have you looking great by tonight. I promise. But I need *you* to promise me you will never ever try to layer your own hair again."

"Are you kidding me? If you can fix this, I'll be your customer for life."

"Deal."

"I'm gonna leave you to this—" Colt gestured to the neon nest on Holly Camden's head, "—and go get Jax."

"Who are you?" Holly asked, like she'd just noticed he was standing there.

"Uh, Colton. Avery's boyfriend and I just took a job with your cousin, Brock. Can I assume since you're here he might need a little help with chores today?"

"Oh, I'm sorry. Did I interrupt you two? I was in crisis-cowgirl mode."

At that moment some other woman, Melony, Colt assumed, swept inside. "So sorry I'm late. Early snows are terrible for cornfields." When she noticed Holly, she blinked several times. "Wow."

"Yeah, I know, Mel."

"Maybe put the hat back on 'til I'm ready for you," Avery instructed.

"Good idea." Holly jerked the hat back over the monstrosity of her self-made hairdo. She turned back to Colt. "They could definitely use some help. The snow took down three fences and Brock's trying to plow enough to get the feed trucks through. We weren't quite ready for snow this early."

"That's what I figured." Making his way to Avery, he pulled her close. "Good luck, sugar."

"This I can handle. Is it awful that this might be exactly the break I need? I'm trying not to show how excited I am." She spoke into his chest to keep Holly from hearing.

"She did it to herself, babe. If the opportunity presents itself, nothing wrong with jumping on it and givin' it a ride."

"See you later, cowboy." That impish grin heated his blood.

"Give me a call when you want me to come get you. Oh, damn, that reminds me." He grabbed that bag of hers, which looked damn near big enough to hold a calf, and dug through it until he found her phone. He entered his number on her favorites list.

"Are all cowboys so invasive?" she asked Holly and Melony as she shook her head at him.

"What?" he huffed. "You need my number to call me."

"They are," Melony assured her. "Trust me. If something needs to be done nothing stands in their way, which can be nice...and it can also make you want to pluck every hair on their head out by the root."

"On that note, I'm leaving." He brushed a kiss on Avery's cheek and lifted his hat to the other ladies. Looked like she'd be busy most of the day. He tried not to lament that fact.

Twenty minutes later, he was exiting the truck at Pearl's trailer. His new home away from home. He tried to decipher how he felt about that. Knocking on the door, he waited until Chase opened it. Colt's eyes zeroed in on a deep purple marking peeking out of the ridiculous turtleneck Chase was wearing. "Yeah, that ain't working, stud. Good effort though." He pointed to the hickey.

Chase rolled his eyes and backed up for Colt to enter. "How you feeling, Miss Pearl?" he asked as he crossed the room to warm his hands by the fire. She was sitting in her usual chair, snuggled up close to the flames.

"Tired, but that's always the case. Where's Avery?"

"Cutting somebody's hair and demilitarizing someone else's."

"One of them YouTube videos?" Pearl asked knowingly.

"Yes, ma'am."

"Kids these days, I swear. Well, I'm glad you're here, honey. Sally just left. She's going home to see about Theodora, but then she said she'd be back. She made cider. You want some?"

"Sounds good, but I'll get it. Can I get you anything?"

"I'm still cold. Could you grab me another blanket?"

"Sure thing." Colt grabbed one of the quilts off the couch and shot a disappointed glare at Chase, who should've made sure his aunt wasn't chilly. The kid offered up yet another eye roll, more dramatic this time, and disappeared into the bathroom in the hall.

Colt bundled Pearl up and poured her another cup of cider along with one for himself.

"Colton!" Jaxon bounded in from the back of the trailer carrying what appeared to be a plastic serving tray. When he spun it Frisbee style, Colt pulled it from the air.

"No shield throwing inside, little man. You ready for our tractor ride?"

"I haven't had no accidents," he vowed readily.

"Attaboy. Go find some warm clothes and your coat and hat for me." Jaxon scampered back down the hall. "Miss Pearl, I want to ask you something."

"Oh," Pearl's hands covered her mouth. Delight danced in her eyes. "You want to ask for Avery's hand. I just knew when I saw you."

"Uh...na...uh...now...no," he spluttered. Downing a shot of the cider, he wondered if Pearl was aware he hadn't even known her niece a week. Seeing as he was sitting there effectively asking to move in with her, maybe it wasn't too crazy she thought he was proposing. "No, now that ain't it. I wanted to know if you'd be willing to rent out that other trailer on your property. I could help out around here more if I was close by and I wouldn't mind getting to see Avery more. Plus, I got a job at Camden Ranch, which as you know ain't too far from here."

"I hadn't ever really thought about renting out Lester's trailer. That'd help with the medical bills though, wouldn't it?"

"Yes, ma'am. And I'll pay you twice the price I was paying for the motel a night."

"Oh, now, you don't need to do all that. You sure Avery's okay with this?"

"I'd say she's real good with it."

"Well then, absolutely. When can you move in? Lots of Les's furniture is still in there. I didn't have the heart to get rid of it. Probably still a bunch of his crap in there, too. Man never did throw anything away. I dust and sweep on occasion, or I did 'til I got sick, so it's not too bad."

"I could move in right away, ma'am, and I sure don't mind cleaning it up. I appreciate you letting me rent it. I'm gonna take Jax with me to the ranch, but you call me if you need me and I'll come right back." He took her cell phone off of the TV tray by her chair and entered his number the same way he'd done with Avery's.

"I just have one condition about this renting business."

Figuring he was about to be told to stay the hell out of Avery's room at night, he hated that he was about to tell yet another lie. He wasn't staying out of her room unless she was the one who asked him to. "You name it."

"While you're here, will you think about marrying my sweet Avery? She deserves a good man and I know that's what you are."

Colt had been called many things in his life. Bastard son. Dumbass. Coward. Hothead. Womanizer. Jerk. But never in the past thirty-four years had anyone called him a good man. "You may be wrong about that, Miss Pearl."

"You know, Avery's mama and me had a falling out when I married my Lester. He was a cattle rancher, too. We used to have a lot more land than I have now, but Ev Camden always came through for us when we needed to sell some off for the money.

"Les was more than a little rough around the edges. His daddy was a horse's ass. Awful, hateful man. But not my husband. Now, he drank a little too much and played the field a little too hard before we met. Liked to get into bar fights, too. Lord, it took me more than a day or two to break him of that. Elaine kept telling me he would break my heart and ruin my life.

"She had a habit of making decisions in the moment and then blaming the men she'd made them with if there were lifetime consequences. She swore Les would turn out just like his daddy. Said she'd never speak to me again if I moved up here with him. It took me years to realize she was being awful to me out of fear. That's why she wanted Avery to come up here and take care of me and why she wanted her to take over my little shop and make it shine. She thought she owed me." Pearl shook her head at that. "I loved my Lester 'til the day we put him in the ground and I love him still. He never did me wrong. Always took such good care of me, protected me. Even when times were tough, he never let me down. I miss him so much I can't see straight. He was a good man. Even if no one else saw it, I knew. I can always tell. I'm not wrong, Colton. You're a good man, too."

The story sank slowly through Colt's mind, bringing him a little bit closer to being the man he wanted to be. Maybe his whole life he'd been waiting on someone to give him a chance to be something other than Mick Camden's bastard son or almost a Holder. Maybe this was his chance. "People who know me best call me Colt, ma'am, and I will do as you asked. I'll think about me and Avery. She deserves better than me though." He kept telling her he'd figure things out but the truth of it was she'd always deserved more than he was.

"If she deserves better, Colt, then be better."

Jaxon rushed back into the living room wearing an odd combo of short-sleeved and long-sleeved shirts. He did have on jeans, but he was wearing two different boots. Pearl chuckled. "Why don't I get little Jaxon ready and you can go get a look at the trailer."

"You sure you don't need my help?"

"Now you sound like Avery. I'm not a complete invalid."

"I never said you were. Trying to be a better man is all."

Pearl beamed at him. "Naw. You be better for my Avery. You're just fine by me."

Not wanting Pearl to believe that he questioned her ability to wrangle the boy, Colt left and headed over the fifty paces or so to Lester's former trailer. The door was unlocked. He stepped inside and hit the light switch. There were boxes of newspapers and ranching and cattle magazines from the last four decades scattered around and stacked on the kitchen counter, but the place wasn't nearly as bad as he'd envisioned. He'd seen enough of those hoarding shows on television to give him pause.

The living room was sparse but had a decent plaid sofa and an old box television set. He worked his way down the hallway. The trailer was smaller than Pearl's. It had two bedrooms to her three, but the kitchen was a little bigger. No washer and dryer. What was meant to be the laundry closet was stacked high with boxes and other junk. He shook his head at the old tractor motor shoved in the back corner. That almost explained the case of motor oil he'd located in one of the bathroom cabinets.

Flipping on more lights, he stepped into the master bedroom. Another old TV set and a king-sized bed with two TV trays as bedside tables. The bedroom across the hall held nothing but a stack of feed pallets, old mattresses, and broken furniture. Sighing, Colt closed the door to that room. He'd deal with getting rid of it all later.

Currently, he just needed a working kitchen, bathroom, and most importantly a bedroom. He stacked the stray boxes from the living room and kitchen into the unusable bedroom. The space already seemed less cramped.

On top of one of the boxes, he picked up a small stack of papers with a compilation of dates on the tops. Flipping through them, he noted the same signature over and over again. They were land sale contracts. It appeared Lester had indeed sold off his ranch fifty acres at a time to Ev Camden over a thirty-year period. *Ev Camden always came through for us.* "Yeah, well Ev's nothing like his brother then," Colt spoke to the cold air surrounding him.

Locating a washrag in one of the kitchen drawers, he scrubbed down the countertops and flushed the commode a few times to make sure it worked.

Calling that good enough, he headed back across to Pearl's trailer to pick up Jaxon. He needed to head out to the ranch.

When he returned, Jaxon was dressed in long underwear, a flannel shirt, a pair of overalls, two pairs of wool socks, and a thick leather pair of small cowboy boots. Pearl was pulling a stocking cap on his head and had a cowboy hat on the counter for him. Clearly, she knew how to dress a little rancher for a day on the range.

"Do I really gots to wear all of this?" Jaxon sighed out.

"You do if you want a tractor ride. It's freezing out there, little man," Colt informed him. "You ready?"

He struggled to get the cowboy hat over the cap but finally managed it with a grunt. When it was locked in place, he headed toward the front door. "I get to ride in your truck."

Colt started after him when Pearl touched his hand. "Before you go, would you mind doing one more thing for me?"

"Hey Jax, hold up," Colt called. "Anything, Miss Pearl. What do you need?"

"Well..." She fidgeted with the fringe on the shawl she was wearing. "It's Chase," she mouthed.

"Is it about that Kami chick?"

"In a way I'm sure it is."

As if he'd been cued to do so, at that moment, Chase slunk out of the bathroom and disappeared into the boys' room. Realization slowly locked into place. Fuck. "He in there the whole time I was over in the other trailer?"

Pearl nodded.

"How many times has he gone in there today?"

"If he's actually using the bathroom that much, we need to get him to the doctor," Pearl stated knowingly.

"But that ain't what he's doing."

"I don't think so."

Colt considered for a few breaths. No guy wanted to be called on doing that. Ever. Especially at sixteen. On the other hand, there was only one bathroom and he lived with two women. "For now, let's leave him to it. He's not doing any real harm. I'll think about the best way to approach this, but nothing's coming to me at the moment. Hopefully he'll be playing football soon and that'll give him something else to do with...well...with his hands."

"That sounds fair. I just wanted to make sure he wasn't acting oddly. I never had kids of my own."

"Not odd at all, but he could probably be more discreet."

———

Avery methodically wove the foiling comb through Melanie's long blonde locks.

"I've never colored it before," she stated again.

"This is going to give you a little depth of color and make it shine. You want Tucker to notice right?"

"Definitely."

"Then that's my only goal," Avery vowed.

"Have you all heard from Natalie since she left on her honeymoon, Holly?" Melony asked.

Holly lifted her head from a hairstyle magazine circa 1984. "Aaron sent Dad a pic of the two of them on a ski lift because Dad kept calling and they kept not answering. I'm sure it's not the only pic he's taken, but it's probably the only one that's G-rated."

Melony and Avery both laughed.

"Where are they honeymooning?" Avery asked.

"Vail, which is so weird because until she fell in love with Aaron, she never wanted to leave the ranch. I'm so proud of her."

Avery offered a kind smile but thought it an odd comment. Why would going on your honeymoon make your sister proud?

Before Avery could come up with something else for all of them to talk about, the mailman stumbled into the shop. "I got a delivery for an Avery Hale."

"Oh, just set it there." Avery gestured to the counter so she wouldn't have to stop Melanie's foil.

"Looks like a bunch of business files, a few magazines, some brushes, and some of them metal wands you women-folk curl your hair with."

Avery's mouth hung open. "I mailed that before I left Oklahoma. I thought it was lost. Did you open my mail?"

Melony nodded, sliding her hair out of Avery's grasp. "He opens everyone's mail and most everything that gets shipped is at least a month late. It's ridiculous." She made no effort to keep the mailman from hearing her. Avery wanted to feel bad for him, but she was rather irritated.

The mailman left and Holly sighed. "Never ever mail order anything here. One time my cousin's wife, Hope, ordered sexy lingerie and he opened it and delivered it to her at the drug store in front of everyone."

"Oh my gosh."

"Yeah," Melony agreed. "And my mom mailed out the invitations to my wedding two months before and no one in town got theirs until a month after. We had to go door to door asking everyone in the Glen to come."

"Why doesn't the town fire him?" Avery asked.

"No one else wants the job, plus he's like a hundred and eighty-seven or something, so Tucker's dad would feel bad about firing him,"

Melony explained. She would certainly know since she was married to the mayor's son.

"He's nuts, and I'm a psychologist so it means something when I say that," Holly quipped. "At five o'clock this morning, he came bustling up the snowy road to my house hollering about some certified letter from Oklahoma. I thought Dec was going to bind and gag him."

The words certified letter and Oklahoma shot pure terror through Avery's veins. The blood that followed it ran ice cold. She swallowed and tried to figure out a way to warn Colt before he got out to the ranch. Chill bumps scattered down her arms. Bile lodged in her throat. Her heart stumbled over its next beat. "Oh, goodness. What was it?" *Please don't say anything about Mick.*

"No idea. It ended up being for Dad so he wasn't even at the right house."

"Oh." She managed to do the next four foils, measuring her breaths and willing her heart to find a normal rhythm. "There. All done with your color. I'm just going to run to the restroom while this sets, then I'll start on yours, Holly."

Grabbing her phone from her bag, she sprinted to the bathroom praying with everything she had that whatever that letter was it had nothing to do with Mick Camden's death or his deranged will.

As she shut herself behind the door it occurred to her that Melony and Holly could probably both still hear her. One of the things she wanted done to the shop was to have a thicker bathroom door installed so she couldn't hear the customers. She texted Colt instead, trying to explain what she'd heard.

When she'd been in the bathroom long enough for it to be considered odd, she whispered a prayer that he hadn't walked into some kind of ambushed inquisition and forced herself to go out and do her job.

As she put a smock over Holly's head and combed out her disastrous hair, she couldn't help but think it had been selfish of her to ask him not to tell the Camdens. If they found out some other way, it would serve her right. She kept her cell phone in her pocket, something she'd been taught never to do in Cosmetology school, desperate for him to text her and tell her everything was fine.

But those frigid hands of despair gripped her once again as she coaxed Holly's hair into something she could work with. Colt couldn't leave. Not yet. Hopefully not ever. Why couldn't she keep him? The world had already taken so much away.

Her heart, which wanted him to stay forever, and her brain, which logically knew he would have to leave, were completely at odds.

Attempting to escape the fear, the way she'd kick off the covers of her bed on hot Oklahoma summer nights, she focused on Holly. "Okay, so what were we trying to do, exactly?"

Holly cringed as she studied her hair in the mirror. "I wanted to add in some highlights, which was clearly a bad idea. And then I wanted bangs and layers, also a bad idea."

"You would look great with some layers and highlights. It's just there's a lot of red in your brunette, and when you tried to highlight your hair, it pulled orange and pink. That's the problem with the over-the-counter colors. They're too strong. How about we get you back to your original color and then I'll add in a few highlights?"

"You are my hero."

Avery forced a laugh. *Doubt a real hero would ask a member of your family to lie to you directly.* "I'm just a stylist. Nothing more."

CHAPTER TWENTY

"Man, you are a lifesaver," Brock vowed yet again. He handed over the keys to one of the John Deere tractors, complete with a snow-plow attachment.

"It's no problem. Like I said, I appreciate you letting me bring him along." Colt gestured to Jaxon, who was currently enthralled with a few of Brock's son's action figures.

"You kidding? He fits right in. We got enough Camden grandkids running around here we probably won't even notice him. Take him for his tractor ride and then bring him back over here before he freezes. He can play with Nate and Evan and we can run the feed trucks."

"Sounds like a plan," Colt agreed.

"I'm gonna go get Natalie's herds fed. Call me if you need me."

"Brock," Hope called from upstairs. She sounded like a dying frog. He grimaced.

"Scratch that. Let me go clean her up, and then I'll figure out how to be everywhere at once."

"Hey, let me get the feeding done. Yours and Natalie's. You go take care of her. If you can keep an eye on little man after he's had his tractor ride, I'll do everything else." *Be better*, Pearl had told him. The two words that had lodged in his mind. Wasn't this the kind of thing brothers should do for each other?

"You sure?"

"Positive."

"She usually rallies around lunch. I can come out then."

"I don't believe for one second that you wouldn't cover for one of your cousins if his wife was in the same shape."

Brock's brow furrowed. He blinked a few times like maybe he was seeing Colton in a new light. "Yeah. I have done that. More than a few times."

"Then the world owes you one, right?"

"Maybe so."

"Come on, Captain America," he called out to Jaxon, "let's go find the tractor." Colt didn't have to say his name twice, but a sudden thought stopped him in his tracks. "Hey, have you used the restroom since we got here?"

Brock chuckled as he left the kitchen. "There's one of those kiddie seat things in the bathroom down the hall."

"Go use it before we get on the tractor and you're sitting in my lap," Colt ordered.

Soon enough, they were out on the tractor in the cold. Jaxon was having a ball while Colt methodically plowed the feed truck runs and then cleared a path to the gravel road so getting on and off of the ranch wouldn't be quite so treacherous.

He caught Jaxon's hand before it landed on the clutch. "Boy, you're gonna dump us out in the snow and wreck Brock's tractor. I'm trying to get him to like me."

"I want to drive it. I can do it," Jax insisted.

"All right, but I do the clutch. You can help with the wheel. Deal?"

"Deal."

Colt managed to keep the steering wheel from going too far one direction or the other by guiding it with his knees. Jaxon didn't notice, so all was well. When he managed to get them to the other half of Brock's land, the part that had been willed to him, he called himself several choice words for his interest in the snow-covered fields that extended farther than his eyes could see.

There was an unused barn boarded up. He kept them in the groove created by the feed trucks and drove a little deeper into the land that currently belonged to him. Another half mile or so in, Jax got wiggly. "You ready to go back, little man?"

"No." A deep yawn contorted his face and he laid his head back against Colton's chest. Smiling at that, Colt tucked him closer and took over the steering.

They came up on a low rock wall no more than three feet off the ground. The snow barely covered the bottom half. As he drove on, he saw that it was a large, raised dirt platform of sorts. It looked like an old gardening set up with raised boxes, half rotten, full of dead weeds. In the center was an ancient rusted porch swing set in tall pillars.

Colt wondered who'd built that in the middle of a ranch and what the woman who'd asked for it to be constructed had looked like. Was it one of his great-aunts, or maybe a great-grandmother he'd never known? Another thousand yards or more away, there was a large white clapboard house that had been boarded up. It looked to be a hundred years old. Brock's house was newer and larger, but this one had multiple chimneys and windows. Colt told himself to calculate the land in dollar figures. The Holders needed the land willed to Colt to be worth nearly the same amount as the land willed to Brock so they could exchange deeds without having to exchange money. But Jaxon was asleep on Colt's chest and the roar of the tractor muted the world around him. All he could do was estimate the value of the land by the amount of life it already held and the amount it could continue to sustain.

Dollars were a fleeting entity to any cattle rancher. Hard work, food you put on the table, a warm willing woman waiting on you at home by the fire, little ones you taught to rope and ride before they were weaned, an old hound dog or two that came when you called them, stars in the navy blue sky, and rocking chairs on the front porch —those were things he wanted to hold in his hands and never let go.

The rumble of the tractor put him in mind of the men who'd plowed this land before him. Men whose lives were indelibly inter-woven with his own even if they'd never know of his existence. Men he wanted to prove himself to even if they were in the ground. Mick was an anomaly among the Camdens. He'd come from better stock than his father. He wanted to hear the old family stories. He wanted to know them, to have been a part of it all.

Eventually, he parked the tractor in the shed and carried a sound-asleep Jaxon on his shoulder back to Brock's house.

When he eased inside, he discovered something else he and Brock had in common. His brother's broad grin, complete with dimples, was an exact duplicate of his own. The freezing cold air trapped in Colt's lungs burned his chest before he managed to let it escape.

"The tractor with the cover on and the combine gets them to sleep every time," Brock chuckled.

"He made it a good long way. Hung with me while we plowed all of your cousin's land and most of yours. Didn't fall asleep 'til I got to mi... uh the other half...over there."

Brock didn't appear to have noticed his misstep. Colt called himself a dumbass again. "Go ahead and put him on the couch. Evan's napping, too. Hope'll be down in a second. She kept some soup and crackers down. You mind feeding with me?"

"So I can open gates for you?" Colt knew what he wanted.

"That depends. How old are you?"

"What?" Why would he want to know that?

"I'm just curious."

"Thirty-four in April."

"April, huh? I'm a little older than you, so you get gate duty. I mean unless you really mind."

"I don't mind." Checking his phone to make sure Pearl didn't need him, he saw a text from Avery. Panic slithered over his skin. Why the hell was Ev Camden getting certified mail from Oklahoma? *Shit*.

The lawyers and the probate judge had been very clear that they were willing to let Colt handle this his own way. Had they gotten impatient? Surely the Holders owned enough of that county they'd named after themselves to keep city officials at bay. Wasn't it possible that the letter had nothing at all to do with Mick or Colton? He didn't want Avery to panic. Texting her back to say nothing seemed amiss, he prayed he was right.

———

Avery spun Holly Camden around to see herself in the mirror. Pride welled through her chest. The side-swept bangs covered the regrettable set Holly had tried to give herself and the color was a gorgeous deep auburn, just a few shades lighter than her natural shade. She'd evened out the layers Holly had hacked into her hair, blending them in to help frame her face. Now that she had all of her curling irons back in her possession, Avery finished the style by curling the ends and adding a little hairspray.

Holly looked amazing. She squealed and then jumped out of the chair and hugged Avery for all she was worth. So far, it had been a pretty good day. Melony's hair had turned out great, too. Thrilled with her new looks, she'd tipped Avery twenty-five dollars. If only Colt would text her back...

"You fixed it!" Holly cheered. "Thank you, thank you, thank you!"

"Hey, that's my job. You look great. I love the color. To keep up the side-swept bangs, make sure to blow dry it the opposite way and then flip it this way to give yourself lots of height."

"I will. I owe you big time." Holly grabbed her bag and whipped out her wallet.

"It's one hundred for the cut, color removal, and the foil." Avery hated this part of her job and hated herself more for hoping for a big tip.

"That's it?" Holly's brow knitted. "I pay twice that in Lincoln. Here." She thrust two hundred dollar bills in Avery's hands. "Trust me, Dec will probably drop by to give you more when he leaves the clinic, which is where I'm headed. Thank you so much, Avery, and I meant to tell you this earlier, but I really like Colton. He seems nice. Is it weird that I feel like I already know him? I mean I just met him and all, but he reminds me of someone. I can't figure out who."

"Oh. No, that's not weird at all. And he's great. Pretty sure I'm already so far in I'll never find my way back."

"Been there. Said that. Married it, in fact. Best decision I ever made. Trust me, no one's relationship, in the history of relationships, has ever had more at stake than mine and Dec's did when we first started dating. Deportation could've been involved. If it's meant to be, it'll find a way. My mom always says, if it isn't happy it isn't the ending."

"That's really lovely. I like that."

"Yeah, never tell her I said this, but Mom's advice is pretty much always spot on. Anyway, I'll see you tonight at the concert, right? Sally was all over town yesterday telling everyone about how you and Colton met at the funeral home and he's your date for tonight."

Avery squeezed her eyes shut but couldn't quell her laughter. "We didn't exactly meet at the funeral home."

"I figured, but God love Sally for her stories."

"We are supposed to come tonight as long as my Aunt Pearl's feeling all right."

"Send her love from the Camdens and hopefully I'll see you later. I owe you a drink."

CHAPTER TWENTY-ONE

"Of course." Brock sighed as he drove the now empty feed truck back through the pasture. They were coming up on a pair of fighting bulls.

Colt nodded. "It's inevitable."

"Yeah, I know, but I'm about done with that one on the left."

"He not getting his job done?"

"No and all he does is fight and tear down my fences. Got no idea when I'm gonna get around to replacing him though. Luke's wife, Indie, announced this morning at breakfast that she's expecting, too. That means all of the Camden wives are knocked up."

"Sounds like y'all are getting the job done then." Colt laughed.

Another one of Brock's grins spread the width of his features and Colt could swear he was looking in a mirror. His nervous system pricked and his mind tangled. The confession threatened to spew from his mouth. He hated lying to Brock. He assumed not many men met their brother at thirty-four years old. There certainly didn't seem to be any kind of protocol for this and ultimately Avery would always be the most important thing in his world. That realization doubled the frantic case of nerves crackling down his spine.

"Yeah, we ain't ever struggled in that department. Problem is we're running short handed all the way around. I've got to figure out when I can get to a sale or an auction. Need it to be sooner than later."

"I don't mind going with you or in your stead if you can't make it. I've been buying and selling for the Holders for years."

"I may take you up on that."

"Just tell me where I'm going." Colt studied the bulls locking horns. "No animal with a higher degree of job satisfaction than a breeding bull. You'd think they'd be too damn happy to fight." He told himself he shouldn't enjoy joking around with Brock as much as he did.

Brock's laughter carried the same deep tones Mick's had without any of the sneering coldness. "Ain't that the truth. Too tired, too. You know, my dad used to say that about them and their job satisfaction. Between that and a few other things you've said, I swear it's kinda like you grew up around here." A note of challenge played in Brock's tone. His statement rung close to a question. What did he know? Colt ordered himself not to panic. He'd promised Avery he'd keep his mouth shut and he intended to do just that.

"Maybe lots of ranchers talk that way."

"Maybe so." Brock's expression said he didn't actually believe it. Colt searched for a subject change. "Hey, you taking Hope to that thing at the bar tonight, or is she too sick? I'm taking Avery as long as Pearl's feeling all right."

"Uncle Ev and Aunt Jessie swear they're gonna keep all of the grandkids. I feel bad they always include mine, but we're all supposed to go since Dec's putting on the show. Hope's looking forward to it, so I hope she's up to going. To tell you the truth, I'd just as soon stay tucked up on the couch with her at home, but I'd never tell her that. Guess that means I'm either firmly settled or I'm getting old."

"You ain't old yet and there's nothing wrong with settling down, although I never would have said that a week ago. Kinda been thinking about getting myself settled lately."

"Oh yeah? Things going that good with Miss Pearl's niece?"

"Yeah. They're going real good. Few complications I have to figure."

"I brought a shit ton of complications to the table when Hope and

I started dating. They seem kind of ridiculous now. I was a stubborn fool."

"What'd you do?" Colt had never had such an open conversation with any other man, except maybe his Uncle Gentry, and somehow this still felt like more. He wondered if Brock talked so openly this way with his cousins.

"Let my pride run the show. Kept something from her I shouldn't have. Basically acted a whole lot like my old man in a way."

"Guess you can't much help whose blood you're carrying." As badly as he wished that wasn't the way the world worked.

"That's not true," Brock was quick to correct him. "You just have to decide to rise above your raising. And you have to keep on deciding it until it's an automatic thing. Uncle Ev taught me that. And a few weeks ago, I finally figured out I'm nothing like my father at all."

"How'd you figure that?"

Brock studied Colt as he eased the truck forward now that the bulls had decided that they could either back away or lose a horn apiece. He shrugged. "Found out a few things I never knew. Gave me some perspective."

Colt had no idea what to do with any of that, so he asked something he'd wanted to know ever since he'd arrived on Camden ranch. "For as much as you've said about hating your old man, I'm guessing he's never met your kids." He methodically spoke in the present tense.

"Hell no. Sick bastard's never coming anywhere near my babies, and just so you know, I include Hope in that."

Sick bastard. The word *sick* ricocheted through Colt's psyche until it lodged in his skull. That was distinctly different from calling him an asshole or a shitlicker, another phrase they shared. What the hell had Mick done to him? Adjusting his hat, giving his mind a moment to settle, he nodded. "Yeah. I feel the same way about Avery."

"You mean about not wanting your dad to know her or about her being your baby?"

Fuck. Brock was too easy to talk to. The innate familiarity was far too accessible. "Being my baby. I just want to take care of her."

"Works fine by me. Looks like I might've finally found a long-term hand." Brock's smirk was familiar as well.

"Yeah. Maybe so." He shoved the words through the bile singeing his throat. The idea of telling his Uncle Gentry that he'd taken a job as a hand at Camden Ranch indefinitely would've been comical if it weren't completely insane. Trying to imagine telling Brock who he really was and that he was currently the *holder* of half of his land and pretending that Brock wouldn't be pissed to hell and back was equally nuts.

"So, how 'bout you? You get along with your old man and your family down in Oklahoma?"

If Brock had landed a fist in Colt's gut it would've left him more air than his question had. Avery's tender grin danced in the periphery of his mind. He grasped for an ounce of truth in a pound of lies. "I hate my old man but I get on with the rest of my family okay."

"Guess we have that in common, too, then."

"Guess so. Hey, uh, I know you said you played ball in school," Colt was eager to change the subject. "Did you catch the Bedlam game last weekend?"

"Yeah, we all watched it down at Austin and Summer's place. Between that and the Huskers game, their swear jar was full enough for Austin to buy himself another ten acres."

Colt forced a chuckle as relief swept air back into his lungs. "Maybe I oughta put in some retroactively. Surprised you all couldn't hear me all the way up here."

Another one of their duplicate grins creased Brock's face. "You and I both know you can't win 'em all."

"Yeah, but knowing it and believing it are two different things."

"Ain't that the truth. Grab that gate for me if you don't mind."

Eventually all of the cattle were fed and checked. Colt helped Brock string two fences before they headed up to the house so he could pick up Jaxon.

"I hope he wasn't too much trouble."

Hope's smile was forced. She stared at him like he was some kind of specimen under a microscope. *Shit.*

"He was no trouble at all. It was great, actually. He kept the boys entertained and I actually got to sit down."

"I appreciate you lookin' after him. Guess we'll see you tonight. You ready to go, little man?"

"Jaxon, why don't you go help pick up the toys first?" Hope reminded.

"Sorry. Shoulda made him do that. Kind of learning this babysitter routine trial by fire," Colt offered.

"I think it's so sweet you're helping Avery out like this." This time Hope's grin was genuine. "If Brock and I can help with Miss Pearl, please let us know. I took dinner over there a few weeks ago, but I can do more."

"That's mighty thoughtful of you, Mrs. Camden. I'll let you know if I think of anything."

"Please call me Hope. I mean...you should call me Hope, right?"

Brock wrapped his arm around his wife's shoulder and pulled her close rather forcefully.

"Sure. I guess. Whatever you prefer." Fuck. What had been in that letter? They knew or at the very least suspected. The only question was how long would Brock let Colt keep lying.

"Oh, that reminds me," Brock released his wife. "We usually pay hands on Fridays. Since you helped me work those calves the other day, I wanted to pay you." He stalked to a desk in the kitchen and pulled a checkbook from the drawer.

"You can do that later," Colt offered without thinking. *Idiot.* What kind of ranch hand wouldn't want to be paid for his work sooner rather than later?

"Nah, it's fine." Brock methodically wrote out a check and then handed it to Hope. She glanced over it before giving it to Colt. What the hell?

"I'm dyslexic. Just always like her to make sure I'm giving you the correct amount and everything," Brock explained.

"Oh yeah?" He stared down at the check made out to Colton Holder, a man who didn't exist. The check could never be deposited. Clearly he was losing his poker face because his half-brother had volunteered the information about his reading issues. Relaxing his features, he tried to look unaffected. Was his brother trying to coax a confession out? Not yet. Colt was determined. "Thanks for this. I'll see you tonight."

As soon as he got Jax loaded in the truck, Colt called that damned lawyer's office. Man had been dry humping his last nerve for two weeks and the one time he actually needed the guy he didn't answer his phone. Reminding himself not to curse in front of Jax, he touched Gentry's name in his contact list.

"I was just checking the weather up where you are," his uncle said without any preliminaries. "Y'all got a storm. Still warm down here." For as long as he could remember his uncle had been fascinated with weather all over the Midwest.

"Yeah, it's fu... It's colder than a witch's ti... Uh—" he glanced over to Jax in one of those booster car seats staring at the fields full of cattle as they slowly made their way off the ranch, "—it's cold. Not snowing anymore though. Sun's out now."

"You okay, son? Sound kinda like you got a mouthful of manure. You get caught in the wind or something?"

"Nah, I ain't that dumb. Listen, did you or Uncle Barrett send some kind of certified mail up here?"

"I haven't sent a thing. Barrett hasn't either far as I know. Why would we send you something certified mail?"

"Not to me. To the Camdens."

"Oh. No. Nothing I know of. We're all on hold 'til you say go. How do you know they're getting certified mail?"

"Long story."

"Did you get a look at the land yet?"

"Yeah."

"And?"

Another round of self-hatred filled Colt's gut. "Not entirely sure, but with the lake on Tex Monroe's land and the amount of acreage up here, I'd say it's almost an even draw. Land in Holder County is worth a little more but not much. I didn't get to see all of mine."

"Yours, huh?"

"For the moment it is, ain't it?" Gall held his jaw in a tense set.

"That's what the will says."

CHAPTER TWENTY-TWO
Brock Camden

"Brock, do you really think...?" Hope leapt as soon as she heard Colton's truck crank.

"Yeah, baby, I do, but maybe don't be quite so forceful about making him feel like family. I gave him several opportunities to come clean. Clearly, he doesn't want us to know yet. Simmer down for me."

"I did a bunch of research while you were gone."

"Of course you did." Brock shook his head at his wife. You could take the girl out of the library, when she was too sick to work, but you could never take the librarian out of the girl.

"Stop teasing me. I'm sick and it's all your fault." She rubbed her hands over her belly. There wasn't much of a bump yet, but she was showing quicker than she had with the other two. Still took his breath away to see her full of his baby.

He wrapped her up in his arms. Her breasts were swollen twice their normal size and tender. He debated asking her to stay home with him tonight. No reason the boys couldn't still go on to Uncle Ev's so he could have a whole evening alone with her. "I'm sorry you're sick, but I'm not a bit sorry you've got another one of my babies in there." He stepped back and placed his hand on top of hers.

"I looked up the Holders in Oklahoma," she continued on.

"Do we have to talk about it all right now? Let's let it ride and see what happens. Come take a shower with me."

"Brock, he's your brother...maybe." She whispered the words so the boys didn't hear her. "I have no idea how you're handling this so well."

"After finding out what Mick did to Natalie, I couldn't learn anything about him that would shock me. Colton wants to get to know me. I'd really like to know him, too. I kinda always wished I had a brother." He shrugged. "And now I know where my dad was going those few blessed weeks he'd leave town every year. I shoulda known there was some reason he was interested in checking our wheatgrass land down there so often. Mick never wanted to work."

"Are you going to call your mom and ask if she knew?"

"Hell no. She divorced him years ago. Why bother her with that information now? He hurt her enough for a lifetime already. Colton will hang out up here long enough to get to know us and hopefully we'll keep in touch after he leaves, but it's got nothing to do with her. I don't want anyone to know just yet."

"I know, but...it's...strange. There a tons of Holders in Holder County, Oklahoma. I mean dozens and dozens of them. Huge family but not one mention of a Colton *Holder* at all."

"And what about Colton Camden because I know you looked that up, too?"

She nodded. "I found a few newspaper mentions of him being arrested for fighting. I even saw one of his mug shots. It's definitely him. What if he's more like Mick than you think he is? What if it's not safe to have him here?"

"I have no plans to leave him unattended for any lengthy period of time, but he's a good guy. I can tell. Look at how good he's been to Miss Pearl's niece. Not a lot of men who'd take on all that."

"Yeah, but did you see his cheek and his knuckles? He's been fighting since he got here."

"Hope, please, I want to see where he plans to take this. Let's just give him another day or two before we confront him. He's been nothing but polite with you and he took excellent care of the little guy he had over here today. My dad never cared that much about me. That kid is Avery's little brother and he took care of him like he was his own. Give him a chance."

"He *was* really sweet and Jaxon absolutely adores him. He talked about Colton all morning. But if he's so nice why won't he come out and tell you why he's here?"

"I keep trying to put myself in his boots. What would I do if Mick had told me about him instead of the opposite? I have you and the boys and an entire ranch to take care of, so I couldn't exactly show up in Oklahoma and spend a week or two trying to get to know him, but I think I would have wanted to. It's a heck of a thing to drop on a guy. I can tell there's a thousand things going on in his head...things he wants to ask me but doesn't know how. I have to go with my gut and my gut says to give him some time to get comfortable with me. Let him tell me at his own pace. My whole life, I've been judged for things Mick did. I won't do that to him, not yet. Not until he proves otherwise."

Hope's sweet grin said she'd go along. "You sure you're not just stringing him along because you need a good hand?"

Chuckling at that, Brock plucked an apple out of a bowl she had set on the counter. "That too. He's a Camden. Gotta be a good cattle rancher, right?"

"Have you talked to Uncle Ev about him yet?"

"Not yet. I figure I'll get Colton to hang out with all of us tonight at the concert. One quick way to figure out how much like Mick he might be is to see how much he drinks. I want to know that before we push this any further."

"Did you see how guilty he looked when you handed him that check? I almost felt sorry for him."

"Me too. I wish he'd fess up. I hate he's stewing on this so much. It's not his fault. It's Mick's. 'Sides, it'd be nice to have someone to talk to about all of the shit *our* dad has put this family through."

"You can always talk to me."

"I know, baby, but you didn't live it. Maybe he did."

CHAPTER TWENTY-THREE

Avery slid the super cute boot cuffs she'd purchased in her former life up her favorite pair of black leggings. As she shimmied into the loose purple ruffled top she'd packed away, certain she'd never have occasion to wear it again, a full-force grin formed on her features. Something akin to a springtime warmth eased the chill she'd become so accustomed to feeling.

The sensation was still somewhat foreign. The way it seemed to permeate her body pinked her cheeks. The low-cut collar of the shirt teased at her cleavage and the long top skirted low on her thighs. Well aware that her grin belonged to the man in the cabin next door getting ready, she tried to formulate some scenario where he could tell the Camdens who he was and still be able to stay in Nebraska. Once again, she came up empty.

It had been so long since she'd gotten ready for a date she'd almost forgotten how. The entire night was surreal. How had her life changed so much in just a few days? The custody fight ahead of her, paying for Aunt Pearl's medicines, all of the complications that demanded her attention, seemed to hover just out of reach that night.

They were in Lincoln or at the very minimum several hundred fence posts away on Camden Ranch. If she were being completely honest with herself, she would admit that it was the fierce might and steady determination of Colt that kept them at bay. He'd called his cousin Meridian about the custody case. She was looking into everything. All there was to do for the moment was to wait.

"You look so pretty, little one," Aunt Pearl said as she whisked into the room. The warm glow in her cheeks helped ease Avery's mind further. She gently untangled a curl in the back of Avery's hair. Whenever she did something like that, gave her some calm maternal touch, Avery felt like her mother was just a little closer.

"Thanks. You sure you're up to me going out tonight? I feel bad. This is two nights in a row I'm leaving you."

"You act like I haven't lived alone for years. I'll be fine. You're leaving me with two strong boys and my best friend, who looks after me almost as well as my favorite niece."

"I'm your only niece, Aunt Pearl, and I'm not sure Jax qualifies as a person who can look after you."

Pearl's mischievous giggle seemed to melt a little more of the snow outside. "I was aware of both of those things. But if any of those villains attack my trailer, I'll bet you little Jaxon will be on it with his shield that used to be one of my better serving trays. I want you to go out and have fun tonight, Avie. Leave all your worries here. Trust me, they'll be ready for you when you wake up in the morning. Nothing can be done about any of them tonight so you go out and enjoy yourself."

"You and Daddy are the only people who still call me Avie."

"Well, maybe we don't want you to forget your whole life before your mother passed away."

"I don't have time to think about any of that. It feels like a lifetime ago. That's where it has to stay."

"Oh my dear child, you listen to your Aunt Pearl. Every moment of your past is the foundation for your future. You don't have time to *forget* that. Besides, Elaine wouldn't want you to forget all she taught you."

"I wish she'd taught me how to deal with everything going on."

"Honey, no one can teach you exactly how to handle life because no two lives are ever the same. I can tell you this though, you're not going to do everything right. It's all part of the dance, my little ballerina.

There are a few missteps, a lot of practice, endless work. It always broke my heart that you approached your dancing like all of the hard work you put into it was for those three minutes on stage.

"That isn't the way life really works. Without all of those hours at the barre, you couldn't have performed onstage. All that practice meant something more. All any of us can really hope for is that we get to smile more often than we frown. Life isn't about those moments when the spotlight is on us, sweetheart. It's about all of the moments leading up to it. You put in all of the effort to make the life you want, you make adjustments when it doesn't go quite the way you hoped, and then you smile because you gave it your all and you know deep in here —" she touched Avery's chest, "—that you did your very best even if you never got to stand in the spotlight."

Something fissured inside Avery. She needed help, not just from Colt but from someone who missed her mother as much as she did. "Can I tell you a big secret, Aunt Pearl? I need you to help me help Colt, but you can't tell anyone what I'm about to tell you."

"Is Colt in trouble, Avie?"

"No. It's not like that."

"You can tell me anything, just like when you were a little girl." Pearl took a seat on Avery's bed and patted the spot beside her.

"You mean after Mama finally got over herself and started to bring me up here." Avery settled beside her, grabbing an old throw pillow and placing it in her lap.

"All a part of the dance. None of us manage life perfectly."

"Holder isn't Colt's last name."

"I take it that's of great significance."

"Yes. Because his real last name is Camden." She half loathed the name, certain it contained spikes that would prick her tongue if she spoke it too loudly.

Her aunt nodded.

"He's here to tell Brock Camden that they're brothers and their father has passed away."

"Mick Camden was an awful, spiteful, evil man, Avery. You need to understand that."

"I do. I mean he hasn't told me much about him, but Colt hates him so much I know he must have been a terrible person."

"Why do you think Colt hasn't told Brock who he is yet?"

"I asked him not to. It was such a stupid, selfish thing to do, but I know how badly he wants to get to know Brock and the Camden family. He's helping me so much. I wanted to do something for him." She shrugged. "I wanted him to have a chance to know his father's family before he has to tell them that Mick died and he's his illegitimate son."

"That isn't selfish at all."

"I know, but that wasn't the only reason I did it. I asked him to wait because I can't bear to think about him leaving me here and going back to Oklahoma. Once he tells the Camdens everything, there will be no real reason for him to stay in Nebraska."

"Do you not believe you're reason enough? I've seen the way he looks at you, just the way your Uncle Les used to look at me."

"We've known each other less than a week. He has all of that land and family down there. They own one of the largest ranches in Oklahoma. They own an entire county for that matter. Life is so much easier there."

"Life isn't easy anywhere. I know this isn't what you want to hear, but you're going to have to go back to that barre, baby girl. Go back and work and fight for what you want. If that's Colt and he needs you to help him figure out life with or without the Camden family, then you help him do that. You're going to have to really watch and pray so you know which steps to make. Listen for the music. It'll be there guiding you on. The Camdens are good people and I know you don't even want there to be a possibility that he might go back to that big county in Oklahoma, but he needs to be honest with them."

"I know. He hates that he's lying to them."

"Now, let me tell you something, Avie. Your man looks a great deal like his father. He's nothing like Mick at all, but he and Brock favor each other so much that I guessed this secret as soon as he said he was trying to get work at Camden Ranch.

"I've been running the beauty shop in a small town for more than half of my life. I know things. And I can tell you this, too. Mick Camden made a showing out here several weeks ago. Things didn't go well, from what I heard. I'll bet Brock is at the very least suspicious. The time will present itself when he needs to tell them who he is. You're going to have to help him make the leap."

"How do I know when?" Avery worried her lip with her teeth and kept her eyes trained on the lacey pillow, afraid of what her aunt would say.

"How did you know when to leap on all those stages?"

Avery lifted her head and let her mind travel backward in time to her performances. "The tempo of the music changes. You feel the momentum. You can feel it in your stomach. You push from plié. Split quick and hard. Deep breath. Stretch high and leap. Trust that you're strong enough to keep from collapsing. It's all about the timing," Avery concluded.

Pearl nodded. "You feel it in your belly and you push when you need to. Take a deep breath and trust that he's not going to let the two of you collapse no matter which family he thinks of as his. And yes, dear one, it is all about the timing. Did you ever think maybe it's you he'd like to belong to instead of either the Camdens or the Holders?"

"That seems like an impossible thing to wish for in such a short amount of time." Avery hated how often she had to remind herself that she was the adult now. She couldn't only be an employee or a big sister. She now needed to become the shop owner and the stand-in mother.

"I knew your Uncle Lester one day and then spent a magical night in a hotel room with him. Mmm, never forget that."

Avery wrinkled her nose but bit her lips together to keep from taking away from her aunt's fond memory.

"I moved up here with him the next weekend. That's part of why your mama was so up in arms." Pearl chuckled.

"And you never regretted it? Even when you had to sell off the land? Even when times were hard?"

"Never for one moment. Good times, hard times, didn't matter. There was no one else on earth I wanted to go through any kind of times with."

"Thanks, Aunt Pearl." Avery threw her arms around her aunt, knocking her wig askew. "Oh, I'm sorry." She immediately righted it.

"A hug from my girl was more than worth it. Now, go have a good time with your cowboy. Tonight isn't for confessions. Tonight is for the two of you."

———

Colt eyed Chase cautiously. Dude was twitchy as a horse's tail surrounded by flies. He pulled back the curtains and checked the yard for the fourth time. "What time did you tell her to be here?"

The sheer panic that flashed in the kid's eye said Colt's guess was spot on. "Did you read my texts or something? You're taking this whole being my stand-in dad thing a little far. Avery likes you. You don't have to use me to get to her."

"I'm not using you to get anything and I didn't read your texts. You remind me a lot of myself at sixteen. I'm guessing you told her to come over and *help you babysit*." He made liberal use of finger quotes. "I'm just curious what time you told her we'd leave."

"You said you were leaving at 6:30, so I told her to be here by 6:45."

"See, that was your mistake. Women are never ready on time. I was betting on another fifteen minutes, but then I saw your aunt go into Avery's room. Once you factor more women into the equation, the time expands exponentially. Look, there's a math lesson for you, too."

"I suck at math."

"I wasn't too bad at it. If you need help, give me a shot."

"Can't you tell Avery to hurry or whatever? I don't want her giving Kami the third degree." He sank down on the sofa beside Colt.

"What makes you think either one of us will be okay with you having her here while we're gone?"

"You really don't seem to get this whole you're-not-my-dad thing."

"Speaking of me not being your dad, can I give you a little advice as a friend?"

"Even if I say no, you're going to, so go on with it," Chase huffed.

The boy was catching on. "Seeing as how you're sharing a bathroom with your aunt and your sister, maybe try not to be in there quite so much." He pretended not to notice the heat scalding Chase's features. "I'm sure sharing a bedroom with a four-year-old is a pain."

"You have no idea." If Chase had rolled his eyes any harder, they would've lodged in his skull. Colt felt genuinely sorry for him.

"For tonight, keep in mind that you're supposed to be helping your aunt and keeping up with Jaxon," Colt reminded him.

"Kami likes little kids. She wants to be a preschool teacher."

"Ah, so Jax is your bait."

Chase offered him another one of those eye rolls that revealed the whites of his eyes. "She's not a fish."

"Maybe not, but she's sure as hell got you all kinds of tangled up."

"Aunt Pearl and Sally will be here. We're not going to do anything but hang out."

"You still have to ask Avery for permission. That's another thing about being sixteen. You're so damn sure you can run your life just fine without any interference from anyone else. But a whole bunch of people a lot smarter than you or me figured out that when sixteen-year-olds are allowed to run their own lives, more times than not they steer right into a ditch."

A knock sounded on the front door. "Guess I'll be asking for forgiveness not permission." Chase sounded far too pleased with himself.

"Or your sister's gonna come out of that room and the situation is gonna blow up in your face right in front of Princess Kami."

Avery followed Pearl into the room. Colt stood. "Damn, baby, you look incredible."

The lamplight shimmered in her eyes. Delight curved the corners of her mouth, only making her more beautiful. "Thanks. Who's at the door?"

"Chase invited a friend over."

"A friend? You're supposed to babysit Jax." Avery jerked the door open. But it wasn't Kami standing on the porch. It was Jessie Camden. Colt's stomach bottomed out somewhere in the vicinity of his boots.

"Mrs. Camden..." Avery gasped. She spun to send Colt a frantic look.

He stood but had no idea what to say. Jessie grinned at them both. "I just wanted to drop a big pot of my vegetable soup and some bread by. I knew you and Colton were heading out tonight, Avery, and I've been meaning to get a pot of this out here. Thought I'd stop by and let the grandkids drive Ev nuts for a while, and that way you have dinner ready."

"Oh, goodness." Avery accepted the pot. "You didn't have to do this. Thank you so much. Come on in."

"Pearl, how are you feeling, honey?" Jessie's grin was kind but she kept an eye on Colt.

"I'm fair to partly cloudy most of the time. Have you met Avery's boyfriend, Colton?"

Jessie never faltered. "I have. He's working for my nephew. Brock's so pleased to have a hand that knows Herefords from heifers he can't see straight. Seems ranching is in Colton's *blood*."

Ranching might've been in his blood but the comment had ripped the air from his lungs. He attempted to smile but was certain he came up short.

"I keep telling Avery, Colt will find his way around Camden Ranch," Pearl stated knowingly. Avery clung to Colt's arm. It certainly seemed most everyone knew and yet, the dance went on.

"We're pleased he's there. You know I think of everyone on my ranch as family," Jessie commented.

"I do know that," Pearl agreed like she was reading lines from a script. Colt's stomach churned.

"But I'm also mighty protective of my brood."

Avery's eyes closed. The veiled threat hung in the heated air surrounding them. Before Pearl could respond, there was another knock at the door.

Jessie smiled. "I need to get. Got a house full of grandkids, like I said. Pearl, honey, you know if you need anything at all I'm just a few fence posts away. You give me a call and either me or Ev or one of the kids will be right over." She squeezed Colt's bicep as she walked by. "You know, family is a lot like my vegetable soup. Every ingredient makes the others a little better but it does always take time to simmer. See you all later."

Jessie waved as she headed out the door and Kami ducked inside. Avery stalked to the kitchen, set the soup on the stove, and then let her head fall into her hands.

"She knows," Avery mouthed when Colt wrapped her up in his arms.

"I think she knew from the get go. Brock's suspicious, too."

"What does that mean for...us?" She choked on the two letter word that meant the world to him.

Colt assured himself yet again that if he was doing this for her, he wasn't a coward. "Nothing."

She lifted her head. Those crystal-blue eyes reflected his own terror back to him. "I need to know what happens when you tell them. I need to know when you're going to tell them. I can't... I don't know how..." She shook her head. "I don't know how to help you if I don't know when you have to tell them."

"Hey," Colt delicately cradled her face in his hands. He'd never let her down. He'd never walk away. "I'll figure something out."

"I used to say that all the time, too. I believe it was you who told me that sometimes we can't figure it out."

"That ain't at all what I said. I told you that sometimes every one of us needs some help. Together we will figure this out. And the custody thing and the medicine and the will and anything else this world has dished up lately. Together, Avery. Me and you. *We* will figure it out. Now, tonight, for me, let this all go. The Camdens seem willing to let me go on keeping this from them so let's take them up on their offer. It's like I told you, there's nothing wrong with jumping on opportunity when it saddles up and giving it a ride. Tonight, I'm taking you out and we're gonna have a good time. I'll deal with tomorrow, tomorrow."

"I'll try." Her voice faltered.

Colt drew her back to his chest. "Together, baby. We can do this together. Now, let's go harass Chase about inviting girls over without your permission."

That earned him a timid grin. "I can probably do that."

When they arrived back in the living room, Avery's gaze shot from Kami to Chase and back again. When it returned to Kami, it immediately zoomed in on the matching hickey on her neck, which she'd made precious little effort to cover.

Colt chuckled under his breath.

"Uh, hi, I'm Avery. Chase's big sister. And you are?"

"I'm...Kami, Chase's girlfriend."

"I see. It's funny Chase hasn't mentioned you to me at all. In fact, it seems he completely forgot to mention that you were coming over tonight."

Chase shot Colt a pleading look. Colt mouthed the word, "Boom."

Kami preened like a peacock in a beauty pageant. "I was just going to help Chase look after his sweet baby brother. I'm excellent with children. I babysit every weekend. I have tons of experience. I could probably even teach you a few things. Someday, I'm going to be an amazing mother."

"Yes, well, let's just make certain *someday* is a very, very long time away," Avery ground out. She paced to Chase, jerked him into the hallway, and got in his face even though he was an inch or two taller. "She can stay as long as you two remain in the living room with Pearl and Sally. And so help me if either of you have more of these—" she jerked the collar of his shirt away from his neck and drove her fingernail into the purple skin, "—when I get home, I will show her every single picture in your baby book, the home movies mom made of you doing the potty dance, and I'll tell her all about how you used to have a penchant for putting rocks up your nose."

Colt choked back laughter. Chase looked ready to maim.

"That's probably sufficient." Colt eased Avery away from her brother. "See, your sister doesn't take a lot of shit offa anyone. If I were you, I'd keep that in mind."

"Yeah, I know."

Avery whirled back around before Colt could put her in the new coat he'd purchased that afternoon. "And play whatever Jaxon wants to play even if he wants you to pretend to be Red Skull. Got it?"

"Yeah, fine."

Kami laughed as she bustled over to Chase and laced her fingers through his. She stared up at him like he was the King of Cowboys. "I really like those boots, Chasey."

"Chasey?" Avery sputtered through laughter.

"Bye, Avie," Chase taunted.

"We're leaving." Colt accepted another hug from Jax, who'd been wishing him goodbye for the last half hour, and finally got Avery in the coat.

"It's so warm. Thank you so much."

"I told you keeping you warm was my job. Now let's go before Chase's face actually catches fire and he melts through the sofa."

She was still worrying that lip. Colt knew Jessie's appearance had done nothing to soothe her nerves. The thing was he couldn't quite tell if Jessie had meant her visit to reassure him or to scare him away.

"Who used to call you Avie?" he asked as he cranked his truck and let it warm.

"Chase was being a twit. My dad still calls me that, but it doesn't bother me."

"I'm just glad it wasn't some other guy I was gonna have to hunt down and string up."

She gave him that mischievous grin that could unlock the gates of heaven or send a man straight to hell for the sinful thoughts it gave him. "So possessive," she teased.

"Guilty as charged, but darlin', I know you like it."

"I do. I shouldn't, but I do."

"Why the hell shouldn't you? You have all these damned rules in that head of yours. So many of 'em they make me dizzy. Why can't you let yourself like what you like?"

"I'm supposed to be more evolved than that."

Colt snorted. "Nothing wrong with liking the fact that I'd beat the piss out of any man who so much as let his eyes slip below your face."

Though she was visibly trying to be in that moment with him, she couldn't do it. "Do you think whatever was in that certified letter is how they found out?"

"I have no idea, honey. I'm more than curious, believe me. Also wonder how much of the story they actually know. Did they just figure out I'm Mick's kid or do they know he ain't with us anymore?"

She fidgeted constantly with the long ruffled hem on her blouse. Colt deeply appreciated the low V-cut of the neckline and the fact that he could get his hands up that loose top without anyone being the wiser. "So, you don't think they know about all of the stuff in his will?"

"If Brock knew someone had given away half of his land, he'd have plenty to say about it. There wouldn't be any of this letting me be until I want to talk, which seems to be the way he's handling everything. To a cattle rancher, the land is everything. It's where you come from and where you go back to. I figure that's why Mick wants to be buried over there. It's more than what we do. Not to sound too clichéd but it's who we are. It may just be dirt to some, but to a rancher it's his blood."

"So, that's why the Holders are so protective of the county lines then? I remember when your uncles got into it with Charett County when they wanted to redraw the lines last year."

"Hell yeah, that's why we were up in arms over it. That and the fact that they were trying to make an illegal eminent domain claim that was a bunch of horse shit. It's Holder land above all other. Since my great-great-great-great-great-granddaddy set his flag down on it, that's been Holder land and it'll keep right on being Holder land as long as any of us are alive to see to it. I'd bet you a dozen Benjamins the Camdens feel the same way about Camden land."

"I've never had a dozen Benjamins to bet on anything." She tried for a joke.

"The money's another way I know Brock doesn't have a clue his land is mine for the time being. A cattle rancher's land *is* his security. Cattle market is a fickle bitch. Only two things a rancher ever wants is a warm, willing woman in their bed and to own the ranch next door."

"There are a lot of cars here." She changed the subject so quickly, when he pulled into Saddleback's parking lot, he was shocked there wasn't an audible record scratch.

"Guess whoever the Original Sinners are they put on a good show." He shrugged.

"You're kind of distantly related to the lead singer."

"Yeah, I gathered that when Brock mentioned the only reason they're coming tonight was because of Dec, whoever he is."

"Declan St. James is Holly Camden's husband, which actually makes her Holly St. James, but he's still part of your extended family."

"Don't really care about any of my relations tonight, baby. Only person I want to pay any attention to is you. You look good enough to eat. Plan to do just that once I get you in bed after this shindig."

CHAPTER TWENTY-FOUR

Colt escorted Avery into a wall of people. "Wow," she gasped.

"Shit," he spat. Brock had the right idea about staying home. Sardine real estate offered more room than the packed honkytonk.

"Not a fan of crowds I take it?" She scooted closer to get around three cowboys clogging the doorway.

"I'm a cattle rancher. I like wide open spaces and neighbors I only have to see in town."

A waving hand caught his attention. Brock was standing at a table. He pointed to two available seats.

Avery drew an audible breath. "Guess we're sitting with them. I hope I don't slip and say something stupid."

"I've got you, baby." He shot her a wicked look as he guided her toward the designated Camden table. "If I have to, I'll slip my tongue in your mouth to hush you up."

"Very funny."

"You rather I slip something else in there?"

"Would you behave?" she scolded.

Laughing at that, he shook his head. "Not in this lifetime or the next, so you need to go on and get that thought right on out of your head." He pulled out her chair. "Uh, Avery, I know you've met some of them, but just in case, this is Brock and Hope. You already know Grant. This is Luke, Austin, and I'm afraid I'm out of names."

Grant smiled. "This is my wife, Katy. That's Luke's wife, Indie, and that's Austin's wife, Summer. And this is our baby sister, Holly." With each introduction, he pointed around the table.

"How's your aunt, Avery?" Hope leapt in as soon as Colt took the seat beside Avery.

"She's been really good the past two days. I think she must've missed Sally. She has another treatment next Tuesday. I just keep praying they're working."

A man dressed in an apron appeared beside the table, holding a sloshing pitcher of beer. "Bring a pitcher for the table, Ed. All of the Camden girls are drinking water this evening," Brock requested.

"What do you want, baby doll?" Colt whispered in Avery's ear, remembering the promise that they wouldn't drink in case Pearl needed their help later.

"Just a club soda."

"We'll take a club soda and a Dr. Pepper. Be happy if you kept 'em full," Colt added to the order. For some strange reason his brother looked oddly pleased at that.

"This is a bar. I make money on liquor. You sure you don't want nothing *in* that soda?" The bartender, on the other hand, was highly offended.

"Ice."

A few of the Camden boys chuckled as the bartender angrily carved the drink order in a notepad and grumbled about wishing he could charge for ice. "What about to eat?"

"Camden Ranch provides all of the beef here, so it's all good," Grant explained. "Baby has a hankering for a rib-eye, Ed." He rubbed his wife's rather round belly. "I'll take one, too, rare."

Colt couldn't help but smirk at Avery as the rest of the Camdens ordered burgers and steaks. She glanced over the five items available on the menu, all beef.

"You are in cattle country, sugar," he whispered.

"Yeah, I know, and ever since I had that stupid hot dog all I can think about is meat." Before Colt could open his mouth, she had a finger in his face. "Do not make some kind of lewd joke."

Brock, who was seated on the other side of Colt, laughed. "You did set him up beautifully."

"She keeps doing that and then gets mad when I take her up on it."

"What can I get you two?" Ed asked.

"I'll have some of whatever he gets," Avery explained.

Colt rolled his eyes. "What is it with you and my food? We'll both take a filet. Do hers medium well. I'd prefer mine still mooing. Baked potato, load 'em up with the whole deal. Oh and make sure hers has plenty of bacon."

Avery stuck her tongue out at him. With the quick cock of his eyebrow, he didn't even have to say anything that time. She blushed all on her own.

A dude dressed in black leather pants made his way to the table.

"Oh, hey, baby." Holly beamed. "There's four counties worth of people here."

"Pretty sure they're just here to see you, love." He winked at her. Colt rolled his eyes. The guy had a British accent and he was a little too smooth. Avery elbowed him. "You staying out here, or do you want to sit on stage with me?"

"I'll stay out here. Oh, hey, this is Avery and Colton. Avery's who fixed my hair."

Declan St. James shook Colt and Avery's hands. "I owe you a debt of gratitude. Dear God, I've never seen anything that color. She spent half the night either crying or yelling at me."

Avery laughed. "I do what I can."

"You do it well. Any requests we can play for the two of you?"

"Really? You're taking requests?" Avery seemed thrilled.

"Sure. Why not." Dec grinned at her.

"I'm a huge Garth fan."

"Damn perfect woman." Colt brushed a kiss on her cheek. "I was scared for a minute you were gonna ask for something like Enya."

"I grew up in Oklahoma. Obviously, I love Garth Brooks."

"I didn't know you were from Oklahoma. Did you know Colton before you moved up here?" Hope asked.

"I know some of his cousins, but we actually met here at this bar."

"I will see if I can work in some of Mr. Brooks's greatest hits. Anything else?" Dec asked again.

"Anything she wants to dance to, I'm game," Colt vowed. All of the women at the table swooned and Avery painted a tender kiss on his jawline. *Take that, leather-pants.*

"I will see if I can't keep you two on the dance floor." Dec took his wife's hand and tugged. "Come back with me for a few minutes. I miss you." Holly followed after him.

Conversation lulled into awkward silence as the drinks were passed around the table. Colt didn't seem to be the only one guarding his words. Tension laced itself into a tight knot in his gut. The letter, the check from his brother, Jessie's appearance, every realization the Camdens had made shortened his time with Avery. He had to figure out a way to stay with her.

"So, Indie, you thinking it's gonna be twins again?" Austin asked his sister-in-law.

"Luke and I made a deal," she stated pointedly.

"Do we have to talk about that right now? It's not twins. I can tell," Luke huffed.

"You cannot tell. And I'm holding you to our deal, Luke Camden."

"I'm fine with it, but I don't want to listen to their shit talk." Luke gestured to his brothers.

"What was the deal?" Grant asked.

"If it's another set of twins, he gets a vasectomy."

Colt tried to hide his cringe. He knew there was nothing wrong with getting one. It just made him squeamish to think about someone with a sharp blade down there. Luke's brothers and cousin had a similar reaction.

"I used to think I would love to have twins before I started taking care of my brothers full-time. Now, half of my daydreams are about hiring a nanny," Avery admitted.

"Oh honey, believe me, we all have thoughts like that." Summer reached out and squeezed her hand. "But then they come out of you these tiny little balls of soft, sweet cuteness and they cuddle up to you and you sign on to do it again. It's insanity, but I want another one after this one."

Austin waggled his eyebrows. "Sign me up, baby. I'm always in the mood for making babies."

"Oh yeah, like I was worried you wouldn't be up for it." Summer rolled her eyes and the table erupted in laughter.

"Hey, I do what I can, too." Austin stuck the tip of his tongue between his teeth and laughed.

"You want any kids, man?" Brock asked Colt.

Since he'd spent the better part of the last few minutes wondering how in God's name he was in the middle of a conversation about having babies, it took him a second to formulate an answer. "Never really gave it much thought." What the hell was she doing to him? Suddenly, an idea sprang to his mind, a way to reassure Avery, which was his only goal that evening. "If she wants 'em, I'm game."

Holy fuck, what had he just said? Avery stared up at him like he'd sprouted another head. For a moment he wondered if he had. He did seem to be having an out-of-body experience. Cold sweat dewed on his neck and his heart detached itself from his chest and found a new home in his throat.

The good Lord took pity on him. His steak was placed before him. Shoving food in his mouth was a sure way to keep from rattling off other nonsensical shit about investment plans or retirement or something.

"You've actually thought about us having kids?" Avery whispered. Every eye at the table was on him, so her whisper hadn't been quiet enough to keep her words from them. Brock leaned in a little closer.

Shit. "Yeah, I guess." He inhaled a bite of steak he'd torn away from the whole.

Her mouth hung open for far too long. Eventually, he cut another piece of his steak and offered it to her on a fork. Her acceptance of it stirred his blood, freeing him of a little of the panic centered between his shoulder blades. "Now chew, baby doll." Again, she complied. Damn, but his cock liked that. No one had ever affected him the way she did.

Maybe having babies wasn't a terrible idea. The thought had always terrified him before...made him think of his own father and mother and all of the ways they'd managed to screw him over. And yet, much to his shock, the thought of Avery swollen full of his baby did mighty things to him. Of all of the emotions it stirred, fear wasn't one of them.

As everyone was finishing their supper, Dec's band took the stage. They opened with some old school John Michael Montgomery.

A tender grin spread across Avery's beautiful face. The lights in the bar lowered. The spotlight glinted off of her hair, casting a halo on his angel. Her bottom lip slipped through her teeth. Hope glimmered in her eyes. If his baby wanted to dance, all she had to do was keep looking at him like that. Pleased leather-pants had kept his word on the dancing music, Colt offered his hand to her. "And would my ballerina care to dance?"

"You really don't mind?"

"Dancing with you is the only reason I'm here, sweetness. Now come on." Guiding her through the throngs of cowboys pulling their dates into their arms, he found them a spot as far away from the Camden table as he could get them. As soon as he drew her to his chest, the brittle tension in his bones eased. He clung to his saving grace, reveling in her closeness, in the soft pressure of her face against him, her arms around him. "You okay?" he breathed the question over the shell of her ear. She shivered in his arms, making him ache.

"Are you?"

"I am now."

The music flowed through her curves as they started to sway. He closed his eyes and willed away every other person in that bar. He wanted to get lost in her, to feel her body move with his own. As more and more people joined the dancing crowd, he tucked her tighter to him, keeping the world at bay.

Marriage and babies and his family, they could all just take a fucking number and wait outside. He had everything he'd ever wanted in the world in his arms.

Time itself could wait on him to make certain she understood he wasn't going anywhere without her. She nuzzled her cheek against him. "I've got you, baby," he soothed.

"I know."

———

Avery let the rhythmic drumbeats vibrate under her feet. Colt's warmth and protection surrounded her. If she could've swayed back and forth wrapped up in this sanctuary of muscle for the rest of her life, she would've jumped at the chance. He filled her with a certainty she had no business trusting.

"Lift your head, baby." The silky rasp of his voice liquefied the need in her veins. She did as she was told. "Need a hit of those lips." His hand cradled the back of her neck and angled her face upward until there were only millimeters between their lips. His breath was hot and hungry. She wanted to close the distance, to meld their mouths, but she remained steady, waiting on him to come to her.

"Have no damned idea how I ever thought I'd be able to resist you. You knocked me on my ass as soon as you opened that door." He smirked instead of kissing her. Needy oppression had her so hungry for him she could hardly stand it, she arched even closer. "There's my girl." His lips were on her skin, easing the worst of her desperation as he dragged innocent kisses along her jaw and cheek. Then the warm flesh of his lips skimmed against her own. Every touch of his hands, of his lips, of his cock, took immediate possession of her. Her body became a willing slave to his caresses. This time was no different. The heat between them vanquished the sensuality, turning it into rampant craving. Colt inhaled her.

Her fingers dug into his biceps, clinging to the only solid thing that kept her knees from collapsing. A hungry growl lodged in his throat as his tongue parted her lips, demanding more. His hand slowly climbed under the loose ruffles of her shirt.

"Colt," she breathed his name as his lips trailed to her neck. Whether it was a warning to stop or a plea for more, even she wasn't certain. He gripped her backside, pressing his burgeoning erection into the cradle of her hips. "Yes." She gave herself over to carnal hunger.

"The things you do to me. My God, I burn. I fucking burn for you," he groaned in her ear just before spinning his tongue along her lobe. His hand climbed higher. His lips returned to hers.

She steeped herself in his flavors, the coarse salt from his steak, the sweetened confection of his drink, and there beneath all of it was her Colt, that liquid chaser of pure sin she craved above all else. His fingertips traced along the tops of her leggings.

Every nerve ending in her body honed in on the sensation of his touch on her fevered skin. One singular brain cell tried to force a warning through the haze of lust that had taken over all rational thought. People were going to see them. That particular brain cell joined in the hymn of gratification the rest of her body was already singing when his fingers dipped below the waistband of her leggings and massaged his desires into her pliant skin.

Back and forth, lower with each pass, his fingers became a metronome of need in tune to her rhythms. The band bled seamlessly from John Michael Montgomery to Garth Brooks. It was her favorite song. With another grind of Colt's cock against her, she temporarily forgot the title.

His thumb encountered that spot where her thigh met her mound and she was certain the dance floor beneath her feet had turned to quicksand. Clinging to him was her only hope. "What if...?" the two words were lost in her own moan.

"No one can see us, sugar. We're hidden in plain sight and remember what I told you before—I don't give a fuck who *can* see. Garth ain't the only one who's shameless for his girl."

"Oh...mmm," breathed from her lips to his neck. A low groan of male pleasure vibrated throughout her body.

"You're already dripping for me, aren't you baby?"

She nodded against him. This slick heat gathering in her panties, preparing her for him, the only perceptible feeling besides the rasp of his callused fingers against her skin. "I swear you make me wet every time we kiss." Her trembled whisper elicited a grunt from his lips.

"And what shall I do with my wet, needy girl?"

Lost in the music and the low bass tones of his voice, she couldn't formulate an answer. Anything that involved him owning her thoroughly would do. "Make it better," she begged softly.

"I'm gonna make it feel better, baby, but not yet. Not 'til I'm good and ready. I want you to let it build for me. I want you to ache with it first."

She still had no idea how he managed to read the scripts of all of her darkest fantasies. She occasionally wondered if he was a figment of her imagination, and yet he stood there before her, keeping her pressed tightly to his body as his hand cupped her mound. He blocked them from sight with the broad width of his shoulders and might of his torso.

"Sweet little peach, so juicy for me. I could make you come right now, couldn't I, honey?" His middle finger teased at her clit and a full-body shiver shook through her.

"Please."

"No, sugar. That's only for me. Only I get to see you like that. This is just the appetizer. Soon I'll take you to my bed and ruin you. Make you scream for me. Take everything I want and then take more. All fucking night I'll have you."

"God...yes...mmm..." She breathed the nonsensical pleas against his lips. His fingers continued to taunt the apex of her slit, the teasing touch making her swell and pulse. He wasn't the only one burning. She rocked her hips forward. The fierce rigidity of his cock strummed his fingers deeper. Her moan was entirely too loud given the venue. Thankfully, Dec hit a deep note, his gravelly voice covering her hunger.

Her nipples were tightened pebbles urgently pressing into Colt's chest, begging for his fingers, for his mouth, for attention in any way he agreed to give it.

"Naughty girl," he scolded and moved his hand from her clit to her backside, punishing her for trying to take more. "That what you want, sugar?" He jerked her so close she could feel the denim ridge of his zipper line between her folds.

"Yes," she whimpered.

"You're breaking the rules, sweet baby. Have to come on my fingers before I give you my cock. Your sweet little pussy's too tight for me otherwise."

Her heart beat entirely too fast. A mass of bodies pressed in around them. The air was so hot and thick she couldn't breathe. "Now." Impatience surged through her. They needed to leave. She couldn't stand it. Necessity dictated that he take her now.

"Not yet. My little ballerina's gonna dance all for me. Still not over you up and thinking you could do that for other men."

If that's what he wanted, that's precisely what she would give him. When the music picked up pace and Garth disintegrated into Luke Bryan, she lifted her head and smirked. "You want me to dance for you, cowboy? Watch me."

Spinning around, she pressed her backside to his crotch and ground to the backbeat. Her shoulders flowed with her hips, shaking her tits back and forth.

"Oh hell yeah," slipped between his teeth as he gripped her hips and rocked with her. He wasn't lying. He really could dance. The fast song had most couples fleeing the dance floor. There was more room, so she took it. If he needed his world rocked, she was the woman to do it.

"Hold on tight, cowboy."

He spun her back around, keeping to the beat, his hungry gaze locked on hers. "That won't be a problem." Shock shimmered over her skin when he whirled her around once more, locked his hand to her belly, and continued to rock.

Some dude in a black cowboy hat approached. So lost in the music she'd forgotten their audience, it took her a moment to catch on that he was trying to cut in.

"You can't be that stupid," Colt ground out. "The only thing I'd let go of her for would be to beat you into the ground, fucker."

Avery spun back around and looped her hands around his shoulders. "Deep breath, cowboy. I'm all yours."

"Don't ever forget that."

CHAPTER TWENTY-FIVE

So damned thirsty for his baby he was certain he was going to lose his mind, Colt kept her dancing in his arms. The slower songs seemed to lure more couples on the dance floor, but the way Avery rocked that sweet little body during the fast ones set his predatory ways to full tilt. His need to satisfy her hummed in his blood, drowning out every other thing pressing in around them.

The Camdens were still there, dancing on occasion, enjoying the music, and sometimes singing along. Leather-pants pulled Holly up onto the stage for some Savage Garden song Colt had heard before but didn't really know. The crowd went wild though, and his band carried the song for him while he kissed her for the last half.

At the end of "Free Falling," Avery grabbed his hand and pulled him back toward the table. "I'm thirsty."

"Then let's get you something to drink, sweet thang."

Between the dew gathered on her face from their dancing and the light in her eyes, he swore she glowed like a fallen angel he was meant to catch before she hit the ground. The demons he'd carried for as long as he remembered willingly bowed to her. Damn, but he was done for.

"You all look great out there," Brock complimented.

"Have to keep her dancing or she gets antsy," Colt teased.

"Would you hush?" She downed the rest of her soda water. He handed over his Dr. Pepper, certain that's where she was going next. She giggled and took a few sips.

He lifted his hat, trying to regulate his internal temperature. The lights in the room were turned up higher while the band took a break. Holly hurried away from the table to find her husband, Colt assumed.

"Where did you learn to dance like that, Avery?" Hope asked.

"Oh, I used to dance for the Oklahoma City Ballet Company. I've always loved to dance." Avery shrugged, like her years of practice weren't really worth much. Colt shook his head. If it was the last thing he did, he'd make her see how amazing she was.

The heat was still oppressive as men lined up at the bar to get more drinks for their dates.

"Hey, man, I meant to ask you, who'd you piss off? Somebody got a hold of your face." Brock's question was far too calculated. Colt's gut twisted with a knowledge he wanted to trap away with the might of his fists.

Avery's lip went right back between her teeth. Terror took up residence in her eyes. "Nah, nothing like that. Just a klutz. Opened my truck door into my face."

His brother didn't look like he believed that, but he didn't argue. Clearly, unless someone forced his hand, Brock was going to let him come clean when he was ready. One quick glance at his baby assured him he was far from ready to talk.

"We're going to have to go home before I overheat." Katy picked up Grant's hat and started fanning herself with it. "This baby is like carrying around a furnace."

"Then let's go, peaches. I've been trying to get you home all night."

With a grin that said she was gonna give her husband what he was wanting, Katy shook her head. "I think there's only one more set. I don't want to hurt Dec and Holly's feelings."

"Patience ain't ever been my virtue, Katy-Belle," Grant warned.

"I am aware. But you'll survive another few minutes."

Colt chuckled at the exchange. It sounded like something he would've said.

All of the Camden men had their sleeves rolled up. The heat was relentless and he'd be damned if he was going to return to the dance floor without his hat, so Colt followed suit.

Rolling up his sleeves quickly, he chugged the remaining Dr. Pepper in his glass and appreciated the slap of ice against his whiskers.

A shocked gasp escaped Avery's lips. He set down the glass, prepared to ask her what was wrong, when he saw Brock staring at him, his mouth hanging open as well.

He followed the path of his brother's eyes straight to the cigarette scars on his inner arm—almost exact duplicates of the ones on Brock's arm. Damn near the same locations *and* dimensions. Brands they'd never asked for but had been forced to wear.

"Holy fuck," vaulted from Grant Camden's mouth. Luke's eyes were the size of saucers. Indie's and Summer's mouths hung open as well.

There was far too much certainty in his brother's knowing gaze, like the missing piece of the puzzle had just been snapped into place. Hope's quick breath was tunneled, trapping both him and Brock together in a moment they couldn't escape.

People at nearby tables all witnessed the shock at the Camdens'.

In Colt's peripheral vision, he noted Avery's harsh swallow. Her hands wrapped around his bicep and slid down his arm like she could somehow wash away the marks of Mick Camden. "Uh..." The tremor of her voice vibrated in his soul.

Not yet. He couldn't do this now. Not fucking yet. He needed more time with her.

"We should...go home...and check on...the boys," she pled, the words coming out in small bursts. He couldn't fight his way of this, couldn't pound out his fury with his fists. He could only run from what was inevitably coming. Too many people now held the knowledge he so desperately wanted to keep at bay.

Nodding, he grabbed their coats, laid them over the evidence, forced a half-wave to his family, and rushed her out into the freezing cold.

The thin air stung his lungs. His head spun. He had to get her away. He had to cling so tightly to her he'd have the strength to face them when the time came.

———

The panicked certainty that the entire Camden family now knew beyond a shadow of a doubt beat against Avery's skull. There had been no question in Brock Camden's eyes. She'd known it would happen eventually but hadn't mentally prepared herself for it to be that night.

Her Aunt Pearl's advice echoed in her head. She was supposed to help him know when it was time to tell them. Her world that he'd just begun to stitch back together began to pop. Weary threads unraveled quickly. She didn't care when the right time might be. All she wanted was him with no ending date stamped on their future.

"Say something," Colt demanded as he forced the cold truck engine to get moving before it was ready.

"What happens now?" she asked as he pulled out of the lot.

"He doesn't have enough Mick in him to have called me on it in front of all of them but I'm gonna have to say something soon."

"What does that mean? He doesn't have enough Mick in him?"

"He's got a fuck ton more patience than I ever have."

"Do you think we should go to Camden Ranch? Do you want to get it over with tonight?" The words she'd forced out of her mouth tasted like acid.

"Eventually we will but not tonight. I've been stewing on this for weeks. He can deal with it for one more night. Tonight is for us."

"How soon are you going to leave after you work out everything with the land?"

"Avery, whatever comes next, I have no intention of leaving you."

Intentions were no more tangible than smoke from a fire. Wispy wishes that may or may not waft away. Life never seemed to follow one's intentions, she knew. If only she could erase the last five minutes of their life... undo it all. If only she could fall back in his arms and dance again, free of this debilitating knowledge.

She pled to the universe itself that Brock Camden was as good and sweet as his brother. That he wouldn't hate Colt for lying and wouldn't blame him when he found out what Mick had done with the land. That he would maybe even want his brother to stick around.

The soft rumble of toothpicks rolling in Colt's ashtray brought her back to the present. He tossed one between his teeth. It anchored her to the present, to the realization that while the future was full of unknowns she had this moment, the here and now. It would have to be enough.

"I could keep fucking driving," he spoke around the toothpick. "Not stop 'til we figure out how to make this work."

"I can't run away with you, Colt, as much as I wish I could. Too many people depend on me. I can't abandon them."

A harsh nod was his only response.

Camden Ranch loomed in the distance, far too close. Its expansive fields ready to swallow them whole. There simply weren't enough fence posts between their land and her aunt's to keep them safely away. There wasn't enough time. There would never be enough time.

CHAPTER TWENTY-SIX

Gall thundered in his bloodstream, surging through him with each beat of his heart. Anger, always much too accessible, clawed under his skin. Why did his whole life have to be so damn fucked-up? Forever severed in two pieces that would never fit together. Why couldn't he have the things he knew she needed? Land to give her a home. A house with room for her brothers and any babies she might want. Cattle to raise and sell to put food on the table. Why couldn't he just have her?

He was standing at her door a heartbeat after he parked the truck next to the trailer. Lifting her into his arms, soaking in the comfort of her, he strode toward the trailer that wouldn't be his home for nearly long enough.

"Colt, I have to go check on the boys and Aunt Pearl. Please. I'll come over as soon as I get them all to bed."

Unfit to be around her brothers and her aunt, he begrudgingly carried her to the porch of the other trailer and set her on her feet. "I ain't gonna be able to wait long, Avery. I need you too damn bad."

"I know. I'll be quick."

He stared after her, cursing the cold chafing his skin, as she disappeared back into a life he'd had no business trying to insert himself into. He'd never fit. A man like him could never have a home.

He waited for her in the empty trailer, pacing from the living room down the hall to the bed and back again. Back and forth, up and down, seeing nothing before him until a light shone through his bedroom window.

He watched her silhouetted figure whisk into her room. His own personal North Star. She picked up something and disappeared from the room again. *Come back.* The plea turned to a boulder in his throat, threatening to strangle him.

He worked his jaw to keep from falling on his knees and begging whoever the hell ran this fucked-up world to give him this one thing he needed. His molars ached, but the stabbing pain in his chest muted out any other pain.

Suddenly, she returned to her bedroom. He watched her graceful movements as she lifted a tissue out of a box on her bedside table. She sank down onto her bed. He stared at her, desperate to sear every bit of her into his mind. Her body shivered and she brought the tissue to her eyes.

Clutching his chest, utterly gutted, he watched her cry. No. Not because of him. He wasn't worth this. His self-appointed job had been to keep her from sadness and he'd failed at that like he did at everything else.

Storming out of the back door of the trailer, he moved toward her window. The bedroom portions of the trailers were mirror images. The door from his room led him to a door to hers he'd never noticed before.

He knocked softly. The boys shouldn't know he was there. He had to do right by them for as long as he could. He watched her push something away from the door and throw it open. She fell into his arms, her tears searing his skin as she sought out his lips.

He kissed her with everything he had in him. Stepping inside, he kicked the door shut. Tonight, he decided, he would only give. There would be no taking. He would worship her until the moment the Camden family dragged him from her bed and forced him to confess his sins by the might of their shared family name. A space heater roared in the corner offering them a slight sound barrier.

His hands slipped under that tempting top that displayed his baby in all her beauty. He lifted it over her head, needing to feel her soft skin against him. Needing the reassurance of her.

Her fingers flew through the buttons of his shirt, as if she was thinking the same thought. She jerked it down his arms and he eased his hands away from her waist only long enough to fling it away. Her full breasts were swollen over the satin cups of her bra, her nipples needy for his mouth. Her alabaster skin streaked with pink heat from emotion and a need only he could soothe.

He cupped her breasts, lifting their heft, letting the lace trappings spill through his fingers. Another convulsive breath shook through her. "Let me make it better, baby. Let me have you."

"Don't you think they'll come here? Don't you think they'll say something now? So many people saw."

"No one is going to keep me from you tonight. You hear me? No one."

Her hands splayed over his chest as she rocked forward, her body begging on behalf of her mouth. Lifting her back up into his arms, he carried his sweet baby to the bed, cosseting her softly against her sheets.

He eased the black tights down her legs. His mouth watered as he encountered the wet satin covering her pussy. "So fucking beautiful. So damned perfect." He grunted out his anger that this was temporary, that the world was going to drag them apart.

Tracing his thumb over the satin, he watched her writhe so needy what was left of his heart shattered. How could anyone need him so much? He was nothing. She was everything.

Dispensing with the tights, he lifted her leg and planted a kiss in the arch of her foot before he painted kisses up her calf. A sheen of sweat still clung to her body from their dancing. He wanted to drown in the flavors of her.

Suddenly, she sat up. That determination was back in her eyes. She gripped his belt buckle. "Not yet, baby."

"No. Now. Please, Colt. Let me taste you. I need to know. I want to memorize the way you taste." Her eyes closed. Her tender voice carried the crushed remnants of the good-bye that hung between them, a broken wind chime he wanted to tear from the very earth itself. "Please."

Fucking hell. She was a broken bottle of pure perfection spilling herself willingly out for him. He let her continue. She worked the belt loose and popped the snap of his Wranglers. Her palm and fingers danced over the fabric enclosing his swollen cock. A low grumble vaulted from his mouth. He couldn't wait any longer. There was no time. He could spend every waking moment of the rest of his life in her presence and it would never be enough time.

Jerking the zipper down, his cock swelled to the top of his briefs. She pulled the elastic away and spun her tongue over his head. "Jesus Christ," gasped from him.

The warm wet rasp of her cleaning his need from his head spiked his blood. Pushing his jeans down for her, he threaded his fingers through her hair, watching the black and purple cascade over his hand. "More," he demanded. "Take more."

A low hum of adamant approval vibrated down his shaft. The room spun and he forgot to breathe. He watched her cheeks hollow as she pressed him to her throat. The muscles there contracted against his slit. A low growl of nonsensical curses slipped from his mouth. Breath returned to his lungs only when she retreated.

"I knew you'd taste so good. I knew it." She went back for more. Her lips a harsh pink from the force of her suction. The fingertips of her right hand wrapped around his shaft. The others teased at his sac. His eyes rolled back in his head, insatiable for the tight pressure of her mouth and gentle caresses of her fingers.

"You like my cum, sweet baby? I'm gonna fill your mouth full of it, then I'm gonna do the same thing to your pussy. You're gonna take it all like a good girl. You like to swallow, sugar? It's a damned good thing because I'm about to come right down your throat."

"Yes." She breathed the single word over his cock, releasing him with a brief wet pop before returning to her work.

"So fucking good. My God."

Her focus never wavered. Yet, his vision clouded. Clearly he wasn't alone in his intention to satisfy.

He lost himself in the velvet heat of her mouth, thrusting into her, unable to stop himself. Too damned weak not to take everything she offered.

He forced himself to concentrate on her, not on the overwhelming sensations. Ecstasy danced in her heavy-lidded eyes as she lapped at his cock. It was then he understood. What he wanted to take she needed readily to give. In that moment he knew how to be the man Avery Hale needed him to be.

He'd spent his whole damn life looking for something he was missing—something to fill the hungry void at his center. This was it. They fit together. The two distinctive pieces of himself only fit when she was between them.

"I love you, Avery," spilled from his lips. His body jerked and convulsed as she sucked him harder, inhaling him, healing him, mending their pieces together.

She withdrew, rubbing his crown with her thumb. "I know. I love you, too." On her next suckled draw, he lost it all, filling her mouth with everything he was, everything he might ever be.

Still not enough for her.

So keep trying.

When he was spent, he eased her mouth away and climbed into bed beside her, cradling her in his arms.

"That was a dumbass time to say that, wasn't it? I'm sorry."

She grinned at him, still licking her lips, still driving him wild. "For us, it was the perfect time to say it."

———

That dark heat shadowed his eyes again. Avery welcomed its appearance. She needed both his sides, the light and the dark.

"I'm gonna spend all night making you come, baby. Every possible way I can think of," he warned.

"Good, but we have to be quiet. I don't want to waste one moment we have together."

"I'll be right back." He stood and she wanted to demand that he return.

"Where are you going?"

"I have one condom in my wallet and that ain't gonna be near enough. Tonight you're mine. Any way I want you. As many times as I want you. I'll be right back." The way he covered her in the quilts and sheets, making certain she stayed warm, brought another round of hot emotion to her throat. He sprinted out into the freezing night wearing nothing but his loosened jeans and boots. She hoped the heat that existed between them would keep him warm until he returned.

Anticipation tangled her in knots in the moments they spent apart. He wanted this night to be about them. She wouldn't ruin it by demanding some kind of plan for the next day or the one after that.

Tonight, she'd show him just what he meant to her. Slipping out from her covers, she silently tiptoed to her dresser and dug until she located a short satin nightie, in crystal-blue, complete with a ribbon that tied under her breasts. She'd purchased it two years before. It was almost too small now. Her cleavage was barely contained. Colt Camden would certainly approve.

The ruffled satin skirted her backside, revealing a hint of the globes of her ass. The soft fabric whispered over her skin enlivening every nerve ending and making her breathless.

Raw sexuality and her own femininity coursed through her. Realization of her own power bolstered her courage. All woman. All his. And they could figure out the forever part together, just like he'd said. No matter what it took, no matter how hard she had to fight, they were meant to be together. She would find a way.

"Holy mother of all the saints," growled from him. A slap of freezing cold air pricked at her backside. She spun to face him as he eased the door shut. His long legs ate up the distance between them. "This for me, baby?" The trace of his rough fingertip over the swells of her breasts elicited an earthquake inside her.

She managed a nod.

"So fucking beautiful. My God, I will never deserve you."

"That isn't true, Colt. I ache...my whole body aches for you. Don't you feel it when we're together? Don't you feel how life makes sense...?"

"When I hold you in my arms?" His voice was raw. "I feel it, sweetheart. Believe me, not a damn thing in this world makes a lick of sense unless you're mine. Now come here to me. I have so many plans for you tonight."

His fingers threaded through her hair. He angled her head upward but he paused with mere millimeters between their mouths. She could feel his hot breath tickle her lips.

Her frantic heartbeat timed the seconds. "Kiss me," she whimpered. She needed to erase the turbulent emotions displayed in his eyes.

His lips brushed hers in a quick rush but then he slowed, sweetening the kiss. His right hand clasped her backside, dragging her closer, but he lifted his head. "I intend to take my time with you tonight, beautiful. Savor every soft little moan you give me. Savor every single thing about this. I'm gonna be the lover you need, Avery. I'm gonna take everything I want from you because I finally figured out you need to give it."

"God, yes," she vowed. He understood. The few short days they'd spent together had granted him access to the tender pieces of her soul that she'd kept locked away for so long she barely recognized them.

Her hands skated down his chest, reveling in the masculine hair obscuring the tattoos there. She spun her thumbs over the disks of his nipples. His abs locked tight. A grunt sounded in her ear. Her fingertips traveled farther south until she traced the waistband of his boxers in his still-open jeans.

"Stop, baby." Defiance shot through her bloodstream. What would he do if she refused? She desperately wanted to know. Keeping her eyes locked on his, she dipped her fingers underneath the elastic and teased the head of his cock. The spike of pleasure within her soul was dangerously beautiful. She needed more. She needed to cede her pleasure entirely to him. Her very existence depended on it.

His hand closed around her wrist. Control was locked in every hard line of his body. "I said to stop," was the only warning she received before he turned her, planted her side to his chest, and used his free hand to swat her ass. Once. Twice. Three times. The hot sting rushed wet heat to the lips of her pussy. "Do you need more, or can you be a good girl for me?"

"Oh God," she choked. Her lungs refused her breath. Every nerve ending in her body zinged with the knowledge that he understood. Her pussy throbbed. *I need more.* She craved another sweet shock of bliss from his hands.

"Answer me, Avery."

Riding higher on the love she now understood than on the tangible lust between them, she stared him down with what she hoped was a perfected sex kitten pout. "More," whispered from her.

The clap of his massive hand against her fleshy backside drew a low, hungry moan from her lungs. His strength kept her upright.

"That was four. Count them for me, honey."

Another slap.

"Five," wrenched up from the depths of her soul. "Six. Seven." He stopped.

"That's my sweet, dirty girl. I told you I had no issue paddling my angel." Releasing her wrist, he slipped his hand under the hem of the gown. "Spread your legs. Show me how wet that made you." This time she complied readily. A primitive growl was her reward when he found her tissues drenched. "I'm gonna lick up every drop of your honey from every single fold." His gruff warning sank slowly through her mind. Her eyes closed and she honed in on his two callused fingertips that traced back and forth between her lips but refused to enter her. The rough glide along her most sensitive skin rendered her mindless.

"Now that you're behaving, go sit on the bed and wait for me."

CHAPTER TWENTY-SEVEN

Colt inhaled the breath rapidly expelling from her lungs.

"Go," he commanded and she obeyed. He'd been a fool every single time he'd been with her. Worried his beautiful city girl was just too delicate for his wild Holder cowboy ways. It had all been bullshit. She craved him the very same way he was certain he couldn't go on without her by his side.

Every doubt about who the hell he was disintegrated in the hungry heat in her cool blue eyes. He was hers. That would always be what mattered. And he knew her. Knew what she required to come completely undone. Knew what it did to her when he held her pleasure fully in his hands.

Tomorrow held nothing but unknowns. Tonight, he held her.

Toeing out of his boots, he stepped to the bedside table and gave her a wicked grin. Her eyes goggled. The delicate lace on that nightie that was sin incarnate fluttered with her rapid breaths.

"What's in here, sugar?"

Her teeth sank into her bottom lip. He slid the drawer open, knowing what he'd likely find. He wasn't disappointed. A stack of romance novels, what appeared to be a large vibrator in a black silk bag, a hot pink clit massager, and a bottle of some kind of organic lube.

Grasping the clit massager, since it was out, he stared her down. "When's the last time you used this, baby?" Her eyes closed. "Answer me."

"A few nights ago." Her whispered words were barely audible over the space heater in her room.

"First night I kissed you?" he asked unnecessarily. He already knew.

"Yes."

He set the vibrator on her pillow, shucked his jeans and boxers, and then picked it back up. "Thinking about me while you used it?"

"Yes," rushed from her this time.

"But it just wasn't as good was it, baby? It wasn't as good as my big hard cock filling you to overflowing was it?"

"God, no."

"Left you wanting didn't it?"

She gave him another nod. Her eyes locked on his package. He gave himself a long stroke. Her lips parted in intrigue and a shivered squeak escaped her lips.

"We can't have that." Settling his back against a few pillows he propped against the headboard, he spread his legs and summoned her with his index finger.

She crawled on her hands and knees, sex-kitten style, to him. His cock pulsed its adamant approval. "So fucking sexy, baby doll. Come sit right here."

She settled between his legs. He positioned his cock between the lush cheeks of her ass. "That's it." Her soft succulent curves melded against his hardened chest. Sweeping her hair off of her right shoulder, he brushed one slow kiss and then another up her neck. Her fingers located his thighs. She clung to the tight muscles there as her body trembled from the scrape of his teeth and the prick of his whiskers.

Chill bumps scattered from the thin silk strap of her nightie down her arms. He relinquished the vibrator in exchange for cupping her lace covered tits. She was delectable.

The lace abraded his palms as he pressed it into her pliant flesh. Her nipples obediently throbbed out a plea for more. Her back arched.

She buried her face into the side of his neck, covering her own needy moan.

The firm globes of her ass tightened against the fierce strain of his cock. The blow job had done nothing to ease the sharp need he always had for her.

He swore he would've sold his soul to make this night last for a week. "I love your tits, Avery. My God, honey, they're incredible. So thick and heavy. Do they ache, baby? They needing to be sucked?" Her flesh overflowed his palm. Back and forth, he rolled her nipples between his thumb and fingers. Her breath stuttered and her body writhed against him.

"Yes. Now. Please," she begged. A wave of pure need rolled through her body.

"I have every intention of getting my mouth all over them, sweetheart, but right now I have other plans. Watch me." With dedicated precision, he slowly pulled one end of the ribbon keeping her covered in nothing more than a slip of satin and lace. Centimeter by centimeter he tugged the ribbon loose.

A ragged moan sprang free from her. She was much too loud. He loved the need-you noises she made for him but waking up the whole house wasn't going to work.

He clamped his left hand over her mouth and used his right to finish untying her. "Quiet, sugar."

The garment separated in agonizingly slow increments under the weight of her breasts, catching on her nipples. Her breath hitched from the slight pain.

Colt freed her. He released her mouth and cupped her breasts, reveling in her hot flesh in his hands this time. "I'm going to make it all feel better."

She clamped her legs together and rubbed them back and forth desperate for friction.

"Hurts doesn't it, sugar? So damned needy tonight aren't you? But if you don't stop that, I'm gonna turn you over my knee, remind you who's in charge. Now, be nice and quiet for me."

Grabbing the vibrator with his right hand, he returned his left to her mouth. Switching the toy onto its lowest setting, he drew soft circles with the tip over her mound. Her moan hummed against his hand. Her body writhed like he'd shot her full of pure adrenaline.

"I love you bare for me, baby. Pretty little pussy." He continued to taunt her mound with the toy.

"Please, Colt. Please," made its way past the loose set of his hand to her mouth

"Please what, sugar?"

"I hurt."

He hummed his approval in her ear. "Your greedy little snatch needing to be filled, naughty girl?"

He pulled his hand away from her mouth in time to hear, "Please."

"Not yet, honey. Not 'til I get good and ready." He hinted at the apex of her slit watching her begin to bloom for him. "Feels so good doesn't it? How much can my girl take?" He turned it up to its next setting and slicked the smooth silicone with the dew weeping from her slit.

Keeping her head cradled to his shoulder, he tempted the hood of her clitoris with the vibrator. Her nails dug into his thighs. She whimpered out his name.

Her hips rocked back against him constantly as he slowly pressed the toy closer to where she craved the vibrations. "Use your fingers to hold yourself open for me," he ordered.

Once again, she complied. Her submissive desires couldn't have been any more obvious if she'd inked them onto her skin. Sensuality spilled from her pores. Perfection personified.

When she revealed that slick pink pearl timidly pulsating, he let a low growl of appreciation loose from his lungs. He circled the toy against her until he located the spot that had her digging her heels into the mattress. "It's right there isn't it, sugar? Hurts so good right there."

The vibrator shook against her clit. She shook harder. Her moans were constant now. His body rocked with hers as he thrust against her ass-cheeks. Thoughts of coming all over her backside had him clenching his jaw so tightly his molars ached with the effort of denying himself.

Abandoning her job, she relinquished her slick folds and arched forward.

"Need to come, sweetheart?"

He was certain her tight-lipped moans were meant to be a yes. He watched her nipples tighten and pulse, a harsh pink against her pale skin. Strands of black and purple laid against his chest and tumbled over her shoulders as she swayed with need. The air was thick with the scent of her arousal. The old pillows crushed behind his back as she tensed.

In a fit of wild abandon, "Please. Please let me come," wrenched from her in a throaty plea.

His cock throbbed against her back as he pressed harder still, covering the vibrator and her pussy with his hand. She turned to him and he captured her moans with his mouth. Her body went rigid. Her legs trapped his hand and the toy between them. Their teeth bumped from the franticness of the kiss as she finally broke free on a wail that he swallowed.

Her body continued to jerk and pulse. He switched the toy off and tossed it aside so he could cradle her in his arms. "Most fucking beautiful thing in the whole world watching you come for me."

She chased her breath and buried her face in his neck once again.

"I've got you, baby. I'll always have you." He prayed she understood the vow. No matter what happened with the Camdens, he wasn't walking away. "Just breathe for me."

———

Utterly limp with satisfaction, Avery lolled against Colt's substantial shoulders.

"I've got you," he whispered again. And he did. As many times as she'd fantasized about someone else wielding her vibrator, the reality of it had been unfathomable. He was so in tune with her body she swore they'd made love a thousand times before. It made no sense that they'd only known each other a few days. Her life made no sense without him in it.

Gently, he cradled her in his arms, rose up on his knees, and laid her out before him. The dark hunger was still alight in his eyes. He was insatiable just as he'd warned her he would be. It was yet another thing she loved about him.

No matter how many times he made her climax, she was certain she would always crave the heat and hardness of him plowing into her the same way she would always need the rough scrape of his voice and the warm muscle he enveloped her in so readily.

Her body gave another convulsion as he layered himself over her and plundered her mouth with a hungry kiss.

Lowering his head, he nibbled and licked the underswells of her breasts, once again rendering her breathless.

"Believe my baby said she needed these tended, didn't you, sweetheart?"

She scooped the heft of her own breasts into her hands and offered them to him, a willing sacrifice. "Please."

His stubble scraped against her fevered skin as he spun his tongue around her right nipple and then her left. Back and forth until she was nothing more than a writhing pile of pure desire. His scent clung to the pillows threatening to collapse against her face.

Mercifully, he drew her right nipple into the hot, hungry need of his mouth and sucked with fervor. The ball of tension he'd just released with a toy began to weave itself back together behind her mound. She would never get enough.

Desperate for every inch of his skin to connect with hers she thrust against him. The wiry hair on his thighs taunted her own. The fevered strain of his cock rasped against her tender clit. His sac laid against the slick folds of her pussy. Every pillow of muscle in his abdomen and chest moved against her soft, willing flesh.

Her fingers dove through his hair as he sucked, eager for him to take more of her but she was denied. With a wicked smirk, he scooted down her body. He painted a trail of fire with his tongue over her stomach.

When he spun it in her navel, her breath caught. Chuckling at that, he gripped her thighs and positioned his head between them. "What did I tell you I was going to do when I got you nice and creamy for me?"

She bucked in his face, almost embarrassed at her own insistence that he taste her. Sinking her teeth into her bottom lip she tried to recall the warnings she'd been given. "That you would taste me." He'd said something like that. She was sure.

"Not just taste you, beautiful. Devour every drop of honey from every fold." True to his promise, he licked and suckled the sheen of sweat gathered between her lips and her thighs. Tempting her further, he planted open mouthed kisses on the tender hollows on either side of her mound. When he'd washed her clean from one side, he moved his ministrations to the other.

Her eyes closed. Ecstasy sizzled from the tiny spot where he sucked at her skin outward through her limbs. It came in waves of excruciating pleasure.

When she was certain she would die if he didn't give her what she desperately craved, he slicked his tongue with her cream, delving deep between her lips.

"You taste like heaven," he groaned before going back for more. He crammed his tongue deep within her channel, devouring her. Unable to remain still, her thighs locked against his jaw. The rough stubble of his beard rubbed her raw. He jerked his head away, wiping away the sheen of her moisture with the back of his hand. She bit her lip to stifle a whimper as he rose from the bed. His darkening eyes were almost as arousing as his touch.

Three long strides and he was checking the lock on her bedroom door. Next, he switched on the fan in the bathroom, further muting any sound. Finally, he lifted one of her favorite scarves from the chair in the corner piled with laundry that wouldn't fit in her tiny dresser.

Her heart dislodged from her chest and made a quick leap to her throat. The savage glimmer in his gaze served as a warning. Waves of awareness washed over her, crashing in her belly as he stalked closer. "Do you trust me, baby?"

"Yes," she answered readily. She had no doubts.

"You real sure about that answer?"

"Is that going to be a blindfold or are you tying me up with that?" If he needed proof that she wanted to do more than dip her toes into his preferences, that she wanted to dive in headfirst and bathe in every flavor of his kinks, that she needed to feel the very things she'd only experienced in her darkest dreams, she thought her question might prove that.

He stood over her backlit in the glow of the lamp, all shadows, ridged angles, and might. "Yes or no, Avery." All cowboy.

Tension sizzled from his dark, eager gaze to hers. "I trust you completely."

"Good girl."

Those two words. The things they did to her. The unrestrained need they summoned from the primal depths of her soul. The way they quieted her mind and starved the constant distress she carried until it disintegrated into nothingness. The way they choked out her every insecurity. A gush of wet heat saturated the lips of her pussy.

"Lift your head, baby." He seated himself on the bed beside her. She watched him roll the scarf into a three inch strip of cloth as she complied.

A moment later, he fixed the scarf over her eyes, robbing her of the view of his dangerously handsome physique but granting her the ability to place her own pleasure fully in his hands. She fixed an image of him in her mind and expected him to locate something else to bind her hands.

She should have known he never did what was expected. If he did, he would have gone running as soon as she rattled off every reason they shouldn't be together. Colt Camden was not like any other man. He was more. He was everything.

His rough tipped fingers slipped slowly over her breasts, circling her nipples. She felt them pucker and throb. Her breath tangled in her lungs, preventing her from begging him to soothe their strain.

"Mm, sugar, do you hear that? Do you hear the way your breath changes as soon as I lay my hands on you? Does mighty things to me. Makes me want to fuck you just like this, then turn you over, paddle your ass while I do it again. Fuck you so hard every single member of my family living on that ranch next-door hears you screaming my name."

"Oh God," she whimpered. "Do it. I want it. Please."

"And there's my naughty girl," he leaned and breathed the admonition over her ear. His hot breath ignited her. Her entire body erupted desperate for him to fulfill his threats. "You want that, sweet baby? You want me to fuck you raw. So hard you feel it with every step you manage tomorrow?"

"Please," she begged. Her body writhed. Her head turned right and left, back and forth. The cool pillow caressing her cheeks did nothing to tame the wildfire he continued to kindle. Her knees bent and straightened one after the other, so desperate she couldn't remain still. Her hips rocked against the mattress.

"Done. Take a hold of that headboard, baby, and don't let go until I say."

Wrapping her fingers over the cold wrought iron spindles of her bed, she quelled a moan with a quick, "Yes."

"Yes, what?" he scolded as he drew her right thigh over her left, exposing her ass as he pressed her knee to the mattress taking advantage of her flexibility. His hand rubbed a circle over the tattoo on her backside, a question of consent he pressed to her flesh.

A gasp of realization escaped her lips. "Yes...*please*," she challenged, craving what she knew would follow.

The firm smack of his hand on her backside elicited another desperate moan from her lips. "Yes, what, baby?" He massaged away the sting. The rough glide of his hand over her heated skin, tender from his force made her ragged with need. This time she refused an answer altogether. "You like testing me, sugar? Think I won't follow through?" Another strike. Another eager moan. Then one more before he soothed the skin this time. Fresh arousal wept from her slit.

"Say it for me, honey. So you can sit down tomorrow."

This time the hungry groan lodged in her throat. "Yes, sir," slipped out around her own needy noise.

He eased her right leg back and then spread them wide. She gasped when he dragged his knuckles through the sopping wetness between her thighs. "Do you feel how wet and needy you get for me? It hurts doesn't it, angel?" Two callused fingers stroked over the swollen lips of her pussy. "Hurts right here, all for me doesn't it? I know it burns, honey. Throbs. Aches for me."

She sank her teeth into her lip. Every nerve ending was overly-sensitized, attuned to his touch. She could see nothing. She could feel everything. "Yes, sir," she whimpered.

"I know it's there, sweetheart. I'm gonna draw it out and make it feel better."

"Now," she finally demanded.

A dark chuckle sounded from somewhere nearby but the mattress lifted, no longer constrained by his weight. She heard him rustling to her left. Before she could tell him there were more scarves in her closet, she heard a familiar pop and then another. The soft swish of leather hitting the floor made its way to her ears. Unable to place where she'd heard that sound before, she strained to hear what might be coming next.

Suddenly, soft, silky strips of fabric with distinctive edges fluttered over her naked body. Her eyes widened behind the makeshift blind-fold. Ribbons. Specifically, the ribbons on an old pair of toe shoes he must've found in the corner. Holy fuck.

She wondered if her cowboy intended for this to carry as much weight as it did for her. No longer a slave to toe-shoes. No more hours at the barre. No longer trapped in her former life. He'd broken her bounds, torn the ribbons. She would dance in his arms, only for him. He would set her free and make her fly.

He let the silk glide over her mound. A quick gasp turned to another whimpered moan as he spread her legs again and let the fabric tease at her wetness.

Her pussy clenched, so anxious for his fullness she was half-certain she was going to die.

His knuckles made another exploratory survey of the sticky dew covering her swollen lips. A primal groan brimming with raw male longing came from him. Pleasing him was an aphrodisiac like no other. If her mother knew Avery had discovered this about herself, she would roll over in her grave. And yet, Avery didn't give a damn.

Those rough-skinned fingertips that she swore played her body like a fine instrument trailed down her legs until he caught her ankle.

The ribbon circled once, twice. He wasn't binding her hands. No. He was fastening her legs wide open all for himself. She felt him loosen the ribbon around her ankles and then her heel pressed into the mattress. "If you don't want this, say so." His voice had lost a little of his dominating edge but the need weighed heavily in every word.

"I want this," she vowed. She heard the silk rub against the iron footboard until she was bound.

"Keep your hands on the headboard or I'll tie those, too," he informed her. Again, she complied. Every cell in her body rejoiced at her willingness to allow them what they'd craved for so long.

He made quick work of her other ankle. She tried the ribbons and found herself able to move her legs a few inches but no more.

"Do you have any fucking idea how beautiful you look bound for me, baby?" His hands trailed slow paths up her legs and abdomen. "I could come all over you just looking at those fuck-me thighs spread wide for me."

"You're more than welcome to come all over me, cowboy, but you better *fuck* me first," she demanded.

"And there's my little spitfire. I'll do whatever I please to you *first*, sugar. Never forget who's in charge when I get you like this. And right now, I want those gorgeous tits wrapped around my cock. Then we'll see about me coming all over you."

The mattress on either side of her lowered under his weight. He straddled her midsection. Her back arched in an effort to bring the top of her belly to meet his ass but her movements were halted by the ribbons at her ankles.

"Anxious, honey?"

CHAPTER TWENTY-EIGHT

Colt couldn't believe he had her like this. He'd known this was what she needed. He just couldn't rectify the knowledge that he was lucky enough to be the guy who got to give her this freedom, this space to relinquish her pleasure fully.

Scooting back and leaning down, he traced a slow, torturous circle around her left nipple with his tongue and let his rock-hard cock tease at her pussy.

She tried to rub against him insistently complete with a frustrated gasp of need. "Look at you trying to grind that little pussy on me. What do you need to come around first, sweet baby?"

"Your fingers," she whimpered. "Please, Colt." She dug her heels in literally and managed to rub her swollen mound against him. Victory had her pursing her lips. He knew if he tore off that scarf covering her eyes, he'd be greeted with a smug look that said she'd gotten what she wanted.

"You think you can handle my fat cock right now, sugar. You take it." He thrust hard and fast, filling her to overflowing, owning every tight inch and taking more. He allowed himself one brief moment to experience her walls tightening around him with nothing between them.

"Oh yes!" she gasped before the air ripped from her lungs. She was so wet he knew he wouldn't hurt her and she wanted to play the game.

He jerked back out of her and plunged in again, even faster this time. A strangled moan choked from her.

He pulled away and crawled up her body. "Open your mouth," he demanded.

"Oh, God."

"I didn't tell you to call him yet. Yes sir, and then open your mouth."

"Yes, sir," she obeyed. He slicked her lips with the head of his cock soaked in her own juices.

"Lick," he ordered. Her tongue darted out and danced at his slit. "Good girl. Now suck your sweetness offa me. Lick me like I'm the best damned thing you've ever tasted." Once again, she complied.

"Tastes so good doesn't it, baby? Makes me hungry for your sweet pussy." He eased his length away from her face and slid down her body. "Since I've got you spread so nice and wide for me, think I'll have a taste."

Slowly, he dragged his tongue up her slit and down. Going only millimeters deeper the next time he repeated his motions. Then once more just a little deeper until every breath she managed held a plea for more. "So sweet, but that's all you get 'til you can be a good girl for me."

She protested but he crawled back up her body then drew her ample breasts together, so tight her nipples almost touched. Using one hand to hold them where he wanted them, he used his other to squeeze the base of his cock, desperate to choke back his own need.

"Hold your tits right here, baby. Do as you're told." She always kept him on his toes. Damned perfect woman. He had no idea if she would willingly comply like his sweet damsel that needed to be freed or if she'd balk, anxious for punishment. If she tried that again, he'd have plenty to say about it.

She seemed to be considering. A half-second later, her hands slid from the headboard to her tits. She scooped their weighty heft together and presented them to him like the gift they were.

"Good choice, sugar. You're learning." With that he grabbed the lube he'd found in that drawer full of naughty toys and squirted it in the enticing line centered between the most gorgeous rack he'd ever seen. "Been wanting to fuck these tits ever since I first laid eyes on you."

He made one slow glide of his cock in the valley between her breasts slicking himself in the lube. He pulled out, leaned down, and blew a cold rush of breath across the stiff peaks. He pressed between them again, reveling in the soft grip of her flesh against him.

She shook. Her back arched offering him more of herself. He took with greed, pressing until the head of his cock nestled in the hollow of her throat, moving faster with each pass.

"Colt. Yes," she whispered as she gave herself willingly over to his needs. "Please let me see. I want to see us like this." Her request was earnest. If she wanted to see how incredible they were together, he would never deny her. Easing the blindfold off of her head, he leaned forward, slipping his cock away from her tits, and brushed a kiss on her forehead.

"So fucking beautiful, Avery. My God," was all he could manage.

Her eyes were alight with intrigue as she watched him work. But when her gaze moved to his, he slowed. "I love you," she whispered. "Thank you for knowing what I need even when I'm too ashamed to ask."

Suddenly her breasts simply weren't where he needed to be. They didn't join them. "God, baby, you fucking wreck me. I had a whole damned plan," he confessed in a haggard choke. "Now all I can think about is being deep inside of you."

"I know I wanted this but now I just want you inside of me with nothing between us. Please. I need you."

Sweet baby. He'd never deny her anything she truly wanted. Pulling his cock away from her chest, he leaned back and tugged the ribbons at her ankles, setting her free.

"Look at me, baby," he ordered. "If that's really what you want, say it again. Say you don't want me to wear a condom."

"I don't want you to. I just want you. Please. I promise I don't have anything or whatever. I've never...not used a condom."

"I know, sugar. I'm clean, too. Tell me you know if I got you pregnant I'd never do what my father did. I'd never leave you. I'll be there every single day for you. If we do this, it changes every single thing. I want that. I want this. I want us forever. But I have to make sure you do, too."

"I do."

All of his rules, all of the pretenses, every facet of making love that existed previously between them shattered with those two words. Two words he had every intention of hearing her say at the end of an aisle sometime soon.

"Nothing else is ever going to make sense, Colt. I know it won't. It never has, not until I met you."

Laying out over her, becoming her constant shield in the storm, he cradled her face in his hands, tangling her hair between his fingers. "I love you, Avery, so fucking much."

"I love you, too." Her body rolled sending shockwaves over his from every touchpoint of their skin.

"I don't want to hurt you, baby. You're so tight," he grunted as he dipped himself between her warm, wet lips allowing her only his tip.

"You could never hurt me. Please. I need you. I need to be full of you."

"Jesus," he murmured against her throat as he painted kisses there on the tender skin that smelled like his own personal sweet cream confection. He pressed further. Her eyes closed. She had to still be tender from his earlier force. "Can you take a little more for me?" Her walls tightened anxious for his fullness just like she'd said. She was just so tight.

Her legs splayed farther for him, an invitation to be the man he became with her. "Give me more. All of you."

With that, he sank himself deep inside that sacred pool she offered him so sweetly, washing away everything he'd ever understood about the way his world worked. Redemption existed there. He knew. From that moment on, he swore he would be the man she needed him to be, no matter what it cost.

As he made another slow, reverent dip, relishing the heat and the silk of her channel, he saw himself making love to her hundreds, no thousands of times. His entire future lay before him. Her back arched.

Her cheeks pinked with heat. Her body drew him deeper, fitting him like she'd been made for him alone. Their love palpable between them. His everything.

Bracing himself on his elbow he continued to rock, retreating slightly and then burying himself to his hilt. A ragged groan shuttered from his lungs. "You're so incredible, so beautiful," he offered the feeble supplication.

"Colt... I'm going to... I can't hold it back..." she gasped breathlessly.

"Let it go for me, sugar. Let me feel you come around me. I'm gonna fill you full of my seed. I want to see it drip from your lips when I'm done." There was no safeguard between them. He wanted her to know his every thought.

Her body tensed. His name hung on her lips. She came in racked tremors. Her body milked his own in tight pulls he couldn't withstand.

"Christ...mmm..." he growled. "If you want me to pull out, say so now."

"Fill me full." Her soft whisper summoned his climax instantly. He spilled himself deep inside her. Each hot spurt burning away another dose of shame he refused to exist in any longer. He didn't have to be a Holder. He didn't have to be a Camden. He only had to be...hers.

Making a tender withdrawal from her when she shifted, he indulged himself in the sight of her swollen folds dripping with his cum.

His smirk increased as he watched her attempt to walk to the bathroom to clean up and then watched her delicately tread back to the bed.

"Proud of yourself?" she teased and snuggled up on his chest. He covered them in her quilts and blankets.

"Yeah. I am aware that makes me an asshole though."

"It doesn't. I love feeling where you were when I walk, knowing what I can have again and again."

"Whenever you need it, baby, you just say the word."

Her sweet giggle was followed by a yawn. "Looks like I need to put my girl to bed. Pretty sure I just wore her out."

"I don't want you to go to the other trailer. Stay with me tonight."

"I was hoping you were going to say that. I'll just sneak out in the morning and come in the other door."

"I knew falling in love with a bad boy would have its perks. You're good at sneaking around." She looped her fingertip in small circles over his chest.

"I *was* a bad boy but I want to be a good man for you, baby."

"You are. The very best kind of man. I love you so much."

"I love you, too."

"I'm still a little worried about what happens tomorrow or Monday when you go to work, assuming you still have a job at Camden Ranch."

"It doesn't matter what happens. I'll figure out some way for us to stay together."

She brushed a kiss on his chest. "*We'll* figure out some way."

He smiled at that. Leaning upward he switched off the lamp and then cradled her once again.

"Can I ask one more thing before we go to sleep?" she whispered.

"You can ask as much as you want, sugar bee."

He felt her grin against him. "Will you promise you'll always be that demanding in bed?"

He planted a kiss on the top of her head. "Nope."

"Nope?"

Chuckling, he traced his index finger over her cheek, across her shoulder, and then down her side. "Sometimes I'll be worse."

"Good. And when I want you to be sweet and gentle will you always do that?"

"How about I promise that I will always be the man you need me to be."

CHAPTER TWENTY-NINE

Never before, in all of his years, had Colt hated the sunrise so viciously. He'd spent every moment of the previous day in her presence. The only time he'd been away from her was to help Chase practice for his football tryout the next day, since the ones Friday had been cancelled, and to pick up Pearl some cough syrup from the drugstore. Avery had parked herself on the porch and watched them toss the ball back and forth, refusing to be out of his sight.

Every time a truck had passed by Pearl's land, bile had climbed up his chest. He was certain Brock would show up and demand to know why he'd lied. But his brother never came. No doubt he was waiting on Colt to show up at the ranch for work Monday. They shared enough of the same blood for Colt to figure out his plan.

While he scrambled eggs and cooked bacon for everyone for breakfast, he tried to let the pops of oil sooth him.

He had a plan. When he got to the ranch that morning, he'd give Grant the money for Chase to play ball before everything went down. Then he'd come clean. His time was up. His entire future would depend on a brother he'd always wanted but still didn't really have.

Pearl had fielded three calls for the beauty shop the day before. People asking if Avery had any appointments available. It seemed

Holly Camden had raved about Avery's miracle-working at the salon. Everyone else wanted in. For the first time since she'd moved to Nebraska, Avery's morning was fully booked. The selfish part of Colt loathed them all for taking her away from him. Another part was sick and tired of the Camdens dictating everything, even if it had worked to their benefit this time.

He voiced none of that as he drove her to the salon after breakfast. "I still could just keep driving." His offer held every note of a plea.

"You know I can't do that. My brothers are counting on me to make us a life here."

"I know. Sorry. Just can't fucking stand any of this. I'm just gonna tell him everything and let the cards fall where they may. I'll get a job somewhere else nearby."

She gripped his hand. "I hate this, too."

The word sounded so strange coming from her. His baby never hated anything. "I thought you didn't..."

"Yeah, well, the only thing that could ever make me hate anything is the thought of losing the man I love. It's the only emotion strong enough to be a balancing force."

"I don't want to be the reason you hate anything, Avery. You are not losing me. I will not let that happen."

Parking near the door of the Cut 'n' Curl, he used their joined hands to pull her to him. "I'll pick you up this afternoon."

"We have to go get my car before you go."

The inevitability strangled him. "I am not going anywhere. I meant what I said. I'm going to come up with something, some way for us to stay together."

"I kept thinking that all weekend. That we'd figure out some way for us to stay together. Then I realized how selfish I was being. You can't take the cattle rancher off of his ranch. I would never ask you to give up who you are to be with me. You'd be miserable. It would never work."

"Stop," he snapped. "Stop fucking telling me goodbye. We're not doing that." Unable to listen to her tell herself they could never be together, he captured her attempted good-bye with his lips. Once again, he memorized the flavors of her mouth, softly exploring her. He would find some way to have her forever. Come hell or high water, there had to be a path forward for them.

When she finally pulled away, she flung herself out of the truck and refused to look back.

Sitting there in the car, he called his cousin, Meridian, again to see if she'd made any headway on Avery's custody case.

"She's definitely got an uphill battle. He's the father. The courts are going to honor his wishes. The best thing we can do is try to talk him into joint custody, like I said."

"He never had anything to do with him until her mother died. Never even saw the kid in four years as far as I know."

"Yeah, I heard you the first time you told me. Congratulations, by the way."

"For what?" What in God's name could she possibly be congratulating him for? He was about to ruin the only thing he'd ever really needed because of his father.

"For finally falling in love. I barely even recognized your voice when I talked to you before. Who knew a trip to Nebraska to find your dad's family would change you so thoroughly? We shoulda sent you up there years ago."

"Yeah, well, Mick's still somehow fucking me over from the grave. Some things never change."

"Maybe so, but sometimes the most fucked-up shit in this world can still get us where we're supposed to be."

"If you say so."

"How 'bout I come up there and take a look at these papers in person?" Meridian offered.

A renewed sense of hope tried to light low in his gut. "I have to figure out some way to stay up here with her. There are no jobs in this town except the one I took which I'm sure I'm about to lose."

"Why are you so sure they're going to blame you for all of this?" Colt recognized Meridian's lawyer tone.

"No one ever wants to look their father's mistakes in the eye. I've been lying to them. And how well do you figure your daddy or Uncle Gentry or any of the Holders would take to the news that they'd lost half of their land by order of a man they all hated?"

"Well...none of that...I mean...it still doesn't mean any of it is your fault."

"Pretty sure that's lawyer speak for 'you just lost the case.'"

By the time he drove under that ridiculous Camden Ranch sign promising that everything would be fine, he'd amended his plan. He'd throw himself at the mercy of his half-brother. He'd give him back his land and the land in Moore in exchange for letting him be a hand on Camden Ranch for the rest of his life.

Colt would never own his own land anyway. It would be a small price to pay for staying with her. He tried with everything he was to believe that. *Cattle rancher without grass to sell is more worthless than you already are.* Mick's taunts stabbed through him once more.

His gut swirled ominously with every yard his truck advanced. Nothing like driving yourself directly into the vast unknown. He parked outside his brother's home and sat in the cab for far too long, unable to march himself onward.

The two fragmented parts of himself went to war: half desperate to know how exactly this would all go down, the other half determined to sit his ass right there in the field and refuse to move unless someone figured out a way for him to stay with Avery forever that included being able to provide the life for her she deserved. His current pay at Camden Ranch was a quarter what his Uncle Gentry paid him.

Eventually the freezing cold wind urged him onward, sweeping him to the front door. There was a note attached to the door with a magnet. His heart slowed as he unfolded it. The wind almost yanked it from his grasp. Turning his back to shield the note from the elements, he read: *Hey Colton, I'm going to be in Lincoln most of the day with Hope. She has a doctor's appointment and wants to look for some baby stuff. Run the feed trucks for me and check the calves. Keys are already in the trucks. We'll talk tomorrow.*

Air rushed back into his lungs. He had another day and apparently he still had a job. He could hold her again all night in his arms. Nothing would happen before tomorrow.

Climbing back in his truck, he called Avery to explain.

"Are you serious? He's not even there?"

"He's not here and my cousin Meridian is gonna come up to help you with Jaxon's custody case. Don't give up on me yet, baby."

"I'll never give up on you, Colt, even if I don't get to have you in my life every day. Come get me as soon as you're done working."

"I'll be there. I love you so much."

"I love you, too."

He made his way to the shed where Brock kept the feed trucks. Before he could exchange one truck for the other, someone stalked up behind him. "What the hell do you think you're doing here?"

Spinning around, he started to explain when his eyes landed on the bartender from Saddleback's. All ability to communicate verbally left him.

"I asked you a question," the bartender demanded.

Colt cleared his throat. "Brock asked me to run the feed trucks for him. Said he was taking Hope to the doctor. Thought you were on your honeymoon."

"I was. We got back yesterday. You're working for Brock now?"

"Yeah, you got a problem with that?" Dude needed to take several steps back. Colt's fists clenched by his sides. His emotions were still twisted like an old roller coaster and his temper threatened to ignite at any moment.

"Maybe."

Flinging open the door to the feed truck, Colt threw himself inside. Beating the shit out of this guy wouldn't solve anything. That was something Mick Camden would do—hit first, ask questions later —and that wasn't the man Colt wanted to be.

The roar of the engine fed his ire. He had a job to do. As he pulled out of the shed, he saw the bartender tug his phone out of his pocket. Colt had a better than decent guess who he was calling. He reached for his own phone, but the bartender was too fast. "Hey, you've reached Maddox 'Mad-dog' Holder, proud Screaming Eagle from the 101st..." He'd gotten to Maddox before Colt.

———

Avery told herself to be happy or thankful at the very least. She'd done three cuts and a color that day. It was almost two and she still hadn't sat down. This was exactly the kind of business she'd hoped to establish in Pleasant Glen. But the time away from Colt made her feel like she was being rent in two. She needed to work. She couldn't stand to be away from him if his only solution to staying there was to not be a cattle rancher. She couldn't allow him to give up the fiber of his being for her.

Her phone rang as she was walking Ms. Bethancourt, a friend of Gretchen Parsons's, to the door. She made it back by the fourth ring.

"Hi, Ms. Hale, this is Susannah from Dr. Sarrington's office. I'm returning your calls in regards to Pearl Roberts's medications."

"Yes. Hi. Thanks for getting back to me. Her insurance is denying two of her medications. I tried calling them but didn't really get anywhere."

"Yes, ma'am. Dr. Sarrington said to tell you that she's going to call the insurance company herself on your behalf. If she can't get them to agree, there is another medication that might work, but she would really prefer for your aunt to stay on the Belinostat. We've just gotten her most recent lab work back and it seems to be working. The numbers are much better than they've been in the past few weeks."

"Really? That's wonderful. Best thing I've heard in...well, a really long time." A modicum of the weight pressing in around her eased its grip. Her shoulders lowered and her lungs filled with air.

"Yes, we agree. Insurance has been denying all of our patients' Belinostat prescriptions lately, so she's going to see what she can do. Would there be any way for you to pay out of pocket for the drug in case Dr. Sarrington can't work this through with them?"

I'll figure it out. The four words that had been her edict for her entire life hung on her tongue. But she wasn't sure she could do it anymore. She wasn't sure there was anything more she could give up. Even if her clientele continued to be this robust, she still wouldn't make enough for the medicine. "I don't think I can." And those words made her want to vomit.

"I understand, ma'am. I'll get back in touch with you after the doctor talks to the insurance company. Perhaps we could talk to the drug manufacturer. Sometimes that works."

"I appreciate your help." That four-word phrase was far more palatable. She didn't have to do everything on her own. Colt had shown her that.

"We'll do everything we can."

"Thank you. Could I ask one more question before we go?"

"Of course."

"Aunt Pearl has a bit of a cough. It's not bad. I just thought I would check to make sure it wasn't serious."

"We'd have to see her to determine that for certain. Does she have any other symptoms?"

"Not that I can tell. She hasn't even complained with the cough."

"I can transfer you to scheduling if you'd like to make her an appointment."

"Should I make her an appointment?"

"I can't tell you that. Maybe just keep an eye on her and call if the cough doesn't improve or if she has a fever."

"I'll keep an eye on her. Thanks."

When she ended that call, Avery checked her voicemails. "Hi, ma'am this is Stever from Steve's Towing and Auto Recovery. We picked up a car registered to a Miss Avery Hale from The Dew Drop." His chuckle made Avery cringe. "Anyways, all four tires have been gone after with a screw driver, I'd say. You give me a call back I'll make sure to get you some new tires and then you can come pick it up 'less you're wanting to sell it to me for parts. I'd have to talk with Steve Sr. to see 'bout that."

She shut off the message before he could rattle off the return number. Her head fell into her hands. She couldn't imagine how much four new tires for her car might cost. Once again, she was drowning in numbers, too high for her to even count.

At that moment, she heard the jangle of boot spurs on the old linoleum flooring. Lifting her head, she stared at her own knight in shining armor, or even better, her own country boy in dirty cowboy boots.

"What's wrong with my girl?"

Everything. "Nothing."

"Not nothing. Talk." He came around the front counter and guided her into his arms.

"You kind of got one of your wishes. They did tow my car."

"That's a good thing. I know you didn't want me telling anyone where it was. That's why I let it ride. I'll pay to get it out and that way I don't hafta try to find a second set of arms to go out to that club with me."

"Yeah, except those men you beat up slashed all four of my tires before they had it towed."

"Fuckers. Did the tow yard call you or someone from that club?"

"Stever from Steve's Towing and Auto Recovery called. Apparently, he works for Steve Sr."

"Stever, huh? This should be fun. Give me your phone."

She watched Colt return the call. "Yeah, this is Colt Camden. You've got my girlfriend's car there. The one with the slashed tires." He paused for a moment. "Yeah, actually, I am a relation to Ev and Jessie. They're my aunt and uncle." Another pause.

Avery couldn't believe he was saying that out loud. Thankfully no one else was in the shop. "No kidding. No, her car was taken. Not sure how it ended up out there. If I could get it back for her, I'd be much obliged. See, she's kinda pissed at me because I'm the one that left it unlocked. I'm in the dog house. Can you help a guy out?"

Avery shook her head at him. Unorthodox hero, through and through.

"Yeah, put four new snow tires on it and get her some chains as well. We'll pick it up in a little while. I'll throw in an extra Benjamin or two if you can get it done quick since you're not gonna charge me for the tow." Colt grinned. "Good man. We'll be there before you close tonight."

"You do not need to get me new tires," she fussed as he ended the call.

"I keep telling you I'm always going to take care of you."

She threw her arms around him, wishing she could crawl inside his coat or, better yet, into a vacant bed with him. "I can't believe Brock wasn't there today. That's so weird. Did any of the other Camdens say anything to you?"

"One of them. The bartender guy."

"Bartender? Oh, you mean Natalie's husband, Aaron."

"I guess. Pretty sure he called my cousin Maddox but he won't out me. Holder strong and all that. I didn't even see anyone else on the ranch today. Pretty sure that was planned. I can't find it in myself to care. I just want to spend every moment I can with you. The rest will come later."

"That sounds perfect."

"Let's go find some lunch and check on Pearl, then we can go see Chase's tryouts together. Kinda curious to see if Grant will speak to me."

"Okay, but I need to wait for Sally to get back."

"That mean we're all alone in here?" His smirk spoke volumes.

"Yeah." She couldn't help but grin, despite everything they had going on.

"Come with me." He grabbed her hand and half-dragged her to the back room.

CHAPTER THIRTY

Brock Camden

"Do you have any idea who it is you've hired?" Aaron demanded of Brock as he helped Hope out of the car.

Sharing a knowing wink with his wife, he nodded. "Yeah, I know exactly who he is. How long you been outside my house waiting on me?"

"A while. Are you sure about that? I called an old buddy of mine and he refused to say much, but I can assure you that guy is not Colton Holder."

"No, he isn't."

"And you're okay with that?" Aaron's gruff army-earned tone struck Brock as mildly humorous.

"I'm fine with it. Just wish you hadn't called anyone on my behalf."

"Not sure if you remember, but I was a Green Beret. I don't fucking mess around with men who are going to be around my wife, working on her ranch."

"He would never hurt Natalie." Brock found it mildly odd how defensive he was of the brother he didn't quite have yet. They needed to talk. Soon.

"How do you know that?"

"Because I know him."

"Yeah, you keep saying that."

Brock opened the front door and guided Hope inside. He wasn't surprised when Aaron followed after them.

"Brock?"

He blinked several times. His keys hit the entryway floor as his mind shorted out. "Mom?" If Hope, the most angelic woman on the planet, had backhanded him he was fairly certain he wouldn't have been more shocked than he was to see his mother standing in his house.

"Oh, Mrs. Camden, it's so nice to see you. We didn't know you were coming." Hope scooted into the room and threw her arms around his mother.

"Hi, sweetheart. Jessie let me into the house. I haven't been here long, just enough to perk a pot of coffee. I brought you several bags of the Gypsy blend you like from Mac and Molly's. They send their love to both of you."

"You're so sweet. Thank you. Mary, this is Aaron Weber, Natalie's husband."

Brock studied his mother's reactions. Had she known what Mick had done to Natalie and never told him? Ever since he'd found out, he'd longed to call and demand to know but couldn't bring himself to do it.

She gave him a smile. Guilt weighed heavily in her eyes but he had no way of knowing if it was in regards to Natalie or to why she'd suddenly shown up at Camden Ranch.

"I wish I were here just to see you. I've missed you so much," she confessed.

"We've invited you up several times and you refused to come," Brock reminded her. Aware he was being indignant he couldn't force himself to stop.

His gut had been twisted in knots most of the day. He'd told himself it was the situation with Colt that was bothering him, but that wasn't it exactly. He'd worried it was Hope or the baby, but the doctor had assured him both of them were healthy. There were even ultrasound pictures of the blob that would become their little one in Hope's purse. They were both ecstatic. Instinctively he knew this was it—whatever his mother was here to tell him, that was what had rubbed him raw.

"I suppose I've always felt a little out of place up here, Brock. This was your father's family and his land."

"Yeah, well it isn't his anymore. It's mine and he's never coming back here, so we'd like you to come up and visit more. Ev and Jessie don't mind either."

"I know. I spent some time with Jessie this afternoon. She seemed pleased to see me."

"We all want you to visit more," Hope vowed. "But what did you mean you wish you were here just to see us?"

"Well, I need to tell you something and I didn't want to do it over the phone."

"Have anything to do with Mick?" Aaron demanded.

"Hey, this is my home not a battlefield so watch it," Brock threatened Aaron. Not a brilliant thing to do to a former Beret but he couldn't find it in himself to care. "What is it?" he asked his mother.

"It's about your father."

"What's he done, now? He finally in prison or something? Honestly, Mom, I don't care."

"He's not in prison. It seems he...passed away."

"What?" Shock bolted up Brock's spine. His father hadn't been human enough to die. The information wouldn't compute. A sense of relief danced before him but he couldn't quite reach it, not yet. He'd have to see the bastard in a box to believe he was gone. Even if he were, Brock was certain he would haunt his worst nightmares until it was him in the ground.

"He died in Oklahoma a few weeks ago from what I've been able to figure out. I haven't been able to get the body back to Gypsy Beach to bury him. I've been blocked at every turn by some lawyer representing..."

"The Holder family," Brock concluded for her.

"That's why he's here," Aaron stated knowingly. Brock had almost forgotten he was in the room. "And this is precisely why I will not allow him anywhere near Natalie." With that, he stormed out of the house.

CHAPTER THIRTY-ONE

"Oh my gosh, Colt, look at him! He's doing really well." Avery squealed in his ear.

Chuckling at her, he pulled her closer. They were sitting in the stands of the Pleasant Glen High School practice field, watching the kids play. Pride welled deep in his soul. Chase was going to be all right. Kid was a natural on the field. All he'd needed was to find his place in this world and it looked like he was well on his way.

Kami was sitting in the stands as well, cheering Chase on every time he landed a long pass right into the receiver's arms. "So, I guess she really likes him," Avery whispered.

"Yeah, I might've misjudged her. Still hope she doesn't break his heart."

"Heartbreak is a part of life. I don't think you can escape it."

The pain that haunted those beautiful eyes cut him to the quick.

Grant Camden was down on the field watching the players but hadn't so much as acknowledged Colt. Every bizarre moment of this day turned the screw of tension tighter and tighter in his gut. Something was coming—he could feel it—and the rest of his life hung in the balance. All he could do was wait, and patience had never been his virtue. He was trying. God knew, he was trying.

As long as Avery was beside him, he could deal. He hoped.

An hour later, Chase raced up the stadium steps and swept his sister, and not his girlfriend, up into a sweaty embrace. "I made it. I'm starting quarterback. I never would've been a starting player back home."

"I'm so proud of you." Avery appeared to be holding her breath while squeezing him back.

"See, sometimes it pays to play ball in a small town." Colt razed his hair.

Chase released Avery and offered Colt a genuine grin. "Thanks for helping me practice and giving me rides and paying for the team fees and everything. I really appreciate it."

"My pleasure. Maybe just give your sister a break every now and again for me."

"You got it." With that, he turned all of his attention to Kami.

"Ready to go pick up Jax and get your car, sweetness?" Colt guided Avery toward his truck.

"Yeah, I guess so. Chase, don't forget I need you to watch Jax and Aunt Pearl in a little while. Is Kami giving you a ride or do you want to go with us?" Avery called.

"I'll give him a ride and help him with your aunt and brother," Kami volunteered.

"Yeah, we got it, Avery. No worries," Chase offered.

Avery, who'd clearly expected an argument from her brother, seemed shocked by his quick agreement.

"He's got a purpose and a place, two things every human being needs."

Colt noted Grant making a quick escape to his truck in the parking lot. He was about to approach him with the money for the booster fees and uniform, but the man got in the truck and flew out of there like a bat out of hell. "Guess he doesn't want to chat."

"This whole thing is so weird. I can't stand to think about you leaving, but all of this waiting for the other cowboy boot to drop is killing me."

"Agreed. Let's get out of here. I ain't gonna force anything. I'm trying to learn some patience."

"I like your impatience." She quirked one of those grins that always turned him inside out.

"Trust me, sugar, I'll never have any patience when it comes to wanting you. You ain't gotta worry about that."

An hour later, Colt followed his GPS program down a half dirt, half gravel path that was supposed to get them to Steve's.

"Is this actually a road?" Avery kept one hand gripped around his bicep and the other on the door handle.

"I guess it is in Nebraska."

He spent the better part of the next hour shooting the bull with Stever. With every exchange the price of the new tires decreased, but Colt wished the guy would shut the fuck up so he could get back home with Avery.

His heart had lost all ability to find a steady beat. The strangeness of the day—Brock's disappearing act, Grant's avoidance of him—had lodged a brick of tension in his stomach. Every shift of his body pressed the sharpened edges forward to pierce him from the inside out.

He took Avery out to dinner, but his mind would only rest when he was looking at her. She brought breath back to his lungs. She was his saving grace.

As he followed her back toward her aunt's trailer—she in her car, he in his truck—his cell phone rang. He glanced at the screen. Maddox. Finally. "I've been trying to call you all damned day," he snarled.

"Yeah, I know, but if I'd answered, you would've tried to talk me out of what I'm doing and that wasn't gonna happen."

"What's that supposed to mean?"

"Where are you?"

"In Nebraska," Colt huffed.

"No shit. Where in Nebraska?"

"About fifteen minutes outside of Pleasant Glen coming from the Wyoming side. Why?"

"Come on to Camden Ranch. We'll meet you there."

"What?" Colt's heart refused him another beat. The blood in his veins froze.

"Dad and Uncle Barrett and Meridian are standing in Ev Camden's kitchen. I'm out on the porch. You need to be here."

Colt slammed on the brakes, his truck narrowly missing Avery's car. He cursed under his breath.

"It's gonna be good, man. I swear. Just come on."

"What the hell are all of you doing up here?"

"Well, Triple A gave me a call this morning. I didn't tell him who you were, but the thing about him is that he was pretty much the best intelligence officer in the army. He has a way of figuring out everything you're not saying. I knew you were had. Let's get this hammered out. Plus, we all want to meet Avery."

"Who the hell is Triple A?"

"Aaron. He's married to Natalie Camden."

"Thought he was a bartender."

"Yeah, well, before that he was *the* army of one."

"Have you said anything to them about the land or Mick?" Colt demanded.

"We didn't say anything about Mick, but someone else did. Get here fast, man. We got some shit to shovel our way out of. But you ain't doing this alone. Holder strong, man, you know that."

Maddox ended the call. Colt stared at the Oklahoma tag on the car in front of him. He'd follow her anywhere. But this time she would need to follow him. He called her and asked her to come with him to Camden Ranch. The other boot was on a downward spiral.

Time to face the reckoning.

———

After Colt's phone call, Avery drove on, seeing nothing before her but an empty road. Somehow that seemed fitting. If the Holders were standing on Camden land, they'd reached the end of the line. She had no idea what the night would hold or what her life might look like tomorrow. Her stomach bottomed out somewhere near her ankles and the boulder that had set up residence in her throat was expanding. The only way out was through.

The music had reached a crescendo, her body had taken up its position, and it was time to make the leap. Split hard and fast. Half here. Half there. All his. She pulled onto Camden lands and prayed he'd somehow be able to catch her, that together they could avoid a total collapse.

They parked their vehicles and Colt clung to her as they slowly walked toward the largest house on Camden Ranch. In his other hand was that briefcase she'd first seen in his hotel room.

She stared up at an old farmhouse. Smoke billowed from the chimneys. The front porch lights guided them on. How could anything that looked so peaceful levy so much heartbreak?

If it's not happy, it's not the end. Avery wasn't so sure about that. Maybe that was true for people who got to live places like this, enveloped in so much land nothing could touch them. But for someone with nothing to call her own other than the man pacing beside her with terror in his eyes, that just wasn't the way it worked.

Brock opened the door and offered a kind smile. That was something. She clung to it. Maybe he didn't hate Colt for lying to him.

"You okay, son?" one of Colt's uncles asked him. She couldn't recall which Holder he was but the resemblance was there. Deep concern was carved in the light lines on his face.

"Not really, Uncle Gent. Why the hell are you here?"

"Sounded to me like you needed someone to let the Camdens know what kind of man you are. Barrett and I intend to do just that and we have an offer for you. This must be Avery." He extended his sun-worn hand.

"Yes, sir," she barely squeaked out.

"Avery." Meridian Holder rushed toward them. "How did I not figure out that you were his Avery? How are you? I was so sorry to hear about your mama."

"Thanks. I'm...not really sure how I am. Why are you here?"

"Colt called me about your custody case. When we get all of this hashed out, I'm gonna take a look at those papers you were served. Deep breaths for me. Uncle Barrett's about to give Colt something he's always wanted. I'm excited. Now come on." She gestured for them to follow her and, helpless to do anything else, they did.

Ev Camden was seated at a large dining room table with Barrett

Holder, patriarch of the Holder family. Meridian took the seat on Barrett's right. Gentry settled on his left.

Jessie and Holly were seated beside Ev, going through papers. Brock remained near Colt in what was hopefully a show of support. Hope was seated in a chair nearby with an older woman Avery had never seen. Aaron and Natalie were packed in as well.

The woman beside Hope walked toward them. "This must be Colton."

"Uh, yes, ma'am. Can I ask who you are?"

"I'm Brock's mother, Mary."

"Oh."

Avery was beyond certain the word fuck was meant to come out next, but he bit it back in honor of his present company.

"I'd love to hear this whole story from the beginning if you don't mind, Colton." Ev's request was politely wrapped in an order and everyone in the room knew it.

"Yes, sir. Uh, well, Mick's my dad. Kind of know you already got that figured out."

Brock slapped him on the shoulder. "No one's pissed about that, man. Keep going. We have to get to the bottom of all of this. Ev got a tax assessment on the land in Moore two days ago. Seems we no longer own the lion's share." Oddly enough, Brock didn't seem angry or even annoyed. He was smiling.

Disbelief, tempered by a touch of hope, filled Colt's hazel eyes as he stared at his brother. "Mick died a few weeks ago."

For some reason, Ev's head snapped around to stare down Natalie's husband. "Please, for the love of all that is good in this world, tell me you were really in Vail."

"I had nothing to do with him dying, sir. Unless I hit him harder than I thought. You have my word," Aaron vowed.

Colt's brow furrowed. "You the one that beat the piss out of his face?"

"That'd be me."

"Nice shot, kid," Gentry complimented. "Been wanting to do that for years."

Colt shook his head. "Anyway, he showed up in Holder County a few weeks ago. I saw his car in my mom's driveway and I stayed away, just like I always did when he came around. But one evening, she called me and said Mick had slumped over at the supper table. She called the ambulance, but by the time they got all the way to her house on Holder land he was gone. Massive heart attack. They said his liver was the root cause." Colt rattled off the details with no feeling, like he was reading a grocery list. Avery clung to his hand.

"No one's surprised by that either. Keep going," Ev commanded.

"Couple of days after he passed I found out I'd been made the executor of his will. I knew he had another family, but I never guessed he'd fuck us all over so bad, I guess."

"Oh, Dad loved nothing more than to ruin people's lives," Brock assured him.

"Yeah, well. Meridian went over the will with me and Mick left me half of your land here on Camden Ranch."

"He did what?" Brock stepped back like Colton had slapped him. Avery gnawed on her lip. This was where everything got ugly. She knew.

"There's more. He left Uncle Barrett half of your wheatgrass property in Moore. Guess that's what that assessment was all about. But he left you prime grazing and watering land that borders Barrett's part of Holder Ranch. It's in Holder County but belonged to someone else. We'd been leasing the land for years. The Holders need it back to keep the ranch running the way it's supposed to. His will also dictates that he be buried here on Camden Ranch."

"Like hell he will," Brock spat.

CHAPTER THIRTY-TWO

There. He'd done it. He'd told the Camdens everything he was supposed to. Now, he just wished they'd go on with whatever they were going to do about it. He didn't have anything left to give. All he cared about was finding some way to stay with Avery. Reaching into the briefcase he flung the stack of letters on the table. "He left you all letters. I didn't read them."

"He can't give away land that isn't his to give," Brock spat.

"I never took his name off the land in Moore." Ev spoke into his own hands. "I honestly forgot. My only goal was to get him the hell away from Natalie. The land in Oklahoma never even occurred to me."

"What the hell did he do to you?" Colt finally demanded of Natalie. Somehow she played a bigger piece in this than any of the others.

Every Camden eye darkened. Aaron looked ready to murder someone, likely him. Avery's hand flew to her mouth. "Oh my gosh. Natalie, I'm so sorry. I promise Colt had no idea it was something like that."

"Did you become a mind reader all of a sudden?" Colt tried to temper his words but came up short.

"Holly said she was proud of you for going on your honeymoon. And then Aaron hit Mick when he was here." She rose up on her tiptoes and whispered what she suspected in his ear. Colt slunk down into a nearby chair. His blood ran hot and then freezing cold. He was going to vomit.

"Holy fuck." *Sick bastard.* Now he understood. His father had molested Ev's daughter. Dear God. No wonder her husband was so protective. Any hope he'd ever had of having a family had gone up in flames because of Mick. Finally locating words, he offered up the only fitting response. "I'm so sorry. I swear I'm nothing like him."

"Yeah, I know, but I'd kind of like to know if there are more of you we should be expecting." Natalie sighed.

"I think it's just the two of us." Colt gestured to Brock.

"Never put anything past Mick," Brock huffed. "But that brings me back to him giving you half of my land. The land wasn't his to give. It was taken from him when Uncle Ev ran him off the ranch for what he did to Natalie. He's had no land up here for years."

The terror that had been his constant companion for the last two days finally gave way to devastation. Had Mick really believed he was giving Colt something, or had he arranged this whole farce to show his bastard son once again that he owned nothing and *was* nothing? Brock was right. He should know better than to put anything past Mick. He was being fucked with from the grave.

"That may or may not be true," Meridian corrected. All eyes turned to her. "I'm sorry, Mr. Camden, but Mick never signed anything stating that the land belonged to you. If we chose to fight this, I'd say half of the land will be granted to Colt."

"But we have no intention of taking all of this to court." His uncle Barrett's words somehow carried all of the weight of the Holder family. They always did. "Brock, Colt will sign the land back to you and Ev, and I will gladly give you back your half of the wheatgrass property in Moore. All we want is for you to sign the land in Holder County back to us."

A fire lit in Avery's eyes. She jerked her hand out of Colt's and erupted. "Exactly. You all want everything to go right back to the way it was before Mick Camden died. Well, let me tell you something about the way it was before. His other son, who's every bit as much entitled to his property as you are, Brock, gets left with nothing to call his own. But that's just fine with all of you. No skin off your back, right? All he wanted was to get to know you," she fumed at Brock. "And you—" she turned on his uncles, "—you let him work your land like some kind of employee. I thought being a Holder meant family. My whole life I heard how the Holders take care of their own, Holder strong and all of that nonsense. Well, clearly you don't.

"And you," she snapped at Ev. "This whole town lives and breathes by what the Camdens say and do. Ev Camden is the salt of the earth. Do you have any idea how many times I've heard that? And yet here you are taking everything from a *Camden*. All he wanted was a family and all of you have cut him out completely. You make me sick."

Complete disbelief rocked through Colt. No one had ever stood up for him like that. Once again, his fallen angel had held the ground between him and ruin. For some reason Jessie, Holly, Natalie, and Hope Camden were all trying to hide smiles. The men, however, were stunned to the point of silence.

His uncle Barrett recovered first. "She's right."

"I am?" Avery seemed genuinely confused. Colt pulled her onto his lap, clinging to the only thing that would ever make any sense.

"You definitely are," Meridian agreed. The Camden half of his family didn't seem to agree.

"And I appreciate that you're willing to stand up and defend my nephew. You've proved yet again that an angry woman is more dangerous than an angry bull, but that works out all right by me. Colt's needed someone to set his boots firmly on the dirt for him for a long time, so for all that Mick Camden did, it seems his parting gift to Colt was you, my dear. I suppose I have to appreciate that. But you didn't let me finish. Gentry and I are here to give Colt back the land that was his mother's. One fifth of Holder Ranch is yours, son. You've earned it."

"Holy fuck" was the only phrase Colt's tongue could locate. His own ranch on his own family's land. All his. For most of his life it was all he'd ever wanted, until he'd met Avery.

Before he could respond, her cell phone rang. She jerked it out of her pocket. "What's wrong, Chase?" All of the fire that had colored her cheeks moments before bled from them in an instant. "I'll be right there. Call an ambulance."

"What happened?" Colt set her on her feet and stood to follow her.

"Aunt Pearl won't wake up. Chase is freaking out. I have to go." She grabbed her purse and sprinted toward the door.

"I'm going with you."

"No!" She turned back to trace a hand down the side of his face. "Don't. Colt, I love you so much, but you have everything you've ever wanted now. You have a home and a ranch all your own, so go live your life." Hot tears streamed down her face. She shook her head. "I have to stay here. Please don't follow me. I can't stand it. I can't...I can't... watch you go. I can't tell you goodbye. I just can't tell anyone else I love goodbye. Go back to Oklahoma and be the cattle rancher you were always meant to be. I want that for you. It's like you said. When someone hands you an opportunity, you jump on and ride. They just gave you what you always wanted, what you deserve. I won't stand in the way of that." With that, he watched her race out of the kitchen and flee to her car.

"Son, you go get in your truck and you go after her, now. If her life is about to go from barely together to completely apart, you need to be there waiting to put all of the pieces back together." It wasn't either of his uncles giving orders this time. It was Ev Camden.

"Yes, sir. I plan to do just that." He wasted no time getting to his truck and was on her tail a minute later. Avery was the family he'd chosen, not one of the two he'd been born into, and whatever was about to happen with Pearl, he needed to be there to help her rebuild her life.

Three hours later, he sat with his head in his hands in the ICU waiting room. He'd been denied entry to Pearl's room. Avery had refused to come out.

"Got you a Dr. Pepper." Brock held the bottle under Colt's face and he lifted his head.

"Thanks." He accepted the drink.

Brock took the seat beside him. Ev Camden and Chase took the ones opposite him.

"Have you seen her?" Brock asked.

Colt shook his head. "They won't let me back 'cause I'm not family."

Brock grunted his disdain at the rule. "Not family, huh?"

"Seems to be the way my life's always gonna work." Exhaustion tugged at Colt's eyelids. He leaned his head back against the cold concrete wall and took a swig of the soda. His body was hollow. His current life much like the wall behind him. Without her warmth. Without her soft curves that evened out his rough edges. Without her sweet giggles or stubborn determination. Without her.

"I read that letter Mick wrote me." Brock's exhausted voice jerked Colt back to the present.

"He have any pearls of wisdom for ya?" Aware he was being crass, Colt didn't have enough energy left to care.

"Can't get pearls outta a shitsack, so no. He was a rotten bastard to the very end."

"Can't say that surprises me."

"Me either. Hey, how did Dad come to buy up property bordering your ranch without the Holders knowing about it?"

Weary of guarding the stories, Colt drew a deep breath and willed himself to explain. "Did you know Mick ran gambling rings in North Carolina and Oklahoma?"

"It did occur to me a time or two that as soon as we got kicked off Camden Ranch he never did have a job. I never wanted to know any details."

"Used to take small-time bets. Since beating people shitless was his favorite pastime, he was a natural bookie I s'pose."

"When you say small-time bets, what's that mean exactly?" Brock was mighty curious about the details. Colt supposed he owed him all he knew about their father.

"Took bets on horse races at the local tracks, never the big ones, pool games at the local halls, took 'em on high school football and baseball games. Hell, my mom told me once, he'd even take a bet from a bystander on a poker game."

"Well, that explains something I've been wondering about for years."

"What's that?"

"Why he was so hell-bent on me playing football in school even though I couldn't read well enough to pass any of my classes. I thought he'd threatened the principals and teachers to get them to pass me. Hell even the superintendent was in on it. I bet that wasn't it."

"You figure he let them in on the cut in exchange for passing you?"

"Makes sense doesn't it?"

"Once you let motherfuckers start to slide..."

"They get to thinking they can ice skate," Brock concluded for him. "Rotten to the core, like I said. So, you figure he gambled his way onto that land your family needs?"

"Guy that owns the land had a problem. He'd bet on a pissing contest if somebody'd throw in the ante. He was putty in Dad's hands I guess. He got in way too far and got the shit beat out of him. I have no way of knowing if Dad got somebody to do that or if he just knew it was going to happen and leapt at the right moment. He paid off Tex's debts in exchange for the property."

Brock shook his head. "His letter wasn't worth a pile of manure. He said he figured if you ended up getting my land it'd serve me and Uncle Ev right and if I ended up taking it back it'd serve you right. He was fine either way."

"What the hell fucked him up so bad?" Colt demanded.

"He was a bad seed," Ev interjected, "and then our mother always babied him. Let him get away with anything. Never tell your grand-daddy I said this but he used to compare us all the time. Everything was a competition. When it came to ranching, I almost always won. I loved it when I was a kid but when Jessie had Grant and I looked at my two boys both so different, I realized how much damage it had to have done to Mick to always be compared and always come up short. Mama felt sorry for him. He was a disaster from the get go."

"Maybe we oughta put that on his headstone." Brock shook his head.

Ev edged forward. His worn Wranglers grating against the ancient wool seat of the waiting room chairs. "Can I ask you a few things about all this, son?"

Colt nodded. "Yes, sir."

"How long ago did he fix his will this way?"

"Lawyer out in North Carolina said he'd signed it about a month ago. He got Tex to keep letting us use the lake until he'd heard that Mick had died. Got no idea how he knew it was coming though."

"Oh, I knew he knew his time was up when he showed here a few weeks ago. It was his farewell tour. When he kept wanting to be forgiven I figured some doctor somewhere told him he didn't have long. But I got another question. Did uh…did my brother meet your mama when he was down there looking at our land in Moore?"

Since some kind of story on how his parents met wasn't often afforded to the bastard kid, Colt shrugged. "I honestly don't know, sir. That seems about the right time though don't it?"

Ev nodded. "Yeah. It does. And that land was the only thing my brother ever put forth any effort into us getting. For a moment, when he'd talked my dad into buying, I thought he was finally coming around. Fate's a crazy thing."

"What's fate got to do with this Uncle Ev?" Brock asked before Colt could.

"Oh," Ev grinned. "It's just that Lester Roberts, Pearl's husband, was the one who told your granddaddy he ought to go down to Oklahoma and look at buying up some land for backlotting back in the day. Dad was curious but not interested enough to go himself so he sent Mick. Thing is, if Avery's uncle hadn't mentioned it you likely wouldn't be here, Colt. And it looks to me like you and Miss Avery are near 'bout ready to walk down the aisle."

"I know they won't let you back there but have you gotten to talk to Avery yet?" Brock offered Colt a consoling smile.

"No. She won't come out of there."

"Sounded to me like she thought you ought to take your uncles up on their offer."

"All I ever thought I wanted in this whole fucked-up world was a piece of land to call my own. Now I got it and I can't have it and her. Without her, I don't want it."

"Well, I'll say this, you fall in love like a Camden. Like Uncle Ev said, it's only been a couple days and you're ready to walk down an aisle. You think she'll move back to Oklahoma with you?"

"She can't." The harsh reality clawed at Colt's chest. The next time he saw Jaxon's father, he'd strangle him with his bare hands. "Hey," he turned to Chase, "where's Jax?"

"Hope's looking after him," Brock explained. "Chase wanted to come out here with me. We'll take care of everything until Miss Pearl gets out of here."

Chase continued to stare at the brown speckled flooring under his sneakers. He hadn't spoken.

"You okay, man?" Colt asked him.

He lifted his head. "I need to talk to my sister." Colt watched him march to the nurse's station. "I'm Chase..." he faltered for a moment, "...uh, Roberts. Yeah, I'm Chase Roberts. My aunt Pearl *Roberts* is here and I need to see her. Now."

"I'll need to see some I.D.," the nurse ordered.

"I don't have a license. My big sister is in there."

"His last name ain't Roberts is it?" Brock whispered.

"Nope," Colt shook his head.

"She's my aunt and that makes us family and I'm going in."

"I suppose it's all right." The nurse glanced around like someone would scold her as soon as she let down her guard.

Colt and Brock shared a grin. Kid was definitely going to be all right.

———

Avery had cried herself out of tears. When the door slipped open, she barely managed to lift her head. Chase offered her a sweet smile. "Hey, sis."

"Chase, how did you get here?" She didn't really care. She was thrilled to see him. Standing, she let him embrace her, thankful she wasn't alone in this any longer. They both stared at their aunt. Her ashen face slightly sunken. The first responders had given her oxygen. She'd rallied in the ambulance. The emergency room doctors had given her steroids. It had helped her breathing some but she'd been asleep for the last hour.

"Brock brought me." Chase squeezed her tighter.

"Brock's here?"

"Yeah, he's sitting out here with Colt and Mr. Camden."

Colt's name took another vicious stab at her already deflated lungs. "Colt shouldn't have come. He needs to get packed to leave."

Chase released her and stepped back. "You're just as stubborn as Mama."

"Thank you." Avery continued to try to swallow the ever-expanding ball of despair lodged in her throat.

"I didn't mean that as a compliment and I have something to say. I want you to actually listen to me this time."

"I do listen to you, Chase."

"You half listen to everyone. No one's voice talks louder than Mom's in your head. I see how much you doubt everything you do. You shouldn't be so hard on yourself."

Avery longed to tell him that he had no idea what he was talking about. But when her brother drew himself up to full height and took a deep breath, she knew he had something he needed to get off his chest. "What's going on, Chase?"

"I think...no, I know you should move back to Oklahoma with Colt."

"I can't do that. Our life is here with Aunt Pearl. She needs us." Avery tenderly traced her fingertips over her aunt's features trying to ease their strain.

"Once she gets better, we can take her with us. You shouldn't have to give up anything else for us, Avery. You already gave up everything you worked so hard for back in Oklahoma."

"You know Colt's land is not anywhere near your old school. It wouldn't get us back to our old life."

Chase's eyes darkened. "I'm not being a selfish brat. I know sometimes I can be but I'm not saying this because it's what I want. I want you to have a life with Colt. You're so happy when he's around. I want you to have that...happiness, or love, or whatever. You deserve that, Avery."

"Chase," she breathed his name as she threw her arms around him. "Thank you for saying that."

"So, we'll go when Aunt Pearl gets out of the hospital then? We'll move back with him and you can get married or whatever?"

Avery couldn't believe he was offering to uproot their whole life all over again. She didn't want to tell him the real reason they couldn't go. "What about Kami and football? You're the starting quarterback."

He stared at the cream colored cabinet over their aunt's bed, refusing to meet her gaze. "It's okay. I don't mind. I'll be a starter next year or something."

"Chase, I made a huge mistake. Randy talked me into signing papers saying I wouldn't take Jaxon over the state lines without his permission. I'm so terrified he's going to get custody of him. And if that happens, I want to be nearby so I can see him occasionally. I can't move back to Oklahoma. I have to stay here with Jax and you and Aunt Pearl."

Chase's mouth dropped open. His brow furrowed. "Wait, do you mean he tricked you into signing something saying you wouldn't take Jaxon away from here?"

"Kind of. He told me if I'd sign it..." Avery gasped. "He told me if I'd sign it he wouldn't sue for full custody of Jaxon. But he did. He broke his own contract."

"Yeah, so that's fraud. I may suck at math but I'm good at government and law."

"It still doesn't matter." The flicker of hope was immediately doused with cold reality. "He's sued for full custody now. I'll have to be up here for the trial. They might give him primary custody but I don't think they'd keep me from seeing him. It's just like I said. I have to be here. I wish I could figure out why he even wants Jaxon now. For years, he never even saw him."

"He did used to come around some but he only ever really spent time with Mama, not Jaxon."

"How did I not know he came around?"

"You were busy with Samantha and the shop and all that."

"Sorry I wasn't there for you more. I should've been."

"Stop. You're a great sister. I know I give you hell but I love you. Life kinda sucks since Mom died but I never would've survived it without you. I'm gonna help you figure out this bullshit with Randy, too. All he ever talked about when he came over for supper was Mom's shop. It was weird."

"Chase, do you know how Mom met Randy?"

"I think he's an accountant. I know he worked for the real estate investor who owned the mall where Mirror, Mirror used to be. He helped her with her taxes."

Avery's conversation with Sally rushed to the forefront of her mind as fragments of realization slowly snapped into place, piece by piece. The slap of the gavel on the probate judge's desk echoed against her skull. The liens on the shop she hadn't known existed. *"Like I said, the state inspector and I are friends."*

"What kind of friends?"

"The kind who keep each other from getting lonely on cold winter nights."

"Oh my, God," she gasped. Her heart flew against her rib cage. Blood rushed from her head to her feet. She gripped the bed to steady herself.

"What?" Chase stepped to Pearl's bedside. "She didn't move. Is something wrong?"

"No. Well, maybe. Can you stay with her for a few minutes?"

"Yeah, I'll stay. Will you talk to Colt first?"

"That's who I'm going to talk to." Sprinting from the room, she ran toward Brock and Colt but stopped short of propelling herself into Colt's strong arms. It would be easier to get him to go back to the life he deserved if she didn't let herself soak in the contentment that came from those arms. And she wasn't certain this was going to work.

"Baby, listen to me, please. I don't want the Holder land. I want you. I'll find some way to make a life up here for us."

"Colt," she choked. Shaking her head, she dug deep and forced the words from her mouth. "I will never allow you to give up your dreams for me. I won't. But I do need your help. And if I'm right, I might be able to move back with you. I don't know how to figure out all of this but I think it might be Randy's fault the courts took Mirror, Mirror. I have to prove that he stole tax money from my mom. That might get me custody of Jax and then we could move with you if you want us to. Do you think you can help me?"

He gave her a slow nod. "I'll help you do anything in the world. You know that. What did Randy have to do with your mom's shop?"

"I didn't know he had anything to do with it. Chase just told me he was the accountant for the real estate investor who owned the strip mall where the shop was. I didn't know until Mama died that there was a tax lien against the shop. I thought Mom must've mismanaged the money but now I'm not so sure.

"What if Randy didn't do her taxes correctly and that's why the county took back the shop? They leveled it a few days ago. Samantha said investors had rushed to buy the land. Something about this feels weird. Something isn't right. I just know. The mailman delivered a big box of paperwork from the shop that I didn't have time to go through before we moved up here. Can you go through it with me? Maybe there's some proof in there. I have no idea how to follow a paper trail or anything though."

"I know somebody who can help you," Brock volunteered. "Tell me how Pearl's doing and let me and Colt go get you the people you need to figure this out."

"You'd do that for us?" A mix of shame and appreciation swirled in Colt's hazel eyes. Avery tried to memorize the color. If she was wrong and this didn't work, she wanted to remember the caramel color when he was happy and the hickory tone when he was thinking something through and then the shadow of dark whiskey when he needed to take possession of her body.

"She has pneumonia. She told the EMT's she stopped taking her medicine when she thought the insurance wasn't going to pay. They think she's going to be okay. I should have been watching her more closely. They have to get the fever to break before we'll know..." Avery squeezed her eyes closed shutting away a vision of the future she wanted no part of.

Colt wrapped her up in his arms while her eyes were closed. "We'll know what happens next," he concluded for her.

She managed a slight nod. Her lungs drank in that scent of his cologne and of leather. Her entire body honed in on the scent she'd come to associate with being home.

"I am not leaving you, Avery. Not here in the hospital and not here in Nebraska."

"I don't have any energy left to argue with you," she confessed. The moments of fervor over figuring out Randy had dissolved.

"Good. I have one question about all of this with Randy. What do the taxes on a hair salon have to do with custody of his son?"

That was the biggest piece of this bizarre puzzle, the one she couldn't figure out. "I have no idea but maybe if I can prove he did something wrong it'll make him look bad. You know like what you were saying when you rescued me from...that awful place." Brock's presence erased the name from her tongue.

"That awful place?" Brock's brow furrowed.

Worn raw from the events of the night, Avery let the shame wash over her. She lifted her head. "I tried to get a job dancing at the Dew Drop because I needed money so badly. The owners tried to keep me from leaving. Colt saw my car in the parking lot and came in to rescue me. That's what really happened to his face." The brick wall stacked with tension that had been framing her in ever since her mother's death crumbled slightly. Not living under the constant shadow of lies felt awfully good.

Brock shook his head. "Wish I'd known you needed money or that he might've needed help getting you out of that place. If Colt needs some muscle, I'm there." Brock grinned. "I'm not gonna let anybody pick on my kid brother."

From some buried place inside her, a giggle sprang free from Avery's lips. "You may be his big brother but he's taller than you," she teased.

"You see why I love her?" Colt goaded.

Brock laughed at his own expense. "Believe me, I know how good it feels when someone you love goes to bat for you. I wouldn't be standing here having this conversation with you two if it weren't for Hope going to bat for me with the whole school board in Gypsy Beach, North Carolina. Now, tell us where this box of paperwork is and we'll go see what we can do about whatever happened with your mama's hair shop."

"Thank you so much." Avery released Colt and hugged his brother for all she was worth.

CHAPTER THIRTY-THREE

Torn, Colt debated what to do. He couldn't stand to leave her at the hospital alone and not knowing what might happen with her aunt for the next few hours, but if she was right and there were a few skeletons in Randy's closet that could be exhumed maybe, just maybe, they could move back to Oklahoma together. He could have it all. The land he'd always wanted and her by his side.

He could give her a good life, the kind of life she deserved. She'd never have to worry about the boys' lunch money or Pearl's medical expenses. He'd open her up any kind of hair salon she wanted tucked safely behind Holder County lines where nothing could touch them. It was a long shot but he was taking it.

"I don't want to leave you here, baby," he confessed. His brother lowered his head and stepped back, giving them space.

"We have to figure all of this out about Randy before the trial. I'll be okay."

"I'm gonna stay up here with her." Chase stepped out of the room. He held his shoulders high. Determination was chiseled into his jaw. Kid looked like he'd matured a half-dozen years in the last few minutes.

Avery's seeking gaze met Colt's. Her teeth sank into that lip. He knew what she wanted. They both needed to prove to Chase that they believed in him, believed he could make the decisions of a man instead of just a kid.

Colt offered him his hand. "You take good care of her. I'll be back as soon as I can."

"I will." Chase gripped his hand with more force than was really necessary but it thrilled Colt to no end. Avery visibly refrained from informing both of them that she could look after herself, a sacrifice to her brother. Colt winked at her.

"The box is in my bedroom." She dug in her pocket and handed over the keys to the trailer.

"I promise you, Avery. If there's anything on this guy, I know the people who can find it," Brock vowed. Colt had no idea what he had up his sleeve but just then he was willing to bet his very life on his big brother.

"Uncle Ev, we're gonna head back to the Glen and figure something out about all this. You want to come with us?" Brock asked his uncle.

"Did I hear Avery say Pearl wasn't taking her medicine 'cause she couldn't afford it?" Ev started to pace in the waiting room.

"The insurance company was denying a few of them," Colt explained. "Spooked her I guess. It kills me for Avery and Pearl. No one ought to have to fight for the medicine to stay alive."

"Amen." Ev nodded. "I think I'm gonna stay up here. I need to talk to Pearl as soon as I can."

Brock cleared his throat as they made their way onto the elevator. "Why don't you ride back with me? I'll bring you back up here. I have a few more questions about all of this if you don't mind."

Feeling lighter than he had in weeks, Colt nodded. "I'd be much obliged. I have a few questions myself."

Brock's new F-250 Dually was parked near the entrance.

"You have any idea what it is we're supposed to find in these papers?" Brock began his questions as soon as he turned the key.

"Not really. I keep trying to remember all of the stuff she's said about the old shop and what little I knew about that area of Oklahoma City. Randy, the guy she's talking about, is Jaxon's dad. That land down near where the hair salon was hit a boon last year. Went full on commercial instead of residential commercial. Investors started buying it up. Prices skyrocketed. I'm guessing Avery thinks her mama got taken advantage of."

Brock pulled out onto the street. "I don't know that much about real estate. S'pose it's possible. What was all that about a custody suit?"

"Randy filed for full custody of the little guy. Kills me to think about her having to lose anything else. She signed some kinda paperwork agreeing not to take him across the state lines without permission."

The moonlight glinted off of Brock's eyes as he turned to study Colt. "So, what's your plan if this works out in Avery's favor?"

"Meridian basically said there's a better chance of her getting struck by lightning twice than of her getting custody of Jaxon away from his father. I don't want to make plans just yet."

"Sounds a little like a Hail Mary pass from the end zone."

"You got that right."

"Caught one behind my back senior year. Ran it all the way in. So, anything's possible. Probably made our old man a fortune." Brock shook his head.

Colt sighed. "Galls me he made money offa you playing. That ain't any kind of father."

"Mick wasn't any kind of father. Wonder if he ever made bets on your games. Didn't you say you were also a wide receiver?"

"Yeah. Guess he might've. He wasn't in Oklahoma as much as he was with you, but you already know that."

"Was it Avery that kept you from telling me who you were right off?" Brock asked abruptly.

"Nah." Colt couldn't bring himself to tell even one more lie no matter how much ego he was going to have to eat to tell this truth. "At first, I wasn't sure if you were gonna be like Mick. I wanted to know that before I went about offering to give you back your land. I knew you weren't as soon as I saw you with little Evan. Then I wasn't sure if your uncle was like him. But more than all of that I kinda wanted to get to know you before I dropped the load of manure, so to speak. Guess I sorta always wanted a brother."

Brock offered him a kind smile. "Oh yeah?"

Colt shrugged. "Yeah."

"Me, too. I always had my cousins but it's not the same."

"Same goes."

"Hey, you know he's your Uncle Ev, too. And Evan is your nephew."

"Gonna take me a day or two to wrap my head around all that. I got Mick's stubbornness about me."

Brock chuckled and changed lanes to exit onto the long road between Pleasant Glen and Lincoln. "That ain't necessarily a bad thing. Depends on what you do with it. How come you seemed so convinced I was gonna hate you once you did tell me?"

"I just figured no one ever wants to have to look their father's mistakes in the eye."

"Fuck that," Brock huffed.

Shocked by his adamancy, Colt stared his brother down. "What the hell does that mean?"

"I spent the last few weeks working out how in God's name Natalie could ever forgive me for what my father did to her. Somehow she has. I point blank asked her about it right after her wedding. She said I wasn't my dad and that no one ought to have to answer for their father's sins.

"See, she used to hate me and I never knew why until it all came to light about Dad molesting her. She started to apologize to me for being hateful, but I wouldn't let her. Jesus, if anyone had the right to be hateful it was her. But she didn't want that hate in her. She wanted to be done with it. I didn't want the hate I have for Mick in me either. You aren't a mistake, man. You need to get that through your stubborn head right now. Nothing that Mick did is my fault, or your fault, or Natalie's fault or anyone but Mick's fault. Stop taking that on yourself. Trust me, it won't get you anywhere worth being."

———

Avery returned to sit at her aunt's bedside, too exhausted to hope she could ever really have Colt forever. The sense that Randy was to blame for her financial ruin was nothing more than a suspicion from her weary mind. She'd probably just sent the man she loved off on a wild goose chase.

She stared down at her aunt's lifeless form. If there was any chance her intuition was right, she had to try though, didn't she? If by some miracle she could secure custody, then she could move back to Oklahoma with Colt.

There beside the hospital bed, she closed her eyes and silently prayed for strength, for wisdom, and for a few more days or months or years if God was extremely generous with her aunt.

Chase squeezed her hand. Her eyes blinked open. "She's gonna be okay. I just know," he insisted.

"I hope so." The memories were right there, so close they still left brutal, jagged cuts if she allowed herself to feel them. She was here again. Her aunt's lifeless expression so close to that of her mother she had no choice but to allow the memories to sever her in two.

"What happens if she doesn't...?" she had to ask him. She had to know. Her mind wouldn't allow her to plan anything beyond her next ragged breath. She couldn't seem to understand what happened if her aunt didn't pull through.

What happened if her suspicions about Randy were wrong? What happened when Colt left? What happened the day after that and then the one after that? She couldn't do it again. She couldn't bury her own flesh and blood and survive it this time. She couldn't.

"Then we're still gonna be a family, Avery. Even if it's just you and me. We're gonna figure this out."

"I thought that was my line." Her smile fractured the stream of tears trailing down her cheeks.

"You always leave out one important part, sis. The *we* part. *We're* gonna figure it out."

"You sound just like Colt."

"Good. Don't ever tell him I said this but he's pretty cool."

CHAPTER THIRTY-FOUR

Colt flipped on the lights in Pearl's trailer. For the first time since he'd arrived in Pleasant Glen, the trailer was empty. The life it usually held existed only in the past and the future held nothing but unknowns. The present was nothing more than a memorial to what once had been. His footsteps echoed, reminding him of everything he had to lose.

"Kinda like a loose BB in the chamber ain't it?" Brock didn't seem to care for the empty trailer either.

"Yeah. It kills me to think Pearl might not pull through this."

"You know Miss Pearl saved me from Mick's fists more than a time or two. She'd chew him up one side and down another. She hid me out in the Cut 'n' Curl one time when he was after me for breaking a bowl and waking him up. She went after him with a broom another time. She's tough. Don't give up on her yet." He smiled as he placed a few of Jaxon's action figures in a nearby laundry basket. "Kinda crazy to think about all Miss Pearl did for me and then for my brother to be marrying her niece. That and what Uncle Ev was saying about the wheatgrass land."

"I ain't convinced her to marry me yet."

"Then let's find this paperwork and see if we can at least fix it so you can be in the same state together."

Colt led Brock back to Avery's bedroom. For the first time, he noted the details of her life he hadn't paid enough attention to before. Too anxious to get her in the bed, he ordered himself to fall in love with every nuance of Avery and to keep falling in love with her every moment of the next eighty or so years.

She appeared to be running some kind of plant hospice care center near every window. If they ever thrived again, it'd cost God several miracles. It was too cold in that cramped room. There wasn't enough sunlight. The air was stale and too thick to breathe life into much of anything.

There was a small watering pot crammed on Avery's vanity. He picked it up and watered what he could. If she had faith, then so would he.

"She a part-time gardener or something?" Brock asked.

"I think she uses all of this to make medicines and stuff. One of the guys at that shithole strip joint got a punch between my ribs. She put some of this stuff on it." He lifted a screw-top jar. "It stopped aching and it's almost gone now."

"You coulda just told me you got in a fight when I asked you about it." Brock sounded put out.

"I know but she didn't want anyone to know she'd tried to get a job there. That lie *was* for her."

"I get that. Looks like she needs some kind of greenhouse."

"Yeah. I can put one up near the house if I can get her back to Holder County."

A frown creased his brother's features as he nodded. "That the box?" He pointed to a dilapidated cardboard box shoved near the closet.

Colt pulled it open and located three large accordion files labeled Mirror, Mirror. "Guess this is it. Still don't really know what I'm looking for." He slipped a few folders out of the first file."

"Guess we could start with stuff for the IRS but let's not spend too long looking. We need to get all of this over to Aaron." His brother paced in the room.

"The army bartender guy?"

Brock laughed. "Yeah. He's got a shit ton of experience figuring stuff out and he's got friends that do this kind of thing for a living."

"He don't like me much though."

"He needs a little perspective and I think I figured a way to give him that. Might need Natalie's help."

"You think they're still up?"

"It ain't all that late. Let's go see. I'll call her on the way."

A few minutes later, Brock was knocking on Natalie's door while Colt balanced the files of information in his arms.

"Hey." Natalie offered them both a smile. "Bring it on in here." She led them to her kitchen table.

"I really appreciate this," Colt vowed. "And...I'm really sorry...about everything. I don't ever want to spook you.... I just..."

"I'm a cowgirl. I don't spook and I appreciate your apology but you didn't do anything wrong. Mick halfway apologized in that letter you gave me but he also sang his song to the grave. Still seems to think I owe him forgiveness. Aaron's out running with the dogs. I suspect he's on the phone with either T or Griff trying to chill out."

"Unfortunately the rat bastard ain't in the grave yet." Colt sighed. "He's rotting on a table down in Oklahoma. I guess I wish my apology could make up for his lack of one."

"Same goes." Brock sighed.

"Let's see if we can help Avery. Helping other people helps me remember that those parts of my past don't have any rights to my future. Aaron will be back once he's simmered down. He'll probably have all the answers you need in less than an hour but I want to see if we can figure anything out first."

"You still trying to one up your Beret, Nat." Brock razzed her hair and Colt found himself chuckling.

"You know I like to be the best." Natalie laughed.

"Oh, I know."

"She is the best." A low, menacing voice sounded from the living room. Two dogs skirted Natalie's legs bearing their teeth and barking at Colt. Aaron appeared with Maddox.

Maddox offered Colt a genuine Holder grin. "I vouched for your good character." He elbowed Aaron.

"He's all right." Aaron called the dogs off. "I guess."

"Aaron," Natalie spoke through her teeth. "What Mick did isn't his fault."

"Speaking of that," Brock spoke up. "Hate to bring up any bad blood but seemed to me at the wedding you all had a few weeks ago it was your foster parents we all met."

"Your point?" Aaron's brow furrowed.

"I kinda figured your own dad must've fucked something up bad enough to have lost custody of you."

Realization lit in Aaron's eyes. "You reminding me that I wouldn't want to be held accountable for my parents' actions?"

"Something like that, and asking if you could help a brother out." Brock quirked a grin.

"A brother or *your* brother?"

"My brother." Brock's vow was weighted with adamancy and concern. Colt was deeply touched.

"Yeah, all right, fine." Aaron settled at the table. "The truth of it is that it still irritates me that I'm not the one that killed him after what he did to her."

"Hey, you want to take credit, you got it," Colt offered. "I don't blame you."

"Can't we just be glad he's gone?" Natalie's impatience perforated her words. "He can't hurt any of us anymore. Let's be glad of that." She offered Colt a smile. "Brock told me about your arms." If only that had been the worst of it. Colt refused to speak that into existence in light of what he'd done to Natalie. His rat bastard of a father just wouldn't ever take no for an answer. He always wanted power over everyone. Colt hoped he died knowing he was a worthless piece of shit with no power at all.

"Show me what we're working on here." Aaron gestured to the folders. "I'll call Griff and T in the morning if I need some help."

Colt and Brock watched Aaron go through paper after paper and stack them in neat piles. Colt scrubbed his hands over his face determined to stay awake as the night wore on.

Aaron held up a stack of paper. "Her mother, Elaine, held a mortgage on Mirror, Mirror Salon. Here are all of the proofs of monthly payments. For the last four years, she paid them electronically. Doesn't look like she was late too often."

"Yeah, she owned the salon but I think the rest of the shops in that mall area were rentals," Colt added.

"Interesting."

"Okay, she's written three checks to Randall Buttridge Accounting services each April for the last three years. I'm betting she thought those were going to end up in the hands of the IRS. But here is the lien on the property and the rapidly mounting fees." Aaron showed Brock and Colt the letters.

"Don't seem to me that the state would let that go on for three years." Colt's mind raced through possible solutions or scenarios. Every time Aaron revealed something new, it tripped and restarted trying to sort through the endless possibilities.

"They wouldn't have unless she was making payments, but I don't see anything indicating that she had a payment plan with the state. I need T's help. Accounting isn't my specialty, it's not in my lane. You want to introduce me to this guy, let me tie him to a chair and interrogate the piss out of him, I'll get you answers. But financial records, that's T-Byrd's specialty. Plus, he's got the tech he needs to run background checks. You heading back to Lincoln tomorrow?"

"Planned to head back now. I'm gonna go get Avery a change of clothes and her toothbrush first," Colt explained.

"Let me get a few hours of shut-eye then I'll meet you up there. We'll go see T. He'll get you what you need. Avery was right though. Something about all of this is sketchy. I can't quite see how any of this has to do with custody of his kid though."

"She's brilliant and beautiful, and maybe that background check will be enough to keep him from getting Jaxon." Colt prayed this would work.

"See, he's a good guy," Maddox piped up before his face contorted with a deep yawn. "He's giving up his wild ways to take on kids and a wife, the whole deal. Personally, I think he's lost his fucking mind, but..." Maddox smirked.

"Someday some woman's gonna knock you on your ass, Mad-dog, and we're all gonna be there laughing ours off at you," Colt informed his cousin.

Aaron grinned, took Natalie's hand, and guided her onto his lap. "When that happens, give me a call, I want to join in the laughter."

Maddox rolled his eyes. "Before you go running back to your woman at that hospital you better get your ass down to the senior Camden's place and take Uncle Barrett up on his offer."

The fissure in his own soul continued to widen. He'd been offered the one and only thing he'd ever wanted and he still couldn't have it. He told himself he didn't want it without Avery but willingly severing the man he'd always been from the man he wanted to be was like separating the marrow from the bone.

"I can't exactly accept their offer until I know what's gonna happen with Jaxon. I can't...no, I won't leave Avery here."

Heavy-duty skepticism formed on Maddox's face. "All you ever wanted your whole life was a piece of land to call your own."

"Yeah, I know, but I don't want it without her."

"Better get you back to the hospital. We can stop by Uncle Ev and Aunt Jessie's on our way." Brock offered him an out.

"I appreciate your help, man." Colt offered Aaron his hand. "She wouldn't accept my apology on my father's behalf but you have no idea how much I wish he hadn't been a part of her life." He gestured his head to Natalie.

"I get that and thank you for saying so." Aaron accepted the handshake.

A few minutes later, Colt gripped the back of one of the chairs at Jessie Camden's large kitchen table trying to remain upright. He swore a thousand pounds of pure exhaustion compressed his spine.

The Holders and the Camdens were still in the kitchen talking at the late hour. They seemed to be getting on well. Colt took that as a good sign.

"How's Pearl, sweetheart?" Jessie asked him.

"She has pneumonia, ma'am. They're trying to get her fever to break. That's all I really know. I'm heading back up to the hospital."

"But you thought you better come by here and try to explain to me and your Uncle Barrett that you're just not too sure you want all that land we're offering unless you can get her to agree to move down there on it." Gentry chuckled.

"Something like that," Colt admitted.

"Well, then how do we go about getting her to agree to move back to Oklahoma?" Barrett bellowed from behind what appeared to be a shot glass of Crown he was sipping.

"It's a long shot, Uncle Barrett. She has to secure custody of her little brother. Right now she can't even take him out of Nebraska."

Meridian perked up at that. "I'm doing my best, Uncle Barrett. Taking custody from a father isn't that easy to do."

"There's a chance his dad did something sketchy with the taxes on Avery's mom's hair salon. I'm going to talk to some people who can help me figure out if Avery's even got a leg to stand on with the courts," Colt explained.

Meridian stood out of a recliner in the living room. "Tell me more about this."

"You want to head back to the hospital with us? I'll explain what I can on the way."

"Sure. Who needs sleep anyway?"

"Your uncles are going to stay here tonight, Colt," Jessie explained. "We are family after all." She patted his cheek and smiled at him with a hearty dose of pride in her eyes.

"You had me figured the first time you saw me didn't you, ma'am?" Colt couldn't help but grin.

"No offense to my sister-in-law but I raised four Camden boys. I know a guilty Camden expression when I see it. And that morning when I was driving out to the table I saw you braced at the end and I thought you were Brock. You two stand just alike. When I got there and saw Brock was actually branding, I knew. Then Nash Tillerson gave Ev a call and said he'd met a Camden who said he was from North Carolina." She winked at him.

"Guess lying's not really my thing." Colt sighed.

"And that is how I know you're nothing like Mick, honey, and that is why you are welcome on our ranch whenever you want to be here."

———

"Come here to me, baby." The tender cadence of Colt's voice slipped into her ears. She was certain this was a dream. He was back in Oklahoma now and she was all alone.

When her body jostled and he lifted her out of the chair beside her aunt's bed and settled her in his lap, reality rushed back into her consciousness. "I sent Chase out to the waiting room. There's a couch out there he can stretch out on. Go on back to sleep. I've got you."

"Did you find anything out about Randy?" Avery buried her face in his neck, inhaling that fully masculine scent that intoxicated her with its warmth and reassurance. She wanted to curl up in it like a fleece blanket and a cup of warm coffee. The very scent she was still certain she was going to have to learn to live without.

"Still working on it. I'm not gonna let you down. I'm gonna get all of you down to Holder county and I'm gonna give you the life you deserve to have."

"I'm scared to even hope that this might work. I'm too terrified to believe I could have you *and* my brothers." She sounded like she'd swallowed gravel for the last few hours but she was too tired to care.

"Get some sleep, sugar. I'll hope for the both of us. I do have Mick Camden's stubbornness and I intend to use it for good."

CHAPTER THIRTY-FIVE

"Colt?" a weak, weary voice called.

Keeping Avery cradled tightly to him, he eased forward. "Miss Pearl, how you feeling?"

"Like hell on a bull's back."

"I'll bet. What's this I hear about you not taking your medicines?" he kept his voice low.

"Who told you that?"

"You told the doctors that. Some of that stuff in that IV must be a truth serum."

Pearl's delicate laughter seemed to rob her of any energy she'd mustered. "Listen to me, tell Avery the deed to my land is somewhere in Lester's old trailer. That'll give you two a little starting out money."

"Miss Pearl, please don't talk like that. We aren't selling your land. You're not going anywhere yet."

"I'm so tired and I miss my Les."

"I know, ma'am." He cleared the emotion from his throat. "But keep fighting for me. Do it for Avery. She loves you so much."

"I know she does. But not as much as she loves you. I heard her last night. When they told her to keep talking to me. I could hear her. She said you were going back to Oklahoma. That's not what you're supposed to do."

"Well, now, what if I take you and my girl and the boys with us? I don't know how to be anything but a cowboy. I've got it in my blood from both sides. I'm a good one, Miss Pearl. I'll give you all a good life. I swear to you."

"All I want is for you to promise me you'll find a way to take care of *my* girl." Her blinks extended in length and her breaths were far too labored.

"I'm gonna take care of all of you. Please hang on for me. Hang on for a little while longer." He kept his eyes trained on the heart monitor. Her pulse was still steady. *Keep on fighting, Miss Pearl. We need you with us.*

A soft knock sounded on the door. A nurse swept in. Brock, Chase, Maddox, and Ev were behind her. "I'm letting them in here for just a few minutes," the nurse explained.

Brock was carrying two bags from McDonald's. His brother had hung through the night with him. Colt still couldn't quite believe Brock had taken him in like he had.

"Looks like you've got your hands full, quite literally," Ev said with a chuckle.

"She's my baby and she's been fighting all by herself for too damn long."

Avery sat up with a quick gasp. The devastation in that small sound was crushing. She rubbed her hands over her face. "How is she?" She climbed out of his lap and held Pearl's hand while the nurse checked her vital signs.

"We won't know for a day or two if the antibiotics and steroids are going to work. Her fever hasn't dropped and her pulse is steady but weak. We'll just have to wait and see. Can I get you anything?"

"No. I'm okay. Thanks for taking such good care of her."

The nurse gave her a genuine smile. "Not many people thank us for what we do, so I appreciate that. Has anyone thanked you for all you've done for your aunt?"

"Oh, I don't need any thanks. I just want her to be comfortable and healthy if we can manage that."

"That's always what we're going for. Take it easy. It's going to be a long few days."

The standard Holder smirk formed on Maddox's features when the nurse asked him specifically if he'd be around for the next few days.

"Yes ma'am. I'll be here. You get lonely you come find me."

Colt rolled his eyes. Everyone caught the nurse slipping him her number. "What?" Maddox said with a shrug after she left the room. "She's gorgeous. I jump out of airplanes for a living. I'd say I could come up with more than a few ways she could help nurse me back to health."

Brock's eyeroll matched Colt's.

"Ignore him," Colt ordered. "He's got one in every state."

"I'm going to refrain from discussing the well-worn path to your bed since your new girl is right there," Maddox teased.

Avery shot him a smirk. "That's so kind of you. I see that he gets his inability to keep whatever he's thinking in his head from coming out of his mouth from the Holder side of the family."

"Oh, now don't be too sure about that, sweet girl," Ev corrected her. "Brock's about the only one of mine that can keep his mouth shut when he should and even he ain't that great at it. It's more than likely his Camden side."

Colt found it oddly disconcerting that he was being claimed by both families. A week ago, he'd feared neither really wanted him.

"Miss Pearl, are you up to listening to your old neighbor for just a minute or two?" Ev moved beside the bed. A weary, worried expression was painted in the depths of his hazel eyes.

"Ev?" Pearl didn't open her eyes. Colt's heart stuttered on its next beat. "Les says to tell you he misses the hell out of you."

Avery trembled. Colt was beside her in an instant. She didn't have to be strong anymore. He'd not only hope for the two of them he'd be her strength as well. Folding her into his arms, he prayed for a reprieve on her behalf.

Ev took off his hat and lowered his head.

Fury shadowed Chase's features. "She doesn't know what she's saying. It's the fever." The statement was an order to the universe Colt knew didn't always listen.

Ev patted Pearl's hand. "Well, Miss Pearl, if you talk with him again, you tell him I miss the hell out of him, too. And you tell him he better save me a big old plot of promised land where we can run cattle together like we did back in the day." He shook his head. "But listen to me for a minute. Let me buy the rest of your land from you. You keep your trailers there and you keep living life just how you want but let me pay your bills. Let me do it for Lester."

"You'd really do that, Mr. Camden?" Avery lifted her head off of Colt's chest.

"Darlin' if I'd a known she needed the money I would've offered months ago. I thought she'd speak up if she needed anything at all. And I have a real good feeling you're gonna end up marrying my nephew so we really are going to be family. There isn't a thing in the world I wouldn't do for you or Pearl. We aren't meant to make it through this life all on our own. Everyone needs a little help on occasion."

"Thank you so much." Avery exchanged Colt's embrace for Ev's. He squeezed her tight and grinned like she was already one of his own.

"I always take care of my kiddos," he informed her. "Aaron and Natalie are on their way here. My son-in-law thinks you need to go with them to talk with his friends. He figures you know more about all that paperwork than anyone."

She turned back to Colt. "I don't understand."

Brock stepped in. "Aaron used to be an intelligence officer in the Green Berets. The remaining members of his old group run an investigative agency of sorts. They're real good at finding out most anything anyone needs to know. They can help you with your custody case but I agree with Aaron, you need to go with us to talk with them."

"I can't leave...Aunt Pearl." Her voice shattered on her aunt's name.

"I'll be here when you get back," Pearl informed her.

Smiles spread the width of every face in the room.

———

The sun had barely vanquished the indigo night sky in Lincoln by the time Avery stepped out of Colt's truck in the business district. She stared up at a five-story brick building still not entirely certain what to say to these people who were willing to help her for no reason at all.

Most days she wanted to dip her soul in the memories of her mother and let them permeate her skin. Just then she wanted to wash them away. People were willing to help if you asked and you accepted it. She didn't have to do it all on her own.

"Thank you for your help," she stated again as she followed Natalie Camden onto the elevator.

"That's what family is for, right?" Natalie grinned at her.

"And thank you for saying that. Colt was a little worried you all would hate him." Avery hoped she wasn't embarrassing Colt but she wanted the Camdens to know how much their acceptance meant to her.

"I hate Mick," Aaron readily volunteered. "But my wife was right. His sons don't deserve crucifixion for the sins of their father."

The elevator opened onto another corridor. They followed Aaron to a corner office. The Aegis Agency was carved on a jet-black sign mounted to the door. De Oppresso Liber was printed underneath.

"What does that mean?" Avery whispered.

"Without equal," Natalie explained. "It's the motto of the Green Berets. I'd say it's pretty spot on."

Stiffening her spine, she expected to step into a posh office full of intimidating men in uniform. Instead she stepped into a cozy waiting area. The walls were lined with framed promotion certificates and scores of medals but there were two worn leather loveseats and a TV set along with a coffee pot full of coffee.

She was greeted by a woman with long brown hair dressed in an army T-shirt and jeans seated on a desk flipping through a catalog of what appeared to be combat boots. "If it ain't Triple A and Mad-dog Holder. If that ain't a team, I don't know what is. How goes it, men?" She hopped off the desk and hugged Aaron and then Maddox.

"Hey, Rylee. We're good. How are you?"

"I'm here. They're all in the back being idiots as usual. Tell them I said to actually get work done. Slackers." She rolled her eyes.

Aaron laughed. "Sounds about right. You picking out new boots for them or for you?"

"For me. I'm interviewing a new client coming by in a little while. I'm heading out of town after that. Go on back." She folded a stick of gum into her mouth.

"Quit smoking again?" Aaron stated knowingly. Avery watched the exchange.

"Can't keep anything from intelligence." Rylee laughed. "Yeah, I quit...again. It's a bitch, too."

"Try the patches," Aaron called as he led their group down a long hallway.

"Is she the secretary?" Avery asked Maddox.

He cringed. "She's their security guard. Don't let her hear you call her a secretary. They still haven't located the body of the last guy that did that."

Aaron popped open a door. Avery peeked around Colt and Brock to see four incredibly well built men on their toes and hands pumping out push-up after push-up.

Aaron rolled his eyes, stalked into the room, and placed his boot on top of one of the men's back. He pressed down as the dude pushed up and groaned out, "You are a motherfucking asshole."

"Get up and figure shit out. Isn't that what your clients pay you to do?" Aaron chided.

"Yeah, but Smith said he could out push-up me and Griff so I can't quit now."

The man in the back corner, who Avery assumed was Smith, laughed.

Aaron shook his head and pointed to Colt and Brock. "Pick one and jerk them upright."

Before they could follow orders all four of the men were on their feet. The one with an imprint of Aaron's boot on his T-shirt grinned. "I'm T-Byrd. You must be Avery." He offered her his hand. "And this must be Colt Camden. It's a badass name man. Not gonna lie to you."

A guy with jet-black hair rolled his eyes. "I'm Griff. He's an idiot. Ignore him."

"And this is Smith Hagan and this—" Aaron roped his arm around the last guy's neck, "—is Voodoo. Who let you off your leash, my friend?"

"Fuck off, Triple A. Thought you wanted us to put our skills to good use for the Camdens with their permission this time."

Natalie and Brock both laughed. Avery had no idea what they were talking about. "I, uh, hate to rush anything but I kind of need to get back to the hospital soon."

"Sorry. Ignore us. Come on back here and let's see what we can figure." T-Byrd led them to another room with a large table and a massive computer screen on a desk in the corner.

Colt handed over the files of paperwork he'd gotten out of her room the night before.

"All right, from the beginning tell us what you suspect and why you suspect it. Even if it seems unimportant tell us," Griff ordered.

"Okay, well, my mother opened a salon in Oklahoma about twenty years ago," Avery began.

"We need more than in Oklahoma, sweetheart. *Where* in Oklahoma?" Griff barked.

Avery watched Colt's eyes narrow and his jaw flex. "Watch it," he snarled. "I don't need any kind of medal to knock your ass to the ground."

Griff looked amused.

Natalie sighed. "Okay, could you all just back the testosterone train up? Colt, simmer down. He's doing his job. Griff, stop being an ass," she snapped.

All of the Berets started laughing. Aaron grinned at his wife. "I love you."

"I love you, too." She blew him a kiss which he caught in the air and brought to his chest.

Avery beamed at that and laced her fingers through Colt's. "Sorry. It was in Slatern Hills just outside of Oklahoma City. It was the first finished building in what was to become a strip mall. She saved up enough to get a mortgage on the building. I was really young at the time but my understanding was that she had some kind of deal with the investors who bought up the land on either side of the salon. The salon was always profitable but the first few years were rough. But once a boutique and a yoga studio went in on either side of it and we made a name for ourselves, it made good money.

"I never knew much about the books. I know my mom wasn't good with numbers. My brother Chase told me last night that Randy Buttridge was actually my mom's accountant. See, I just thought he was my little brother Jaxon's dad. I didn't find out until after Mama had passed that there was a lien against Mirror, Mirror. Two weeks after her funeral, the city took it away from me. Now it's been leveled. I think Mom might've..." Shame slithered under Avery's skin. She couldn't quite manage to voice this part. Colt squeezed her hand. Realization formed in his kind eyes. "How 'bout I take it from here? Think I just put it all together."

"Thank you."

"Seems maybe Avery's mom traded something other than cash for the help with accounting from Randy. Now he's trying to get custody of the little guy away from Avery when he had no interest in him before now."

"No." Avery shook her head wanting to make sure she told them everything she knew. "Apparently, he did see Jax more than I realized in the last few years. Chase says he came by when he was in town and that he was always talking about the salon with Mom. Something just feels off about all of this. Mama paid the taxes. I remember her talking about how much it cost her but then the state said she didn't. If Randy was supposed to do her accounting, isn't it possible he kept the money she gave him or something?"

Another round of that infuriating hope fizzled in her belly. Instead of wishing it away this time, she clung tightly to Colt's hand and prayed the hope would be enough to convince these men to help her.

"You ever heard of a county taking possession after filing a lien so quickly?" Griff asked T.

"Never."

"Well, I don't actually know when the lien was filed," Avery explained.

"I do." T held up a piece of paper from the file. "Something about all of this is jacked up. Trust your gut. You're right. What I don't know yet is why he'd steal from your mother and then want his kid back, but trust me, I plan to find out. Men who accept alternative payment for their services aren't typically interested in the kids that are created in the...transaction so to speak. Strange case."

"You mean, you think I might could keep Jaxon with me? Maybe Randy will go to jail or something."

Everyone in the room offered her a kind smile. "That'll be up to the courts. But we will do everything we can to get you enough rope to hang him with," Smith offered.

"Thank you all so much."

"That's what we do." T winked at her.

"He managed to get a temporary custody hearing next week."

"Then we'll work quick. You get back to your aunt and let us get to digging." T cracked his knuckles. "Finding skeletons in closets happens to be our specialty."

"Can I please hug you?" Avery could hardly believe she had a fighting chance to keep Jaxon with her forever.

T glanced from Avery to Colt and back again. "He kinda looks like he's had a rough night. Let's just shake on it."

Avery giggled at Colt while shaking T-Byrd's hand.

"Told you I was possessive as hell," Colt spoke through his teeth.

"And I told you I liked that." She brushed a kiss on his cheek.

As soon as they arrived back in the intensive care ward, she rushed to her aunt's room. Chase grinned at her as soon as she swept into the room and washed her hands.

"Her fever broke," he announced proudly.

Relief washed through her, cleansing her of the terror that had taken up residence in her chest. "It did?"

"Yeah. The antibiotics are working. They think she's going to be okay."

Turning to Colt, she threw her arms around his waist. "You know what, Colt Camden, I'm pretty sure I was all out of miracles before I met you."

His deep chuckle echoed through the hollow emptiness that had pervaded her soul, filling in the gaps and soothing the raw wounds. "Same goes, sugar. Believe we already decided life works better when we're together so that's how we're gonna keep it."

"No. Don't say that yet. I want you to promise me that if they can't find anything on Randy and I have to stay here that you'll still go back to Oklahoma…and do…all of the cowboy things you were born to do."

"This'll probably be the one and only time I ever flat out tell you no when you're wanting something, so listen up. No, I will not under any circumstances go back without you."

CHAPTER THIRTY-SIX

A few days later, Meridian and T-Byrd were leaned up against the wall outside a courtroom in the Lincoln County courthouse. They both appeared ready to maim.

Avery paced back and forth until Colt was afraid she was going to wear a groove deep enough to swallow her whole in the ancient hardwoods.

"Deep breaths for me, baby," Colt tried again. "You're nervous enough for the whole damn county."

"What if this doesn't work? What if...what if it isn't enough? Or the judge doesn't listen? Or Randy makes up something? Or he's wrong?" she mouthed and discreetly gestured her head to T.

"He ain't wrong. He showed you all of the evidence last night."

Jaxon was currently safe at Ev and Jessie's house playing with Evan. Avery had been afraid to send him to school. If this didn't go the way they needed it to go, she wanted the chance to try to explain the unexplainable to him. Brock and Hope were there to support Avery and Colt.

"We're gonna get this over with and then go get little man and take him out for Runzas with as many fries as he can pack in that belly of his. Then I'm taking him to buy every Captain America toy I can find in that toy store near the hospital," Colt promised.

In true Meridian Holder hellcat format, she was shooting Randy smirks that said she was about to hang him by his own scrotum. Her briefcase contained the necessary paperwork to extradite Randy back to Oklahoma to stand trial for tax evasion and fraud. She'd managed to talk the Pleasant Glen sheriff into waiting to arrest him until after this trial.

Randy didn't know that yet but still looked sufficiently terrified. This was going to work. Colt refused to believe anything else.

Pearl had rallied. As soon as she was released and was healthy enough to travel, he planned to pack the whole family up and tuck them safely behind Holder county lines.

Avery's cell phone rang as the clock slowly chewed through the minutes before nine o'clock. "Sally? Is everything okay?" Her eyes goggled. "They just went ahead and sent him up here?" She scowled.

Brock and Colt shared a confused glance.

"Okay, yeah, I'll tell him." Avery ended the call.

"What's wrong, sugar?"

"It seems the funeral home in Oklahoma got tired of waiting on you. Burt from the funeral home in Kempton called Sally to tell me to tell you your father's body was delivered there last night. So...he's here."

"Guess we'd been so busy with all of this and Pearl in the hospital we forgot to figure out what to do with the sonuvabitch," Brock huffed.

"Let's get through this before we make any arrangements," Colt decreed.

Before anyone could agree, the doors to the courtroom were opened by the bailiff. Colt wrapped his arms over Avery's shoulders. "Let's go get our boy."

———

The pounding of her heart in her ears muted all other sound. Avery mentally rehearsed what she was supposed to say when the judge spoke to her.

Meridian seemed so certain this would work. Avery tried not to think about trying to explain to Jaxon that he had to go live with a man he barely knew.

"And Miss Avery Hale, you are representing yourself, is that correct?" the judge asked.

Avery stood. "Uh, yes, ma'am, with legal counsel by Meridian Holder."

"Who does not have a Nebraskan state license, correct?"

"Yes, ma'am."

She asked some question of Randy that Avery couldn't quite make out over the roar of panic consuming her. Meridian elbowed Avery sending her into action. "Uh, I, uh, I would like to present newly obtained evidence against Mr. Buttridge's character, your honor. It's an arrest warrant and extradition papers from the state of Oklahoma."

"What?" Randy seethed.

"Permission granted to submit this new evidence, Ms. Hale."

Meridian shoved the paperwork into Avery's clammy hands. She managed to get it up to the bench.

"My client has rights, your honor," Randy's lawyer clamored. "Let me see those."

"Sit down, Judson. He hasn't been arrested yet. He'll get his rights read to him and I'll get them to you in a minute," the judge huffed. "Looks like your client is to be arrested for tax evasion and fraud. Be difficult to take care of a child while he's serving time."

Avery tried to suppress her smile. Colt winked at her.

"I'm going to assume this is your expert witness," the judge pointed to T-Byrd, seated on the other side of Meridian.

He stood. "Master Sergeant Thomas Byrd, ma'am."

"Impressive and thank you for your service to our country, Master Sergeant Byrd. Now, since we're all interested to hear what you managed to dig up on Mr. Buttridge, get up here and start talking."

Avery supposed county courts in the middle of ranch land USA weren't quite as by the books as the one she'd been to in the big city.

"Gladly, ma'am." T was sworn in and took a seat. "Several years ago, Avery Hale's mother, Elaine, owner and lead stylist at Mirror, Mirror hair salon had a rough year. She, like many of us during the economic collapse, was struggling to make ends meet. It seems Mr. Buttridge approached her about possibly buying the property the salon was on and allowing her to rent it back from him. His brother, Richard Buttridge, owned the shops surrounding the salon and they were looking to buy as much land in Oklahoma as they possibly could as cheaply as they could when the real estate market crashed. Together they own several real estate investment firms along with a few shell companies.

"Avery's mother had no interest in selling but couldn't quite cover the property taxes on the salon that year. Randy came up with another suggestion. If Elaine would agree to a romantic affair with him, he would pay the taxes on the land for her."

The judge glared at Avery.

"Remember we're not trying the character of a dead woman, your honor," Meridian snapped.

"And you remember I can throw you out of this courtroom, dear," the judge warned. "Continue."

"Before he paid the taxes, it would appear that Randy struck a deal with Fred Miccick, a tax assessor for Oklahoma County."

"What kind of deal?" the judge demanded.

Avery shifted in her seat causing the uneven legs of the chair to clunk against the wooden floor. The sound reverberated through the room. Every eye turned to her and she wanted to melt into the stupid wobbly chair itself.

T cleared his throat. "I have provided both you and the Oklahoma City sheriff's office with enough suspicion to secure a warrant of Mr. Miccick's bank records, which the state of Oklahoma has secured. Do you know any other county tax accessor in the Midwest who can afford to vacation in Fiji and to own three Maserati convertibles?"

"No. I don't. How exactly did you come upon this evidence, Master Sergeant Byrd?"

"His Instagram account, your honor."

Her eye roll gave Avery another boost of confidence.

"Continue on."

"It would appear that Miccick used his ill-gotten gains to change the appraised value of the land Mirror, Mirror salon occupied along with the value of the other storefronts in the same strip. This allowed Randy Buttridge to pay next to nothing on the taxes the first two years he kept this deal with Elaine. I was able to access the payments made by check from the public records domain. In the following years, Elaine got sicker, he took the money she gave him to pay the taxes and instead of paying for the land, he allowed a lien to be placed on the property but kept Elaine from knowing about it by making a few irregular payments to the state. He would occasionally pay a little on it to keep the tax commission from leaning too hard on her."

"Any truth to this, Mr. Buttridge?" the judge turned the questioning on Randy.

"I refuse to answer that."

"I had a feeling. Okay, that gets us the fraud charge. But surely even the original amount of the owed taxes was less than it appears Mr. Miccick was paid off."

"I don't think Mirror, Mirror salon was the only property he was being paid off on," T explained.

"I see. Nonetheless this is nothing more than a temporary custody trial, Master Sergeant. What does any of this have to do with the child in question?"

"This is where it gets interesting, your honor. In a sealed packet of more than seventy individual papers from Buttridge Financial that Randy had Elaine sign just two days prior to her death, I located documentation of a twenty-five million dollar trust fund set up for Jaxon Buttridge, by the Buttridge family of Nebraska. I'd like to point out that the other sixty-nine documents were mostly nonsense. Nothing more than typed words she signed her name to."

"You're suggesting that she was tricked into signing agreement to this trust for her son under duress and not being of sound mind or body?"

"I am suggesting that and the trust is a little different than most. Jaxon doesn't get the money when he turns eighteen. The person who has primary custody of Jaxon on his eighteenth birthday does. As I'm sure you know, all of the money deposited into a trust is not taxable, however. Basically, Avery's mother birthed Randy a tax shelter. It would appear that he didn't want to be bothered with the kid until it was absolutely necessary so he left Jaxon with Elaine.

"When she died, Randy showed up at the funeral saying he wanted to spend more time with Jaxon. It took him less than two weeks after Avery Hale moved Jaxon to Nebraska for him to demand that she sign paperwork agreeing not to take Jaxon out of the state. He threatened to file for full-custody if she didn't sign it once again proving he didn't really want to care for the kid he just needed to keep access to him."

"Is that true, Miss Hale? He threatened you if you didn't sign the paperwork?"

"Yes, ma'am." Avery nodded.

"Did you know forcing someone to sign anything by way of threat is illegal in the state of Nebraska?"

"Not really, ma'am. I was still trying to figure out how to go on after my mother's death."

"I see." The judge continued to go through the paperwork T had provided her.

"As long as Avery never took Jaxon out of the state, he was always accessible. Randy assumed Avery could take care of him and he had many years to obtain custody. I suspect that when he met a man claiming to be Colton Holder and began to understand that Avery and Colt were falling in love, he panicked. The Holder family carries a great deal of weight in the state of Oklahoma, ma'am. They own one of the largest cattle ranching companies in the Midwest."

"Assuming your conjectures were proven to be true in a trial that would mean that the Holder family could financially fight on Ms. Hale's behalf to keep custody of her brother, correct?"

"Correct. It was less than forty-eight hours after he met Colt at Avery's home that he petitioned for full custody."

"None of this even matters, your honor." Randy's lawyer finally went to battle. "Jaxon is my client's son. He has every right to him. Having a trust fund for your child is not illegal. Besides that, this *is* all conjecture. None of it has been proven."

Avery's head started to swim. Her cheeks felt like they'd been held to a lit match. She pressed her palms to the table in front of her willing the cool laminate to permeate her veins. A maelstrom of fear swirled ominously in her belly. She was going to be sick. Why hadn't T told her the night before that Randy had filed because of Colt?

"That is true, Judson, but I have a warrant for your client's arrest on suspicion of tax evasion by way of dishonest reporting and fraud." The judge's sharp tone sliced through the cloud of confusion drowning Avery. "Miss Hale could also press charges for signing under duress. These are all very serious claims and I will be turning Mr. Buttridge over to Oklahoma authorities."

Avery slumped in relief. Colt's eyes closed and he squeezed her hand.

"However," the judge continued. Both Avery and Colt snapped back to attention. "This is only a temporary custody trial. The rest will be left to the state courts. For now, I am granting a stay to Ms. Hale. Jaxon will remain in her custody until your client faces trial in Oklahoma. Based on the outcome of that trial he can petition for custody again at a later date."

What? No. That wasn't how this was supposed to work. Avery leapt to her feet. "But he's a horrible person who let the state take my mother's shop so he could level the entire complex and build a mall! He used my little brother to swindle money away from my dying mother and then used him to hide money from the government."

"Ms. Hale, take your seat. This is a civil trial. Those are criminal charges. I've done all I can and all I will do. Considering the way your mother went about having your brother I'd be thankful you were just granted custody."

Meridian's chair flew backwards colliding with a desk behind the one where they were seated as she leapt up. "My client seeks permission to move the dependent to Oklahoma. She's to be married there where her future husband owns an extensive amount of land."

"Denied, Ms. Holder, and she is not your client. The dependent may not be moved from the state of Nebraska until a permanent custody hearing is held and she is granted custody. You're not hiding the child away on Holder land." Once again, the harsh thwack of a gavel decided her fate.

Avery's head weighed more than ten bowling balls. It swayed on her shoulders. The room went fuzzy at the edges. The future she'd stupidly hoped for went black with the blink of her eyes. She collapsed into Colt's arms.

CHAPTER THIRTY-SEVEN

Colt Camden had been sucker punched more times in his life than he cared to remember. Several of them had come from the hands of his father. None of them had ripped the very air from his lungs the way the banging of that damned gavel had.

How in the hell did it work out that he didn't have to pay for the sins of his father, an abusive child molester, and she had to pay for those of her mother who really hadn't done anything other than try to keep the business she used to provide food for her kids thriving? It made no fucking sense.

He squeezed Avery tighter to him. If he just held her with enough strength, maybe he could somehow erase the insanity of this fucked-up universe.

Unable to see anything beyond the devastated expression in Meridian's eyes, bile rode on the utter disbelief that shot to his throat. Randy wouldn't have pulled the trigger on the custody suit if it weren't for all of his lies. She really was better off without him. Some part of him had known all along.

There was only one thing that didn't make any sense. The one and only thing that kept him clinging to her, to the only place he'd ever really belonged. Clenching his jaw, he forced his mind to move slowly in reverse. He'd been so careful. He'd corrected her every single time she'd called him Colton *Holder*. "I never introduced myself to him as anything more than Colton. How the fuck did he know?"

Meridian's brow furrowed. Avery lifted her head and scrubbed her fingers over her eyes. "I can't figure that out either. He only ever saw you at Aunt Pearl's and you never said your last name. How did he know you came from the Holder family?"

T came into focus as he edged closer. "I'm sorry, Avery. I'm telling you there's more to this. I just didn't have access to all of the information I needed to prove it. That tax accessor is making a killing and Randy is in this deep."

"You're right," Meridian gasped. "Colt! He knew who you were before you ever got up here. I have to go back to Oklahoma. Avery," she squeezed Avery's arm, "this isn't over yet."

Hope and Brock made their way over. Sorrow etched both of their expressions. Hope rubbed her hand up and down Avery's back.

"I have to go get Jax. I have to try to explain to him that we can't move to Holder Ranch. He was so excited to learn to be a cowboy." Avery shook her head and headed toward the doors.

"Baby, wait. Maybe don't tell him yet," Colt followed in her wake. She spun back. Her eyes closed in abject defeat.

"Colt, I love you so much but I can't keep doing this. I can't let my brothers live in a constant state of limbo. Go back to Oklahoma. I have to stay here."

"Hope, baby, would you mind taking Avery back to Uncle Ev's? I need to talk to Colt," Brock asked.

Before he could inform his brother that he had no intention of abandoning the love of his life when it was his fault she was in this situation, Avery nodded. "Thank you."

"I really don't think now's the best time for whatever it is you have to say," Colt huffed to his brother.

"I'm pretty sure it's now or never. Trust me."

For some unfathomable reason, the earnest look in Brock's eyes had Colt agreeing.

An hour later, he followed Brock inside Saddleback's. Every collision of his boot heel with the hardwoods tightened the knot of fury slowly coiling in his gut. How the hell had he managed to fuck things up so badly?

Brock directed him to the small table in the back, the very table he'd sat at when he'd first arrived in Pleasant Glen, the very table he'd stood from to go search the bulletin board when she'd swung that door into his ass and had knocked his entire world off of its axis.

Brock returned with two shots of Jack and two cold glasses of Coca-Cola. "My cousins never spent enough time south of here to appreciate a Jack and Coke."

Colt didn't particularly care which liquor had been chosen on his behalf as long as it served to burn away any piece of his day so far.

"That was the biggest bunch of bullshit I've been witness to in a long while." Brock sighed as he took a slow sip of his drink.

"That what you wanted to tell me?" Colt was awash in confusion. He'd allowed himself to hope more than he ever should have. Now he couldn't go forward and he couldn't go back.

"Nah, I just thought it was a decent opener."

"I can't fucking believe I did this to her." Words began to spew from Colt's mouth. He'd never had a brother willing to listen to him rant so he took the opportunity. "I fucked her whole life up because I couldn't keep my hands off of her. She kept telling me we were a terrible idea and I didn't listen. Such a dumbass. Always have been. Jesus, I'm just like him. Go in and take whatever you want."

"You done telling yourself a manure load of lies now?" Brock seemed perfectly willing to let Colt go on if he felt the need so he did.

"I kept fucking telling myself Mick had finally done something for me, something good. I was stupid enough to believe something real was going to come from me coming up here and telling you what he did. I was dumb enough to believe I was going to get a real life and that I'd be able to give her a life where she didn't have to worry constantly about where her next meal was coming from."

"How 'bout now?" Brock wore a bemused expression.

"Why not?" Colt drowned the rest of his diatribe in a sea of whiskey and Coke.

"I've half a mind to get Austin to put you up on a few of my bulls' backs and let you hit the dirt hard enough to knock some sense into you."

Colt's grunt was a perfect echo of his brother's.

"Since Austin ain't here, how about you shut up and listen to me for a minute? The fact that you wanted to give her the kind of life you just said you wanted her to have means you ain't nothing like Dad. And if you'd get your head out of your ass for a full minute you'd remember what you just told me in the courtroom. You never introduced yourself as Colt Holder to that shitlicker. He knew who you were when he saw you, not after he talked to you."

"Doesn't mean it ain't my fault. If he hadn't ever seen her with me, he wouldn't have done this." Another round of self-hatred slithered down his throat along with the fizzy, alcohol-laden drink.

"You really believe that he'd let her go on endlessly with the key to the kind of money he has hidden in a trust fund for Jaxon?"

"Hell if I know."

"Exactly. You don't know. Now simmer down. I got something to ask you and it's important."

With everything he'd lost that day, Colt was almost shocked to realize if his brother needed something he'd do whatever he could to help. "What do you need?"

Brock half chuckled. "Well, I could use someone to help me run my half of Camden Ranch. My kids could use an uncle. I could use a friend, someone who knows his ass from a hole in the ground, who can tell me when I'm being a stubborn dumbass like my old man. Someone to have a beer with when the cattle market decides to fuck us all over and someone I can pour one for when either the Pokes or the Huskers manage to beat the Sooners. I could sure as hell use a brother, not a cousin, a real brother who thinks kinda like me and looks out for the Camdens the same way you always looked out for the Holders."

Realization poured over Colt slower than molasses in January. "Are you asking me...?"

"'Fore we bury the bastard let's you and me stick it to him one last time."

———

"Avery!" Jaxon wiggled back and forth on Ev's shoulders. Ev set him down and he flew into his sister's arms. She squeezed him just as tightly as she squeezed her own eyes shut. Crying in front of him was not happening. She had to be strong. "Are we moving now? I'm gonna be a real live cowboy. Colt's gonna get me a horse. He said so."

Jessie and Ev seemed to have realized something was wrong. "We can't actually move with Colt, buddy." Avery's voice quaked. Her hands shook so violently it took her two breaths to realize the earth itself wasn't moving. It was simply that her heart was breaking.

"Where's Colt, sweetheart?" Ev asked tenderly.

Hope squeezed Avery's shaking hands. "He's with Brock. They pulled into Saddleback's."

"I'll be back in a little while. Hope, go find one of the boys and get them to take Jax on a tractor ride." Ev pulled his cowboy hat on his head and shrugged into a quilted Carhartt jacket hung by the kitchen door.

"You going to do what I think you're going to do, Everett?" Jessie asked as she started a pot of coffee.

"Should've already done it."

"I know. I told you that a week ago. Go on now."

"I'm going, woman, and I'm bringing all of my kids and my brother's kids home with me. Might want to put another roast beef in the oven."

"Already got four in there. This ain't my first Camden rodeo." Jessie smirked.

"I don't understand. What are you going to do Mr. Camden?" Avery managed to ask.

"Don't you worry, arling'. We're gonna take good care of all of you," Jessie answered on her husband's behalf. "Jaxon, honey, go with your Aunt Hope and find your Grant. Tell him I said to take you on a long tractor ride. Avery and I are gonna have a cup of coffee and do a little chatting."

"You're my aunt?" Jax demanded of Hope. She beamed at him.

"I plan to be very soon. Come on, sweet boy. We're gonna make you a cowboy just like Colt and Uncle Brock, okay?"

"Okay!"

"You shouldn't promise him..." Avery started.

Jessie shook her head. "We're going to do just that."

CHAPTER THIRTY-EIGHT

"I know your uncle's offer is worth a thousand times what I'm offering." Brock kept saying shit like that. Colt still couldn't believe a man he'd barely known two weeks had just offered him half of his cattle ranch complete with a house.

He couldn't seem to recall how to make his lower jaw connect with his upper. When Ev Camden dragged a seat up to their table and sat down, Brock smiled. "Figured you show up once you realized what I was going to do."

"Boy, I've known you since you was shorter than them calves in your fields. I knew you were gonna do this as soon as you figured out who he was. What I don't know is what happened in that courtroom this morning."

"They granted Avery temporary custody but if Randy manages to get out of the charges in Oklahoma he can come back and try to get Jaxon later. Avery isn't allowed to move with him," Brock supplied.

"Like I said last night, as soon as you start letting worthless pieces of trash put dollar signs on kids to get out of paying their taxes, there ain't no coming back from that. Surely, somebody somewhere will figure out he's better off with his sister."

"I don't know, sir. Randy's in the back of a police car on his way to

Oklahoma but clearly he's lining the pockets of city officials." Colt still couldn't wrap his head around it all.

"Question is, son, what are you gonna do about it?" Ev asked pointedly.

"He's still half-thinking Avery'd be better off without him," Brock huffed.

"Lord, he is your brother ain't he?" Ev sighed. "Why in the world would that be the case?"

"T figured out that Randy went ahead and tried to get custody because of the Holder's money," Brock continued to supply answers.

"Brock, son, I know you're new to this whole big brother thing but I'm fairly certain Colt can answer for himself," Ev scolded.

Both of the Camden brothers laughed.

"I never introduced myself to that motherfucker as Colton Holder. I got no clue how he knew who I was but T says that's why he went ahead with this," Colt explained.

Ev waved the bartender over. "Get me one of them things my boys are drinking, Ed." He settled back in his seat. "Now, tell me this, if at any point in the future this manure wagon planned on taking little Jaxon away from your sweet Avery how exactly do you figure she would've been able to even hire a lawyer to do battle with the likes of Buttcrack or whatever his name is?"

As Colt recalled his own name for his mother's boyfriend—ass wagon—he couldn't help but chuckle. Must've gotten that from his father's side of the family. "She's brilliant, sir. She would've figured it out."

"She is brilliant, son. Smart enough to see right through you and know that deep inside you're one helluva guy. But she also needed some help. Help you gave her. Help you're going to continue to give her. There ain't a single one of us that can predict the future. That's shaky ground no matter where you're standing. But you can give her a steady hand to hold on to no matter what. She'd be just as lost without you as you'd be without her. She's the one who made you believe you belonged somewhere. Now, why don't you take your brother up on his offer and remind her that she belongs in your arms and that the two of you, and those boys, and any you might put in her belly in the years to come, belong on Camden Ranch."

"I can't believe you'd give me half your ranch." Colt finally said exactly what he was thinking.

"I had a brother in this life," Ev huffed. "I hated him from my first day of school. He was two years older than me. I had a crush on Emma Sue Whethers. Don't tell your Aunt Jessie."

Brock chuckled. "You were only five, Uncle Ev."

"Still though. Anyway, Mick knew I liked her. He kept flipping the skirt of her dress up while we were on the playground. He made her cry and all he did was laugh and push her down in the dirt. Tried to show me her little underthings. I knew then and there he was full of nothing but nasty. I got so mad I threw him down on the ground and beat him senseless, even though I was smaller. I hated him for it then and I hate him still even if he is gone. So, if God sees fit to give you a brother you admire, who knows what's right and does it, who'll have your back when the world serves up its worst, take hold of that. Appreciate it. It ain't something all of us get."

"I have to talk to Avery," Colt choked. His big brother had just thrown him a life preserver and he knew if he somehow lost his grip, Brock Camden would dive into the freezing cold waters he was trying to outswim and pull him back to shore.

"Can I make one more suggestion, son?" Ev grinned.

"Of course." Colt leaned toward his uncle anxious to soak up every word of advice.

"Maybe talk with a ring in your pocket. Every now and again a woman likes something that shines on her finger to remind them you're gonna be there day in and day out. That you ain't ever gonna waver, ain't ever gonna fall, and that you ain't ever gonna let her down."

"I already bought her a ring. Last week while she was sitting with Pearl up at the hospital. I got stir-crazy in that tiny room so I went for a walk downtown and found a jewelry shop. I was gonna give it to her tonight. I figured we'd be celebrating. But what if I can't do that? What if I can't figure out how we can keep Jaxon with us?"

Ev slapped him on the back. "I didn't say that you were gonna fix it so the world only ever worked out her way. I said you were gonna be there standing beside her no matter which way it works out."

Turning back to Brock, Colt offered him his hand. "All that stuff you said you needed, you got it. Maybe we could keep each other from ever acting like Mick."

Brock accepted his handshake. "You got it, brother."

"You think maybe I could see the house. I've have an idea about how to propose."

Broad grins spread across both Ev and Brock's features. "Aunt Jessie already had me and Luke pull all the boards off the windows for you. I had the power and water turned back on, too. Guess she knew this was how it'd end up."

"Woman's damned frightening with what she knows," Ev vowed. "Come on. Let's go see if we can't get you all set to rights."

————

A cloud of despair had weighed on Avery all afternoon. She had no idea where Colt was driving them on the ranch and why he seemed so happy about it.

"Shouldn't we go back to Aunt Pearl's and get you packed to go home?" She couldn't stand for him to put off his life any longer on her behalf any more than she could withstand the paralyzing thought of him leaving her behind.

"Say something like that one more time and I'll stop this truck and turn you over my knee." He didn't sound like he was teasing.

"Where are we going then?" she huffed.

"It's a surprise. Simmer down for me."

Simmer down. She rolled her eyes. Life continued to screw both of them over and he wanted her to simmer down.

His truck lurched and bounced over the rough terrain. The tires slid over a cattle guard and any kind of grip on reality continued to elude her.

Where did they go from here? She'd debated asking Hope if maybe Brock could keep Colt on as one of his ranch hands but refused to take advantage of the Camden's generosity or to ask Colt to give up anything else for her. She'd done enough taking. Now was the time to give. She had to make the leap alone. Her aunt had been wrong. It wasn't his job to keep her from collapsing. It was hers. It had always been hers alone.

He pulled up beside a large, wooden, two-story house. Avery had seen a lot of Camden Ranch in the last few days but she'd never been this deep onto the property. About fifty feet away from the expansive front porch were ten raised garden boxes. They held nothing but dead leaves now but she couldn't help imagining what it would be like if they were full of green life-giving plants. In the center of the boxes was an ancient wooden swing that looked like it hadn't been moved in the last decade. With a little love and care the entire place would make a beautiful home.

"Come on, baby." Colt hopped out of the truck before she could demand to know where exactly they were.

When he opened her door and offered his hand, her brow furrowed. "Who lives here and why are *we* here?"

"I told you this was a surprise. You get no clues. Now come here to me." He half yanked her out of the cab of his truck.

The second step on the porch gave a welcoming creak when her ballet flat pressed down. She couldn't help but smile. It reminded her of the stair creaks in her mother's old home.

Colt pushed open the door and ushered her inside. Ev, Jessie, Brock, and Hope were standing by a roaring fire in the living room. They all smiled at her.

For a moment she was afraid this was some kind of intervention. What on earth was going on?

"So, I was thinking," Colt began, "we obviously need furniture but you brought all of yours up from OKC and I got a house full down in Holder County and then your aunt's got a bunch. We need a sofa and some recliners." He pointed to the empty floors in the living room.

"And a big flat screen up here for watching games," Brock pointed over the mantel.

"Exactly." Colt took her hand and guided her into a large kitchen. Everyone followed after them. "Uncle Ev says this table's been here for a while but it's big enough for us and the boys and Miss Pearl to use.

We won't have to use those folding ones your aunt has. Brock and I can build a bigger one if we need to. Turns out Mick yelled at both of us about building shit so we both learned to do it."

"Colt? What on earth are you saying?" Avery couldn't listen to him go on and on like this. His life was in Oklahoma. Hers was a few hundred fence posts beyond this house in a cramped trailer with her aunt.

"Look out that door there." He pointed to a vacant plot of grass painted in the fading colors of the sunset. "I'll put you a greenhouse there. Them trees make a natural snow fence so it's a good spot for it."

"Colt, did you hit your head or something? This isn't our house." She knew him better than to believe he'd show her something she couldn't ever have. He loved her too much for that. What was he doing? "You are moving back to Oklahoma without me." To her shock, he swatted her backside just as he'd promised right there in front of his family.

Ev rolled his eyes. "Yep, he's a Camden through and through."

"Would you just look for me, please?" Colt ordered.

When she turned back from staring out the kitchen door, he was down on one knee. Her mouth opened just in time for every ounce of air in her lungs to expel in a gasp.

"Brock offered me half of his land, baby, and this house is included on this half of the ranch. We're going to run it together, like brothers. The way it always should have been. Until my dying day I swear to you I'll make you a good life here. I'll work day and night to care for you, and the boys, and your aunt, and this land, and the animals here. I'll make you proud, Avery. I promise you that. Will you please marry me?"

"Oh my gosh." She couldn't process any of this. "What does that mean? What about Jaxon and your family? What about Holder County? What about Randy? What happens if..."

Before she could formulate one more question, he stood, pulled the ring from the box, and pushed it on her finger. "Look at me," he commanded.

Since her body seemed to be hardwired to his orders her mouth closed and she stared him down.

"I don't have a single clue what our future holds, sweetheart. I'd love nothing more than to be able to tell you Randy will rot in jail in Oklahoma and you'll never have to see him again but I can't promise you that. The only thing I can tell you is that no matter what happens I will be right beside you and no matter what comes I will fight day and night to make sure Jaxon stays with us until he's old enough to do it all on his own. I told him one of us would be there every day when he gets home from school. I intend to keep my promises. Please, for one moment, stop worrying about all of the what-ifs and say yes. Let's do this life together. Nothing even makes sense any other way."

———

She stared up at him with tear stained eyes. "Yes," quivered from her lips. "Yes, I will marry you and I will fight right beside you for the rest of my life." She threw her arms around his neck and in that moment Colt knew for all of the shit he'd shoveled in the last three decades because of his father he'd finally gotten everything right.

"I know you hate your dad and I know he did awful, unforgiveable things." She squeezed him tighter. He lifted her off of the ground intent on keeping her flying. "But he gave me you and I'm so thankful for that."

"Here, here," Ev Camden agreed.

Colt settled her back on her feet.

"What are you going to tell your Uncle Gentry?" she asked.

"That mind never does stop worrying does it sugar? I knew I had to keep you dancing lest you get antsy."

"I can't actually believe this is happening. Would you stop teasing me?"

"Not now and not any time in the next eighty years or so. Hope that's okay."

That sweet, mischievous grin that had been absent for the past few days formed on those lips of hers. He bit back a hungry groan. "I guess it's okay."

"Good. And I called Uncle Barrett and Uncle Gent and my mother. They're going to keep Holder Ranch divided between the four brothers until their kids are ready to take ownership. They were all fine with the deal as long as we agreed to get married down on Holder Ranch so they can all see it. Be hard to get that many Holders up here."

"And we get to live here? I mean you get to have your own land and cows and stuff just like you always wanted?"

Colt shared a quick grin with his brother. "Listen to me, sugar, about thirty-seconds ago when you said you'd marry me I had everything I ever needed. But yeah, now I have everything I ever wanted, too."

Avery turned to Brock and threw her arms around his neck this time. "Thank you."

Brock embraced her gently. "That's what family is for. And listen, it's like Colt said, we're both pretty good with a hammer. He said you'd been wanting to redo The Cut 'n' Curl. You just pick out what you want and we'll get it renovated for you, okay?"

She nodded but Colt still didn't get the impression she believed any of this was real.

"And even if Randy gets Jaxon we'll still be here so we can still see him maybe." That was his girl. She had to figure out every contingency.

"We'll be right here come hell or high water, sugar. And if I have to personally dismantle the entire court system in the state of Nebraska to keep that shitsack from getting our boy, I will."

After a thorough investigation of the house, Colt packed Avery up in the truck and drove her back to the trailer by way of the grass instead of the roads. It was all his land now.

When he stepped into the trailer, he smiled. "Miss Pearl, get your hat on, we're moving."

CHAPTER THIRTY-NINE

"Remember how I taught you to saddle the horses?" Colt asked Chase whose face was contorted in a deep yawn.

"Kinda."

"Most mornings we'll be saddling up to check the herds but since it's winter and there's snow on the ground we're gonna run the feed trucks first. Sometimes, I'll let you feed with me but sometimes I'll want you on horseback so you can really see 'em while I feed 'em. Got it?"

"And we have to do all of this before I go to school?" He sighed.

Colt chuckled. "Someday, you'll figure out how blessed you are to have a job that requires you to be on horseback instead of riding a desk."

"I guess I kinda like it. How come Avery gets to stay in bed while we're out here freezing our asses off?" He watched Colt tighten the cinch on the saddle.

"She ain't in bed. She's making you and me and Jaxon and your aunt breakfast and she gets to stay nice and warm because she's my wife and you're just my brother-in-law," he teased.

"You're not married yet."

"I wasn't finished with my list. She also already has a job and since you got your license and Ev Camden graciously let you have one of the old ranch trucks to drive around town whenever you want, you need to earn gas money."

"Yeah, but you and Avery still won't let me drive on the gravel roads when it snows."

Colt rolled his eyes. "You gonna be this chatty every morning? We're trying to keep your smart ass alive. You learn to steer the horse, I'll teach you to drive on the gravel roads."

When they returned to the house from feeding, Colt warmed his hands by the fire he'd built before he'd headed out. "Still cannot believe this is my life." Avery grabbed a half-dozen pieces of bacon she'd pulled from the skillet with a pair of tongs and laid them out on a paper towel covered plate. "I live on a cattle ranch. I eat red meat on a daily basis. I've also never been happier in my whole life."

Colt winked at her. "Well, maybe that's what was missing all along, sugar."

She burrowed her way into his unzipped coat and shook her head against his flannel shirt. "Nope. *You* were missing all along."

"Am I taking Pearl to Lincoln for her treatments today or are you?" Colt tried to get his day in order. He still had fence to fix on his newly acquired land and there was a bull sale he was going to for Brock the next day.

"Actually, I have five appointments today so Sally is taking her. I've never seen her excited to go to chemo. I guess it is a lot of hours to sit and talk."

"I'm having visions of Thelma and Louise. You sure they're good to drive all the way out there?" Colt didn't want to think about what kinds of trouble the two of them could get into.

Avery giggled. The melody still made his cock stand up and take notice every single time. "They'll be okay. The roads are cleared and they're so excited I don't have the heart to tell them no."

When Colt's cell buzzed in his pocket, Avery dipped her hand down to extract it.

"Mmm, little to the left, baby," he whispered in her ear.

Her eyebrow arched in intrigue but she handed over his phone. Meridian's name was displayed on the screen.

"Are you and Avery still planning on coming down next weekend?" Meridian demanded as soon as Colt answered the call.

"Yeah. I desperately need Rio and I'm delivering the papers on Tex's land to Uncle Barrett, why?"

"Randy waved his right to a jury trial. They've set a bench trial for next Friday."

"Is that a good thing or a bad thing?"

"It's not a good thing. Looks like he might also have a few judges on his payrolls."

Another round of hatred stabbed through Colt. "So, it's not going to be a fair trial no matter which was we slice it."

"I don't know yet. I did just deliver enough evidence to bury him under the state penitentiary."

"You sound like the cat that just caught the canary."

"I plan to be the hellcat that catches the jailbird."

"Don't get my hopes up Meridian," Colt warned. "If he's got a judge under his thumb..."

"I'm calling that T-Byrd back. Maybe he can help me get the judge recused."

"I can't go on thinking he's ours if that ain't always gonna be the case," Colt admitted.

"Definitely don't count your chickens but does the name Seth Corbale ring a bell?"

The name did ring a bell. It was also not a name Colt ever thought he'd hear again. "Ain't that the shitlickin' secretary to the assistant city manager from Charett County that I beat the piss out of for mouthing off about a fake eminent domain deal in Holder County? The one Uncle Barrett threatened to gut like a trout because you figured out he was trying to get the Holder County line pushed back ten miles?"

"That's the one."

"What's he got to do with this?"

"I'll tell you the rest when you get here. If I can get a different judge, this is going to be so, so sweet."

Colt told himself to take it with a grain of salt. They'd been too sure they had Randy dead to rights last time and it had all been for naught.

"All right, tell me this, are we allowed to bring Jaxon with us or we still aren't allowed to take him out of the state?"

"You can bring him with you. You just cannot declare permanent residency as long as he is Avery's dependent in any state other than Nebraska."

"Got it. We'll see you in a few days."

CHAPTER FORTY

Avery rearranged herself on her stomach with her feet up in the air on her old bed in their new room. The kitchen door swished open and then shut. The flow of water from the kitchen sink meant he was washing up. She grinned.

"Baby?" he called.

She bit her lip and tried not to giggle. "Up here."

Two of her favorite sounds made their way to her ears, the thud of his boot heels and the jangle of his spurs. Anticipatory bliss centered in her chest and arrowed out to all of her limbs.

Wiggling, she made sure the knit leg warmers she was wearing, with nothing else save her engagement ring, covered only her calves and tried to squeeze her boobs together with her inner arms without making it obvious she was doing so.

While she was still arranging, a low growl sounded from the doorway. "Damn, baby."

The fire in Colt's eyes burned her exposed skin. He licked his lips. "Keep wiggling like that for me. Let me see that pretty ass jiggle." He gripped his cock, still concealed in the dirty Wranglers he was wearing and tugged, showing off how ready he was for her.

The giggle she'd been trying to quell sprung free. "I believe I was informed that the only things cattle ranchers really want are a warm, willing woman in their bed and to own the ranch next door. Pretty sure you have both, Colt Camden."

"And I am one lucky sonuvabitch. My God you are so fucking beautiful. Pearl and Sally not back yet?" He stalked closer.

"They just left Lincoln. Won't be here for a nice long while."

His long legs carried him to the side of the bed in two quick steps. His eyes were still trained on her ass. "And the boys?"

"Chase is picking up Jaxon but not for another blissful forty-eight minutes."

"And how hot and wet is my naughty little ballerina?"

"I've been thinking about you all day. Why don't you check and see for yourself?"

"Oh, honey, trust me, I intend to." With that, his fingers worked through the button-down shirt she'd ironed for him. His boots and his jeans were next. Avery wondered if there would ever be a moment when the sight of her fiancé naked didn't take her breath away.

Powerful and dangerous, yet with her and the boys, so tender and kind. Impatient for his hands on her skin, and to feel his fullness she went up on her knees, arched her back low, and wiggled her ass in the air.

A low rumbled groan thundered from his lungs. Balancing, she reached her right hand out and slipped her fingers through the slit in his boxers. She spun her thumb over his head, loving the way his body always reacted to her touch.

Breath hissed between his teeth. His muscles tensed, all sinew and raw strength. His jaw tightened. When her mouth watered, she thought of another thing she required. Rearranging so she was seated with her rear end on her feet, she eased his boxers down and licked her lips.

He gave her that hungry grunt she'd longed to hear ever since he'd fucked her sweet and slow this morning, rocking her body with his own long before he covered her in their sheets and blankets and went to work with his brother.

"Hungry, sugar?" His husky voice pooled in her belly and liquefied the need surging through her veins.

"For you."

"Can't have that." He stripped out of his boxers and took one last step bringing his package to her face.

She splayed her hands wide across his pecs first, feeling the ripple of his muscles drawn tight under his skin.

Leaning forward she spun her tongue around his head and teased his slit. "Shit. That's so damn good. Take more, baby. Please."

The fact that she could make this man, this cowboy, beg, that she could leave him breathless and senseless always catapulted a balance of unending love and power throughout her.

Tracing her hands down his abs, she teased at his base with her fingers. "Avery, now, baby," he warned.

The dance, that she so loved, began. "I don't think we have quite enough time for me be naughty." She refused to resent that.

His low chuckle stirred her hunger further. "Then you better get me between those lips, sugar bee. 'Cause when you're finished, I plan on being between the lower set."

Dragging her tongue from his root slowly up his shaft, she flicked it back and forth at his crown listening to the breathy string of curse words that flew from his lips.

His fingers tangled in her hair and tugged her head back gently. Every nerve ending on her scalp throbbed out a single plea: *more*.

"Clean that up like a good girl." He pointed to the pearly bead of precum gathered at his slit. Anxious for his flavors, she licked him clean and drew him in.

———

There was just no fucking way this was his life. How the hell had he gotten so lucky? He watched her cheeks hollow, felt the hot velvet of her tongue as she sucked him. The only thing in the whole fucked-up world that made sense sat before him on her knees. Damn.

When her fingers gently teased at his sac, he knew he had to stop her. They didn't have time for more than one round and he was coming in that tight snatch.

He never would've asked her to but she'd voluntarily gone on the pill. Fairly certain they should've let a full month go by before they'd completely stopped using condoms both of them had decided to let the cards fall where they may. If together they created another Camden grandbaby, they were okay with that.

She sucked harder. His mind spun. "You suck like a fucking dream, sugar, but stop." He backed away. That pouty little looks she gave him with her lips covered in his need, sent a fresh surge of hunger throughout his musculature. "Have I ever left you wantin', baby doll?"

She shook her head.

"And I never will. Get back up on your knees like you were. Keep that head low. Show me how wet sucking my cock gets you."

Both aware that the boys would be home soon, she shook that luscious ass in his face.

"Spread your legs more for me, sweetheart. Let me see that pretty pussy wet and ready for me."

He traced his fingers over her swollen lips and teased at her backside. A jolt of desire shook through her. He groaned his approval. Dipping two finger deep inside her, his eyes rolled back in his head. "Always so ready for me. Such a good girl." He knew precisely what she longed to hear from him. The walls of her pussy cinched tight against his strokes.

"Yes. Please take me." Her begging flooded him with primal urgency.

"You still trying to break the rules, baby?" Again, he knew what she wanted. That knowledge racked like heavy weights in his balls and yet it always served to free him of everything wrong in the world. His saving grace, through and through.

She turned her head back to stare at him. Dark fire alight in those crystal-blue eyes. He ran his free hand over her soft curves. She'd put on a little weight now that she no longer had to worry if the boys had enough to eat. That thick ass and full hips drove him wild. She was pure feminine perfection and she was his.

"You know I like to break...mmm...oh God yeah..." she tried to flirt as he strummed her G-spot. He gave her a wicked grin.

"You like to break what, sugar?"

"The rules," she managed in a breathless pant.

"I am aware." He strummed, knowing her rhythm, knowing her needs until she fisted the quilt underneath her and his name hung on her lips.

He popped those tattooed lips on her ass that encouraged him to smack it, keeping her from coming. "Not 'til you're on my cock. You said you wanted to break the rules."

"Yes." She writhed. He was burning precious minutes. He knew but she was simply irresistible. Every single thing about this life they were creating together was better than anything he would ever have allowed himself to imagine.

Her pussy milked at his fingers. She was so close. "It's right there, isn't it?"

"Please, Colt."

When she tensed and cried out his name loud enough for his brother to have heard, he granted her a reprieve. Easing his fingers away, he pulled her back and plunged into her depths. She came on his thrust. His every fantasy a reality. How had he ever gotten so lucky?

"Hey, sugar bee?" Colt sighed contentedly. He ran his fingers through her hair, reveling in her soft rhythmic breaths cascading over his chest. The boys would be home soon but he had to ask her something first.

"Hmm?"

"I want you to be my wife."

She grinned against his skin and traced her fingers over his tattoos. "Well, that works really well because I'm wearing your ring and I really want to be your wife."

"But I want it now. I'm tired of putting off anything good in this life." He wondered what she'd make of that.

"You mean you don't want to wait until spring? You want to do it here instead of on Holder Ranch? I need to see if my dad can come up."

"No, I want to do it down there. I just want to do it next weekend. Unless...you were one of those girls who had a big fancy wedding all planned out. If that's what you want, I'll wait. It's fine."

She lifted up on her elbow. Her hair fell in a wild cascade over her shoulder. Her sex-stained lips still puffy from his cock. "I didn't have time to be one of those little girls. I was too busy trying to take care of my mom. The only thing I ever dreamed of was a man who would love me and let me love him fully. After that, I dreamed about the kind of man who would give me babies and help me raise them. The kind who plays ball with his kids in the yard after he finishes feeding and checking cattle. The kind who would teach his kids to be a rancher just like him."

"You dreamed about marrying a cowboy?"

"No. I didn't even know how to dream up a man as amazing as you are. You had to become my reality before I even knew I was allowed to dream at all. No one ever tried to help me pick up all of the pieces of my life before you. I was always the one picking up everyone else's."

"Baby." Colt cradled her gently. "I love you so much."

"I love you, too. I want to marry you right now but if I have to wait until next weekend I guess I'll survive. I want to be like the Lancasters though."

"Who are the Lancasters?"

"They're the sweet old couple that I did the makeup and hair for at the funeral home. You remember that day."

He remembered. He would always remember the first time she raced into his arms, the first time he knew right where he belonged. "The guy that grabbed your ass. I'm still pissed about that, just so you know."

She erupted in hysterical giggles. "Yes. Him."

"So, you're saying you want me to grab someone else's hind quarters after I'm gone?"

More giggles shook her sweet little body against his. Perfection. "So help me, Colt Camden."

"I'm teasing you. They're the ones that died in each other's arms at ninety-something years old, right?"

"Yes."

"That sounds like a plan. And you're sure about next weekend no matter the outcome of the trial?"

"I'm sure. We stick together, side by side, no matter what, right?"

He closed his eyes, inhaled that spicy femininity that perfumed the air after he'd had her, and reveled in the fact that she finally believed in him and in them. "Forever, baby. No matter what."

"Then make me Mrs. Colt Camden, forever."

CHAPTER FORTY-ONE

Late that afternoon, as the sun sunk low on the horizon, Colt heard a knock on the kitchen door. He patted Avery's backside. "Hop up, baby doll."

She begrudgingly crawled out of his lap in their new recliner. Chase was upstairs doing homework. Pearl was in her room resting after her treatment. And Jaxon was over at Austin and Summer's playing with J.J. and little Hank. A chicken was roasting in the oven, filling their home with scents that made Colt's mouth water. Life was just the way it was supposed to be.

But the breath escaped his lungs in a quick huff when he opened the door for his brother who was carrying a shovel. "Guess we need to bury the dead, huh?" He'd been putting this off.

"Casket's on its way here," Brock explained. "Think it's high time we stop living in his shadow."

"Let me get my boots on."

Chase made his way down the stairs. His eyes flitted from the shovel, to Brock, and then to Colt. "I'll help you."

Colt braced his boot on the shovel head and broke the ground in the back corner of the Camden's family plot. Brock followed suit six feet away. Ev was beside him. With every rhythmic dip of the shovels, Colt tried to reconcile where he was with where he'd come from.

Life was bittersweet. He knew. There would always be a splinter of sadness in every moment of blessing. It was the bittersweet that had earned him the calluses on his hands and the determination in his heart.

Hope, Jessie, and Avery made their way to them, each carrying a warm thermos of cider. There would always be a sliver of moonlight even in the darkest night.

"Can I help?"

Colt and Brock both turned their heads. Natalie stood before them carrying her own shovel. Colt started to tell her that she didn't have to. He wanted to bury the bastard on her account but he understood she needed to dig. She, like him and his brother, needed to wash themselves clean in the dirt.

CHAPTER FORTY-TWO

"You sure you're ready for this?" That was the third time he'd asked her that very question. Avery kept her gaze locked on the passenger side window of his truck. They'd driven under the *Welcome to Holder Ranch Est. 1889* sign ten miles before. How was there even this much land in an entire state? And how did one family own it all? She'd thought Camden Ranch was huge. This was something to behold.

"You make me feel like I'm about to face a firing squad. I've met some of your family. I used to cut their hair, remember?" Truthfully, meeting the entire Holder family was a little intimidating.

"It's just...there's a lot of them," he eased. When he threw a tooth-pick in his mouth, she knew he was nervous.

"Do you not want them to meet me?"

He stared at her like she'd lost her mind somewhere in the miles of dust and green grass behind them. He jerked the toothpick back out of his mouth. "Why do you even say shit like that? No. Wait. Better question. Where do you even come up with shit like that? Of course I want them to meet you. If for nothing else, I want to show you off and brag to all of my cousins that I'm marrying the world's most beautiful woman." He winked at her.

"You are so full of bullshit, cowboy."

"Careful there, sugar, you're getting to sound an awful lot like a country girl."

"I am marrying a cattle rancher. I now own not one but two cowgirl hats and my fiancé does things with steak and butter that I swear I would eat three times a day without complaint. Pretty sure I'm a country girl."

Colt laughed at her outright. "Oh, baby, we got so much more to do 'fore you're a country girl."

"Like what?"

"My brother and all of my Camden cousins say you can't be a country girl 'til you're baptized."

"You mean like at a church? I think my grandmother had that done to me when I was a baby."

"Nah, not in a church. Nekkid in a lake with me." He waggled his eyebrows at her as they passed a landscape dotted with more cows than she could count. The prairie fields expanded so far to her right she couldn't see the end of them.

She laughed. "I think I'd prefer to wait on my baptism until the lakes aren't frozen over."

"I s'pose I'll allow that. We got to teach you to rope, too."

"Well, I managed to rope you and I wasn't even holding a lasso." Pure bliss took fifth position and leapt into her favorite dance deep in her belly.

"You don't need a lasso to rope me, sugar. You just show me them titties and I'll come running."

Avery shook her head at him. An expansive house came into view. "I'll keep that in mind. But would you please behave while we're in front of your family."

"I could but if I did they might not recognize me." That sinful half grin formed on his features and she momentarily debated asking him to pull off near a few of those hay bales and let her straddle his lap in the cab of his truck. Surely, that was another requirement for being a country girl.

"What's that devious little grin for?" he asked.

"Nothing," she cooed.

"Not nothing. Talk."

"Just thinking about putting off meeting all of the Holders long enough for us to get busy in the truck."

He readily produced that low, hungry grunt she loved. "Wish you'd decided that about two minutes ago. My Aunt Leigh's on the front porch. She saw my truck." He pointed to the house only a hundred yards away now.

"Maybe some other time then."

"Maybe? That ain't gonna be a maybe, sugar. Plenty of room on this big-ass ranch to get lost after the sun goes down."

The quick clicks of the parking brake shot her slight case of nerves into overdrive. "What if I can't remember all of their names?" She willed her pulse to calm.

"There ain't gonna be a quiz, sweetheart. And I ain't gonna leave you with 'em. Deep breath for me. They're all dying to meet the woman who finally settled me down."

Before she could respond his aunt was beside his door. He leapt out and hugged her before he released Avery from the truck.

"Aunt Leigh, this is Avery Hale, my fiancée."

His aunt folded her into an all-encompassing embrace. "Lord have mercy, I never thought I would hear the word fiancée coming out of that child's mouth. I am so thrilled to meet you, Avery." She wrapped her arm over Avery's shoulder and guided her up the steps to the house. "Now, I know it's been all kinds of crazy with Colt and him being a Holder or a Camden or whatever but I want you to know, I have a tremendous amount of experience in dealing with Holder men. I married one, put up with three of his brothers, and birthed another four of 'em, heaven help us all. If Colton ever gets out of hand, you just give me a call and I will personally drive up to Nebraska to set him to straights if that's called for."

Colt rolled his eyes. Avery giggled. "I will definitely keep you on speed dial, Mrs. Holder."

"Honey, there are enough Mrs. Holders floating around here, just call me Leigh. And if you forget someone's name once we get in here you just point and I'll whisper it in your ear." The sense of warmth Avery had come to associate with being in Colt's arms or being with the Camdens pervaded her soul here as well. Perhaps, she would always be a misplaced Oklahoma girl or maybe she could count both ranches as her home.

When Colt eased her away from his aunt so he could wrap his arm over her shoulder to pull her close as they stepped into the onslaught, she understood, wherever he was, she was home.

Three hours later and two moments before his Aunt Leigh broke out his baby book, Colt managed to escape with Avery. "Get in the truck, baby. Let's get out of here."

She readily complied but he knew as soon as that lip went between her teeth something was wrong.

"I'm sorry. Jase and Hudson were just teasing about taking me to Scarlet A's tonight." He intended to dress them down before the wedding Saturday. No one was going to make his baby doubt him.

"It's not that. I was just wondering why your mom wasn't there."

So, that's what was brewing in that mind of hers. "Being there when I need her hasn't ever been one of her specialties."

"I'm sorry." She scooted closer in the truck and nuzzled her head against his shoulder. Then she brushed a kiss on his cheek, making him grin.

"Just so long as you know I'm not going to be that way. If you or the boys need me, I'm gonna be there," he vowed.

"I do know that. She'll come to the wedding, right?"

"No idea. You want to go by her house and see if she's home?"

"Is that a good idea? I don't want to bother her."

"It's what she's wanting. If she ain't gonna be the center of attention, she don't put forth much effort. She wants me to come to her."

"My mom had a little of that going on, too. I'd like to meet her if you don't mind."

The afternoon was wearing on when Colt pulled onto the far east side of Holder Ranch. Avery studied the fields as they passed by. The hay bales cast long shadows across the prairie lands. The windmills spun on just as they always had.

The bright Oklahoma sun glinted in her crystal-blue eyes. He dug behind her seat until he located a Pokes baseball cap.

With one of those intoxicating grins, she pulled it over her hair. "Damn beautiful, woman," he grunted.

She shook her head at him. "Colt, can I ask you something?"

"Anything, sugar bee."

"Is this the land you gave up for me?"

There, in the middle of a dirt road at least a hundred years older than he was, he stomped on the brakes. Cradling her chin in his rope-callused hands, he lifted her head until she had no choice but to look him in the eye. "Listen to me, Avery. I did not give up anything for you. If it weren't for you, I'd still be wandering around this earth trying to figure out where the hell I'm supposed to be. I don't give a damn where I ranch so long as you're right there beside me. If it weren't for you, I wouldn't have a real brother to run a ranch with. So, no, this isn't the land I gave up. This is Holder land. And as much as I love both sides of my family, my God, baby, I love you more than life itself, more than any piece of land anywhere. You got that?"

This time her beaming grin spread the width of her face. He decided the gates of heaven couldn't look any more beautiful than that. "I got it." She threw her arms around him and there in the middle of the land that had raised him, he knew, home was wherever she was standing with open arms to bring him in.

"Mama, you forget you were supposed to be up at Uncle Gent's and Aunt Leigh's this morning?" Colt didn't feel like making pleasantries.

"You coulda come to see your mama first," she whined. "And this must be Amy. Colton said you used to work out at the Mirror whatever salon where them rich bitches get their hair done."

"Mama, for Christ sakes, do you have to do this today?" Colt seethed.

"Um, it's Avery," she shot him a look that said she had this handled. "It's nice to meet you Miss Holder. And I see you must be looking for a new salon. You know, I could trim up those frizzy ends for you while I'm here. Those home-coloring kits really do strip the life out of your hair if you're not careful, ma'am." She expertly ran her fingers through his mother's hair and let Betsy Holder know she wasn't going to be messed with. Colt swore he fell even more in love with her at that moment.

"Well," his mother smarted but couldn't come up with another retort.

"I'm taking Avery into the city for dinner. We're staying out there since we have to be at the courthouse first thing in the morning. We just came by to say hi." As always within the first five minutes of being in his mother's presence he was looking for an escape.

"Well, sit down for a few, son. Anson's on his way over. He'd love to meet Amy."

"It's Avery, Mother. And no."

"Who's Anson?" Avery mouthed.

"Boyfriend slash asshole," Colt grumbled.

Before he could get her out the door, Ass-Wagon himself pulled up in his Audi douche-canoe. Colt ground his teeth. The dude's hair was so slick, he was shocked he didn't slither up to the front porch.

As usual, Anson attempted to out-grip Colt in a handshake. Colt flexed. The ass-wagon's eyes bugged as he attempted to pull away and Avery giggled hysterically.

"Oh, this must be Amy." Anson attempted to rub the ache out of his right hand with his left.

"It's Avery. A-v-e-r-y," Colt spelled out. Annoyance rocketed up his spine. They needed to leave.

"Right, right. And you met her when you went up to see your father, right?"

Far too many smartass answers tempted his tongue. Colt pulled Avery close and inhaled her sweet scent in an effort to calm his nerves. "You know what, why not? Let's go with that. We'll see you two at the wedding."

"What wedding?" Anson looked genuinely confused.

Colt shot his mother a hateful glare.

"Colty is marrying *her* up at Barrett's place on Saturday. Mick's family is all coming."

"Oh, yes. I'll have to miss it. Actually, I was going to invite you both Saturday evening to a gallery showing of my vulva and breast pieces. It'll be out near Tulsa."

Colt choked on his own saliva.

"A showing of your...what?" Avery gasped.

"Jay-sus." Colt coughed.

"They're all from my *man's interpretation of womanhood* collection," Anson went on to explain.

"I see." Avery's jaw cocked to the side and her eyes narrowed a half-notch.

Colt found himself anxiously awaiting whatever was about to come out of that mouth.

"You know, since we're getting married that day and will be at our reception and then in our hotel room that night, we'll have to miss it. Besides, I, personally, am more than a little tired of seeing *boys* trying to interpret women. Guess that's why I'm marrying a cattle rancher." She grabbed Colt's hand and he scooted them out of his mother's house.

"Have I told you today how much I love you?" he asked as he cranked the truck.

"You have but wow that was something."

"Sorry about her."

"Hey," she squeezed his hand. "You're not your daddy and you're not your mama either. You're you and you're mine."

"Nothing else I ever want to be."

"Some sick part of me kind of wants to see this artwork."

"Please, baby, please, please do not make me take you to one of his pussy parades."

She dissolved into another one of those piles of sweet giggles righting every wrong in his world.

———

They'd been outside of Holder County for ten minutes. A steady tide of memories washed over Avery with every mile they advanced toward Oklahoma City. Her whole life had happened right here. If only she'd known her future awaited her behind Holder County lines.

As the residential streets began to bleed into four-lanes the breath washed from her lungs. "Colt." Her voice shook.

"What's wrong, baby?" He slowed the truck.

"Will you turn left here?" She pointed to the upcoming road at the traffic light.

"Sure." He never questioned her, only signaled and changed lanes.

"Take the next right," she pled.

He did. When the stone fixings that held the gates of Resurrection Memorial Cemetery came into view he squeezed her hand. "Am I turning in here, baby?"

She managed a haggard nod. He parked the truck and let her guide him to the grave. She couldn't afford a headstone so there was nothing there but a simple marker.

"Take your time, sugar. I'll be right here." Colt whipped his cowboy hat off and lowered his head. Avery knelt down to trace her fingers over her mother's name.

"I'm getting married, Mama." Her voice fissured. "I know you used to think that was a stupid thing to do but I am." When the tears she'd tried to dam back spilled free, Colt pulled a handkerchief from his pocket, knelt down beside her, and wiped them from her cheeks.

"See, Mama, he's such a good man. He takes such good care of me and of Chase and Jax. He's going with me tomorrow." The winds whipped her hair to the side and pricked at her skin. Colt eased out of his coat and blanketed it over her shoulders. His scent filled her lungs and gave her strength to go on. "He's going with me to fight Randy for Jaxon. Well, really the state is fighting Randy. It's complicated." She shook her head.

"Did you know, Mama? Did you know what an awful man he was? I keep thinking you didn't. You couldn't have known. But he is." She eased the handkerchief from Colt's hands and wiped her eyes again. The cold concrete remained unmoving and unhearing but she kept talking. "And even though Randy is an awful, hateful man Colt is going with me to fight him. Most of his family is coming, too. The Holders and the Camdens. They're good people, Mama. I...I just wanted you to know that I'm doing what you asked. I'm taking care of the boys but I'm not doing it all by myself. So many people are helping me. I love you so much, Mama, but you were wrong. People out there will help you if you let them. And they'll love you and let you love them. I wish you'd known that." She pressed her index and middle fingers to her mouth and laid the kiss on the stone beneath her feet. With that, she turned and once again, let Colt ease the blows the world had levied.

A few minutes later, he had her back in the truck.

"Where are we going now?" she asked as she dried the last of her tears.

"I'm taking my baby to get a chai tea latte since I don't know how often I'll be able to get you one back in Nebraska."

"I love you so much."

"Same goes, sugar."

CHAPTER FORTY-THREE

A woman in a blue pantsuit flew by Avery almost knocking her into the wall in the Oklahoma City Courthouse that morning.

"I hate the city," Colt huffed as he steadied her. He tucked her deeper inside the barrier of Camdens and Holders all set to watch the upcoming trial.

"Same goes," Brock agreed.

"Avery, sweetheart, you want me to go find you a ginger ale? Looks like you might have a nervous stomach over all of this blasted ridiculousness." Aunt Leigh patted her back. "Men without sense God gave goats trying to take Holder land and take our little Jaxon. I've of a mind to get after them with my good broom and then Gentry's shotgun."

"Ain't that the truth. Oh here, honey, I've got some of Everett's Tums right here in my pocketbook." Jessie handed over the medicine.

"They trying to out-mama her or something?" Brock spoke through his teeth.

"Aunt Leigh's been trying ever since Avery told her about her mama dying. When you brought Jax and Chase in this morning, she near 'bout lost her mind. She's wanted grandkids forever now. My baby's nervous because they won't leave her alone." Colt made certain only his brother could hear him.

"Mama, I wouldn't let anyone hear you threaten anyone with a shotgun right here in the big city courthouse." Maddox rolled his eyes.

"Maddox, honey, I do not remember addressing you in any way at all." She licked her thumb and scrubbed something off of Maddox's cheek. He jerked backward and ground his teeth.

"Don't talk back to your mother," Gentry ordered no one in general out of habit, Colt supposed.

"All right you all can come on in. Just keep quiet." Meridian opened the courtroom door where the trial was being held. She introduced them to the assistant D.A. who'd be handling the evidence this time.

Colt found it distinctly odd to be viewing a trial instead of participating in it, especially since the very way their lives worked was why they were there fighting. There wasn't a thing they could do or say to change the outcome of this one. This was Randy Buttridge against the state of Oklahoma.

He ushered Avery down one of the rows of chairs for spectators, seating her between himself and Brock. Jase and Wyatt Holder were on his side. Grant and Luke Camden were on Brock's. Colt would've loved to have seen Randy Butt-crack try to get to her.

She skipped gnawing her lip and had her fingernails in her mouth instead. He grabbed her hand. "It's gonna be fine, sugar. Deep breaths for me."

When Randy was brought in, what little color was left in his face drained away as he eyed the four rows packed full of cowboys ready to watch his ass be tried.

"Boy better hope he goes right on to the jailhouse," Grant Camden huffed under his breath.

"You got that right," Austin agreed from the row behind them.

Jase and Ford Holder both lifted their hats in agreement. Colt's uncle Wyn, patted Grant's shoulder in solidarity.

"There's a back alley to this place," Colt's cousin, Memphis, whispered.

"Would the lot of you hush," Leigh commanded.

"I'll bail every one of 'em out." Uncle Barrett didn't seem to care who heard him. "Sometimes there's ass that needs to be whupped. That's what he gets for trying to take my nephew's boy and my land. Sorry piece of cow shit."

Ev Camden looked like he agreed.

Everyone stood as the judge entered. A broad grin spread across Meridian's features. All of the color bled from Randy's. That was good enough for Colt.

The judge nodded to the crowd. "Judge Roberts has recused himself from this trial. It would seem there might have been a conflict of interest so I have stepped in."

Meridian spun around. "Yeah, a conflict of interest that involved Judge Roberts getting a new boat from the defendant."

The trial began. The assistant D.A.'s heels clicked ominously as she paced. "Based on bank record evidence supplied to the courts, three years ago, six subsidiary companies all under the Brookdale Real Estate Group umbrella, a company owned and operated by Randall James Buttridge, wrote a total of fifty-seven checks to several people in top-level positions in both Oklahoma City and Norman, your honor. The combined total of those checks was 2.5 million dollars."

The judge gave nothing away but a nod.

"Copies of those checks are also in the evidence files," the assistant D.A. continued. "This practice continued this year as well. Bank records were subpoenaed from the county employees. Not only does it appear they were accepting bribes from Brookdale Real Estate subsidiaries but there were checks from other businesses as well. Upon further investigation all of the money came from one of the thirty-seven registered businesses all owned by either Randall Buttridge or his brother Richard."

"What were you paying our city officals for exactly, Mr. Buttridge?" the judge demanded.

"My client refuses to answer that until he's called to the stands," his lawyer huffed.

"Fine. Continue."

Colt tried his damnedest to follow along but tax evasion and one company owning a half dozen others made precious little sense to him. Jaxon wasn't brought up at all.

Avery's brow remained pressed into a permanent furrow.

When the assistant city manager was called to testify, things got more interesting. He sang like a songbird about how he'd turned a blind eye to tax assessments he knew were reported incorrectly.

"They offered him a plea," Meridian explained quietly.

Another hour ground on but then Colt's uncle, Barrett, took the stands. Every Holder and Camden in attendance sat up a little straighter.

"Sir, can you tell the courts what you received eighteen-months ago regarding your land in Holder County?"

"I can. I received a certified letter informing me that the bordering county was to access the East end of Holder County under eminent domain stating it was needed for a new highway to join the counties."

"And your response, sir?" The D.A. quirked a grin.

"That they could take any piece of Holder County from my family over my cold dead ass and when they pried my shotgun outta my cold dead hands."

The judge looked mildly amused. Colt knew his uncle wasn't exaggerating.

"And you hired your own lawyer to investigate the claims, correct?"

"I hired my niece, Meridian, who's the best damned lawyer in this state or any other. Only a Holder's gonna represent Holder land."

Meridian cringed. Leigh and Barrett's wife Sara both shook their heads.

The D.A. audibly cleared her throat. "Well, can you explain to us how Meridian stopped the acquisition of you land?"

"My nephew, Colton, overheard some S.O.B. running his mouth in the Broken Bowery. Colt figured out that there never were plans to build any kind of new road. There ain't no need to build another road to get out to my ranch land. The truckers that buy my cattle can get there just fine. But Colt learned that the eminent domain claim was to be turned over to a third party for private use. He confronted the shitlicker and he may or may not have let it be known that he didn't approve.

"As I'm sure you know, land in Oklahoma cannot be taken for private use. Colt told Meridian what he'd heard and she started digging. When she found proof that there was a private real estate firm's money behind the claim she threatened to skewer them in court and they dropped the claim."

"And do you know the parent company of Peseca Investment, the company that was writing checks to the county planner to help with their eminent domain claim, Mr. Holder?"

"I'm assuming it's one of the dumbass's you got sitting at that table right there. Shit stinks. There ain't no getting around it. I expect his sorry ass got away with something like that at some point. It's like I tell all my boys once you let motherfuckers get to slipping they get to thinking they can ice skate. I'll say this and you can put it right in the record, he ain't gonna get away with it on Holder land. Oh, add this in too. He aint' gon' get away with it up in Nebraska on Camden land neither. My shot gun will travel and that's my family, too."

Brock and Colt shared a discreet grin. Avery hid her grin behind her hand. Meridian spun in her chair to wink at Colt. "That's how Randy knew who you were. You were fighting for Holder land," she mouthed. "He thought you were a Holder."

The judge's expressions ranged from bemused to concerned. You could take the rancher off the ranch and bring him to the city but you couldn't take the ranch out of the rancher. Colton could've told them that.

Another few witnesses were called when finally, the strip mall in Slatern Hills was brought up. Avery sat up straighter. The story was retold. Her mother's name was mentioned twice but only as the owner of the salon. Once again, Jaxon wasn't brought up. But the evidence T-Byrd had found was reviewed. The checks written from Randy to the state in odd amounts were presented. The liens Avery's mother never knew about were dissected. The D.A. painted quite a picture.

Colt's gut continued to roil. He kept Avery's hand tucked tightly in his own. Jaxon and Chase were safe on Holder Ranch with Aunt Pearl, Natalie, Aaron, and a few of Colt's cousins.

There were two additional hours of Randy and his lawyer trying to explain everything away. He was examined and cross-examined. Colt was certain his own eyes were going to cross.

Finally, mercifully, the judge drew herself upward and took a deep breath. "The evidence presented today was extremely tight and leaves no room for error, Mr. Buttridge. This court finds you guilty of seven counts of tax evasion, four counts of bribery, and ten counts of defrauding the government. Your sentencing will be held here next week."

———

With the swing of this gavel, Avery's body went numb. It was over. He was guilty. But what did that mean for Jaxon?

"How long will his sentence be?" she whispered to Meridian as Randy was taken from the courtroom in handcuffs.

"He's looking at a minimum of fifteen but as much as thirty, I'd say. He could get off on good behavior but Jaxon will be with you on his eighteenth birthday, meaning that trust will become yours and Colt's. I know that's not why you did this but..." Meridian shrugged.

"Damn," Colt grunted.

"I think you both deserve it. You were both willing to put Jaxon first. You've both made sacrifices for him." Meridian smiled.

"I have no idea what I would do with that much money other than send him to college and buy you more land," Avery stared up at Colt. "I already have everything I could ever want."

"We'll see to it that Camden Ranch and Holder Ranch are here for another two hundred years," Colt vowed.

Ev slapped him on the back. "So, let me see if I got this straight, son. You beat the piss outta some guy that was trying to steal your land illegally and that guy happened to be working for the man who was her brother's daddy. Tell me this, you believe in fate now?"

Colt turned to stare at her. He braced her chin delicately in the might of his hand. "Yes, sir. I sure do."

"Okay, you know what we're going to do now, right?" Hope and Holly bustled over.

A bubble of thrill burst through Avery. "We're going to buy my gown."

CHAPTER FORTY-FOUR

"There some kinda story here?" Brock asked as Colt drove them toward the tux rental shop on the courthouse square.

They'd come up behind Ziggy Pugh's old El Camino. As usual he was doing fifteen in a forty-five.

"It's Friday afternoon at three o'clock," Colt explained.

"Look at that they even taught you to read the time way down here in Oklahoma." His brother laughed. "But why is he going so slow? My tractor goes faster."

"He takes his wife out for a drive every Friday." Colt couldn't help but chuckle at the bewildered expression on his brother's face.

"There's only one man in that car."

"Yeah, I know."

"It's an El Camino. She can't be in the trunk."

Colt choked back laughter. "That is dark man."

"I'm just saying," Brock explained.

"Her ashes are in the box in the front seat. See, he's got her strapped in. She's been dead for twenty-seven years." Colt whipped around Ziggy illegally across the double yellow line. The Holder County sheriffs knew his truck. It was good to be a Holder and a Camden.

"Jesus. And you think Pleasant Glen is crazy?"

"I never said Holder County wasn't. They're both nuts. 'Course we didn't have to have ribbon cutting ceremonies when they brought the cell towers out here."

Brock gave him their identical smirk "Guess I can't argue with that."

"Hey, thanks for doing the best man thing for me, and thanks for coming this morning to the trial. That meant a lot." Colt finally got around to what he'd been wanting to say all afternoon.

"That's what brothers are for. This is how it's supposed to work."

———

Avery stood in a small guest bedroom inside the largest home she'd ever been in.

"Avery, I look so freaking gorgeous," Samantha gushed as she sidled up to the mirror.

Hope rolled her eyes discreetly. Aunt Pearl shook her head. Avery was thrilled Hope agreed to be her maid-of-honor, saving her from having to ask Sam.

"Aren't you supposed to tell me I look gorgeous since I'm the bride?"

"Well, obviously you do. But I get excited whenever you make my hair look this good."

Avery laughed. "I do what I can."

"I still can't believe you're marrying one of the Holder boys."

"I'm not. I'm marrying one of the Camden boys."

Avery's father came back into the room carrying Jaxon. "Jax was advising me on how to be a cowboy."

"Well, he's learning from one of the best." She beamed at them.

"I gathered that, although I can't quite tell if I'm being insulted. Your fiancé and his brother keep calling me a greenhorn when I ask questions about ranching."

Avery giggled. "They mean it with love, Daddy."

"I'll go talk to Brock," Hope offered.

"Nah, it's fine. As long as he takes care of my girl, he can say it all he wants."

"Oh, I almost forgot. Did Colt give you that check?" Avery asked.

"He tried to. I tore it up. I told him you'd always be my little girl, it was a rare day you ever asked for anything and it was my pleasure to send you some gas money. He said that sounded like you." He paused and quirked his brow at her. "You're sure about this guy? Don't recall you ever being interested in a cowboy the entire time you were growing up."

"I didn't know what I was missing out on. I just wish the time would go by faster. I can't wait to see him. I miss him."

"Well we can't have that, baby doll. I won't have my girl missing me and left unsatisfied." Colt stood in the doorway. She was quite certain there had never been a finer image than her soon-to-be husband dressed in a suit with a black Stetson on his head and freshly polished boots. Her father chuckled when she rushed into his arms.

"You're not supposed to see me yet," she objected even as she wrapped her arms around him.

"You look so damned beautiful and you know I'm bad at rules. I couldn't stand this anymore. I told you I don't want space. I don't like it when we're in the same house but not together. Brock sent me down here because I was driving him nuts. Why'd we decide to have this shindig in the evening, anyway?"

"Because that's when we could get all of the Holders here and you were out riding this morning."

"Well, after this I have to trailer Rio for a long, slow drive back to Pleasant Glen." He pressed his forehead to hers. "Did I already tell you how beautiful you look? Damn, I'm a lucky man."

"You did, but I don't mind if you want to tell me again."

"I can't wait to get you back to our room, sugar," he breathed across her lips. "Unbutton all of them buttons. Run my hands all over my wife."

Her father cleared his throat. "Maybe save that for *after* the ceremony."

"Daddy! I, uh, forgot you were there."

"Obviously."

"Colt kisses Avery lots of times." Jax slapped his own forehead, making everyone laugh. "I say it's okay because she almost never cries no more."

"Well, then that's all I need to know," her father said with a grin. "Now, Mr. Camden, I believe you're supposed to be waiting on my daughter at the end of the aisle."

"Nowhere else I'd rather be. See you soon, sweetness." He painted a tender kiss on her lips. "Love you."

CHAPTER FORTY-FIVE

Being that they'd just vowed to love and care for each other for the rest of their lives, Colt thought the ceremony had gone by rather quickly. That suited him just fine. The wedding was a day. He wanted the life that came after it.

Memphis, who was playing D.J., turned on *Shameless* by Garth Brooks, and Colt drew his sweet baby, looking sweeter than sin on a Sunday all in white, into his arms and started to sway.

"Pretty sure everyone would notice here if you tried to get your hands up my skirt here," she whispered in his ear.

"Mmm, that a dare, sugar?"

"You better not." She giggled.

"Then this better be our last dance 'cause I'm all kinds of out of patience."

"Oh yeah?"

"Yeah."

"I thought you liked to dance with me," she continued to flirt.

"Oh, baby, I love to dance with you but right now, I want to make my girl fly and there's way too damn many people here."

"Well, don't be too impatient. I saved you some time."

Colt was quite certain most everyone could see his prominent erection. The damned tux pants were too tight. He knew he should've insisted on wearing Wranglers. "What's that mean, baby doll?" He kept her head tucked on his shoulder so he could whisper in her ear and his neck kept anyone from hearing her responses.

"Do you know what a garter belt is?"

He had a guess and if that's what she was wearing they were leaving before Garth sang the final chorus. "One of them things that goes around your waist with the straps that attach to your stockings."

"Mm-hmm and I don't have anything on between that and my stockings." She lifted her head. Liquid heat pooled in those blue eyes. When she licked her lips, he was done for. He wouldn't have been more frantic to get her out of there, if someone had set him on fire.

Before he could inform everyone that they were leaving, his Uncle Barrett stepped up. "Soon as this song is over, we need to go over a few things."

"We really have to do this on my wedding night, Uncle Barrett?" Colt fought not to actually whimper as his uncle led them to his office.

Avery walked beside him, giving him those mischievous little smirks that did nothing to help the situation.

"Thought you were working on learning some patience, son," his uncle goaded.

"Not when it comes to her."

"Probably best. But we need to get this done before the Camdens head back to Pleasant Glen." He shoved Colt down at a table, where Brock, Ev, Gentry, Meridian, and a woman he didn't know were already seated. Then Barrett politely pulled out the chair beside him for Avery.

"Thank you, Mr. Holder."

"No problem, sweetheart. If he gives you a moment's trouble, you call me. I'll turn him out with my bulls."

The stained glass desk lamps glimmered in her pale blue eyes as she stared Colt down. "I will keep that in mind, but I doubt he'll give me too much trouble. I think he kinda likes me."

Colt huffed. "You think? What was your first clue, arling'?"

"Well, you're about to sign away like a bazillion dollars' worth of land for me."

"Not quite a bazillion." Colt winked at her.

"Newlyweds." Uncle Gentry rolled his eyes.

Ev and Brock both laughed.

"All right, since we don't want Colt to actually keel over from a pair of blue balls, let's get this done," Meridian teased. Girl was crude when she wanted to be. Had to come from growing up with a shit ton of brothers and cousins.

"It's a distinct possibility, so yeah, let's do this," Colt came right back.

"All right, I have the paperwork from the lawyer in Nebraska with the new lines drawn and the new deeds giving everyone the land that was agreed upon. Colt, you're agreeing that the land you now own must remain in the possession of the Camden family. You're not allowed to sell it unless it is to Brock or one of Ev and Jessie's kids. There's no getting out of it is what I'm saying."

"Good, I don't want a way out. Give me them papers."

"All right, sign there, there, and there. Brock, you and Ev have duplicate papers to sign. Everything is legally binding now. Nothing written in pen this time. And Linda, here, is going to notarize these for everyone. So there will be no more surprises on land ownership."

"Let's certainly hope not," Ev quipped.

"Mr. Camden, Uncle Barrett has signed you back the land in Moore in its entirety. Just sign here and here accepting." Ev read through the papers and then signed them while Colt prayed they would speed this all up.

Brock and Hope were taking the boys back to Nebraska for them. He and Avery had this one night to enjoy being married in every possible way before they went back to being full-time parents.

"Brock, you are signing the land adjoining Uncle Barrett's property to Holder Land and Cattle." She placed the papers in front of Brock, but before he could sign, Uncle Gentry stopped him.

"Now Barrett and I got to thinking and the land you're giving back to us is worth a good bit more than the land Brock is giving Colt. We didn't think that was fair. So," he slid an envelope to Brock and then one to Colt.

"What's this?" Colt folded the flap of the envelope back and revealed a check from Holder Land and Cattle Company. His eyes goggled as he noted the amount. "Uncle Gent, you can't...I mean...I don't need this."

"We wanted to give you a little something to get started on. Plus, that should help with all of her aunt's medical bills."

Brock's mouth was still hanging open as he stared at his own check.

"You just see to it that my nephew and his wife have anything they need to get started and take care of those boys," Uncle Barrett urged Ev. "That's all that matters to us."

"You have my word," Ev agreed.

"And it might take Colt and Avery a little longer to get back to the ranch tomorrow than was originally planned," Gentry explained.

"Why's that?" Colt managed to locate words through his shock.

"'Cause, boy, you gotta pull a long trailer full of stock. No nephew of mine's gonna be all hat and no cattle. You got land, now it's time to put some steers on it. You're a cattle rancher for Christ's sake." Barrett laughed.

Colt stood. "Uncle Barrett, you didn't have to do that."

"I know I didn't but I wanted to. I'll never forget that night Betsy came into Mama and Daddy's house telling us she was pregnant with you. Thought Daddy was gonna explode right then and there. But she was the baby and he'd always treated her as such. 'Course that was before any of us had actually met Mick. I just remember praying that you wouldn't end up nothing like your daddy and I'd say my prayers were answered. I'm gonna help you get set to rights as a Camden. It's a damned good family and I'm gonna treat them as such from here on. You connected us, boy. But to me, Colt, you'll always be a Holder."

"If it's okay with you Uncle Barrett, I'd really like to be both."

EPILOGUE

The Following Spring

Colt bounced his new double C cattle brand in his gloved hands before he branded the first calf born on his portion of Camden Ranch.

Brock laughed at him outright. "You gonna brand it or stand there admiring your initials?"

"Fuck off, man." Working quickly, he did indeed stamp his initials into the hide. "I think Avery should get my brand tattooed on her gorgeous hide."

Brock shook his head at him. "Think I'll let you tell her that. But if she goes for it, tell her to take Hope with her."

"You two idiots gonna keep working calves or are we going to stand here discussing branding your wives?" Natalie goaded.

"Says the girl with the Green Beret logo on the back of her neck," Holly chimed in.

All of the Camdens laughed.

As Austin continued to let calves down to the table one by one, the family worked, just the way it was supposed to be.

"I think you're right," Brock commented a little while later as they stowed the calf table back in the barn.

"About what?" Colt ran his handkerchief over his face.

"About the Angus cattle. We ought to expand. You still think your uncle can help us find a supplier?"

"Sure." Colt couldn't help but grin. "When do you want to make the buy?"

"Let's get them in here now and get 'em fat and happy before winter," Brock strategized.

"Agreed. 'Spect we might better get them here before my niece makes her appearance as well."

"That, too." Before Brock could say more his extremely pregnant wife waddled to the barn.

Colt offered her a grin. "Here. I'll stack some hay bales for you to sit on."

"You're so sweet. Thank you," Hope managed to give him a hug around her massive midsection. "I've never felt more like a breed cow."

"Hope." Brock shook his head. "Stop it. You look beautiful."

"I can't see my own feet."

"They're there. I promise."

Colt laughed at that. "I'm gonna go check on my wife. Chase'll be home from school in a little while. We're all going to get Runzas tonight to celebrate Pearl's remission, right?"

"You know we'll be there," Brock vowed.

"Heck yeah, boy, we're all going," Uncle Ev grinned. "Jessie's up at the house now trying to figure how to write remission on the cake she baked and make it pretty. I told her none of my boys care much what the cake looks like so long as it's in their big mouths."

"I'm offended, Dad. I do *not* have a big mouth," Austin teased. The entire family erupted in laughter at that.

Pleased with his day's work, Colt made his way to his house. Tiny shoots of green in Avery's new garden were just breaking through the soil. And there in the middle of all of the newfound life, was his wife swinging back and forth on the swing.

"Hey, baby, you run out of people's hair to do this afternoon?" Colt slowed the swing so he could take the seat beside her.

Avery giggled. It was still his favorite sound in the world. "I had to go to that conference with Jaxon's teacher, remember? Aunt Pearl's up at the salon doing a few of her old client's hair so I decided to come home and work on the garden."

"How'd the conference go? My boy behaving?"

"Kind of." She shot him a smirk.

"What's that look for?"

"Apparently, Jax has been going around holding up his middle finger and telling his classmates that all of his cousins say it's bad to hold up that finger but that his Colt and all of his uncles do it to each other."

Colt choked back laughter. "Guess all of us need to watch our hands when we're working, huh?"

"It would really be best." She shook her head at him.

"Pretty sure we could blame this on Nate and J.J. though. Clearly my brother's and Austin's kid are a bad influence. They're older and all," he teased.

"Oh, yeah, I'm sure that's the case."

"See, now that's all settled, and we can swing."

"I like that idea. I'm tired anyway." She nuzzled her face on his shoulder.

"Haven't showered yet, sugar." He wrapped her up in his arms anyway.

"I don't care."

"I knew you were the perfect woman first time I laid eyes on you." He chuckled.

"You are so full of shit, cowboy."

He kept her swinging back and forth gently but she was still antsy. He could tell. "Not full of it. Occasionally covered in it though. What's wrong with my girl?"

She lifted her head. "Nothing."

"Not nothing. Talk."

When her teeth started worrying her lip, concern filled his gut. "Is it Pearl? She feeling badly again?"

"No. Aunt Pearl's doing amazing. I promise nothing is wrong. It's just..."

"It's just what, baby? You're scaring me. Talk."

She gave him her sweetest grin. "Don't be scared. Do you

remember a few months ago when we said maybe we'd like for me to go off the pill so our kids wouldn't be so far apart in age from Jaxon?"

Colt halted the swing. "I do recall us saying something like that."

"Right. So, uh...." Arching her back, she dug into the pocket of the jeans she was wearing and produced a pregnancy test. "Just took this."

Colt could see nothing but the plus sign on the test. "Damn."

"Is that a good damn or a not so good damn? I know it's really fast."

Digging through the surprise taking up residence in his mind, Colt could locate no fear. Easing off the swing, he fell to his knees, laid his head in her lap, and rubbed his hands over her midsection. "It's the best kind of damn I've ever said. My God." He hugged her to him. "Do you feel okay? Should you go inside. I don't want you up at the salon so much on your feet like that. You just sit and... be. I'll do everything. Holy fuck."

Avery's entire body shook with her laughter. "I thought you probably already suspected."

"I wondered 'cause your tits have somehow gotten even more magical but I thought maybe I was being given some kind of heavenly reward for being a good cattle rancher, taking care of God's land and all."

That did it, she erupted in hysterical laughter. "You think God rewards you with my tits?"

"Obviously."

"I love you so much, Colt Camden."

"Same goes, sugar. So, my baby's in there." He returned to his seat and kept the width of his hand spread over her belly.

"Yep. After the party tonight, I'm going to ask Hope for all of her pregnancy books."

"I'll read 'em, too. I want to be a good dad."

"You're going to be amazing, Colt. You already are."

"You sure you feel okay?"

"I'm a little tired, like I said, but other than that I'm fine."

"You want to go take a nap? I'll lay down with you."

Her grin widened. "I want to sit right here with my husband and our little tiny baby in my belly."

Willing his heart to locate any kind of steady rhythm, he nodded. "Is it bad that I can't wait on you to have a big huge belly?"

She laughed at him again. "I think it's kind of cool you can't wait for that."

"You kidding me? This is really cool. You think it'll be a boy? I don't know much what to do with girls."

"You take excellent care of me."

"I try."

At that moment, Chase's old truck bounced up the worn grass path to the house. Both of the boys headed their way.

"We telling them now?" He asked her quickly.

Before she could hide the test, Chase was on them. His eyes flitted from the test, to Colt, to Avery. "Ah geez, I am not changing diapers just so you know." Jaxon didn't seem to notice and Avery didn't volunteer the information so Colt kept his mouth shut, still proud of himself when he managed to do so.

"Hey, you." He lifted Jaxon into his lap. "What's this I hear about you raising that middle finger to your classmates?"

"I was telling them *not* to do it 'cause it's bad. You said so."

"Uh huh, but you showing them how ain't too good either. 'Sides I ain't ever seen Captain America do as such."

Jax considered that. "Superheroes don't shoot the bird?" he asked.

"Never," Avery vowed. Chase rolled his eyes.

"K, guess I won't do it no more. It's kinda fun though."

Colt bit back laughter and shook his head. "If you want to keep going over to Uncle Brock's house on Friday nights to watch TV with all of us you'll keep that finger to yourself, little man."

"Fine." Jaxon wiggled down and headed up the porch steps. "I need a juice box."

Colt and Avery laughed. When Chase followed after him, she turned to stare Colt down. "You're going to be the best dad. I'm so scared but also so excited. Everything's going to change."

"Some things will change." He wrapped her back up in his arms. "But this, right here, this land, our home, my love, you and me, that will never change. We're here to stay."

ABOUT THE AUTHOR

Bestselling author Jillian Neal likes her coffee strong and sweet with a shot of sinful spice, the same way she likes her cowboys. In fact, her caffeine addiction is quite possibly considered illicit in several states as are a few of the things her characters do. When she's not writing or reading, you'll find her in the kitchen trying out new recipes or coming up with ~~excuses~~ reasons to purchase yet another handbag or make an additional trip to Sephora. Though she'll always be a Bama girl at heart, Jillian hangs up her hat and kicks up her boots outside of Atlanta with her hunk-of-a-husband and her teenage sons.

For more information...
jillianneal.com
jillian@jillianneal.com

ALSO BY JILLIAN NEAL

THE GIFTED REALM SAGA

Within the Realm

Lessons Learned

Every Action

Rock Bottom

An Angel All His Own

All But Lost

The Quelling Tide

GYPSY BEACH

Gypsy Beach

Gypsy Love

Gypsy Heat

Gypsy Hope

GYPSY BEACH TO CAMDEN RANCH

Coincidental Cowgirl

CAMDEN RANCH

Rodeo Summer

Forever Wild

Cowgirl Education

Un-hitched

Last Call

THE GIFTED REALM: ACADEMY

Free, web serial

www.ingramcontent.com/pod-product-compliance
Lightning Source LLC
Chambersburg PA
CBHW030804260626
47169CB00001B/180